Kendra,
Rock on!
Elle ♡
xo

ANOTHER Postcard

BEST SELLING AUTHOR
ELLE CHRISTENSEN

Dedication

For my husband.
Loving a music woman isn't always what it's
supposed to be.
You've always stood by me.
I'm forever yours, faithfully.

Another postcard with chimpanzees
And every one is addressed to me.

—Bare Naked Ladie

Chapter One

LEVI

"Would somebody put this drumstick in my eye and swirl it around in my brain? Maybe then some of these singers will sound less sucktastic." Matteo twirled his drumsticks through his fingers, scowling at the currently closed door to the sound room. I rolled my eyes and looked down at the music in my hands, not wanting to encourage him, but secretly agreeing.

Since Sheryl, one of the backup vocalists for Stone Butterfly, announced she was pregnant, we knew we would eventually have to replace her, if only temporarily for maternity leave. If we didn't, we'd have to rework all of our music to remove the need for that vocal line and the harmony it created. The more singers a band has, the fuller the sound, and while not all our music called for six voices, it was frequent enough that we'd made them permanent members.

Despite Sheryl's nagging, we'd successfully put it off until the last minute. Unfortunately, it meant that the session musician she and our manager, Noah, had wanted was booked and unavailable. They were pissed when they found out, and I was fairly certain Noah was punishing us by making us sit through auditions. No doubt at Sheryl's suggestion.

It was early afternoon and we'd already been subjected to seven "musicians." Stone Butterfly was a multi-platinum, Grammy-winning rock band. We didn't hold fucking auditions. Don't get me wrong, we jammed with any new session musician to make sure it was a good fit, but outright auditions? Fuck no!

And yet, here you are, dumbass.

"Shut it, Teo. Let's just get this over with so we can get the hell out of here." Simon scowled at Matteo as he plucked out a few notes on his bass. "I've got a date with the lead singer of Lady Luck tonight." His expression morphed into a wolfish grin, and I chuckled. Simon was the poster boy for a Latin lover with his tan skin, dark brown eyes, black hair, and a silver tongue (literally and figuratively. He had a sliver barbell piercing) that had talked many a groupie out of their panties.

Sasha was sprawled out on the piano bench, her feet tapping out a rhythm and her fingers prancing over her stomach, playing the music in her head. She sat up and looked at Simon, cocking her head curiously. "Which one? It's a trio." Simon snorted and then grinned at her salaciously.

"Who said it was only one?" He asked, wiggling his eyebrows suggestively.

Sasha rolled her eyes, then winked and reached out to fist bump Simon as they grinned widely at each other. Yeah, Sasha was the shit. She'd been our keyboardist for almost as long as we'd been a band. She fit right in and didn't go all girly on us, getting offended by our language, partying, and whore-ish activities. Sasha could actually drink a lot of guys under the table and she had the mouth of a sailor, particularly when she played poker. She was all woman, though, with her long, lean body, and stunning face. She could have been a runway model, but, she preferred ragged jeans, and even more ragged T-shirts. Her coppery hair was usually under a baseball cap, with a long ponytail down the back.

I stifled another sigh as the door opened. When I saw it was Noah, I slumped down a little in relief. He stepped into the empty space in front of us and slipped his hands casually into his expensive, gray suit pants. I almost never saw him in anything but suits these days. It was a far cry from the kid I learned to play the guitar with, the one I used to jam with whenever our parents let us. Noah grew up in the rock and roll lifestyle, his parents having their own rock star careers before they settled down on Long Island and focused on producing. Noah and I were both ten, and from the moment we met in school, we became inseparable. He'd grown up playing instruments and singing, and I used to lurk around during his lessons, soaking up as much as I could. Eventually, Noah's parents encouraged me to join him, and we learned to make music together. My younger brother and sister had no interest in the music industry, but they had been our faithful audience and were still our biggest fans.

In high school, we met Matteo, who immediately felt like our brother, and we became a band without really thinking about it. Our natural instincts leaned toward alternative rock, but we dabbled in other genres, refusing to be pigeon holed. As we developed into a working machine, Noah started booking our gigs and managing all of the behind the scenes shit. After graduation, we stayed close, each of us having been accepted into different New York music programs. It allowed us to stay together and perform whenever we had the opportunity. Shortly into our first year, Noah showed up to a rehearsal with Simon in tow and told us he was the brother we were missing. I thought Noah was bringing him in as second guitar, but he handed Simon a bass and stood back to listen and watch. The notion of replacing Noah didn't sit well with me, but I trusted him. And, he was right. *The jackass was always right.* Simon was the puzzle piece we didn't even realize had been missing.

Noah pointed out what Teo and I weren't willing to admit, that he didn't play at the same level as the rest of us. We argued, but in the end, he decided to step out of the limelight and take on the role of manager. He thrived on the business side of things, and it quickly became clear that it was what he was born to do. I could honestly say; I didn't know where Stone Butterfly would be without him. He brought Sasha on board at the end of our freshman year, right before he negotiated our first record deal. She was a brilliant pianist, and when we were feeling a little folksy, we would have her break out her fiddle. When she started sawin' on her fiddle, the devil had nothin' on Sasha Blue.

It wasn't long before we left school behind to go on tour and became a solid group for the next three years, adding Kristi and Sheryl into the mix as backup singers when we headed into the studio to lay down our second album. They quickly became permanent members of the group, instrumental, rather than expendable backup singers. We really hated the idea of breaking in someone new.

Despite the urge I had at that moment to light his ass on fire, Noah was still my best friend, and I respected his position as my manager. So, when he casually looked us over, a small smirk on his face, I refrained from making a sarcastic insult. Instead, I whined, "Can we come out of time out now, Dad?" My tone was dry. "We want to play with the big kids."

Sheryl waddled into the room, glaring at us as she joined Noah. "I don't think you've been tortured enough, but Danny is flipping out about me not being home two weeks before my due date. FYI, I wouldn't be anywhere alone with him for a while, he's pretty pissed at you guys." I almost laughed at the picture in my head. Sheryl's husband was barely five foot seven, and maybe one hundred and fifty pounds soaking wet. Perhaps his level of anger would give him a leg up (pun intended, 'cause I'm awesome like that) to my six foot four and one hundred ninety-five pounds of muscle.

What? I had the right to be a little cocky. It's not like my body happened by accident.

I could see the others holding in their laughter as well, a fact that wasn't lost on Sheryl. Her glare became more intense, but Noah interrupted, diffusing the growing tension. "We've got one more singer for you to see, and I expect you to behave like professionals. It took a lot of negotiating to get her here. She's one of the best in the business and wrangling her away from other potential projects wasn't easy, especially without the promise of more than a three-month gig." Sheryl had informed us that she was considering retiring from performing to be a full-time mom. However, she hadn't made her decision yet, so there was no guarantee that we would have to deal with a permanent replacement. A hassle none of us were eager to deal with.

Sheryl pointed a finger at each of us. "I've known her for years, and Brooklynn is perfect for you guys. So, don't blow it."

Brooklynn? I must have heard her wrong.

"Brooklynn Hawk?" Kristi inquired, her voice cautiously excited. No way did Noah get Brooklynn Hawk. Despite being only twenty-two, she was one of the most sought after singers in the industry. From what I'd heard, she was also a classically trained pianist. Many had tried, but so far, no one had been able to entice her into a permanent spot in a band. Especially, since she'd never been willing to tour. She traveled a little to do session work, but mostly, people came to her and worked in a studio near her home in upstate New York. With that in mind, I wasn't sure what Sheryl and Noah were thinking. As excited as I was at the prospect of working with Brooklynn, with our tour fast approaching, we needed someone who was willing to go on the road.

Noah's face broke into a wide smile, glowing with triumph. "If you knuckleheads hadn't put off getting together with possible candidates, we would have had her contracted six months ago. Obviously, she wasn't willing to wait around for you all to get your heads removed from your asses and she signed a three-month contract for a US and Canadian tour with Unhinged."

"A tour?" I blurted the question in shock. "Brooklynn Hawk doesn't tour!"

"Apparently, she does now," Noah answered with a scowl in my direction. "Now if you're done interrupting…" he trailed off, and I nodded with a one-fingered salute. "Anyway, when Unhinged put their tour on hold indefinitely, we begged her to give us one more chance."

I'd heard about the troubles the lead singer of Unhinged was having. He'd done some damage to his vocal chords, and the doctors were unsure whether they'd be able to repair it. It was a shame, really, Unhinged had real talent and had been steadily rising on the charts.

Sheryl clapped her hands excitedly. "I'll go get her!" Then she spun around like a Weeble Wobble, dangerously close to falling down, and wobbled her way out of the room. Two minutes later, the door swung open and I stopped breathing.

Chapter Two

BROOKLYNN

I was grinning as I stepped into the large studio space. I'd been in the industry a few years at that point and I rarely got star struck. But, dude. *It was Stone Butterfly!* I managed to contain my fangirling to my huge smile as Sheryl introduced me to the band.

"Guys, this is Brooklynn Hawk"—she gestured to me then continued, pointing at each person as she rattled off their names and instruments—"Brooklynn, meet Simon Ruiz, bass, Matteo De Rossi, drums, Sasha Blue, keyboards and anything else she gets it in her head to play, Kristi Davidson, backup vocalist, and—"

"Levi Matthews," the lead singer cut her off and stood. He swiftly approached me and reached out a hand. I gave a little wave at the others, then placed my palm into Levi's. I was completely unprepared for the shock that sparked between us where our skin touched. *Holy shit.* My natural reflex was to pull my hand away but when I tugged, Levi's grip tightened and he grinned, showing off even white teeth, while a single eyebrow arched over one of his aquamarine eyes. I sucked in a sharp breath at the sight of them as they darkened with heat and . . . hunger. My body's reaction took me by surprise, especially after the long hiatus my libido seemed to have embarked upon over the last several years.

Whoa.

It wasn't like he wasn't freaking gorgeous from afar. I mean, the guy could melt the panties off of a nun with his smooth baritenor alone. His reputation and talent reminded me of Jon Bon Jovi, mixed with Dan Reynolds, and a little Billy Joe Armstrong. His versatility was astounding. It didn't hold a candle to the intensity of being right in front of Levi, though. Of touching him. There was intense chemistry between us, but I couldn't help wondering how many women had been recipients of that look. He was at least a half-foot taller than my five foot nine frame, with sculptured muscles that were in no way hidden beneath his long-sleeved thermal and distressed blue jeans, which were molded to his equally drool-worthy legs. I had no doubt the package included a very fine ass. His dark brown hair was cut short, though it was a little shaggier on top, carelessly messy in a sexy, bed-head kind of way. He had a light growth of whiskers along the harsh angles of his jaw line that continued on to form a scruffy goatee around his kissable lips. A straight nose, aquamarine gems for eyes, framed by dark lashes that would make any woman jealous, and high cheekbones all worked together to create a face that belonged on the cover of a magazine.

He also smelled ah-mazing. My girly parts danced in delight, and I had to shut it down before I did something stupid. Sleeping with a member of the band would be a disastrous move, considering that if anything went wrong, it would be my ass on the line. So, I gave him my best "let's be friends" smile and finally managed to extract my hand from his. "It's nice to meet all of you." Levi smirked and amusement twinkled in his eyes like he knew a secret and was just waiting for the right time to spring it on me. When he backed up and took a seat on a stool in front of a microphone, I stifled a sigh of relief as I began to feel less overwhelmed.

"So yeah, that's Levi," Sheryl muttered sardonically. I glanced over in time to see her roll her eyes, but there was also clear affection in them. She turned to me and her excitement was clear as she indicated a stool next to Kristi, slightly behind where Levi was perched. "I have a feeling you're going to fit right in, and you'll all make magic together." I walked over to Kristi, giving Levi a wide berth, and trying to be inconspicuous about it. After I sat and pulled over a music stand, I glanced up to find him eying me with a knowing smile. Butterflies erupted in my tummy, and if I hadn't already been sitting, I think my knees might have buckled. Damn, he was hot. *This is going to be a problem, isn't it?* No, I told myself sternly. I wouldn't let it be. *Good luck with that.*

I looked around at the group, observing their dynamic. The closeness and comfortable atmosphere between them. They were all so different and yet they were a cohesive, solid unit. One of the reasons I decided to work with Stone Butterfly (beyond my school-girl crush on every band member. That's right, even Sasha) was because of the way Sheryl talked about them. They weren't just a band, a bunch of people making music—they were a family. It was something I craved. A normalcy I'd never really known but always wanted to experience.

It certainly hadn't been around when I was growing up. My childhood was…less than ideal, to say the least. My parents weren't fit enough to take care of themselves, much less kids. When I was seventeen, my mother died and my father went to prison. My thirteen-year-old sister Baylee and I were put into foster care. Although we were lucky enough to be in the same town, we were separated because Bailey required a special home. In her pre-teen years, her mental growth slowed down and her maturity level never caught up to her age. She would always need a certain level of care and would never be fully independent.

I'd always intended to go to New York City and pursue a career in music after I turned eighteen. Bailey's foster parents were amazing, and I was sure she would have been fine. But, I couldn't bring myself to leave her yet. It wasn't that I thought she wasn't emotionally capable of surviving my departure. I told myself I was simply waiting until she was older. For her. But the truth was, I wasn't ready to leave her either. She was my only family. I accepted a scholarship to a smaller, local university, and though it was harder to gain the contacts and opportunities I needed, I managed to do it. By the time I'd graduated with my degree in vocal performance, I'd been working as a freelance studio musician for two years. The first year was difficult because I had to travel, but they were short trips, mostly to the city. I managed to work them around school, but tours were out of the question. I didn't want to be away from Baylee for months at a time. At least until she was older.

One day, I received a call from the manager of a rising, young pop star. She'd heard about me from another band I'd recorded with and wanted me to back her up on her next album. With her recommendation, my career took off and I was so busy I was able to become very selective in the jobs I took. Suddenly, artists were offering to come to me. Over the next year, I didn't have school to build my schedule around, so I was able to take on more requests. At twenty-two, I'd already built a healthy nest egg, so when Baylee turned eighteen, I moved her into an apartment and hired Cecily Turner, a home companion, to help care for her. Which meant I could feel safe leaving her from time to time.

Touring still hadn't really been on my radar until Unhinged called with an offer several months later. It was a US and Canadian tour, which meant I could come home often. In any case, Baylee was thriving in her limited independence, needing to rely on me less and less. She and Cecily had grown thick as thieves and were always off on one adventure after another, sometimes even traveling small distances. Like most children, Baylee handled things pretty well as long as she kept certain steady routines in her life, sort of like life rafts that kept her tethered to the shore while she enjoyed the unpredictable waves. But, if things became too turbulent, she regressed to an even more child-like state, confused and often scared of every little thing. At first, I worried that my popping in and out would upset her carefully balanced life but the doctors assured me there were things we could do to keep my presence consistent enough to avoid setbacks. All we needed was a solid plan. I explained things to Baylee as plainly as I could and she was very accepting. In fact, she and Cecily spent more time obsessing over the band and begging for signed posters, than they did about missing me.

Hesitantly, I signed a contract with Unhinged, but it was for a trial period of three months. If things went well, I would sign on for the last six months of the tour. Cecily and I worked with Baylee's doctors and therapists to come up with the right combination of activities, such as scheduled, daily phone calls to keep continuity in our relationship. We put it into practice right away, easing both of us into getting used to being apart. It was a lucky break that the members of the band were all from Syracuse, so rehearsals were only a few hours away, still close enough to come home if Baylee needed me.

The whole scenario was playing out beautifully until Travis, the lead singer, started having vocal issues. No sooner had the announcement been made that the tour was permanently on hold than I received a phone call from Noah Andersen, Stone Butterfly's manager. They needed a temporary replacement for one of their backup singers. It was a similar contract, a three-month stint, except this was a global tour, and I was nervous about going so far away. I agreed to go to the city to meet with Noah first, then if I wanted to take the next step, I'd spend some time with the band.

When Noah opened the door to his office, I was momentarily struck speechless by the sight of him. His tall, lean body filled out a perfectly tailored suit, and his neatly groomed blond hair, silver eyes, and classically handsome face, gave him the appearance of the boy next door mixed with a GQ model. A few more muscles and I'd have dubbed him Captain America. You'd think I would have been swooning, but for whatever reason, I immediately felt an easiness with Noah that was more brotherly than physical. *Maybe not* completely *brotherly, the man was seriously hot.* Anyway…

"Brooklynn," he'd greeted with a bright smile and a handshake. "Thank you so much for agreeing to meet with me."

"I'm happy to," I assured him with an answering smile.

He took my elbow and guided me to a small seating area. "Please, have a seat." I sat down on an enormously comfy brown leather couch. Noah lowered his lanky body onto one of the matching chairs and leaned forward, placing his elbow on his knees. "I'm going to be blunt," he said matter-of-factly. "There isn't much I won't do to get you to sign a contract with Stone Butterfly."

I laughed, sure he was exaggerating to keep things light, but I quieted when I saw the serious intent on his face. The determination in his expression pushed me to ignore his lack of bulk and nickname him Captain America anyway. "I appreciate your honesty, Mr. Andersen—"

"Noah," he corrected, his mouth quirked up in a grin.

"Okay, Noah," I agreed happily. Then I took a deep breath and turned the conversation in a more serious direction. "I'm going to take a leap of faith and trust you," I told him. It wasn't well-known that I had a sister because I'd gone to great lengths to make sure she wasn't ever in the spotlight. I couldn't begin to imagine the impact that media scrutiny would have on her life. However, I felt I owed it to Noah to be honest and planned to plainly lay out my concerns. I gave him the basic rundown on my situation with Baylee, the vague synopsis of our history, and why I wanted her existence kept quiet, as well as other anxieties with going forward. To my relief, he put on his superhero cape and came up with workable solutions for each of my fears. He even suggested that since Stone Butterfly was based in Manhattan, that we move Bailey and Cecily to an outer borough or just north of Manhattan so my time with her wouldn't require a several-hour drive when I was home. The tour contract was three months, but they also wanted me there for the six weeks leading up to it for rehearsal, as well as for finishing an album, which would release mid-tour. Noah even managed to turn it into a selling point, mentioning that it would give me plenty of time to get myself and my sister settled in before I took the leap into touring. I was getting more and more excited about the future and I hoped that things with the band would go smoothly.

"Could I persuade you to head over to the studio and meet the band?" he asked hopefully with lopsided smile.

I laughed at his boyishness and nodded. I was also eager see if the chemistry was right.

Speaking of chemistry. My thoughts strayed to Levi—Nope. Not gonna go there. *There is no spark between me and Levi.* I almost believed my own lie. *Damn, it. Focus, Brooklynn.*

Right, chemistry. Breaking out of my reverie, I felt excitement buzzing over my skin. Just in the few minutes I'd spent in the studio, I'd already felt it. I believed Sheryl was right—we were going to make magic.

Chapter Three

LEVI

My heart was racing. It had been since the moment my hand had touched hers, and I felt a shock of electricity. Damn, she was fucking gorgeous. My eyes couldn't seem to stop drinking in the sight of her long black hair, high and defined cheekbones, deep brown eyes surrounded by dark, sooty lashes and a slight tilt, like a natural cat eye. Her plump, pouty lips had dirty images playing on a loop in my mind, imagining how that mouth would look and feel around my cock. It was something I was one hundred fucking percent determined to experience. I tore my gaze from her face and journeyed down. She was wearing a sleeveless sweater that showed off her naturally tan skin, toned arms, and clung to her full breasts. Fitted jeans hugged her curvy hips and endless legs. When she turned to reach for a music stand, I was treated to the sight of her tight, round ass.

You're practically drooling, dude. I surreptitiously rubbed a hand over my mouth, making sure it was all in my mind and I wasn't *actually* drooling because I couldn't deny that it was a real possibility.

As if her outer package wasn't appealing enough, when she first spoke, her warm, husky voice washed over me like a cresting wave of lust that crashed hard on my dick. *And, I do mean hard.* She was a walking wet dream, and fuck, I wanted her. I leaned down beside me and grabbed my guitar off of the stand, positioning it on my lap so it hid my visceral reaction to her. I'd never been this attracted to a woman in my entire life and I was reeling from the strength of it. Glancing to my right, I watched her laugh at something Sheryl said and the sound was like a new form of music, uniquely hers. Turning back to my mic, I saw Matteo and

14

Simon watching her with naked interest and it started an unfamiliar burn in my belly.

"Let's fucking do this," I snapped, scowling at them both. Matteo simply raised his brows, but Simon's face broke into a wide grin, his brown orbs darting back and forth between Brooklynn and me. My eyes narrowed, and I glared at both of them, warning them away, laying claim on Brooklynn before I even realized what I was doing. I dropped my focus to my guitar, but not before I clocked Noah's frown as he watched me from where he was leaning against the wall by the door. There was a lecture in my future. But, it wouldn't make a difference. I'd made up my mind to make Brooklynn mine.

Twisting in my seat, I smiled at Brooklynn and enjoyed the pink tinge that appeared on her cheeks. "Are you familiar enough with our music to just riff with us?" I questioned, even though I was confident she was. Brooklynn had a reputation of being able to pick up just about anything quickly, with flare and precision. She had perfect pitch and a talent for spitting back whatever she heard with total accuracy. But, what made her truly special was the way she made everything hers, adding unique touches that enhanced what may have already seemed perfect.

Brooklynn raised a condescending eyebrow, basically calling me out for being a patronizing jackass. I laughed and launched into "World On End," one of our most popular singles. It only took a moment for the world to fall away, leaving nothing but the music. I closed my eyes, feeling the guitar become an extension of my body, and the lyrics poured out of my mouth like they'd been caged in and were desperate to be set free. I reached the chorus, and as Matteo and Simon added their voices, I felt shivers coursing through me that were always evoked by the magic of harmony. This was why we worked. Despite the different notes, we were one when the music wrapped itself around us.

On the second chorus, another voice joined in and suddenly, the small shivers became full-blown streaks of emotion. If I'd been standing right then, I'd have been knocked on my ass. The music suddenly faded out until all I heard was Brooklynn's gorgeous alto twisting itself around my voice, blending in a way that would make one believe we were put on this earth for no other purpose than to sing together. The song ended, and the last of our notes died away, leaving a heavy silence. Opening my eyes, I was surrounded by faces filled with awe, each of my band mates frozen. I realized that the reason I only heard myself and Brooklynn was because, at some point in the song, everyone else had ceased playing and singing and it had been just Brooklynn and me. Slowly, I pivoted in my seat and sought out her chocolate eyes. She seemed just as shell shocked as the rest of us.

"Marry me," Matteo breathed, breaking the silence. Everyone but me burst into laughter. Just the thought of Brooklynn with someone else made me want to put my fist into something. Teo's face seemed like a satisfying option. I shook it off and tuned into the pulsing energy of the room. There was an edge of hysteria in their amusement, a sort of high that came with making truly inspired music. The same hum of excitement that I was feeling exuded from everyone around me.

A knock on the studio door calmed our revelry and Noah opened it, letting in Sheryl's husband, Danny. He glared at us, but the expression lacked real malice, and I couldn't help chuckling in response. "Sorry for keeping her, Danny," I apologized with a rueful shrug. With an accepting chin lift, he stalked over to Sheryl and lifted her into his arms.

"Danny!" she squeaked. "I can walk." He grunted a response that only she could hear as he carried her to the exit. I swallowed a laugh at the sight of him attempting to go all alpha on his wife. The effect was kind of ruined since he was roughly the same size as his wife and was clearly struggling to stay upright. Actually, I'd hazard a guess that Sheryl out-weighed him right then. Not that I'd say it out loud and risk what would surely be a swift kick to my balls.

"Brooklynn, you're amazing!" she called out. "You'll be great!" Then she was gone and the door slammed shut.

There was more laughter and then we dove back into the music. It was after ten when Simon announced that he was done for the night and off to get laid, eliciting a round of snickers. He just grinned and beat a hasty retreat. The rest of the group trickled out until it was just Brooklynn and I remaining. I was about to approach her when Noah entered the room. It surprised me because I'd assumed he went home hours before, but he must have been working in his office. He made his way over to Brooklynn, who was slipping on her coat but stopped when he was in front of her. Offering a hand, he smiled widely as he shook hers, and the contact annoyed the shit out of me. Brooklynn returned the smile, and when he let go, she stuck her hands in her back pockets, resting her weight on her heels.

"Sheryl was right, Brooklynn," he told her with enthusiasm. Well, as much enthusiasm as an uptight, overly controlled guy with a stick up his ass can muster. I often found ways to fuck with him just to break through his all-business attitude and make sure my friend was still in there somewhere. Generally, it ended with one hell of a hangover. I grinned at the memory of the last time we let loose. I even got him to take a woman home for the night once, though I hadn't been able to get any details from him about it.

"You are a perfect fit. Can I go ahead and have the contract drawn up?"

Brooklynn lit up and nodded. "As long as it includes what we talked about, I'm all yours."

"I think you mean, all mine," I interjected, drawing another frown from Noah and an eye roll from Brooklynn. Though it was followed up by a suppressed giggle. I paid more attention to the latter, prowling over and slinging an arm around her shoulders. Noah studied us with caution, opened his mouth, then shut it.

Finally, he looked to Brooklynn and murmured, "I'll fast track it through the lawyers, so it should be ready in a couple of days. We'll meet and go over the contract and schedule."

"Great," she replied brightly before slipping out from under my arm and slinging her bag over her shoulder.

"Do you have some place to stay?" Noah inquired. He was tapping away on his smartphone as he asked the question and his tone made it clear that he was simply making sure she was taken care of, not hitting on her. So, I didn't clip him in the jaw. Instead, I listened eagerly for Brooklynn's answer and was shocked to find an invitation to stay with me on the tip of my tongue. I didn't bring women to my home. Ever. It was my sanctuary, the place I did most of my writing, where my family came to visit. In only a handful of hours, it had become more and more obvious that this thing I was feeling between us was more than just a desire to fuck her. There was a deeper connection. One I didn't quite understand yet.

Trust me, I was dying to get her underneath me, but I also felt a desire to know her, to simply *be* with her. It was like my fast-paced world slowed down to a manageable speed and I found my calm center. It was scary to be feeling those things so fast, and I was half tempted to shut it the fuck down before it went somewhere I wasn't ready for. It wasn't like I was the manwhore Simon was, but I got around when I wasn't in a relationship. That's where things had gotten sticky before. I tried the relationship thing in the beginning of my career and it had ended in disaster. Music was the most important thing to me and no girl was willing to settle for that. Nor should they.

So, I'd written off relationships for the time being. I was only twenty-three for fuck's sake, I had plenty of time to focus on my career and get to all that other stuff later. My parents had been married for thirty-five years and were still so in love it made my siblings and I gag. Especially my sister Lily, since she was still living at home. My younger brother

Liam and I liked to tease them, but I wouldn't lie and say I didn't want that someday. I didn't think I would ever be able to put someone before my music though, so I accepted the fact that it might never happen. But, for whatever reason, I was sure what I'd been feeling around Brooklynn was worth exploring, even if all it led to was incredible music and some hot, sweaty fucking.

"I booked a hotel for a couple of nights," she mumbled as she buttoned up her coat. "But I lined up an apartment here in the Village in case things worked out. I'll sign the lease in a few days." She bent down to grab her purse from the floor, giving me an excellent view of her ass, and I stifled a groan. She sighed as she stood back up. "Damn, I hate moving."

Noah lifted his attention from his phone and laughed. "You were always intending to say yes, weren't you?"

Brooklynn smirked and cocked her head to the side. "It never hurts to make you sweat just a little, right?" she sassed.

Noah grinned and clapped her on the shoulder. "Come on, I'll walk you out and find you a cab."

I firmly grasped Noah's arm and removed it from Brooklynn. "I've got some things to go over with Brooklynn, Noah," I told him, keeping my tone easy. "I'll make sure she gets home safe."

"Who will keep her safe from you," he grumped with a warning look in my direction.

Brooklynn laughed and winked at him. "I can handle him, Noah." I had no doubt this was true, in and out of the bedroom. And, the thought of her *handling* certain parts of me had my blood thickening.

"We'll see," he muttered as he walked to the door.

Once he was out of the way, I put on my most charming smile and gave Brooklynn my full attention. "Are you hungry? I'm starving. Let's get some food. I know a fantastic diner on 10th street." I took her elbow and steered her toward the door.

"Um, I don't think that's such a good idea," she objected but didn't stop me from guiding her down the hall to the office Noah used when we were recording in that studio. I grabbed my winter coat and scarf from where I'd thrown it over a worn, plaid couch earlier and put it on.

"You want to go somewhere else?" I asked, deliberately misunderstanding her. "I'm game for whatever." Putting my hand at the small of her back, just above the sweet swell of her ass, I once again led her down the hall. This time I took her out the front door and the bite of the bitter February wind immediately stung my face. I wrapped my scarf around my neck and up over my mouth, keeping my throat insulated from the dry, frigid air. Turning toward her with the intent of helping her, I saw she had already done the same. Not really surprising, considering how dedicated she was to her craft. We protect our instruments with the utmost care. Still, I adjusted her scarf as an excuse to touch her and keep her with me for another minute so I could convince her to grab some food.

"Where should we go?" I shuffled from side to side in an attempt to keep my blood moving and stay warm. I couldn't see her mouth, but her cheeks lifted and her eyes crinkled, giving away her smile.

"I'm going to go back to my hotel. Alone"—she emphasized before I could open my mouth to suggest I come along—"and ordering room service before I call my sister and go to bed. It's been a long day."

Disappointment flooded me, but I understood. I knew she came straight from her home upstate to her meeting with Noah, then spent the rest of the day and night jamming with us, and with the grueling schedule we had before us, her days weren't going to get any easier. I nodded, then curled my arm around her shoulders. "Come on, at least let me escort you to your hotel."

She tilted her head back to look up at me and then chuckled. "I'm not used to this."

"Chivalry?" I joked.

Her eyes twinkled with merriment and she laughed again. "No, although it's very sweet of you. But, I meant having to look up to a guy. I'm five foot nine. It's not often that I meet someone who has me crooking my neck to see their face." Her cheeks were already pink from the harsh cold, but they darkened even more, and it was sexy as hell. She dropped her gaze and mumbled, "It—um—makes me feel almost…dainty." She said the last word with a self-deprecating laugh.

I took hold of her chin and tipped her head back again so I could see her gorgeous brown eyes. "I've never been more grateful to be a giant if it makes you feel *dainty*." The urge to kiss her was powerful, but I managed to push it back and instead, tucked her back into my side and walked toward the corner to catch a cab.

We pulled up in front of the entrance to her hotel, and a porter rushed over to open the door. I slid out and shooed the man away then reached a hand back in to help Brooklynn. I used the leverage from pulling her up to tug her into my arms once she was on her feet. "How about lunch tomorrow?" I begged, with exaggerated puppy dog eyes, tugging her scarf down and brushing her hair back so I could see her whole face.

She shook her head and smiled apologetically. "Sorry, I have to meet with my realtor and then make my moving arrangements."

"Dinner then," I insisted, clutching her a little closer.

She sighed and gently pushed against my chest until I reluctantly let her go. "It's not a good idea, Levi. Dating a band member will only cause problems in the long run, and I don't want to jeopardize my job." Her voice was regretful and it was the only reason I let it go. I'd convince her, just not that night.

Without warning, I leaned in and kissed her icy cheek. "We'll discuss it later. Goodnight, beautiful," I whispered. I spun her around and urged her forward. She threw an exasperated look over her shoulder but continued on until she was inside.

Chapter Four

LEVI

Our first rehearsal with Brooklynn was three days later, and even though I'd sent her a text so she would have my number—after badgering it out of Noah, the bastard—I hadn't heard a peep from her in the interim. I knew she was busy with everything that went along with moving her life to the Big Apple. Still, I'd been a little shocked. I couldn't remember the last time I'd had to chase a woman. But, if that's what I had to do to get Brooklynn to give me a chance, I was up for the challenge.

We only had three more tracks to lay down to complete our album *For Your Sanity* before we hit the road, so we had plenty of time to get Brooklynn acclimated to singing with us. She was incredibly talented and it only took one rehearsal for her to fall right in with us, as though she'd always been a part of the band. Sheryl wasn't surprised at Brooklynn's ability, but she'd given me endless shit for accepting an "outsider" so fast. Begrudgingly, I admitted that I was the pickiest when it came to who we worked with. I wanted nothing less than complete cohesion. Playing together needed to be a natural instinct, otherwise we would lose the sound the fans loved us for.

After we called it a night, Brooklynn asked Sheryl to stay behind for a little while to go over some of the music. I didn't want to give her the creep vibe by staying in the room and staring, lost in the magic of her voice and her chocolate brown eyes. That didn't mean I kicked the stalker act altogether. I made my way to the sound booth, keeping the lights off and flipping on the mics. I was watching them through the darkened window when the door opened. Noah poked his head in, and his eyes went from me to the window

23

and back. He pressed his lips together so they formed a straight line, his brow dropping low in a disapproving glare.

He walked fully inside the room and crossed his arms over his chest. "We need her, Levi," he warned. "We have to do everything we can to convince her that Stone Butterfly is who she belongs with. If Sheryl decides to quit and Brooklynn leaves after the contract is done, it will be a bitch to find another vocalist to replace them." He scowled at me, his silver eyes narrowed. "I'd like to tell you to back the fuck off but I know you'll just do whatever you want, like you always do."

I grinned cockily and shrugged. It was true.

That was clearly not the response Noah was looking for and he sighed, obviously frustrated. "At least promise me that you won't pursue her unless you're serious about her. Because if you break her heart, not only will I beat the living shit out of you, we'll keep her and find a replacement for *you*."

It was my turn to scowl. Not because he'd threatened to kick my ass—*in his dreams*—but the level of protectiveness he was displaying toward Brooklynn was a little too strong. The thought that he might have feelings for her pissed me the fuck off. "Do I need to give you your own warning, Noah?" I growled.

His eyes flashed with an unreadable emotion and then strayed over to the rehearsal space once more. When he looked back at me, his face was deadpan. "No. It's crystal clear where you stand, and you know I would never cross that line."

I nodded, somewhat mollified. In all the years we'd been friends—brothers really—we'd never shared an interest in the same woman, so drawing that line in the sand had never been necessary. I suppose I should have figured it was implicit.

Noah turned and stepped into the hall, then reached for the handle to shut the door behind him. Just before it closed completely, he paused. "That doesn't mean that if you break her heart, I won't be the first one in line to pick up the pieces." He shut the door before I could respond. The jealousy eating at me was as unwelcome as it was unexpected. I'd never felt this possessive over a woman, and it was a little hard to swallow. Maybe it was my ego poking at me, annoyed that Brooklynn hadn't fallen at my feet. But whatever the reason, I didn't care for the burning in my gut, the caveman instinct to grab Brooklynn and run off to someplace no one could find us. Nor did I want this new side of me to damage my friendship with Noah.

I sat on a stool and faced the window once again. The girls were packing up. My eyes had just landed on her when, suddenly, Brooklynn threw her head back and laughed. A burning of a whole different nature began heating my body. My every muscle stilled, except the rapidly hardening one between my legs. She was so fucking beautiful and her laughter was as musical a sound as was her singing voice.

It was entirely possible that if I let the jealousy and possessiveness have their way, I would come on too strong and might end up scaring Brooklynn off. No, patiences and persistence were the best tools at my disposal.

Before the girls exited the rehearsal room, I swiftly crossed the hall to the office and grabbed my coat. Then, when I heard them enter the hallway, I walked out, shrugging on my coat as if I'd been working in there and hadn't been watching Brooklynn through a window for the last half hour as though she were an animal at the zoo.

"Ladies," I greeted. "Brooklynn, can I talk to you for a minute?

Sheryl smiled and gave her a quick hug, then slyly winked at me as she strode by.

"What's up?" Brooklynn inquired with a friendly smile. I took her black, wool coat from where it was draped over her arm and held it for her as she slipped it on. Then I wound her pink, knit scarf around her neck and used the ends to drag her close, but not so close that we were touching. Once I was sure Sheryl was around the corner and out of earshot, I stepped in, crowding her, and pushed a wayward strand of her silky black hair behind her ear while smiling with my best "I'm so cute and charming" smile.

"Have dinner with me. I know a great little Italian place."

"No." Her expression was deadpan.

"Lunch?"

"Nope." The *P* popped between her plump lips as she walked away, her hips swinging, keeping my eyes glued to her perfect ass.

I swallowed hard then shook my head to clear it. No worries. Persistence. That was the plan.

Chapter Five

BROOKLYNN

"Brooklynn, don't hold back on that D sharp. You've got the lungs, use 'em." The tinny voice of Stone Butterfly's record producer and label contact, Cooper, piped through the speaker from the sound booth. I'd noticed that he was involved in a lot more aspects than I had expected for his job description, but it didn't seem to faze anyone else, so I didn't think much of it. Besides, I liked the guy. He had a dry sense of humor and a lot of passion for the music.

I gave him a thumbs up and made a note on my music with a pencil. After a week of rehearsals, we were laying down the first of three tracks for Stone Butterfly's album. Sheryl had decided to hand over the reins to me completely for backups on two of the last three songs being recorded. Given how long we'd known each other, it wasn't a surprise to me. She knew I could handle whatever was thrown at me.

Whatever is thrown at you? Okay, so maybe a wrench had been thrown into my reputation for taking everything in stride. An incredibly hot, distracting wrench named Levi Matthews. I wasn't sure how to handle what I felt for him. The desire was almost overwhelming at times. Although, I had managed to stick to my convictions enough to continue to turn him down when he asked me out. Every. Day.

At least I could find solace in the fact that this weakness was successfully camouflaged. I was the only one who knew that I was teetering on a very thin tight rope, hoping to reach the other side, but so intrigued by the unknown below. Even Levi seemed unaware of just how strongly he affected me.

But, I still had my music to ground me, something I was in complete control of.

"Let's take it from the key change, guys," he instructed.

"Hold it a second," Simon called out as he plucked out a chord on his bass. He tuned a string and played it once again again, his face pensive. Then took a pencil and made a mark on his music, before pointing to me with the eraser. "Hold that G sharp out an extra measure. I'm going to add a chord progression here so that you are singing the leading note and on beat four, Levi will resolve the scale on the tonic while you glide up to the fifth and I drop to the root to create a triad in the next key. I think it'll make the transition into the key change smoother and give the G sharp a real punch."

I ran through the music in my head, hearing the way it made the music richer and sexier. "Fucking brilliant, Simon," I beamed and gave him a high five when he stepped away from his mic.

Levi hummed a little and then bobbed his head up and down with a grin. "I like it. Sasha, add a harmonizing sotto voce run on the piano to keep the music flowing so it doesn't get choppy."

Sasha and Simon tested it out on the instruments, then the four of us ran through it. After a minor tweak, we added Matteo, and then Kristi chimed back in after the transition. Satisfied with our changes, we recorded it and then listened to the playback. It was amazing.

In this industry, it was easy to fall into robotic habits, to simply go through the motions. People often lost the magic of it all and suddenly, it became just another job. There was a lot of wasted talent in the world. But with Stone Butterfly, there was always a vibrating hum of electricity in the air when we were making music. We let the magic seep into our bones so that every note came from our souls. I felt it when I walked into the studio that first day and it had been the strongest thing that had pushed me toward signing with them.

"Let's break here for the night, guys," Cooper announced. "I've got Verruca Salt first thing in the morning, followed by Wrong Direction and their—cough—lovely mother."

I slapped a hand over my mouth as I snorted with laughter. He was referring to a young female pop star, who was well known for her over-the-top demands and temper tantrums, as well as a teen brother duo who had a lot of potential, but their super controlling—*typical stage mom*—was always pushing for what she thought was best. She was usually incredibly wrong.

"I wonder what he calls us behind our backs," Matteo laughed.

Sasha snickered. "Cement Cocoon?"

"Wrong, Ms. Blue," Cooper stated. The metallic quality of his voice through the speaker did not disguise his sarcasm. "That reminds me, I need to see you in my office before you go." The muffled sound of a door slamming shut indicated that he'd left the sound booth. It did not escape my notice that he didn't answer our question.

"Being summoned to the principal's office, Sasha?" Simon teased, shaking his head solemnly.

"Fuck off, Simon," she tossed back, grinning. "He's probably going to give me another lecture and threaten to wash my mouth out with soap."

"Well, this is bound to be entertaining," I drawled.

Sasha laughed and shrugged. "It's not really anything new. I refuse to be anyone but me and trying to force it just means I'll push back that much harder." She started to gather her things.

"Aaaaaaand?" I pushed and winked at her. "Give it up, woman."

She rolled her eyes at my pun, then shrugged with an evil smirk. "I did an interview with *Hard Notes* magazine and I'm guessing they sent him the advanced copy today. Apparently, I said fuck more than he would have liked." She rolled her eyes. "Which means I said it at least once."

"That's it?" Levi asked, knowing full well there had to be more to the story.

"Okay, so I had a photo shoot for the article and I guess

he thinks I took off too many clothes."

"Translation," Kristi giggled. "You took *all* of them off."

Sasha winked at Kristi and laughed. "It's not like I showed off the goods. For the most part." She grinned and snapped her violin case shut then glanced back at us over her shoulder. "I was sitting on top of a piano and there was a violin in . . . a strategic position."

The room exploded with laughter.

"He spent hours trying to negotiate with the magazine not to print the more risqué photos and censor your interview, Sasha." Noah's dry voice interrupted our mirth, drawing all of our heads in his direction. I hadn't realized he'd come into the room. As usual, he looked very *GQ*, impeccably dressed in a custom suit with his blond locks in an artfully, messy style. I vaguely wondered if the guy owned a pair of ratty, holey jeans. Or. Jeans at all, for that matter.

"You know I love you, Sasha." He crossed his arms over his chest, his muscles flexing sexily, and frowned. "But do you think you could try just a little bit not to antagonize our fucking producer? I have to negotiate our contracts with this guy."

"What's the fun in that?" she asked sassily as she strode to the door. "Do you think you could try *just a little bit* to relax? Or one of these days, I'm going to stick a can of WD-40 up your ass." She stepped into the hall but before she shut the door, she called, "That'll be easy compared to removing the stick from Cooper's."

Noah rolled his eyes and shook his head, but one corner of his mouth tipped up as though he was fighting a smirk. Then his focus turned to me and his smile turned genuine. "Brooklynn, I want to run something by you."

"Sure." I rested on my stool and waited while he dragged another one over to me and sat.

"I think you should sing Sheryl's part in 'Sanity' on the album."

My mouth dropped open. "Sanity" was the powerhouse song. The single everyone expected to hit #1 on the charts.

It wasn't a duet, but the female vocals were still a large part of the song, and I couldn't believe Noah was asking me to step on Sheryl that way. "No way, Noah. That's Sheryl's part, she earned it," I snapped, jumping up from my seat and shoving my hands into my back pockets while I paced.

Noah looked taken aback by my reaction at first, then realization dawned on his face. "I'm sorry, Brooklynn. I should have told you first, Sheryl is the one who came to me with the idea."

I shook my head, still opposed to the idea, even if I supposedly had Sheryl's blessing.

"Fuck," Levi interjected. "Why didn't I think of that? Brooklynn, this song is perfect for you."

Kristi, Simon, and Matteo all murmured their agreement, reminding me that they were all still in the room. *No pressure, Brooklynn. None. At. All.*

I stopped wearing a path in the carpet and looked around at their encouraging faces. "Let me think about it," I hedged, uncomfortable continuing the discussion in front of everyone. More than anything, I needed to talk to Sheryl.

Noah nodded and patted my knee before standing.

"Hands to yourself, Andersen," Levi growled, and I rolled my eyes.

Noah ignored him. "I want you to start working on it with Levi tomorrow, so think fast."

Huffing, I muttered, "Gee, thanks."

Noah chuckled as he walked over to Matteo and started a discussion.

"Seriously, baby." I jumped at the sound of Levi's husky voice and the feel of his soft lips brushing the shell of my ear. He was standing right behind me, and I bumped into him. *Where the hell did he come from?*

"You would bring so much to this song. Together, it would be fucking mind-blowing." His lips moved from my ear to kiss a spot just below it, and I shivered. He chuckled darkly and the sound slid over my skin right to my panties, making them damp.

"Let me take you out." His sudden subject change threw me for a second, but I quickly course-corrected.

"No."

"I'm not giving up."

I suppressed a smile and, looking over my shoulder, I rolled my eyes instead. "Somehow, I don't doubt that's true."

here.

"Are you sure, Sheryl?" I asked one more time.

Her sigh was loud and clear over the phone. "Is this really about me, Brooklynn?"

"What?" I frowned and slumped down in my over-stuffed, plush blue sofa chair. The normally relaxing seat didn't keep me from squirming uncomfortably, pretty sure of where Sheryl was about to take the conversation.

"I'm starting to wonder if it's not me you're really worried about. You're afraid to sing it with Levi, aren't you?"

"Um—" I wanted to deny it, but what was the point? Sheryl had some kind of magical friendship Spidey sense and always seemed to know what I wasn't saying.

"That's what I thought." Her tone was annoyingly smug. I stuck my tongue out at the phone, the gesture making me feel better even though she couldn't see it until she said, "Did you just stick your tongue out at me?"

"Okay, seriously!" I said with a hint of shrill. "How the fuck do you *do* that?"

"Don't change the subject," she clucked like she was admonishing a child. Admittedly, sticking out my tongue at her had been quite juvenile, but still…

It was my turn to sigh. "Fine, I'm worried about doing the song with Levi. I'm already fighting a battle with myself to stay away from him. This song not only means more time together, but it's a powerful love song. I don't have that kind of will power, woman!"

Sheryl was quiet for a minute. "Have you thought about giving him a chance?"

I pulled back from the phone and stared at it. I knew she couldn't actually see me, it was just a thing I did. Don't judge. Returning the phone to my ear, I sputtered my response. "What are—how can—are you crazy?" My voice was fully shrill this time. No hint about it.

"He's a really good guy, Brooklynn. And even if you guys didn't last, he'd never make you leave the band."

"Maybe not," I grumbled. "But it would be awkward and most likely heart-breaking. We would only be able to work in that environment for so long before one of us broke. And, it's not like Levi is going to be the one to leave."

"I guess." Her agreement lacked any conviction. "Anyway, you're doing the song and that's the end of it. Love you, bye!" She hung up.

I hope she gives birth to a twelve-pound baby.

I checked my watch and decided to call Baylee. She answered on the third ring, and I felt better the minute I heard her voice.

"Hi, sweet girl!" I trilled.

"Brooklynn!" she exclaimed loudly. I laughed and suddenly, my chair was oh-so-comfy again.

"What did you do today?"

I settled in and enjoyed listening to her sweet voice chirping about all the fun things she'd done and was planning for the next few days. Eventually, she took a breath.

"How's the band? Do you like the music? We got the CD and it's so amazing! Cecily and I listen to it all the time!"

"Is it my turn?" I laughed. I told her about the recording session we'd had that day and, toning down my stories a little, we talked about my band mates. After an hour or so, our conversation wound down and Baylee started losing interest in the phone call.

"Love you, Brooklee!" I couldn't help but smile at her nickname. When she was little, she was confused about my name, since I was always saying Baylee to her, but everyone else said Brooklynn around her. She combined our names and it stuck.

"Love you too, sweet girl. Put Cecily on for me."

"Hey, Brooklynn. Judging from Baylee's reactions, I assume recording is going well?" Her voice was full of humor and a matching excitement that she was trying to hide. Cecily liked to pretend she was too adult to obsess over Stone Butterfly, but she couldn't suppress it completely, especially around Baylee.

"It's been pretty amazing. They asked me to work on a song with Levi today. It's not a duet, but it would be just me and him. It's freaking me out a little."

"Holy cow! Are you serious? I don't know how you even speak around Levi Matthews. I would be totally tongue-tied." She giggled. "I'm just saying, he's the hottest man alive. I swear, I'm gonna marry that guy someday."

"You girls," I chuckled, my head shaking. "I'll have to make sure you get to a concert soon."

"O.M.G!!!!" Cecily screamed. "I can't wait!! Thank you, Brooklynn!"

"Okay, Cecily," I interrupted her exclamations. "Calm down, girl. How is Baylee doing with the move?"

Cecily drew in some deep breaths and when she spoke again, her voice had dropped back down to a normal decibel. "Better than we hoped. The Stone Butterfly albums actually help a lot. She listens to them almost exclusively. Not that I ever get sick of listening to them."

"That's great, Cecily." I sighed with the small surge of relief I always felt after a call with Baylee. It chipped away at my ever-present worry for her. We talked for a few more minutes, going over my schedule for the next few weeks and planning some activities in the city we would meet up for.

After the call ended, my head tipped back to rest on the edge of the chair and I stared at the ceiling. Damn, I was tired. My phone chirped, and I lifted it up over my head so I could look at the screen without moving.

Levi: Whatcha doing, beautiful?

Me: Going to bed.

The little typing bubble popped up on the screen, then disappeared, then popped up again, and did the same three more times. Finally, a message appeared.

Levi: So many dirty things running through my head right now…

Me: Like me in my underwear?

Levi: If I wasn't thinking about exactly that, I am now, cruel woman.

Me: Jokes on you, lover boy. I sleep naked.

Levi: ARE YOU FUCKING KIDDING ME????

Me: Yes. Goodnight.

There went that typing bubble again. Popping up then disappearing, over and over until a message appeared.

Levi: Sweet dreams, baby.

I laughed, knowing he had clearly checked his impulse to reply with something wicked. Fate was a bitch for making him so damn appealing and totally off limits.

Chapter Six

LEVI

I barely made it through our recording session the next day from being so fucking anxious to get Brooklynn alone. Don't get me wrong, I was ecstatic to be singing "Sanity" with her, but I would have been lying if I said I wasn't planning on capitalizing on all the one-on-one time. She looked fan-fucking-tastic and my eyes kept turning in her direction. Her hair was down, the thick, straight strands falling down her back or over her shoulder, flirting with her breasts. She was wearing a soft, pink sweater that had just a hint of fuzz. It reminded me of cotton candy, and I had the strongest urge to lick her and see if she tasted just as sweet. Her jeans were formfitting, showing off her incredible ass. They were tucked into knee-high, black boots with a heel that made my mind draw pictures of fucking her in nothing but those boots. It was a good thing I had my guitar in my lap.

We finished our session around one o'clock, but before I could attempt to talk Brooklynn into lunch, she took off with Sasha and Kristi. Matteo clapped me on the back, getting my attention, and I swiveled on my stool to face him.

"Starting 'Sanity' with Brooklynn today?" he asked.

"Fuck yeah. I can't wait to hear her on this part."

"If I didn't know you'd written it before you met her," Simon said as he sauntered over, "I'd think it was written for her."

Matteo nodded in agreement before putting on his thick, leather coat. "I've got plans tonight, but I should be done around eleven. Let me know if you want to catch a late beer."

Simon snorted in amusement, but he was looking at Matteo like he'd grown two heads. "I hope those plans are not a date, dude. Otherwise, it seems I've taught you nothing."

Matteo gave Simon a one-fingered salute as he started toward the door. "She's taking a red eye flight tonight, asshole."

"Ah, so my teachings have not been wasted," Simon jeered. "Nothing like a fast and hard, farewell fuck. Avoids all the messy, morning after bullshit." Simon was still flapping his gums as he followed Matteo out the door. I laughed at their antics, then picked up my guitar and tuned out everything but the music. "Sanity" was an extremely emotional love song. It started out as hard rock, then dropped to a haunting melody, before moving into an upbeat, almost punk rock sound and eventually ending with our natural genre, alternative rock. It changed sound and tempo frequently throughout the song, the same way someone's mind jumps around, making them feel like they are going crazy. The lyrics told the story of lovers who drive each other to the brink of insanity, but can't seem to survive without one another. Their relationship was almost as toxic as it was healing, a balm to their broken souls. The music returned to singing about their need for one another in every refrain. That was the part where it became a duet of sorts with the female vocals was a powerhouse section. It was full of desire, unbridled need, practically fucking with our voices.

Most people who heard it assumed I was inspired by my own experiences, but the truth was, I wrote it based on an ideal. It was a kind of love that I wasn't sure I believed in, but I wanted to and "Sanity" was my way of expressing my longing for that kind of emotional tie to someone. Even if it meant teetering on the edge of crazy, at least we'd hold hands on the fall.

The rhythmic thumping of the drums accompanied me inside my head as I played my guitar and sang through the piece. I made a couple of small tweaks then began singing the chorus again. The woman's harmony twisted around my melody, her line crossing mine, the notes constantly moving higher and lower. I could hear her perfectly and the blend of our voices was unreal.

Suddenly, I realized that the voice I was hearing wasn't in my head. I stopped playing and my eyes snapped open. Brooklynn had come into the room at some point and pulled a stool over to face me. She was half sitting on it so her rib cage stayed open and though she'd been looking at her sheet music, our eyes met the moment the sound ceased. "Amazing," I whispered. I was referring to her beauty as much as her talent. I shook it off and lifted a chin at her music. "Didn't Noah give that to you before you left for lunch?"

She lifted a single, black brow and smirked, her brown eyes twinkling with laughter. "Yes. I looked at it for a few minutes while you were singing before joining you."

I gawked at her. I knew Brooklynn's reputation, and I'd seen for myself over the last couple of weeks how gifted she was. But, "Sanity" was an unbelievably difficult song. The vocal range needed, the quickly changing melodies and tempos, the tight harmonies, etc., meant there weren't many people who could sing this song and do it justice. It had taken Sheryl months to learn her part and sing all three refrains as well as the ending without making any major mistakes. Brooklynn had looked at it for a hot second and jumped right in, singing it like she'd known the song all of her life.

"Your genius would be alarming if it wasn't so damn consistent," I declared with a chuckle.

She laughed and spun on her stool, her legs flying out in front of her. When she was facing me again, she grinned. "Yeah, I'm kind of a big deal." Then she winked and blew me a kiss, Marilyn Monroe style. Just like that, I was hard as a fucking rock, which was saying something since I'd already been sporting an erection from singing "Sanity" with her.

"You're not helping your cause, baby," I growled. "One of these days, you are going to give in and let me sweep you off your fucking feet."

"That's a pretty inflated ego you've got there, Barney Stinson," she snarked, folding her arms, pushing her tits up. A chuckle bubbled to the surface at her reference to a character from a popular sitcom. I did my best not to let my eyes stray down, but it was a losing battle. I had no willpower when it came to Brooklynn. I'd make a shitty Jedi. "Go ahead, look your fill, because that's as close as your gonna get to my breasts." She practically cackled. Fitting, since she'd cast a fucking spell on me.

I tore my eyes away with a groan and looked down at my guitar. "So, let's work on the song, yeah?" I mumbled, changing the subject before I got on my knees and begged. *Haven't even gone on a date and already pussy-whipped.* Fuck.

Strumming my guitar, I closed my eyes before starting the first verse. Brooklynn hummed a little here and there, then came in with her part on the chorus. There were a few times when she sang a different note from what was written—tightening the harmony—and our blended voices were entwined so close, I felt like they were naked and pressed against each other. I halted after one refrain and stared at her for a moment, contemplating. She hummed a few bars before looking up and noticing my intense gaze. An idea was forming.

This song had come from my soul and to anyone else, they might think it was perfect. But, to me, it had always felt a tiny bit hollow. I'd assumed it was because I was singing about something I'd never experienced, a sort of empty longing. Then Brooklynn happened. It hit me that for the first time, the song had taken on a depth that I could never achieve on my own. And, it was a duet. It was always meant to be a duet but I hadn't realized it because no other woman had made the song complete. So, I'd written only a small part for the female vocals, creating a richer sound, but not really a part of the song. Now, I was seeing what this music could be, and it was so far beyond the realm of what I'd written alone. The song was going to be spectacular, and no one would escape it without being touched deep in their soul.

I gathered up the sheets of my music, each one scribbled all over from the constant changes I made. "Come with me," I beckoned as I made my way to the grand piano in the back corner of the room. "Will you play this while we run through it this time?" Her brow rose in question, but I just gestured to the keys. She shrugged and slid onto the shiny, black bench.

Her fingers rested lightly on the keys, just the pads touching the surface. As she began to play, they remained almost floating over the black and white notes unless they were pressing them down for sound. Watching her was hypnotic, and for a moment, I silently leaned on the piano and just listened. After a few minutes, she looked at me with a questioning raise of her brow.

"I want to make some changes to 'Sanity.'"

"Okay, where do you want to start?" She shuffled through the music on the piano, only half paying attention to me.

I grabbed her chin gently but firmly lifting her head so that I could see her beautiful mocha eyes. "I said that wrong. What I meant was: I want us to make some changes. Mostly you, though."

Brooklynn looked confused. "You want me to tweak the chorus a little more?"

Laughing, I let go of her chin and rounded the piano to sit next to her on the bench. "I guess I communicate better through music than talking. Baby, I want to change this into a duet and I want you to write the part, with a little collaboration."

"Are you fucking with me right now?" she sputtered. I shook my head. "But, I'm a backup singer," she protested. "And, I'm the newest and don't forget, temporary, band member. You should be offering this to Sasha or Kristi."

She stood and wandered around the small space by the piano, then stopped in front of me, her hands slipping into her back pockets. "I don't want to rock the boat. Everyone has been so awesome, treating me like I've always been a part of the group. I'm not going to throw that back in their faces by hogging the spotlight—even if it was your idea and not mine."

While her concerns were understandable, they weren't necessary. I'd given Kristi the opportunity to take a bigger part in our music, but she was content with her role and didn't want more work and responsibility. Sasha was . . . well, Sasha. She'd wouldn't give a shit. And, she wasn't shy about the things she felt passionately about. If she'd wanted to collaborate on "Sanity" with me, she would have made it loud and fucking clear. Or, she would have just shown up one day with her part written and told me, *not asked*, that she'd be singing it with me. Yeah, I knew this from experience.

"Trust me, I know my band mates, babe. They will agree with my decision."

She looked at me doubtfully, but when she glanced at the music, I caught the flash of longing and excitement in her eyes. I'd finally scored a win with her. *Levi 1, Brooklynn . . . Let's not focus on that embarrassing number.*

Taking a seat beside me on the piano bench again, Brooklynn bit her lip, trying to hide a smile. I reached out and gently tugged it out. "Don't do that," I warned quietly.

"What?"

"Bite your lips like that."

Brooklynn looked surprised, obviously unaware that she'd been doing it. "Um, okay . . . Any particular reason?"

I leaned in close, so close our lips were almost touching, and I could feel her warm breaths. She retreated a little, but she had nowhere to go if she didn't want to scoot right off the end of the bench and land on her ass. "Because it makes me want to bite it instead. Because it makes me picture those gorgeous lips wrapped around something else. Because it

41

makes me hard as a fucking rock."

Her tan skin made it easier to overlook, but I saw everything about Brooklynn, so I noticed when the blood rushed to her cheeks and her breathing sped up. *Interesting. She was definitely not turned off by my blunt explanation. Good to know.* Her eyes widened and she glanced around, probably looking for a way to escape me as I bent even closer, caging her in with my arms holding on to the edge of the bench on either side of her. I was invading almost every inch of her personal space, but I avoided actually touching her, mindful of her skittishness and not wanting to push my luck. "So, no more biting that lip unless you want me doing it for you," I murmured.

"Music," she squeaked in response. I laughed and moved back to my side of the bench, throwing her one last heated glance before shifting my focus to music. We talked about the feel and sound we were going for and made some progress writing her first verse.

"Do you like baseball?" The question popped out of my mouth without thought.

Brooklynn looked at me with surprise, since the question had come out of left field. (Everyone has to nerd out sometimes, don't knock my puns.) "Why do you ask?"

"Just stockpiling ideas for when you agree to date me."

"Good grief, you never let up." She pushed her hair over her shoulder and tapped her full bottom lip with one finger before answering. "As a matter of fact, I do. I'm a pretty big fan."

"Pleeeeeease, tell me you're a Yankee fan," I begged with my hands clasped like I was sending up a prayer.

Brooklynn laughed and batted at my hands. "Of course."

I blew out a dramatic sigh of relief. "Good. Sasha would kick my ass if I agreed to let a Met fan into the group."

She giggled again and turned back to the piano and plinked a few keys. Pausing, she glanced at me sideways. "Are you?"

"When my mother gave birth to me, the first thing she

did was dress me in a Yankees onesie. My father made sure of it." We continued to talk in between time spent on the music. It was light and fun, just getting to know one another. It only confirmed my belief that this amazing woman was worth pursuing.

.

Chapter Seven

LEVI

My phone beeped, distracting me and popping the little bubble that had been shutting out the world. I almost ignored it, but then I remembered that my sister, Lily, a senior in high school, was going to her winter formal and it was most likely time for pictures. It seemed kind of early for her to be getting ready, though. I picked up my iPhone and stared at the time in shock. It was already after seven. We'd been working for a little over five hours and it had felt like no time at all. Damn.

Sure enough, my screen showed a picture of my little sister in her formal dress, if you could even call it that. I typed in the code to open the messages and scrolled through the many, many, photos she'd sent. I frowned when I saw her dress and with each swipe of my finger, my brow furrowed deeper.

"Wow, that's quite an expression, Levi. I'd hate to be whoever messaged you right now," she teased. My gaze swung up and I couldn't form words around my anger and disbelief. I shoved my phone at her.

"She's basically naked!" I barked.

Brooklynn smirked. "I wouldn't think you'd have a problem with that—whoa!" She blinked owlishly at the screen before lifting accusing eyes in my direction. "She's practically a baby," she said in a low and quiet voice.

"Exactly!" I agreed, not really understanding her reaction but glanced right over it, still hung up on the fact that my parents were letting my baby sister prance around in a fucking dishtowel.

"Kind of young for you, Levi. Don't you think?" Brooklynn's voice had turned sugary sweet, the kind of sugar that looks deceptively tasty but in reality, it's simply hiding—insert the nastiest thing you've ever eaten here—and will make you sick.

"Young for—" Then it hit me. "Fuck no!" I shouted, taken aback as her accusatory tone started to make sense. "She's my sister."

Understanding dawned on her face then morphed into sheepishness. "Sorry, I thought—"

"What the fuck, Brooklynn?" I interrupted furiously. "Do you really have that low of an opinion of me?"

She cringed and curled into herself a little. "No. I don't know where that came from. I really am sorry, Levi."

I blew out a breath in an attempt to expel some of my anger. We needed to talk, but first…

I pointed at her. "Don't fucking go anywhere," I instructed gruffly. "I have to deal with this shit first. Then we'll talk."

She nodded and her quick agreement washed away another layer of my fury. My finger stabbed "Mom" in my contacts and I put the phone to my ear, pacing as it rang.

After the fourth ring, my mom picked up and sighed dramatically before saying, "You just earned me a week's worth of dishes, young man."

It wasn't anywhere near the realm of what I'd expected to come out of her mouth and it threw me off kilter for a half a second. Then I righted myself and exploded. "What the fuck, Ma? Please tell me you did not let Lily leave the house looking like that!"

"Watch your language, Levi," she chided. "You're not too old for a spanking."

I shook my head in exasperation as even more of my ire leaked out. "Sorry, Ma," I apologized guiltily. "But seriously. She didn't wear that, right?"

My mother belly laughed, and I heard giggling in the background. I assumed Lily was standing right there and I immediately knew I'd been played. "Who won?" I asked dryly.

"Me!" Lily exclaimed, having stolen the phone away. "I know your big brother ways better than anyone, dude." I couldn't help laughing, relieved that my sister wasn't out romping around in a scrap of cloth, and equally amused at their antics.

"I bet Mom that you would call within five minutes of getting my text," she crowed smugly. "Mom said twenty and Dad bet you'd just drive here like a bat out of hell without calling. Thanks for being so predictable, big brother! You got me out of dishes and laundry for a week!" She was so excited, it reminded me of when she was a little girl and I could still impress her. You know, before the "older brother" was no longer cool. *It doesn't even matter than I'm a fucking rock star,* I thought grumpily.

"Want to see my actual dress?" she squealed. I smiled, missing my fun, boisterous family. We'd been so busy ramping up for the album and tour that I hadn't been home for a couple of months.

"Absolutely, sugar. I've got to go, but I can't wait to see it."

"Awesome!" There was a shuffle, and I assumed the phone was being passed around, which was confirmed when I heard my mother's warm voice once again.

"Next time, hold your horses, Levi," she huffed. "I gave birth to you, so you should always be helping me win."

"I'll keep that in mind for next time, Ma," I laughed. "Everything going okay?"

"Ain't nothing but sunshine," she replied, making me even more nostalgic for home. She's been using that phrase for as long as I could remember. Fitting because she had the sunniest personality out of anyone I'd ever met.

"That's great. I'll try to get home this weekend."

"I know you're busy with all the prep, and we understand but we would love to see you." Her tone was warm and comforting, not guilting me, just a subtle reminder that I was loved. It made me determined to go home at least once before we went on the road. "Love you, darling boy."

"Love you too, Ma. Give my love to Dad and Lily. I'll see if Liam can take a couple of days and come home with me." My brother was in his third year at Columbia University. I loved having him near and we tried to grab lunch at least once a week.

"I'd love to have both my boys home!"

We said our goodbyes and hung up. Not thirty seconds later, my phone dinged with a text. My beautiful sister was all dolled up, looking like a princess in her purple, floor-length dress. I chuckled over the whole thing again and muttered, "Much better." Although, I wasn't exactly happy to know she'd have some hormonal little bastard drooling over her all night. I specifically remember telling her she couldn't date until she was at least thirty. Dad and Liam had backed me up. Then Mom overruled us all and let her have a date to the dance. *Traitor.*

"I take it she didn't end up wearing that dress?" Brooklynn asked, and I grinned when I looked at her and saw her amused smile.

I shook my head and strolled over to the stool where she'd gathered her things, then sat and waited for me. Handing her the phone, I lifted my chin in a gesture for her to take a look. "Apparently, my 'older brother' instincts have become predictable. They had a bet on how I'd react to the first *dress.*" The last word came out with a disgusted grimace.

Brooklynn chuckled and handed over the phone. "She looks gorgeous."

"Yeah," I agreed, taking another look at the picture. "She's a pretty amazing sister, too. She's going to fucking love you," I said absentmindedly as I locked my phone and slipped it in the pocket of my jeans. When I raised my head, Brooklynn was gaping at me. "Don't give me that look, Brooklynn. Even if you never give in to my request for a date, which you will eventually, you'll meet them when they come to some of our shows."

She visibly relaxed, but still looked a little

uncomfortable. "I just, um, I don't do families very well."

I raised an eyebrow at her comment. We'd talked a little about her sister's situation. Her sister was a little developmentally delayed. They were each other's only family, and she'd practically raised her. Not only was it easy to see how much she loved her, it was obvious that she took amazing care of her. "I don't believe that," I challenged softly. I took hold of one of her slender hands and brought it up so I could place a kiss in her palm. "Everything about you tells me that you'll fit right in."

She snatched her hand back and her laugh had a bitter edge. "Well, you're wrong." Standing from her stool, she crossed her arms in front of her chest and watched me with a blank expression and shuttered eyes. "Look," she began, the only indication that she was feeling anything coming from the irritation bleeding into her tone. "I'm really sorry about what I assumed before. It was thoughtless, and if I'd taken even a moment to think before speaking, I would have realized what a stupid thought it was. You were right, you've never given me any reason to cast you in a villainous light."

"Thank you." I left it at that. I'd been fired up about it before, but now I just wanted to move on. And, I wanted my Brooklynn back. I didn't recognize this cold, emotionless woman. I grinned when something popped into my head and before I could check the impulse, I blurted, "People often assume the worst when they are jealous."

She glared at me, the spark of irritation lighting a fire in her eyes, and she shoved her hands onto her hips. "Don't flatter yourself, Barney," she snapped. *There she is.* Anger was better than nothing at all.

"My mistake," I remarked, holding my hands up in an "I surrender" pose.

Her countenance mellowed completely and she was back to being the sweet, funny, insanely hot Brooklynn I was used to. She bent down and grabbed her bag and coat, then we walked to the office to grab my outerwear as well.

Just inside the door, I put my hand on her arm to halt her exit.

"Dinner?"

"Nope."

"Lunch tomorrow?"

Brooklynn sighed and turned to walk away, but there was a smile flirting around her mouth.

I grabbed her arm to stop her again, pulled her inside and shoved the door shut. Walking her backward, I crowded her up against a wall. Having caught her by surprise, she didn't protest when I dove my fingers into her hair and angled her head. I didn't give her any time for her mind to catch up, covering her mouth with my own. She gasped, and I took advantage of the moment, my tongue entering her mouth to lick and tangle with hers. I groaned at her taste, it was fucking incredible, and I knew I was instantly addicted. Her hands had been at her sides but they slowly crept up over my chest, to hold on to my shoulders as though they were the only thing holding her up.

I combed my fingers through her hair and then they traveled down to splay across her back, pressing her body forward and flush with mine. Fuck, she felt good. My erection was on the brink of exploding, so hard it was almost painful to breathe. I had to stop before I reached a point of no return. I knew I could seduce her right out of her clothes at that moment, but she'd never forgive me. No, we'd fuck when she wanted it with a clear mind. I backed off of the kiss and then slowly withdrew completely. She was dazed and mussed up, looking like she'd just been thoroughly kissed. It was a look I hoped to see on her more often.

I cupped her face and waited until the fog dissipated from her chocolate orbs. "How about I cook you breakfast?" I grinned roguishly and winked.

"Are you kidding me?" she scoffed at my cheesy line.

I just shrugged and grinned. *It was worth a shot.*

Later that night, I was on my couch, ignoring the TV because I couldn't get Brooklynn off my mind, not that this was a rare occurrence. My phone taunted me from the coffee table in front of me, next to my propped-up feet. I stretched out and picked it up, using my finger to open it as I sat back into the cushions.

Opening my messenger app, I tapped on Brooklynn's name.

Me: You're thinking about me right now, aren't you?

Me: I can sense these things.

It took a few minutes, but eventually, the little bubble popped up to let me know she was responding.

Brooklynn: You caught me.

I grinned smugly.

Brooklynn: I was thinking about what I wanted to eat and you came to mind.

My jaw hit my lap when it fell, and my dick wept with the idea of her bee-stung lips wrapped around it.

Me: I'm willing and available to satiate your hunger anytime, baby.

Brooklynn: Good to know. If I ever have a desire to eat you, you'll be the first one I call.

Me: Were you about to call??

Logic told me it wasn't the case, but I couldn't help hoping.

Brooklynn: I did make a call actually.

How had I missed it? I instantly went to my missed calls and saw it was empty. No voicemail either.

Me: When? My phone doesn't show a missed call from you.

Brooklynn: Why would it? I called and ordered takeout from the little Italian place you recommended. It gave me a chance to break out my language skills. I'm good with my mouth like that.

My head fell back against the couch, and I groaned in frustration. I lifted my phone high so I could see it and tapped out another message.

Me: One of these days, your teasing is going to cause you to find yourself tied to my bed with my tongue in your pussy, and I won't let you come until you've apologized for each and every one.

It took a long time for her to respond, and I dropped my cell into my lap, wondering if I'd gone too far. Then I felt it vibrate, and my head flew forward as I opened it back up to see her reply.

Brooklynn: Tied with what?

Me: I prefer soft materials to the traditional handcuffs.

Brooklynn: I'll keep that in mind.

Fucking hell, the woman would be the death of me.

Brooklynn: Food is here. Good night, Levi.

Me: I'll comfort myself with the knowledge that you'll be thinking of me as you savor every bite.

I didn't see her answering message until the next morning since it had come through at around two A.M.

Brooklynn: You tasted delicious.

Chapter Eight

BROOKLYNN

We finished the other two songs for the album over the next week, but since Levi and I were reworking "Sanity," Noah got Cooper to push off the recording a week and extend our studio time. We came in early and stayed late, barely able to tear ourselves away from the music. We were going to spend the upcoming week fleshing out the details as a group before laying down the tracks.

Levi hadn't brought up our text exchange from the week before, and at some point, I was finally able to be around him without blushing to the roots of my hair. We'd texted a few more times, but those texts had been low key and platonic, so I'd grown comfortable again. We arrived before the rest of the band to work out some last-minute kinks and were in the sound booth listening to the recordings we'd done when Cooper arrived.

"Hey, Cooper," I greeted.

"Brooklynn," he replied with a smile. "Lovely as always." Then he and Levi did that hand shake-back slap thing that I would never understand.

I'd been feeling guilty the last few days and wanted to talk to Cooper about it. "I hope we didn't cause problems when you booked us extra studio time. I'm sure we displaced some of your other clients."

Cooper waved it off. "It was no big deal." Then he grinned like the Cheshire Cat. "I should be thanking you actually."

"Thanking me?"

He nodded and leaned back against the wall, arms crossed and an ankle over the other. "Yup. Verruca Salt threw the mother of all fucking fits, broke some equipment, and stormed out of here."

"And, why are you thanking me for that?" I asked, confused.

"Because she demanded that Daddy get her a new producer, and when he went to the label, they decided it was the last straw and that she was more trouble than she was worth. Not just her demands. They'd gotten the bill for the damaged equipment."

"The label bought out her contract?"

"Oh, it gets better," Levi added.

My head swiveled in his direction and he nodded, his face lit up with mirth.

"She was so full of herself," Cooper continued and I swung my head back to him. "She agreed to sell her contract back for half its value because she'd make it up when another studio signed her for what she was worth."

Levi and Cooper burst out laughing

"Seriously?" I was shaking my head in astonishment, but giggling right along with them.

"Wait, there's more," Cooper panted as he tried to catch his breath from laughing.

"Oh, this has got to be good," I snickered.

"Daddy was fucking pissed, but she railroaded right over him, like always."

Levi jumped in then. "But the best part? Her tantrums have gotten around and she's pretty much been blacklisted. No label will back her. Her sales were dropping anyway because she was alienating fans with her antics at concerts. Canceling last minute, or stopping in the middle of the show to yell at someone about something she didn't like."

"Wow. I can't imagine how anyone could believe they're above everyone else, that all rules don't apply to them and that she'll never get her comeuppance for being a little snot."

"You're too nice, Brooklynn." All heads turned to the door to find Sasha leaning on the door jam, smirking. "I've met her, she's a little fucking cuntcake with vinegar frosting."

Levi and I lost it, laughing so hard we were holding our sides in pain from the lack of air. Sasha was too, until her eyes landed on Cooper. Her face immediately sobered and she whipped around, stalked out, and let the door slam behind her. Like a typical gawker, I turned back to see his reaction, looking between him and the door, where his eyes were trained.

He sighed and shut his eyes, running his fingers through his messy, mahogany hair. When he opened them, he was back in professional mode. He smiled warmly at me, though. "Anyway, she's no longer a client."

"Well, I'm glad I could be so helpful," I joked, trying to lighten the mood.

Levi stood and stretched. His jeans were low-slung on his hips and his T-shirt rode up a little, showing a sliver of his taut stomach and just a peek at the grooves forming a mouthwatering V. Heat infused my body, dampening my panties and setting off flutters in my stomach. Suddenly, I was transported back to the office, back to being pressed up against the wall, his hot mouth moving over mine. I shook off the memory and shot to my feet, practically squeaking, "Okay! Time to work." Then hurried out of the room.

We never talked about the kiss but his clear blue eyes seemed to burn even hotter whenever they collided with mine. He continued to ask me out every day and every day our friendship grew, making it harder and harder to say no. I kept reminding myself of what was at stake. The more I got to know him, the more I realized that if anything ever happened between us and then it didn't work out, I would be devastated over the loss of his friendship as much as I would be by my broken heart. Singing and writing with him was a contradiction, splitting my feelings. On one hand, it was the most amazing thing I'd ever experienced when it came to creating music. Writing with him was effortless. We came together with our ideas and they almost always gelled right into each other, creating something we'd never even imagined.

On the other hand, it was also an incredibly erotic experience at times, especially when we put our whole selves into the song, singing about love that shreds you to the very brink of your sanity, then heals all of your wounds. I knew it was about us, deep in my soul. I knew. Our feelings were slowly driving me out of my mind. A part of me knew that giving in could put me back together, but I was scared. Instead, I ignored them, never acknowledged their existence. I could tell it was frustrating Levi, but he didn't push me, other than continuing to try and talk me into letting him take me to out. It only made my feelings for him stronger.

My thoughts were interrupted by the noises of Levi, Matteo, and Simon stumbling through the door to the studio, laughing and giving each other shit. His eyes immediately sought me out, like they always did whenever he entered a room I was in. I smiled brightly and he frowned. He started to head my way when I was saved by Matteo, busting out a kickass drum solo. After a couple of stanzas, my mouth opened in shock and I stared at him. It was his drum solo in "Sanity." I didn't recognize it at first because he'd made so many improvements to the initial music we'd given him.

Simon, Matteo, and Sasha had sat in on one of our last working sessions on "Sanity." He wanted them to get a feel for what we'd done so they wouldn't be flying blind on our first rehearsal together. But…hot damn!

"Holy shit," I breathed. "It's fucking perfect."

Matteo lifted a brow, his expression a perfect imitation of mine when Levi had asked if I could riff with them. I laughed and bowed, giving him silent props. His smile grew and he winked at me before dropping his dynamics and tempo, leading into the middle chorus. He stopped and beat out a particularly tricky rhythm a couple of times, then he gave Levi a chin lift, indicating that he was good to go.

Sasha was playing her keyboard with the sound turned way down, so she wouldn't clash tempos with Matteo, and

Simon was doing the same on his bass.

"Sasha?" Levi asked.

She shook her head and bent to open another case. "Let me tune my violin, one of the strings is being a bitch." Holding the delicate instrument, she straightened and looked to Levi. "I brought the cello so we can try both," she informed him.

The strings were the only thing Levi and I had disagreed on when it came to the accompaniment for "Sanity." He thought the lighter strains of the violin would complement the song because it was already so rich and full. My gut told me that the cello was exactly what it needed. In theory, his thought made more sense, but for some reason, I just couldn't let the cello go.

Levi gestured to Simon, who began adjusting his equipment while Levi asked Sasha a couple of questions. I scooted over to Kristi and asked her opinion on a section where she was backing me up and we tweaked our syncopation so it was a little smoother through the transition into the last refrain. Simon played a few notes, then tuned a couple strings a little more precisely until it was exactly what he wanted. I was in awe of these musicians, their work ethic, their passion, their skill. Each one had their own abilities and styles, all unique, but they respected each other's knowledge and opinions and then blended it all together to form one entity. They were what every band should be, what they needed to be in order to last beyond the glitz and glamour that were often nothing but a smoke screen.

Simon began to play, and just like I had been with Matteo, I was blown away by the direction he had taken his solo. It was what we'd written but . . . it wasn't. Just as he reached the end, he was joined by the harmonic strains of a violin. They did a little back and forth before the base faded out and Sasha fell into the music. Her eyes closed and she held the instrument lovingly, reverently, as she lightly swayed side to side. Then, without warning, she launched into the melody of the hard rock verse. A fast and hard beat. Her eyes opened as the bow flew across the strings. Her green eyes were burning with an inner fire, it was an intoxicating sight and it captivated her audiences. For those who weren't close enough to see her soul through those emeralds, the depth of emotion seeped through every pore.

I'd been wrong. The violin was perfect—the music wouldn't be complete without it. Simon joined her once more, and after a moment, Matteo jumped in. As they approached the chorus, Sasha faded out. I glanced over at Levi and saw him staring back at me. He beamed at me, looking excited and monumentally pumped. He crooked a finger at me, and I found myself walking over to him, as though he were reeling me in like a fish on a line. He picked up his guitar, slinging the strap over his shoulder and then added another layer to the already gorgeous composition. When the music reached the right place, Levi and I opened our mouths and laid ourselves bare. As the music crescendoed, I belted out the notes, the harmony tight against Levi's beautiful baritenor. Something was different this time. It was more. More than it had ever been. And it wasn't the drums or bass, or Kristi's descant. Tears sprung to my eyes as the emotion threatened to crash down and pull me under.

We faded out and that's when I noticed what was different. My head whipped around and I stared at Sasha who was now sitting, a cello propped in front of her and her bow creating the most lush and opulent strains. We'd both been right. I didn't know why I was surprised. Just like the crazy changes in style, it would make sense that different instruments would complement different parts of the song. After another couple of bars, everyone faded out and we found ourselves grinning at each other like lunatics.

"From the top," I breathed and flipped around to face the mic.

We went from beginning to end, then picked it apart for a couple of hours. Noah had slipped in at some point, listening quietly from a stool set near the door. It was after midnight when he called it for the night. Energy was pumping through us, and if he hadn't interrupted, it's possible we would have gone head first down the rabbit hole, losing all sense of place and time, lost in a world of our creation.

"I've already put off security and the janitors twice," he informed us. "They want to clean and lock up."

We all groaned as though we were little kids being told they had to leave the adult party and go to bed. He laughed and put hands out in an "I'm sorry to be the party pooper" gesture. "You know you do this for a living, right?" he teased. "But, I'm about to turn into a pumpkin, so let's get out of here."

Levi tossed an empty water bottle at Noah who dodged it with a laugh. "We're right behind you, old man."

"Fuck off, Matthews," Noah shot back with a silly grin.

We gathered all of our shit and straightened up. Since this was Stone Butterfly's local studio, Noah had also commandeered a storage closet along with the office space he used while the band worked out of there. They were able to lock up all of the instruments so they didn't have to lug them back and forth on the subway or in a cab. While in recording mode and tour prep, they spent so much time there that it just made more sense. After securing everything, we stumbled out the door into the cold, all of us still buzzing, high on the incredible energy that had been pulsing through our veins for hours.

Sasha stepped to the curb and lifted her hand. The next bright yellow cab with its taxi light lit screeched up to the curb. Sasha threw open the door and turned back to us, waving at the interior. "Dublin House! Who's in?"

"Fuck yeah!" Simon shouted as he dove into the cab, grabbing Sasha's waist along the way and dragging her in behind him, both of them laughing their asses off. "I'm completely wiped out," I said reluctantly. "Next time."

"I'll hold you to that!" Sasha's disembodied voice yelled.

"Matteo?"

Matteo shrugged. "I could go for some Guinness." He looked back at Levi and me expectantly and raised his eyebrows in mild disbelief when Levi shook his head.

"Don't be a pussy, Matthews!" Sasha yelled from inside the car. "Get your ass in here!"

Simon's voice carried from inside the cab next. "Yeah! Otherwise you'll turn into Noah!"

Noah rolled his eyes. "Oh, for fuck's sake," he grumbled as he walked over and slid into the back seat.

Matteo gave Levi one last questioning glance. I pushed on his shoulder. "You should go, Levi," I encouraged. I went up on my toes and whispered, "Don't be a pussy, Matthews." I chuckled but he froze, not even breathing.

Then after a second he relaxed and called out, "Go on guys, I'll meet you there."

Matteo nodded and squeezed in before slamming the door shut and the cab sped off.

Levi whirled around and grabbed my face between his chilly palms before slamming his mouth down on mine. After thoroughly rocking my world, he pulled back a centimeter and mumbled against my lips, "If you don't want me to drag you to the nearest dark space and fuck your brains out"—I sucked in a breath, suddenly burning hot despite the weather being in the negatives—"then don't ever say the word 'pussy' around me." His voice was gravelly and strained. "I can't even think of dirty talk coming from your sexy mouth or I'll lose all control."

I had no words. Well, I did, but they were all really filthy, and it seemed like a bad time for word vomit of a sexual and naughty nature. He rested his forehead on mine, waiting for his breathing to level out. When he seemed calmer, he stepped back, brushed a strand of my hair over my shoulder, then kissed my forehead. He turned and flagged another cab, giving me his hand when one stopped for us. He helped me into the car and then slid in beside me. "What are you doing? Dublin House is the opposite direction."

Levi shut the door and threw his arm around me, hauling me into his side as he spouted off the address of my apartment to the driver. He kissed my forehead and hugged me a little closer. "I won't be able to relax unless I know you got home safe, and I won't know that for sure unless I take you there myself."

I fought a sigh but gave in to my desire to burrow deeper into him. His embrace was the one place in the world where I felt the safest. *Friends can snuggle, right?* I could almost hear my inner self's epic eye roll. *Denial much?*

Before long, we were in front of my apartment. Levi asked the cabbie to wait and jumped out to help me from the car. He took my hand and brought me close.

"Have dinner with me tomorrow night."

Yes! But, what I actually said was, "I need to learn more ways to say no, because clearly English isn't getting the job done."

He adopted a ridiculous, and extremely adorable, puppy dog expression. "There's a seafood place around the corner of the studio that has the best food."

"Do they have shrimp?"

"Absolutely!" His eyes brightened.

"With garlic butter sauce and fresh bread?"

"Hell yeah!"

I snickered and patted his cheek. "Still no."

He looked crestfallen for a second, making me feel bad for teasing him. But, just as quickly it was replaced with an even more determined glint. "We are making progress, at least."

I didn't respond. He took my hand and walked me all the way to the glass doors where my doorman hurried over to open it for me. "Goodnight, baby," Levi murmured and kissed my lips briefly.

I started to walk through the door when his voice stopped me. "It doesn't matter what language you use, Brooklynn. I still won't quit until I convince you to say yes."

I look back at him over my shoulder and my voice is a

little sad when I say, "Vorrei, ma non posso." Levi's jaw drops, and I leave him there in his stunned state.

I wish I could, but I can't.

Chapter Nine

LEVI

"Dude, she speaks fucking Italian," I lamented with my face resting in the center of my folded arms on the bar. "Did you know?" I asked in a muffled voice.

"Yes," Noah confirmed. "She's fluent. Her sister loved the sound of the language, so Brooklynn learned it to be able to talk to her in Italian."

I groaned. "It's sexy as hell."

Noah sighed and clipped me on the back of my head. "What the fuck?" I yelped, lifting my head and glaring at my best friend as I rubbed the wounded spot.

He shoved a pint at me. "Drink."

I didn't have the energy to argue, so I did as I was told.

"I've got to tell you, Levi. I was really worried about you being a complete asshole. I figured you would seduce her, get bored when the chase was done, and break her heart."

"Don't hold back, jackass," I grunted. I debated the merits of putting my fist in his face, then decided I didn't want to take the chance of being thrown out of one of our favorite bars.

"Levi, I need you to fight all of your natural instincts to speak, shut the fuck up, and listen."

I flipped him off. Sign language, it's universal.

"The point is, you seem different with this girl. It's not just the chase keeping you interested in her. So, I'm going to give you a little gift. Don't fuck me over with it," he growled.

I perked up. A little. I was too drunk to muster more.

"One, we are going to draft a new contract for her. Sheryl's decided to get out of the game for now, and I want to offer Brooklynn a permanent spot with Stone Butterfly."

My head turned and I opened my mouth to ask why this

would help me, but Noah cuffed me on the head again. I didn't speak, but my glare promised retribution.

"Brooklynn is worried about being kicked to the curb if things don't work out between you, right?" I stared at him deadpan. *What? This was me, not speaking.*

Noah looked at the ceiling as though praying for patience, then he took a long pull from his bottle and continued, "I'll have the lawyer draft a contract that makes it impossible for you to be the cause for her dismissal."

My head slowly turned to look at him again. I was paying attention now.

"Just be patient while I get the kinks worked out." His voice was thoughtful and he was twisting his lips between his thumb and forefinger.

"Can I speak now?" I sneered without any real malice.

Noah eyed me speculatively. "If you're about to ask if there was a second thing, I'll save you the trouble and you can keep your trap sealed. Yes, there is." I turned back to my drink, which had been freshly refilled. *Excellent.*

"How much do you know about her sister?" This got my attention. Brooklynn had spoken of her sister from time to time, but for the most part, she was very tightlipped about her past and her family. I filled him in on the little I knew.

Noah ran a hand down his face, thinking. "Look," he said quietly, "She was a bit more open with me because we needed to find solutions to her worries. But, she asked me to keep it to myself, and I won't break her trust."

I was at once irritated and confused. I hated that he knew more about Brooklynn than I did and I was confused about why he'd brought this up if he hadn't planned on telling me anything.

"Here's what I can tell you. She is extremely protective of her little sister and wants nothing more than to make her happy. If Brooklynn truly thought Baylee couldn't handle her having this career, she would quit and leave it all behind." This didn't really surprise me. Brooklynn was one of the most beautiful people I'd ever met, inside and out.

Her level of compassion was inspiring, making everyone around her want to be a better person.

"So, what are you suggesting?" I asked.

"I'm telling you that other than through music, her sister is the way to her heart. That's my two cents, take from it what you will."

I wanted to ask him for more but the stubborn look on his face told me I wouldn't get anywhere. I threw back the rest of my Guiness and gave him a chin lift before stumbling my way toward the exit, waving at my other band mates who were doing shots at the other end of the bar.

My mind turned over what Noah had told me as I sat in the back of a cab, headed home. I waved at my doorman before riding the elevator up to the fourth floor. I had a decent-sized, three-bedroom condo in a Manhattan high-rise. I'd decided to be practical and not waste money on the glitz and glam that usually filled the life of a rock star. Noah's parents had ingrained us all with the importance of staying grounded and being smart with our money. It seemed ridiculous to buy something huge, like a penthouse, for just me. I had a room for my instruments and a small studio set up. The other I used as a guest room for when Liam stayed over or Lily came for a visit. Besides, the house I owned just outside the city was big enough.

When I stepped inside my front door, I was hit with a wave of exhaustion. The high from our studio session had worn off, and I was crashing. The alcohol making me even more sluggish and tired as I stumbled into my bedroom. I flopped down onto my king-sized bed without even pulling back the grey quilt. Grabbing the remote, I pointed it at my floor-to-ceiling windows and pressed a button. Immediately, the glass darkened, becoming completely opaque so when morning came, the sunlight would be blocked out. I tossed the remote on the nightstand, shucked my clothes, and finally crawled under the covers. I dreamed of Brooklynn.

After a week of rehearsals, we'd worked through every kink, every inspired idea, and made a million tiny changes to "Sanity." We poured ourselves into the creative process until the music was simply a part of us. Then, we started laying down the vocal and instrumental tracks.

The first day, Brooklynn and I worked on our separate parts with Cooper and the sound guys. Then they asked us to record an acoustic version, with only my guitar as accompaniment, possibly to be used as bonus material on the album. It was the first time we'd sung it, just the two of us, since we'd started working on the piece as a group. As amazing as it was when it was in full force with all six of us, there was something special about performing it alone.

We sat on our stools and faced the sound booth, singing directly into the mics hanging right in front of our mouths. But, we kept stealing sidelong glances at each other and as we neared the final chorus, we stopped trying to avert our gazes. Instead, our eyes locked and we eye fucked each other as we sang. The sexual tension was almost oppressive, making me hot and stealing some of my breath. I knew from experience that it was those moments, the ones where there were no sound technicians splicing and adjusting everything so that the record is a veritable jigsaw, that created the very best recording possible for the album. Acoustic meant we were singing in the raw, our technique wasn't perfect, the notes weren't exact. Those moments were what made it real, when the listener realized they were experiencing our true emotions.

When the song was done, time seemed to slow and the silence hung heavy in the air. I was so caught up in Brooklynn that I gripped my guitar a little too tight, trying to keep from tossing it away and kissing the fuck out of her. Static sounded through the speakers, making us both jump and breaking the connection.

"That was great. You guys are done for today," Cooper announced. "We'll record another acoustic version with all of you at some point as well."

I swallowed hard, barely listening as I wrestled my desires, trying to shove them back in their box.

"Thanks, Cooper," Brooklynn called then hopped off of her seat and grabbed her bag from the floor before making her way to the door. All the while, avoiding my gaze.

"Brooklynn," I said her name almost as a command, and she paused, turning her head to peek at me over her shoulder. Her long hair was loose and some of it obscured her face like a curtain, making it hard for me to gauge her expression.

I put away my guitar and picked up the case, then strode in her direction.

"Recording today was amazing, baby." I pushed her hair away from her face and studied her darkened, mocha eyes. Her face was slightly flushed, something easily missed if you weren't looking up close. I smiled, trying to keep my smugness from showing. I was even more convinced that she was every bit as drawn to me as I was to her. "Let's go out and celebrate."

"No." She shook her head in emphasis.

"How about another kiss then?" It was a long shot, sure. But, I liked betting on the dark horse.

Her lips slowly lifted into a smile and she chuckled. "In your dreams."

"Oh, Brooklynn," I sighed. "In my dreams, we do so much more than kiss."

She glanced away quickly, but not before I saw the flash of heat and longing in her eyes. Before she could try to leave again, I tugged on her arm, recieving minimal resistance. I didn't push my luck, only giving her a sweet, lingering kiss. Pulling back, I smiled at her soft expression, and she returned the gesture. Then she glanced down and when her head came back up, her face was blank. "Goodnight, Levi."

I tucked a strand of her inky black hair behind her ear

and kissed her forehead. "I'll see you tomorrow, baby. Sweet dreams."

After walking her out and putting her in a cab, I dug my iPhone out of my pocket and dialed Simon's number. I decided to walk home and started that way while I waited for him to answer. He picked up, and I didn't even wait for him to say hello. "Poker, beer, my house."

"Poker? I hardly know her!" he shouted.

"Really, Simon?" I asked, infusing my voice with disappointment. "You couldn't come up with anything better? It's fucking sad, man."

"Fuck you," he laughed. "That's classic shit."

"It's shit all right."

"See you in an hour, asshole. I'll bring pizza."

He hung up and I called Matteo, then Noah, demanding that they get their asses to my house and make sure to bring stuffed wallets. I considered calling Sasha, but I wasn't in the mood to be around any estrogen. Sasha would be fucking pissed when she found out we'd had a poker night without her, though. Then I had a brilliant idea. I pulled up Sasha's contact on my phone and hit call. I was walking through my door when she answered with, "You're not my type, Matthews, so I hope you aren't looking for a booty call."

I couldn't help it, despite my low spirits, I burst out laughing. Sasha could always do that, bring lightness and fun to any situation. Always ready with a quip or sarcastic comment to make us laugh our asses off. "Thanks for the offer, Blue," I drawled.

"I didn't offer, fucker," she said indignantly.

"I need a favor." I ignored her protest and moved on to why I'd called her. "Do you have plans tonight?"

"Not a booty call, huh?" Her sarcasm was thick enough to be cut with a knife.

"Would you stop thinking about fucking me?" I clipped, pretending to be offended. "Am I just a piece of meat to you?"

"Yes, that's exactly what you are to me," she agreed. "Fresh meat that I constantly consider feeding to the sharks in the East River."

"Are you done?"

"Yup. What's the favor?"

"Take Brooklynn out tonight. Maybe you could talk Kristi into joining you."

Sasha snorted. "Yeah right. We leave for tour in like two and a half weeks. When she isn't at the studio, she and her husband are holed up in her apartment fucking like bunnies."

I cringed. "Thanks for the image."

"Happy to help," she said cheerfully. "Anyway, no favor necessary. I was thinking of calling Brooklynn, anyway."

"Great." I grinned to myself. Problem solved.

We said goodbye, and I wandered into the living room with the stack of mail the doorman had handed me on the way in. I dropped onto the couch and set aside all the junk, looked through my bills, finishing with a stack of fan mail. We had a team that exclusively handled it all for us, including our social media. It didn't matter how popular we seemed with the public, there would always be people who didn't like our music and sent their opinions via hate mail. The team collected it from the P.O. box and sorted through the mail, weeding out the stuff that none of us needed to see. It would only be added stress in our lives.

Whenever possible, I tried to go through everything they forwarded on to me and answer as much of it as possible. However, when we were on the road, I had to let our people respond and I was adamant that no letter go unanswered. If I couldn't do it, then the team sent an autographed picture and/or other things. I read a couple of the letters, laughing at one from a seven-year-old boy, who'd colored a picture of me performing and tucked it into the envelope. My head and the microphone were the same size, but my body was tiny in comparison. One of my hands was sticking out, holding what I assumed was my guitar. There were curtains on either side of the picture, more like a theatre stage on Broadway. And there were large circles across the top. It took me a minute to realize they were stage lights. I chuckled again and left the couch to take everything into my music room. I tacked the picture on a cork board filled with similar items and snapped a picture with my phone, quickly posting it with a thank you on Twitter.

There was a loud pounding on my door, and I sighed and sent a silent apology to my neighbors. For some reason, Simon had something against my doorbell. I was turning to go answer the door when a postcard caught my eye. I grabbed it on my way out of the room. Simon, arms full of pizza and beer, made a beeline for the kitchen the second I had the door open. Noah held more beer and entered, Matteo on his heels with yet another case of beer. Two guys from another New York based band Afterdark were just coming down the hall, so I held the door open until they were entering as well, but their arms were full of other shit, pretzels, chips, and . . . oh, I didn't see the beer. I chuckled and shut the door and looked down at the thick card stock in my hand as I followed them. I started laughing, a full belly laugh that had tears leaking from my eyes.

The guys were setting up my poker table in the living room and stopped to look at me like I was losing my fucking marbles. I couldn't even explain since I was still laughing, so I just held it out. Noah took it, and when he got a look at it, he started laughing right along with me.

The front had three hairy chimpanzees, all dressed in various colors of polka dot bikinis, standing in a row with their arms linked. They had big false eyelashes, but they were smiling with the typical toothy monkey mouth. There was a huge wave behind them and the top of the card read, "I think you're SWELL and we'd get along just SWIMMINGLY." It was one of the stupidest things I'd ever seen, but it had attacked my funny bone with a vengeance. It worked its way around and when I had it again, I flipped it over to read the typed message.

Levi,
I love your music. I hope we meet someday.

I was disappointed to see no signature. I wouldn't be able to thank the sender. Still, I added it to my board and then we sat down to trash talk, drink beer, and kick each other's asses for money.

Chapter Ten

BROOKLYNN

I was fucking exhausted. Working with Stone Butterfly was exhilarating, but hard work. After the first day of recording, we'd spent the next four days laying down more tracks, rehearsing, and writing. Then piled on top of all that was the strain of keeping Levi at arm's length. I did my best to try and diffuse the chemistry that was only growing stronger every day instead of weakening like I'd hoped it would. We'd taken to texting a lot and had a habit of talking long after the others had cleared the studio. None of it was really serious or in depth. We learned about each other's tastes in food, music, movies, and all the stuff that makes up a personality. A few times, he talked about his family, and I could tell he expected me to reciprocate but I didn't like thinking about my past, much less talking about it. So, I would subtly shut it down and change the subject.

Sasha and Kristi worked in the studio today, which meant a rare day off for the rest of us, and I knew exactly what I was going to do with it.

Nothing.

I'd curled up on my couch with my Kindle and stayed there, pretty much all damn day. It was dark by the time I drew a bubble bath and as I tested the water temperature, I could already feel my muscles relaxing. I was just slipping out of my robe when my doorman buzzed my apartment. At the same time, my cell phone started ringing. I grabbed it from the bathroom counter and glanced down to see Levi's number flashing on the screen as I ran to the intercom by my door. I pressed the button for the lobby and asked, "What's up, Peter?" Then I quickly swiped across the screen of my phone and said, "Hold on a second, Levi."

"There is a food delivery here, Ms. Hawk," Peter said. I

was stunned for a moment. What the hell? I hadn't ordered anything and I opened my mouth to tell him, but stopped when I noticed Levi yelling my name from where my phone was hanging in my hand at my side.

"What?" I snapped lifted it to my ear.

"It's from me. The food."

I opened my mouth to tell him that I had no idea what was going on. "What are you talking about?"

Levi's husky chuckle sent a shiver down my spine and my nipples hardened, the fabric of my robe rubbing across them. I had to bite back a moan. I wasn't wearing any underwear, so I could feel the wetness from my pussy on my thighs. Damn it! Why did he affect me like that?

"Let's have dinner together."

I sighed. "Levi—"

"Hear me out," he interrupted. "I figured if you won't go to dinner with me, we could at least have it at the same time."

I could practically hear the large crack from him chipping away another piece of the wall around my heart...

After telling Peter to send everything up, I went into the bathroom to drain the tub and watched longingly as the scented, bubbly water disappeared.

"What was that?" Levi asked when the tub made a loud gurgling noise.

"I was going to take a bath."

He groaned. "Fuck, now that image won't go away."

My doorbell rang, and I tightened the belt on my robe before opening it for the delivery guy. "Hold on," I told Levi, then greeted a good-looking, young guy, who couldn't be older than eighteen. "Hi." He looked at me and his eyes lit up, like he'd won the lottery, his mouth curving up into a wide smile, showing off two deep dimples. He was a looker, I'd give him that. Still . . . I felt bad. He was probably the popular guy at school who never got turned down, and I was about to pop the bubble he lived in where he was king of everything. *Poor kid.*

"You can put everything on the counter over there." I gestured to the kitchen area of my open concept living/dining/kitchen area. "And, if you don't hit on me, because I'd hate to have to shoot you down, I'll give you a bigger tip." I smiled. There, that was letting him down easy.

He sauntered in the door with a confident swagger that only cocky, teen0age boys could pull off. After setting everything down, he faced me and leaned back against the counter, his hands gripping the edges on either side. I raised an eyebrow. Really? He was going to ignore my warning?

"Do you really want me to go?" he asked slyly. "Or are you just fighting the attraction between us? Because, I could rock your world, babe." *Oh, good grief.* I started to respond when I heard the faraway sound of Levi's voice. I had forgotten that he was still there.

I brought the phone to my ear. "Let me call you back."

"Is the delivery guy hitting on you?" he demanded, his tone barely containing his fury.

"Relax, he's just a kid." The boy's expression fell for a second, but he was back to his cocky self in no time. "I'm handling it."

"Put him on the phone," Levi growled. I was about to argue but then I thought, why the hell not? Let him be the bad guy.

I held out my phone. "My friend Levi Matthews wants to talk to you," I explained. The kid's face made it clear that he thought I was making it up to get rid of him. "Find out for yourself if you think I'm lying."

Warily, he approached me and took my phone carefully, as though it might explode. "Who is this?" he asked. Then he sucked up his chest and put more confidence in his tone. "You're interrupting a private, *romantic* moment." I covered my mouth, hoping he wouldn't hear my snort-giggle.

He listened for a second then his jaw dropped like a lead weight and his eyes turned into saucers. "Holy shit, you're Levi Matthews," he breathed. Levi's voice was low, so I couldn't hear what he was saying. I was surprised he wasn't yelling at the kid, but by the time he muttered, "Yes, sir," he looked sufficiently freaked the fuck out. "I'm sorry, sir, I didn't know she was yo—no, sir. Yes, sir." I felt a little bad for him, but it was overpowered by the hilarity of the situation.

One last, "Yes, sir," and he was handing the phone back to me and making a beeline for the door. He stopped and said, "Sorry, for swearing ma'am and for treating you disrespectfully," and then rushed out the door, slamming it behind him in his haste.

"Um, that was interesting," I said to Levi. "What did you say to him?"

"It's not important." His voice was still tense with irritation. It sounded like he was angry with me too, which didn't make any sense. "Brooklynn, you were about to take a bath before the food arrived, yes?"

Even more confused at his change in subject, I conceded, "Yes."

"And what were you wearing when you opened the door?" His tone was still dark, and I could hear the spoken warning. Oh, that's what was chafing his ass. I considered lying, but I sucked at it, so I shrugged and told the truth.

"My robe."

There was complete silence on the other end of the line for what felt like ten minutes, though it was probably only a few seconds. "You are so fucking lucky I'm not there right now," he threatened.

"Um, okay." I knew I'd regret asking, but sometimes my brain desserts me. "Why?"

"Why? Because you answered the door for a guy who wasn't me. *A fucking stranger!* Wearing almost nothing!" he snarled. "And if I were there, I'd have you over my knee, spanking your sweet little ass until it was bright red."

I gasped, hoping he interpreted it as outrage, which it kind of was. Mostly, though, it was a shock that his words had shot straight to my core, making me so wet it was running down my legs. I was a little mortified that the idea of him spanking me got me incredibly hot.

Out of nowhere, he took the wind out of my angry sails when his voice took on a pleading quality. "Please, baby. Don't do that. It's dangerous and I can't take it. You'll put me in an early grave worrying."

Everything in me melted, and I slid to the ground and put my head in my free hand. That, right there. The combination of badass caveman and the sweet, romantic man. It was almost irresistible. To be honest, I had no fucking clue how I'd managed to hold out as long as I had.

"Okay," I whispered.

He sighed in obvious relief. "Let's eat. What did you do today?"

"You girls are going to love the new single," I told Baylee and Cecily, who were both on the phone with me. "It truly turned out amazing, and I still can't believe I helped write it."

"That's so cool, Brooklee!" Baylee gushed.

Cecily sighed. "You're so lucky. That is one lickable specimen of a man."

Baylee pretended to gag. "Ewww, yuck, Cecily!" Then she lowered her voice to a stage whisper. "She kisses his poster every night."

"I do not!" Cecily protested.

I laughed, missing them both. Before we took off on tour, I was hoping to be able to have a longer visit with Baylee, rather than just going out there for dinner. Levi had mentioned that he planned to spend the next weekend at home, so I figured it would be a good time to surprise my girls.

I told them the story of Levi sending me dinner the night before, leaving out my physical reaction and Levi's threat of a spanking. Which still turned me on. Ugh.

We talked a little more about working with the band, and

I regaled them with funny stories about the antics of the others. I finally wished Baylee a good night and spent a few minutes talking to Cecily alone.

"You got the itinerary for the touring schedule, right?" I asked.

"Yeah, jeez, Brooklynn, you are going to so many amazing places," she sighed again. "And with Levi Matthews. I swear, one of these days we'll meet and he'll fall madly in love with me."

I rolled my eyes and got back to business. "I'll bring tickets to the Boston concert next time I come up there. I'll book your room for a day before and a day after. I know you'll both want to sight see, and I want Baylee more comfortable with the strange city she's in before coming into the craziness of a concert."

"Okay. Sounds good. Night, Brooklynn."

"Goodnight. Give Baylee a hug and kiss from me."

"Will do."

I'd been lying on my back in the middle of the bed, and after we hung up, I rolled to my side so I could plug my phone in and set it on the nightstand. It was tempting to simply curl up and go right to sleep, but my skin would hate me in the morning. Sighing, I stood and made my way to the bathroom where I washed my face and dressed for bed. Once I was settled under the covers with my Kindle, I stared at the same page for five minutes. My mind wouldn't focus on the words, instead it was replaying my last kiss with Levi, over and over.

My phone buzzed with an incoming text, and I shifted to my side so I could pick it up and read it.

Levi: I was lying here in the buff, with my blankets on the floor because my apartment is so damn hot and it got me wondering. Are you one of those chicks with frozen feet?

I laughed at his question and pointedly ignored the first part of his text.

Me: I generally start out wearing just socks to bed, but it

doesn't take long before they are gone and my feet are sticking out of the covers to cool off.

Levi: One more question. Were you kidding or do you really go to bed in nothing but those thigh-high socks?

Me: They aren't thigh-high socks, perv.

Levi: Oh, sweetheart. In my head, they are. And don't avoid the question.

Me: A girl's got to keep some mystery about her.

Levi: Bullshit. I want to know everything about you. Now, I told you my sleeping attire, you tell me yours.

Me: I suppose it depends on who is in bed with me.

Levi: Since I'm the star of your dreams, I'm going to have to make the assumption that you sleep bare assed naked.

Me: What if I told you I wear a unicorn onesie to bed?

Levi: Still hot. I'll love peeling it off of you to get to the prize underneath.

Me: Put that dirty mind to sleep, Levi. I'm going to bed.

I returned my phone to the nightstand, and after some tossing and turning, finally fell asleep. He'd been right, the jerk. I'd spent every night since our last kiss dreaming about what would have happened after his kiss if we hadn't stopped.

Chapter Eleven

LEVI

I lifted my head from studying my music and watched Brooklynn for a few minutes. She was also bent over staff paper, adding and scratching out whole parts of the song she was working on. After we were finished writing "Sanity," I'd been desperately trying to find an excuse to keep spending time alone together. She'd saved me the trouble when she came to me with another song idea. She wanted my help writing it. I'd jumped at the chance, not really caring if the song was any good. I should have known better. It was amazing. We were almost wrapped on recording "Sanity," so we'd spent most of our extra time working on it.

The song highlighted both her and Sasha, with me singing a complementing, but much smaller part than people would be used to. I was excited about shaking things up. Brooklynn would be at the piano and Sasha would be playing her violin, but the female vocal parts were each strong, neither one overpowering the other. It was the first time Sasha had agreed to sing in the spotlight, rather than just singing backup harmonies from behind her instruments. We'd been trying to get her to take a bigger part for years, but she'd remained adamantly against it. I don't know what Brooklynn said to convince her, but whatever it was, it worked.

"Hey," I said softly.

Her head jerked up, her expression startled, like she'd forgotten she wasn't alone. "Hey," she responded with a sheepish smile. "I forgot you were here."

"I figured."

She laughed and her chocolate eyes strayed to my lips, filling with hunger. I fucking loved it when she devoured me with her eyes like that. But, I needed to focus on something else.

I cleared my throat and tried to be nonchalant. "Now that we've had dinner together a couple of times—"

"How do you figure that?" she snorted speculatively.

I spread my hands out in a "duh" gesture. "We were eating at the same time."

Brooklynn laughed, and I grinned at the beautiful sound. Her laugh was almost as beautiful as her singing voice. Not that my dick could tell the difference. He perked up at the sound of either. Then again, just about everything Brooklynn did turned me on.

"The natural progression is for me to take you out," I said in an authoritative tone.

She sighed and stood, then walked away, shaking her head.

Holy shit. This was the first time she hadn't given me a flat-out no.

The next day, we recorded the acoustic version of "Sanity" with the whole band. We went through it three times so we had multiple versions to choose from. Finally, the door to the recording room opened and Cooper walked in. He grinned and stuck his hands in his front pockets. "That's it. *For Your Sanity* is done. I gotta say, guys, I think this is your best album yet."

We were all grinning like loons. "This calls for a celebration!" Simon yelled gleefully. Laughter broke out, and we all made plans to meet up at Dublin House later that night. Brooklynn and I followed Cooper from the room and into the sound booth. We were going to listen through the raw tracks and choose one of the group recordings to put as a bonus track on the standard album. Then we'd choose one from the recordings of just she and I to put on the iTunes exclusive, deluxe version of the album.

The sound guys cleared out so we could listen without it being overly crowded in such a small room. We started with the duets. There were four different versions for us to pick from. After listening to all of them twice, we narrowed it down to two. Then decided to move on to the group versions and come back to the others with fresh ears.

When all the intricacies of recording a song are completed, you're left with as perfect of a rendition of the song as possible. It's incredible to hear your composition on a recording, the way you hear it in your head. It's surreal. And, it's what sells the albums.

However, there was something special about performing in the raw. There was perfection in the mistakes as long as the depth of emotion was there. I honestly couldn't tell you which I preferred because they were unique and not really comparable. Apples and oranges.

That song was special though. I'd never been so entranced by the acoustic version of a song as I had been by "Sanity." Maybe because there was no hiding behind techs who fixed every mistake. Performing in the raw is just that. Raw. It's gritty and rough, scraping over your wounds, laying you bare to be judged by every person who hears it. The only choice is to give in and let it happen. If you fight it, the performance comes across as contrived and lacking true feeling, the listeners know it's fake. And everything about "Sanity" magnified that experience, because it was so much a part of us. Letting someone see inside your soul is terrifying, and "Sanity" came from deep inside Brooklynn and me. It was a part of us. No, it *was* us.

As we sat there, listening to the six of us give ourselves over to the music, tears sprang to Brooklynn's eyes, and she beamed at me. I wiped away the wetness on her cheeks and tucked some of her hair behind one ear. Then I took her hand and squeezed it gently but didn't let it go.

It was the second recording. Cooper, Brooklynn, and I unanimously agreed. We went back to the duet versions and finally settled on one. Cooper slapped me on the back as we man-hugged, then he pulled Brooklynn up from her seat and enveloped her in a bear hug. Irritation buzzed over my nerves, but I stepped on my impulse to tear her from his arms. Until he'd been holding her for way longer than was necessary. I slipped my arm around her waist from behind and pulled her out of his embrace and back against my chest. Cooper smirked and I glared daggers at him.

"Hiring you was the best decision Noah ever made," he declared, smiling at her.

"I won't disagree with you," she replied cheekily. Cooper laughed and gave us a wave before leaving us alone.

We stood just as we were, Brooklynn leaning against me, secure in my embrace. I was almost afraid to breathe in case it broke the spell. She felt so fucking perfect in my arms.

She sighed and I knew what was coming, so I tightened my hold. Why wouldn't she stay? It was beginning to eat at me more and more, chipping away at my sanity. The irony was not lost on me.

"Let's listen to it one more time," she suggested in a breathy tone. It was fucking hot and it was like moving a mountain to open my arms and let her go.

She turned to the soundboard and hit a button. The first strains of the song hit our ears, and we were both completely captivated, lost in the music. When the song ended, we were every bit as charged from listening to it as we were when we played it. The fact that we were alone in the room was screaming at me. I took a deep breath, and when I smelled her sweet scent, I lost it. The next thing I knew, she was plastered to my body, my hands buried in her hair, and our lips locked in a furious kiss.

Her taste was everything I'd remembered and fantasized about and it fueled my wild desire for her. I walked her backward until she was pressed against the wall and slid my hands down her neck, over her shoulders, all the way down to her ass. I palmed each cheek and lifted her effortlessly, groaning with satisfaction when her legging-clad legs circled my waist. She felt like heaven as my hips bucked forward and ground into her heat. She whimpered, and one of my hands glided to her front and up to cup her tit. It more than filled my palm and I massaged it, reveling in her answering moan. I deepened the kiss and my fingers toyed with her stiff nipple while I thrusts against her pussy in a steady rhythm. She was so hot and the leggings she had on were thin. They could be easily ripped.

I was about to pull the wide neckline of her sweater down and latch on to one of her beaded nipples when the door slammed open.

"Fuck!" I growled as Brooklynn hurriedly dropped her feet to the ground and tried to push me away while straightening her clothes.

"Uh, sorry guys," one of the sound engineers apologized as he backed out, avoiding looking in our direction, but unable to wipe the stupid grin off of his face. "I, uh, didn't know you were—sorry." He disappeared, but the door hadn't even shut before we heard his laughter.

Brooklynn's face was a mask of horrified embarrassment. "Baby—" I started. But she waved me off and went running from the room. *Damn it!*

I decided not to go after her, to give her time to stop freaking out. Diving my hands into my hair, I grit my teeth with frustration and clenched my fingers in the strands. I was still panting and my cock was so hard that every movement I made caused pain. *Fuck!*

All of Stone Butterfly was in attendance at Dublin House that night, including Cooper and Noah, although Kristi left early. Our agent, Ken, even made an appearance. As far as agents go, he was the least slick and unprincipled one we'd met yet, so we didn't throw his ass out. To my surprise, even my younger brother Liam stopped by. Everybody was introduced to Brooklynn, who did her very best to ignore me all night. I got strange looks from everyone at one time or another when Brooklynn so obviously avoided speaking to me or even coming near me. But, this was between me and Brooklynn, and I had no intention of facing her down in a crowded pub. So, I let her get away with it, for the most part. The stubborn side of me found ways to touch her as often as possible, and while she shied away from me, at least she didn't flinch or cringe. I didn't think we'd taken too many steps backward. I wasn't giving up, if that's what she was hoping. Fuck no.

"Levi," Sasha yelled across the table with a grin. "Simon told me about the postcard."

I laughed. "It was pretty hilarious. Apparently, this fan has a thing for chimps."

"You got that from one postcard?" Sasha asked skeptically before tipping back her whiskey and draining the glass.

"No," I said with a smirk. "I got another postcard. In fact…" I trailed off and I dug into my pocket and pulled out a folded postcard.

Matteo snatched it from my hand and unfolded it. It had another chimpanzee, this time sitting in a recliner with cats all around it, including one in its lap, and another on its head. The writing on the top said, *I think you're purrrrrfect.* It was too ridiculous not to be funny.

"What's with this chick and monkeys?" he asked absentmindedly.

"Who says it's a chick?" Noah mused with a sly half-smile. "Levi's got a pretty strong gay fan base."

I winked at him. "What can I say? I'm an equal opportunity heartthrob."

"How are you going to fit all that ego on a tour bus?" he taunted.

"A swift kick to the balls could take care of that in a jiffy," Sasha quipped casually.

Every man within hearing distance cringed. "Uncool, Blue," I grumbled, fighting the urge to put my hands over my crotch to protect my manhood.

Simon scooted his chair closer to Sasha and gave her a lascivious once over. "You going to kiss it better after you cause the damage?" Sasha was interrupted from responding when Cooper's glass slammed down on the table. Her eyes shot to his and she glared before turning back to Simon.

"If it were anybody but you, maybe," she joked, completely ignoring Cooper's growl.

I watched them with interest, my head volleying back and forth like a gossip-hungry chick. *Yeah, I'm shaking my head at myself as much as you are. I'll earn a vagina any day now.* I had no desire to butt into whatever was going on with these two, but I couldn't help wanting to know what the fuck happened. I felt a little better when I saw that everyone else, including the guys, was as curious and obviously in the dark.

"So, chimpanzees, huh? I didn't think you'd be into inter-species relations, Levi." Brooklynn broke the silence, and the tension immediately defused as we all snickered. She grinned, and I felt a tug in my chest. She was so fucking amazing, and I wanted her more every second I spent with her.

Chapter Twelve

BROOKLYNN

I couldn't believe it. Our six weeks were up and we were kicking off our tour the next day with a concert in New York. Well, New Jersey, technically, since it was at Meadowlands Arena. It seemed a little surreal. We'd all gone to see family or friends over the previous weekend, taking some time away from each other before we were together 24/7 for six months. Well, three for me.

We all came back to town the night before and met up at Simon's loft in SoHo for a jam session. It was full of fun and none of the music we played was ours. We ended up challenging each other to play obscure pieces of music. If you told someone to play it and they couldn't, they had to do a shot. It was our rocker version of beer pong. We laughed and joked and simply let loose. It felt fucking awesome.

Levi and I hadn't talked about what happened between us the night of our last recording. He still looked at me with hungry eyes, but he gave me some space. *Some* being the operative word. He still slipped in dinner invitations, even by text when he was at home with his family. It slowly filtered out the awkwardness I was feeling, the normalcy righting my off-kilter world once again.

The buzz from the alcohol and the high from laughter must have lowered my inhibitions because we were certainly more touchy-feely than usual, and I did nothing to stop it. As it got later, the group thinned out until it was only Simon, Levi, and me left. Simon finally stood, told us to lock up, and stumbled to bed. Then we were alone. I had just enough sense to keep from jumping his bones and announced it was time for me to go home. When I twisted my scarf around my head, I fell into a fit of giggles and Levi helped me right it. After he'd buttoned up my coat, he stood still and stared into my eyes. His hand brushed along my cheek and then tucked a piece of hair behind my ear.

"You know, it's our first concert together tomorrow night," he whispered seriously. "I don't see how we are going to have the right chemistry on stage unless you go out with me first."

I stifled a giggle. "It's two o'clock in the morning. We can't go on a date!" His suggestion had sobered me right up, but I didn't let on because I was so very tempted to take him up on his offer. I was already feeling an adrenaline rush in anticipation of performing and pumped for the concert. Going home to my empty apartment was a depressing thought, and I vaguely entertained the idea of saying yes as long as I killed any expectation of it being a date. I would clarify the platonic nature of our evening, and we could go as friends.

"Of course, if we were really serious about our craft," he drawled in a low, husky tone that sent shivers down my spine. "We'd skip all that other stuff and go straight to fucking. Then the sexual tension between us would be so much more realistic."

I sputtered with laughter. Platonic. Yeah, you keep telling yourself that, Brooklynn.

Leaning in, I kissed his cheek and quietly, regretfully, mumbled, "Goodnight, Levi."

Chapter Thirteen

BROOKLYNN

"Are you nervous?" Kristi asked, shuffling her weight from foot to foot with an overabundance of energy.

I laughed and slipped my hands into the back pockets of my jeans, resting my weight on my heels. "I don't get nervous before a performance. For some reason, my anxiety always manifests itself afterward. I generally walk off the stage on legs that are practically Jell-O."

Sasha threw Kristi a sly look before flipping her head over to gather her hair into a high ponytail. "She's been doing this for over a decade and she still fights the urge to throw up every time," she divulged, winking at Kristi after she flipped her head back up. Kristi grimaced and pressed her hands against her stomach, her face a little green.

I laughed as I added last minute touches to my makeup and fluffed my hair in the mirror. Sometimes, for concerts, I put large bouncy curls in my stick-straight hair. It was such a pain in the ass to do, so it was a rare occurrence. My debut concert with Stone Butterfly definitely called for it. My sparkly, purple top was a halter with a deep cut-out in the center, so I double checked the tape keeping my boobs from popping out. Skin-tight leather pants were accentuated with a silver belt that matched my chunky earrings and bracelets, and knee-high, five-inch stiletto boots.

Kristi was equally decked out in a silver tank top, hot pink short shorts and tall wedges. Sasha, though…she was somehow a mixture of the shiny rock star and the laid back, every day Sasha. Her red hair was smoothed back and hung straight and long from her ponytail. Her makeup was dark and smoky, overly made up, like the rest of us, so we wouldn't be washed out in the stage lights. She wore a black T-shirt that dipped off one shoulder, revealing a leopard print strap, and ripped skinny jeans, the tears strategically placed, of course, with neon yellow platforms.

"I gotta say, girls," I drawled. "We look pretty fucking hot."

Sasha blew me a kiss. "Thanks, B. If I swung that way, you two would be my first choice. I don't know how I'd decide." She shrugged casually, but smiled with barely contained humor. "We'd probably end up in a threesome."

Kristi snorted. "Wherever Simon is, his head just exploded."

Our laughter was interrupted by the door to our dressing room opening. Mimi, our stage manager, popped her head inside. "Ten minutes, girls."

We were finally about to kick off our first concert on the *For Your Sanity* tour and it was also the first time Levi and I would be singing "Sanity" for an audience. The song was so personal to us—a part of us—that it was freaking me out a little. The worst feeling in the world had to be baring your soul to someone and having them decide it was ugly.

We'd grown so close while recording that song, and despite his constant invitations (and, you know...those, um, moments of weakness), when we walked out the door, I never relented. But, damn, the electricity between us was only strengthening, and the tension from fighting my desire to say yes, to take a chance and be with him, was wearing me thin. That morning, when we were rehearsing on stage, the lights wrapped us in a cocoon as we sang our song. I was pretty sure that if we hadn't been surrounded by our band mates and crew, we would have torn each other's clothes off and gone at it right there on the stage. But, I withdrew and it was the first time I saw impatience in his eyes, his control slipping and giving me a glimpse of just how deep his barely leashed hunger was. I had a feeling we were both approaching our breaking point.

My cell phone rang, yanking me out of my thoughts, and I saw Baylee's picture flash across the screen. I only had a few minutes, and Cecily knew my schedule so she wouldn't let her call unless it was an emergency. I stepped over to the farthest corner in the dressing room and answered worriedly. "Baylee? Are you all right?"

"Cecily said I shouldn't call, but I had to wish you good luck!" Baylee's sweet voice was filled with excitement, and I sighed in relief when I realized nothing was wrong. I knew I should be firm about the rules of when she could call, but I was so filled with love for my baby sister. She and Cecily were such big fans of Stone Butterfly and were in awe of the fact that I was, if only temporarily, a part of the band. When I spent the previous weekend with them, Bailey had danced around the living room singing their songs all day. Calling to wish me luck was adorable, and I couldn't even muster up a smidgen of desire to admonish her. I also felt bad because she hadn't been able to come to the concert. Cecily was sick, and there was no way for me to take care of Baylee while I was performing.

"Thank you, sweet girl," I sing-songed. "You have no idea how much it helps to have you wishing for me. But, I've got to run and get on stage, ok?"

Baylee giggled and started singing a Stone Butterfly song at the top of her lungs and didn't hear me when I said goodbye. Mimi knocked again before opening the door all the way. "Showtime!" she announced. I tossed my phone onto my dressing table and followed Mimi into the wings on stage right, I felt a spring in my step that hadn't been there before. I determined to make my sister proud.

Our concert was packed with energy and emotion, the audience screaming and clapping, fanning the fire. Over the last couple of years, every time I filled in last-minute for bands who were having concerts in or around New York, they were usually one show, two at the most, and then I was back home and, spending most of my time in the studio. Which was fine with me. I loved the rush of performing on a stage in front of thousands of people. There was nothing like it. But my past experiences had been nothing compared to this. The timing had never been right and I'd never truly been a part of the band.

This time, everything was different. My contract was temporary, but that hadn't stopped everyone from treating me like I'd always been, and would always be, one of the group. I'd slipped right into their groove seamlessly. I was still in awe of the incredible musicians who made up Stone Butterfly. And, this time, I felt like one of them.

Simon and Matteo were already out there, ramping up the audience as Sasha, Kristi, and I walked onto the stage. The lights blinded me for a moment, then my vision exploded with one of those "movie moments" we have in life. The ones where you think, *this can't be real, it only happens in the movies*. But there I was, surrounded by thousands and thousands of screaming fans, under bright lights on a massive stage, and for the first time, I felt like I completely belonged there. I wasn't the odd man out to the musicians I was performing with.

My stunned awe wore off, quickly replaced by confidence. I swung my hips as I walked to the area designated for Kristi and me, while winking and waving at the guys closest to my side of the stage. As I passed Simon and Matteo, they both grinned at me. They appeared easy and loose, having the time of their lives, joking around and being ridiculous with the fans. After I took my place, Matteo began to beat a steady rhythm, and then Simon joined in with an intriguing melody on his bass. Suddenly, Levi jogged onto the stage yelling, "Stop! Stop! You can't start a fucking show without me!" Simon waited for the roar of the audience to die down before he rolled his eyes and played an extremely loud, dissonant chord.

"Dude, you just ruined what could have been the best solo of my life. So shut the fuck up and grab your guitar. I wrote a little something. Watch me for the changes and try and keep up." Laughter sprinkled through the audience and he smirked. Then he began to play again and whatever he was playing segued into the intro for "Confess My Everything," and everyone went wild. After that song was done, we moved straight into the intro for the next song and Simon started singing, "Whoa oh ah ah ah ah whoa ooooh," and the audience enthusiastically joined in.

"Can you guys clap your hands to that?" Sasha shouted as her hands beat the rhythm high above her head.

"Whatever you do, don't stop clapping!" Levi took off with the melody and worked the stage. "Sing it, people!" He stopped singing and kept clapping along as they filled the arena with their voices. "Let's get every person in this arena singing. Can you guys do that?" He laughed as they got even louder. "Keep on clapping. Don't stop! All right, here we go!" He started singing again and they kept it up until the very last note. At the end, he spread his arms wide and exclaimed, "You guys are fucking amazing!"

The show really took off from there. Sasha and Levi joined in on the banter and it added a dynamic that the crowd loved. It was abundantly clear how close the four of them were. From our stools to the right of Matteo's set up, Kristi and I were as dazzled by them as the audience.

Levi was always a charismatic guy, someone you were drawn to, but that night, it was magnified times one hundred. With every song, my body burned a little hotter, and it had nothing to do with the industrial lights heating up the stage.

Halfway through the show, Levi introduced each of the members of Stone Butterfly, leaving me for last.

"I've got someone special to introduce to you!" he shouted into the wireless mic hooked over one of his ears. "Can you all welcome Stone Butterfly's newest member, Brooklynn Hawk?" The arena filled with a deafening roar as they clapped and yelled. He ran over and grabbed my hand, dragging me downstage to the catwalk that split the VIP area on the floor. Once they settled a little, Levi continued. "As you know, this tour is called *For Your Sanity*, which just so happens to be the title of our next album, which will release in June!" He had to pause when the audience went ballistic again, but by the huge grin on his face, it was obvious he loved it. "You guys have no idea how fucking lucky you are, because tonight, we have a surprise for you!" He stretched his arms out wide and grinned. "Are you excited?" He listened for a moment, then cupped his hands around his mouth and screamed, "I can't hear you!!" The thunderous response pulsed with energy, making me practically bounce on my feet with excitement.

"There's a song on the record called 'Sanity,' and I co-wrote it with this fucking gorgeous woman right here. It will debut on the radio in just a couple of weeks." A stage tech ran out, and while Levi continued to tease the fans, they attached a wireless mic to my cheek. "So! Have you guessed what your surprise is?" he shouted. "You guys get to be the first to hear it!" Their response was epic and they went crazier still when Matteo started beating a low, steady rhythm on his floor tom. Then he transitioned into the fast and heavy, hard rock beat. Simon and Levi joined him and a couple of bars later, I opened my mouth and sang the most important notes I'd ever sung in my life.

As I belted out the first verse, the world began to melt away completely, leaving only Levi and me. When he began to sing his lyrics, our lines clashed and emoted the first stage of crazy as our eyes locked. We reached the first chorus and Sasha added her haunting violin to the smooth melody. The cacophony of sounds built up the tension inside me. In the safety of the stage and a huge audience, I finally let loose all the caged passion I'd kept locked up tight.

We were approaching the section with the instrumental solos, and Levi faced the audience, dropping his voice so low, the arena fell silent in order to hear his every word. The audience was mesmerized by him. As he crooned the lyrics about love and a broken mind, he faced me again. When he reached the break, he faded out completely. The audience reacted to Matteo, Simon, and Sasha with the same exuberance as they had when Levi and I had been singing. Sasha finished her solo and we glided into the most intense part of the song. I was wrapped up in the music, I didn't even have to think. My mouth opened and I let every repressed emotion I had for Levi pour from my soul. The cello's rich strains crescendoed, and Levi and I circled each other on the stage. I stared into those aqua eyes, captivated by the dark swirl of need that he wasn't even attempting to hide. Each time we sang together, our voices melded, creating a sound that had shivers coursing through my body. We hit the pinnacle of the song, we held out the notes that clashed like to fractured minds. Then we came to the end, our last notes solemn and sung in unison. The lyrics about giving in to the insanity of love and drowning in the crazy. Levi wandered over to me and his hand came up to cup my cheek. I was overwhelmed by the thick atmosphere, so full of lust and emotion, as though our voices were engaged in dirty, sweaty sex.

The other instruments faded out, and all that was left was the smooth, dark melody coming from Sasha's cello. She pulled the bow slowly on the last note, and it hung in the air, the only sound in the otherwise complete silence of the arena. The lights descended until it was completely dark. I was still glued to Levi's intense stare even though I could no longer see him, I could feel him. The connection was severed when the world around us erupted. The lights went back up and he put on his most charming smile before turning to the audience and throwing his hands into the air. "She's amazing, right?" he shouted, receiving an even louder roar of applause in response.

Performing is like a drug. It's a high unlike any other. Standing before a crowd and touching them with what's in your soul. It's also terrifying. But, the audience's reaction boosted my confidence. My head was buzzing and my skin tingling. Levi and I both took a bow before loping off of the stage for a fifteen-minute break. The moment we were in the wings, Levi snatched me up and twirled around, making me laugh. "You were incredible, Brooklynn!"

He stopped spinning and slowly let me slip to the ground, keeping me close and not letting a single inch separate us. I gasped at the electricity crackling between us, and Levi sucked in a breath before whispering, "Fuck it." He took full advantage of my stunned state, lowering his head and sealing his lips over mine. He didn't give me a moment to react, plunging his hands into my hair and his tongue into my mouth. My brain short circuited and all rational thought got lost in the outage. I held tight to his biceps so I wouldn't fall because with every touch of his tongue, my knees got weaker.

"Save it for after the show and get a room, you two!" Matteo jibed, shoving Levi in the shoulder, causing us to stumble and break our embrace. Heat infused my face, and I was sure I was redder than a tomato. Wrapping my arms around myself, I looked everywhere but at Levi before fully giving in to my cowardice and practically running all the way to my dressing room. Sasha and Kristi were already there when I stepped inside and closed the door behind me. I leaned against it, panting and trying to catch my breath.

Sasha raised an auburn brow and snickered. "I think I need a cigarette after that performance," she teased as she tossed me a bottle of water. I wasn't sure if she was referring to the music or the kiss. She didn't elaborate and since I wasn't sure if she saw the kiss at all, I chose to keep my mouth shut. I gave her a grateful smile and then guzzled down the whole bottle of cold liquid in an attempt to cool off. It was mildly effective and helped to slow my racing heart, but my lips were still buzzing from Levi's kiss, the sensation traveling all the way to my core.

A knock on the door warned us that it was time to head back out, and I took a few more deep inhales until I felt more in control. We took to the stage again and the rest of the concert was as fantastic as the first half. Stone Butterfly had a very eclectic sound, and while their main genre was alternative rock, they liked to mix it up with songs that had a crossover sound. Sometimes a bluegrass feel, or punk rock, pop rock, even a little reggae. It livened things up, made it incredibly fun, and really showcased their versatility.

When the lights descended for the final time, after two encores, I felt like I had just run an ultra-marathon. After exiting stage right, Simon jogged over and grabbed me up in a big bear hug. "How's it feel, BK?" I laughed at his nickname for me, a reference to Brooklyn, New York. "It's official, I'm never letting you go."

Matteo tugged me out of Simon's arms and wrapped me up in his. "Back off, Ruiz," he snarled playfully. "I asked her to marry me first." He grinned down at me and winked.

I giggled and gave Matteo a quick squeeze before letting him go, only to find myself hauled up against a brick wall named Levi. "Move it along, boys," he commanded, his voice filled with warning. "She's taken." I rolled my eyes at his obnoxious statement, but when they both adopted their best sad-puppy look, it made me laugh so hard I actually snorted. I slapped my hands over my mouth in embarrassment, then melted into a puddle when I heard Levi mumble quietly, "Fucking adorable."

Why does he have to be so damn irresistible?

Sasha stepped in between Simon and Matteo, looping an arm around each guy's waist. "You'll just have to fight over me instead," she trilled.

Simon's expression became even grumpier. "Like I haven't tried to tap that for years." She threw her head back and laughed before patting him on the head and giving him a peck on the cheek.

"If at first you don't succeed…" Her voice faded out as she turned the boys and walked them over to the backstage hallway. The door flew back open, bouncing off the wall, and in came a tall, incredibly attractive man with deep mocha skin and a shaved head. His eyes darted around until they landed on Kristi, then his whole face lit up and he rushed toward her, calling her name. She whirled around and took off running, jumping into his arms when they reached each other. Their mouths fused together, and I smiled but glanced away, feeling like a voyeur watching their special moment.

"Brooklynn!" I looked back and saw Kristi waving me over. Levi's arms tightened for a moment, but when I stepped on his foot with the five-inch, stiletto heel of my black boots, he yelped and stumbled back. I joined her, and the man with her smiled at me warmly, making my insides go all gooey. He was almost as hot as Levi, and I couldn't help swooning just a little. Kristi snickered and gave me a knowing look. "This is my husband, Jonas. He has that effect on women."

I laughed and put my hand out. "It's great to meet you, Jonas." He ignored my gesture, grabbing my outstretched hand and pulling me in for a hug.

"I've heard so much about you, I feel like we are already great friends," he said with a wide smile.

Noah walked into the wings and huffed impatiently. "Uh, guys, did you forget the fans waiting on you?" He gestured to the door and waited until we all headed into the hallway and in the direction of our dressing rooms. I had, in fact, forgotten about the VIP gathering after the show and at the reminder, I was suddenly a ball of nerves. A warm hand settled at the small of my back and it immediately calmed me. I didn't have to look to know it was Levi, but when I did, I was bathed in the light of his confident smile. "Just picture them all naked, baby," he said, somehow knowing what I was feeling without my having to say a word. Then his eyes drifted to the couple in front of us and his lips pressed together, forming a straight line. "Well, maybe not Jonas."

Chapter Fourteen

LEVI

In all the time since Stone Butterfly became a rock sensation, the meet-and-greets with fans never bothered me. I won't pretend I didn't appreciate the boost to my ego, but I also loved the way those people were about music. The passion with which they responded to our art made it all worth it. But after that first concert with Brooklynn. *After that kiss.* All I wanted to do was grab her and get the hell out of there. I did my duty, though, smiling and charming the crowd, taking pictures and signing autographs. Around two A.M, they shut the party down, and I breathed a sigh of relief.

Although we were just outside the city, and the concert the next night was in Boston, it was decided that we'd go ahead and travel there in the tour buses overnight. It would be less stressful than going home for a few hours, then loading, driving, doing sound check, and performing a concert, all in one day. It also meant I knew exactly where to find Brooklynn after we were done loading out of the arena.

Technically, the girls had their own bus, but Kristi's husband traveled with the band as often as possible, so she was usually with him. Sheryl had stayed on the chick bus with a couple of female roadies, but Sasha had spent most of her time with Matteo, Simon, and me. Especially since we did a lot of writing on the road, and it was more convenient to be together in one vehicle. Eventually, we shuffled everything around and she moved in permanently. We reconfigured the top level of the bus, which used to be a second living room type space and bunks. We added two walls to create three separate "bedrooms." A back room with two twin beds for Sasha and anytime Sheryl or Kristi wanted to stay there, I had the bedroom at the front, and Simon and Matteo used the center area and bunks as a room. On the first level, we turned what used to be a large bedroom into a music room, soundproofing it and hanging acoustic wall panels, as well as bolting down a drum set, a piano, several stools, and music stands. When Brooklynn joined the group, I made sure Noah didn't give her any other option than to be on the same bus as me. I had hoped she'd be sleeping in my bed by the time we hit the road, but at least she was on my bus, even if she was sharing a room with Sasha.

I was the last one to climb on board. Everyone was sprawled around on the couches with the TV on, though they were chatting and looked half asleep. Brooklynn was curled up on one side of the padded bench seat in the kitchen area. I plopped down into the empty spot beside her and twisted my body so I was facing her. Grabbing her legs, untucking them from underneath her, I settled her feet in my lap. "You really were brilliant tonight, baby," I praised her softly.

She grinned and stuck her arms above her head to stretch, which thrust her tits out, and I quickly moved her feet over an inch before she felt me getting hard beneath them. "We did kick ass, didn't we?" She wiggled her toes a little and looked at me hopefully. Rolling my eyes playfully, I grabbed one foot and pushed my thumbs into the soft underside. She moaned in delight and I stifled a groan. I was dying to hear her make those sounds while I moved inside her.

"I'm beat," Sasha announced and waved before climbing the spiral staircase to the top level. I dug my hands into Brooklynn's feet a little deeper, hoping to entice her to stay downstairs with me a little longer. Glancing over my shoulder, I noticed that both Simon and Matteo were conked out on recliners in front of the flat screen mounted in the back of the bus.

"Have lunch with me tomorrow," I murmured when I

turned back to my companion.

She sighed and dropped her head to the side, resting it on the back of the seat. "How many times are you going to make me tell you that it's not a good idea?" Her eyes were on her hands as she toyed with the hem of her shirt, so I leaned across and gently lifted her chin.

"As many times as I need to before you say yes. But"— I lowered my voice into a warning tone—"I've decided it's time to step up my game." I eased the threat with a wink and kept rubbing her feet.

She lifted her head, eyeing me warily. "You haven't been at the top of your game already?" she asked sarcastically. "Ok, so what does that mean, exactly?"

I sighed in mock disappointment. "I'm not giving away my secrets. How else will I keep you on your toes?" I finished with a little tickle to the sensitive arch of her foot and laughed when she jerked her legs back with a shriek. Both slumbering guys jumped up from their seats, startled and looking around wildly. Brooklynn and I both lost it, laughing riotously until they'd grumbled their way up the stairs and out of sight.

I stood up and grasped her hands, pulling her up as well. Then kept ahold of them and led her over to a wider, longer, and much comfier couch. Without letting go, I lowered myself down and urged her to join me. She resisted a little at first, but I smoothed my thumbs tenderly over the backs of her hands and it seemed to drain away her tension. After she sat, I gathered her into my arms and stretched out onto the couch, settling her beside me. She laid her head on my chest and an arm over my stomach, finally relaxing completely.

With slow steady strokes, I ran my fingers through her long, dark hair, letting the silky strands fall through my fingers. "Baby?"

"Hmmm?"

"All games aside, why won't you let me take you out?" I asked seriously.

She sighed and turned her face into my shirt for a second, then lifted her head so our gazes collided. There were equal parts worry and wistfulness darkening the chocolate pools. "My life…" she trailed off, seeming to be searching for the right words. "It hasn't been—well, I've never been a part of anything like this before."

"A band?" I knew her professional history, so I was confused as to her meaning.

She shook her head. "Well yes, but that wasn't what I was talking about. Stone Butterfly is more than a group of people who make great music. You're one entity, a force to be reckoned with, friends, and a family. I was always working toward my goals and never really took the time to nurture friendships. You all pulled me right in and made me feel as though I belong, that I'm part of the family. It's a new experience for me, and I don't want to lose it."

"What about Baylee?"

Her face went soft and she murmured, "Baylee is the best family, don't get me wrong. The thing is, our childhood. . .well, it's mostly just been she and I for our whole lives, and it's more like a mother-daughter situation. I love her more than anything and would never wish for her to be any different. I've never minded taking care of her. I enjoy it." She paused and took a breath before letting it out in a long, slow exhale. "It's so different than the way I fit with you guys," she murmured. "I'm not responsible for all of you. We support and care for each other." She shrugged and gave me a crooked smile. "It's nice to have people I can lean on for a change, to not always have to be the strong one."

Brooklynn had been pretty tight-lipped about her personal life, and I carefully contemplated what to say, hoping she'd continue to open up to me. "Your mom wasn't around to take care of your sister?"

Her eyes darkened ever more and became turbulent, exhaustion showing in the lines of her face. I had a feeling her state of weariness might be the reason her walls were lowering. Our connection was deepening with everything we learned about each other, and I hoped for more. Plus, it might give me an advantage, some insight into her, so I knew what my next move should be.

She contemplated me for a few minutes, chewing on one side of her plump, bottom lip. I used my thumb to pull it from between her teeth and then tucked some wayward hairs behind her ear. "Talk to me," I encouraged softly.

She scooted down and laid her head back on my chest. I was afraid she'd shut the door and I wouldn't get anything more. Then she spoke, so quietly I had to lean down to hear what she was saying.

"My mother and father were never happy together." I managed to stay relaxed instead of tensing in anticipation. I returned to running my fingers through her hair, and when she settled even more against me, I expelled a little sigh of contentment. "She'd gotten pregnant at sixteen, and their deeply religious parents forced them to get married, then promptly washed their hands of them"—she paused to take a long breath—"and me. Why they stayed together after that is beyond me. Anyway, from what I can remember, my mother tried to take care of me, but she suffered from a darkness that no one wanted to admit was there. My father least of all, and he was a loose cannon with a raging temper. I learned from a very young age to be as invisible as possible and to never, ever cry."

It took a shit ton of self-control for me to remain relaxed, to remain passive, and to simply listen. I barely kept my hand steady as my fingertips dragged over her scalp. But, I was afraid that if I spoke, she'd climb back behind her walls, and I'd have to start all over again, breaking them down.

"I was three when my mom found out she was pregnant again. She cried and cried, and I didn't understand it because I was overjoyed to be getting a brother or sister. My father was pissed as hell, though. It was the first time I ever saw him hit her. He backhanded her so hard, her feet left the ground and she flew backward into a wall. I'm not sure my three-year-old mind had any real comprehension of what had happened, other than being aware that my dad made my mom cry."

Brooklynn's hand was twisting my shirt in a tight grip, and I put my free hand over it, silently attempting to give her comfort. "My mother was never light-hearted. I rarely saw her crack even the smallest smile. But, I did find it particularly odd that she was always sobbing when she had to care for my sister, Baylee. My father never let anyone in our house but he worked long hours, and for a couple of years, my mother got away with hiring someone to come in and help us during the day. Then I got old enough to care for myself and Baylee, and one day, the lady she hired left and never came back."

My heart was aching. I placed a kiss on the crown of her head, before resting my chin there. I felt the muscles in her face shift against my chest as they formed a small smile.

"It wasn't until I was a pre-teen that I started to comprehend just how different my home life was from other people's. It never occurred to me that Baylee wasn't my responsibility. I loved taking care of her, and since my mother spent most of her days locked in her room, there was no one else to do it. When my father was home, he ignored us. Which I preferred anyway."

"Somehow, I managed to stay out of my dad's line of fire until I was fifteen. Then the cutest guy in school asked me to a dance. I managed to sneak some money from my mother's purse to buy a dress. On the night of the party, I told my mom I had a study group and wouldn't be home until late. My father didn't really care what I did as long as I kept to myself, but I knew deep down that he'd be pissed if he knew I'd been out with a boy. Anyway, I made sure Baylee had dinner and was asleep before I left and went to a friend's house to change. I was so stupid," she hissed, clearly furious with her younger self. "I didn't change out of my dress before going home, and when I got there, my dad was still awake. He saw my outfit and he knew I'd lied, and sure enough, he was pissed as fuck. He—well, he broke two of my ribs and—never mind, the details aren't important," she stated with an emphatic shake of her head. I wanted to argue with her, to demand she tell me every little thing her father had ever done to hurt her so I could make a list, find the son of a bitch, and give him the same treatment. But, I knew that wasn't what she needed at that moment, so instead, I silently raged while outwardly remaining calm.

"I certainly learned my lesson, but it was like that day had opened his eyes and suddenly, I couldn't hide anymore. I had to be hyperaware of myself and Baylee at all times. To make every effort to stay out of his destructive path. Being forced to be so vigilant made everything around me come into sharper focus, and that's when I began to notice things I'd been blissfully unaware of. Eventually, I took to sleeping in Baylee's room, so that if she woke up in the middle of the night, she wouldn't be scared and cry. Her room was closer to my parents and I started to notice that amidst my mother's crying and the sound of my father hitting her, there were also"—Brooklynn shuddered, and I ran my hand down over her back a few times—"moans and grunting."

Oh, fuck. My brain stalled and I silently begged for my assumption to be wrong.

"It was pretty obvious that my mom wasn't. . .um, a willing . . . participant in their bedroom activities. Her aversion to Baylee started to become a little clearer. She was a constant reminder of what my dad had done. What he was still doing to her."

Please, please, please. I chanted in my head. I didn't want to ask the question, I was so afraid of the answer. Then, I couldn't wait anymore. I had to know. "Did he touch you, Brooklynn?"

She froze for a moment and my stomach lurched. "No," she whispered. "Not like that. He just hit—well, you know."

I said a silent chant of thanks to whatever rock god

watched over my girl and a tidal wave of relief crashed over me, my insides unclenching.

"It was right around this age when it started to become clear that Baylee had some developmental delays," Brooklynn said, continuing her story. "And we started to recognize the signs that her mind hadn't matured along with her body." She tilted her head back, staring at the ceiling, giving me a clear view of her beautiful face. I was tortured by the deep sadness I saw there. "I think it's what kept our dad from getting physically rough with her, though. I counted that as a blessing, even if I had to take the brunt of his anger for the both of us." Her brows furrowed and she looked directly into my eyes. "I'd do it again and again," she said fiercely. "I'll never regret protecting her." I threw a little of my caution to the wind and tenderly brushed my lips against hers, for only a second. A sweet, warm feeling sliced through me when I saw her expression brighten, if only the tiniest bit.

"Things between my mom and Baylee never improved. Mom pretended that she didn't even exist, never acknowledged her unless there was absolutely no other choice. And"—she glanced away and when her eyes returned to mine, they were drowning in guilt—"does it make me a bad person that I was grateful for her disability? For the fact that it kept her from experiencing all of the things I did at the hands of our parents?"

I cupped Brooklynn's face in my palms and stared deeply into her intoxicating, mocha depths, making sure she knew I was one hundred percent serious. "It makes you an incredible sister, baby. I understand that you wouldn't have chosen for your sister to have these challenges in her life, but since she does, it's okay to appreciate the small blessings it brings."

She shook her head lightly. "I'm not even sure how much Baylee really remembers about the way we grew up. All she ever reminisces about are things we did together." The need to gather her up in my arms and comfort her was hard to ignore, but I was still afraid to push her, so I simply placed another sweet kiss on her lips before guiding her head back down to my chest.

"I was seventeen, just barely finishing up my junior year of high school when I came home and found my mom on the kitchen floor, bleeding from multiple stab wounds in her belly. My dad was passed out beside her, the bloody knife clutched in his hand. Thankfully, Baylee was in an after-school program that day." I heard her tiny sniffle and tilted her head back just a little so I could wipe away the tears making tracks over her cheeks. "I called 911 and did my best to stem the flow of bleeding, but she died on the way to the hospital. She was pregnant again, and my dad found out, he went into a rage. He pled guilty and was sentenced to life. He was stabbed and died in prison last year. Ironic, right?" Brooklynn stared off at nothing in particular and shrugged. "Baylee and I were shuffled off to separate foster homes, but were lucky enough to be in the same town. Her foster parents seemed grateful for my help and let me help take care of her. I spent as much time with her as I could. I didn't want her to ever wonder if I'd left her forever." Brooklynn bit her lip again. "She's all I have."

I gave into the urge and slipped both of my arms around her, giving her a light squeeze. "She *was* all you had," I corrected. Her head popped up, and a little of her natural sparkle was back in her eyes as she gave me a tiny smile.

"Exactly."

I shifted our bodies so we were stretched out on the couch with her lying on top of me. I didn't even have to fight my body's reaction to her position. This wasn't about lust or desire, I wanted nothing more at that moment than to give her the emotional support she needed. I wrapped her into my embrace, and with my hand at the back of her head, I guided her down to rest it just below my chin. I inhaled her delicious scent and felt a feeling of rightness flood my mind and heart.

"Do you understand now?" I heard her ask, her voice

muffled because her face was buried in the crook of my neck.

"Did you think your history would make me not want to be with you?" I queried incredulously.

With a push of her palms against my chest for leverage, she sat up and straddled my legs. Amazingly, this conversation was still too important for me to focus on her position and the proximity of her sex to my groin. *Mostly.*

"No, I meant, so you understand why I can't jeopardize what I have here by dating you?"

"What?" I asked, honestly stupefied by her logic. I pushed her hair back behind her ears and framed her face with my hands. "How would letting me take you out on a date threaten anything?"

"What happens when you're done with me, Levi?" she cried. "I'm the one who'll lose everything. It's not like anyone is going to choose me over you!"

After the concert, everyone in the band had threatened me not to fuck with her. Sasha's vivid description of her retaliation if I broke Brooklynn's heart was a little frightening. Honestly, I wasn't sure they wouldn't kick me out and keep her. The idea made me laugh, but I stopped immediately when I saw her eyes swamped with hurt. "Baby, there is so much wrong with that statement, I don't know where to start." I shook my head unbelievingly. How had she not realized how much everyone had come to love and respect her? She was definitely right—we were her family. Though, I was more like a family friend, considering I wanted to fuck her.

She frowned and moved to climb off of me, but I clamped my hands around her hips to keep her in place. "First of all, if you and I weren't together anymore"—she opened her mouth, and I knew she was going to argue that we weren't together at all but I gave her a pointed look, and she shut her mouth—"you would still be a part of Stone Butterfly. Not only do you have a contract, but everyone else would kick my ass if I made them choose between us.

You're right, Brooklynn, you are one of us. We wouldn't be Stone Butterfly without you anymore."

I slid my hands down to her ass and squeezed her cheeks, dragging her forward until her center lined up perfectly with mine. The fact that we were done with the emotional shit was more than obvious by the size of the bulge in my jeans. Her eyes widened to saucers when she felt it pressing between her legs. "On to my next question," I purred. "Who says I'll ever be done with you?"

Chapter Fifteen

BROOKLYNN

Levi's aquamarine pools grew dark and heavy-lidded as he stared at me. I started to squirm but stopped immediately when I felt his hardness growing even more where I was pressed against it. "I didn't think you were a one-woman kind of guy," I muttered, trying to stay very still and avoid my underwear getting any wetter. I swore since I met Levi, I was keeping underwear companies in business with the amount I had to replace. I should've bought disposable panties. *Or edible ones.* I mentally snarled at the naughty little voice in my head.

When I glanced back down at Levi, he was scowling at me. *Huh?* Had I missed something?

"I am not now, nor have I ever been a cheater, Brooklynn." His voice was hard, but I saw a glimpse of vulnerability and hurt in his eyes.

With a grimace, I apologized. "I'm sorry, Levi. That's not what I meant. Really."

"What exactly did you mean?"

"I guess I should have said, the kind of guy who settles down, has a long-term relationship with one woman. That kind of thing."

Levi's eyes narrowed, his mouth forming a grim line. "Relationships aren't easy in this industry, especially when you're touring," he said defensively. "But just because I haven't had success with it, doesn't mean I'm not willing to try again." He seemed so sincere and even a little eager as he finished.

"I—" I wasn't sure what to say. I was exhausted—physically and emotionally. Everything about this man was practically nuclear to me. My insides were constantly melting and I was sure that one day, I would permanently turn into a boneless puddle of goo. That moment was definitely not the time to be making life decisions, especially in regards to Levi. I feared a nuclear meltdown was imminent if I didn't get some sleep and distance to process our conversation. I glanced at the clock and was shocked to see it was almost five in the morning.

When I attempted to climb off him again, he let me. Bending down, I pressed my hands into the cushions on either side of his head, caging him in. "I'll think about it, okay?" I pecked him on the lips but backed up quickly, before he could escalate the kiss. I meant it, too. He nodded reluctantly, and I made my way to the stairs but paused when he called out my name.

"Brooklynn, I wasn't kidding about stepping it up. Now that I know you so much better, I'm even more determined to have you."

There was something in his tone, a dark promise that caused a shiver to skitter down my spine. Without acknowledging his statement, I headed to the upper level and chuckled when I passed Simon and Matteo, who were passed out in their bunks. Both of them were in some level of random undress, as though they fell asleep in the process of changing. I pulled the curtain across their compartment on the way to the room I shared with Sasha and practically fell face first onto my bed.

In what felt like five minutes later, Sasha was gently shaking me awake. "Tech is in a few hours. I figured you'd want to get some food."

I smiled gratefully and rubbed the sleep from my eyes. When I pulled my hands away, they were smeared with mascara and I groaned, remembering I hadn't so much as washed my face or brushed my teeth before passing out. Sasha laughed as she walked away. "I was surprised to see you in your own bed this morning," she quipped. "I thought he might have finally broken your resolve."

"Just friends," I grumbled, dragging my butt out of bed and gathering up fresh clothes and my shower stuff. Sasha didn't say anything. She just snickered and left the room. I was about to follow when the muffled ring of my cell phone caught my ear. Sighing, I dropped my stuff and went searching for it. I wasn't a messy person, but I couldn't seem to keep tabs on my cell phone. It obviously had legs and always wandered to the weirdest spots. I caught a break when I quickly found it under my pillow. Baylee's face lit up the screen, and I answered, already in a better mood.

"Hey, sweet girl."

"How did it go last night?" Baylee asked excitedly, and I could practically hear her bouncing up and down.

"It was amazing!" I declared as I plopped down on the bed, sprawling on my back. "I can't wait to see you tonight!" Our concert in Boston was at the House of Blues, a much smaller venue than the majority of our stops. The intimacy of the performance and the proximity to New York made it the perfect place for Baylee to come see us. And, since she'd been forced to miss last night's performance, I'd suggested a road trip. Cecily had assured me that she was feeling well enough for the trip. She just hadn't been able to handle taking care of Baylee in an arena of that size, with such a huge crowd, while being sick. I felt like it ended up working out even better.

Baylee squealed in delight. "We just got to our hotel! I want to walk the Freedom Trail and then tomorrow, go to the aquarium and the science museum. Oh! And the swan boats!"

I laughed as Baylee chattered on about all the things she wanted to do while she was in Boston. Sometimes, her child-like innocence was contagious, and I added exploring this city to my never-ending list of "one day" activities. We chatted a little more, and then I asked to talk to Cecily.

"Hey, girl. What's up?" she greeted me. Despite sounding cheery, her voice was a little stuffy, and I felt bad for even suggesting they come while she wasn't feeling well. But, I really wanted to see Baylee, and for her to see the band perform before we took off for Europe.

"Thanks for bringing her up here, Cecily. I hope you don't get worse because of me," I stated apologetically.

"Don't think twice, girl! I only sound like death warmed over"—she laughed and then coughed—"I'm feeling much better. I promise."

"Okay…I hope so. Did you get the passes I had sent to the hotel?"

Noah had promised to send a messenger over to where they were staying and leave their all-access passes at the front desk. "Yes!" Cecily practically screamed, forcing me to pull the phone away from my ear so I wouldn't bust an eardrum. "I can't believe we get to meet Stone Butterfly. Levi Matthews is hot as shit."

"So you've said," I responded dryly, but with a chuckle at her fangirling. Her enthusiasm was pretty hilarious and I wouldn't be altogether surprised if she'd slept with his picture under her pillow. Not that I could fault her logic. Levi *was* hot as shit. Although, I made a mental note to give him a heads up before he met her and she drooled all over him. Not that he wasn't used to that kind of thing. I could only imagine the sheer volume of women who slept on his face. Figuratively speaking. *I hope.*

"Okay, I've got to get going. I'll see you guys tonight before the show."

After hanging up, I hopped out of bed and hit the shower. We had our hair and makeup done professionally for shows, so I tossed the long, black tresses into a messy bun and only bothered with a little mascara and some pink lip gloss. I put on a blue sweater, jeans, and black Chucks, before grabbing my coat and purse, then carefully navigating down the spiral staircase to the bottom level of the bus.

Sasha and Matteo were sitting at the kitchen table, with sheet music spread all over it, deep in discussion. Matteo glanced up when I appeared and winked at me. "Morning, sunshine!" he greeted me loudly, well aware that I was not a morning person. Even though it was currently afternoon, but, you get my point. I winced and scowled at him until he said three beautiful words. "Coffee is fresh."

"I love you," I breathed and blew him a grateful kiss while hurrying over to the steaming pot. Before I could get my hands on it, I was grabbed around the waist and pulled back against a very hard, muscular chest.

"If I'd known bringing you coffee in the morning would gain your love, I'd have been waiting on your front porch every day." Levi's voice was pitched low and he nuzzled the back of my neck. Butterflies fluttered in my tummy and I sprayed a mental pesticide to kill them all off. I'm not usually a vicious person, but those stupid winged creatures loved to wreak havoc whenever Levi was near. *Little traitors.*

I didn't get the chance to respond because Levi spun me around and covered my mouth with his. Stunned, my body reacted before my brain could lodge a protest and I melted right into him. His velvety tongue slipped inside and tangled with mine and I grabbed onto his shoulders to steady myself and keep from slithering down to the floor. Like I said…puddle of fucking goo. His hands slid down to palm my ass and he lifted me up to my toes so we were in the perfect position for me to feel exactly what I was doing to him.

"For fuck's sake. Unless you're going to invite me to join in the fun, I'd rather not be present for your live porn show." Simon's voice interrupted the moment and I jumped, frantically trying to leave the circle of Levi's arms. He didn't let go as his head swiveled toward the door of the bus where Simon had just entered.

"Fuck off, asshole," he growled.

I was still frantically trying to extricate myself from his hold, but he wouldn't budge. I was feeling a little self-conscious. Sasha had pretty much implied that everyone was aware of our tug of war, especially after we more or less made out in the wings after the show the night before. Still, Levi's sudden acts of PDA were throwing me off.

Simon let out a bark of laughter. "She won't even let you take her on a date and you're already pussy-whipped."

I stifled a giggle until I clocked Levi's expression. *Uh-oh.*

Levi's mood darkened further and I gave Simon a "shut the fuck up" glare.

"Simon, don't you have some roadies to flirt with or something?" Sasha interjected. She stood and shoved him out the door, following closely behind.

I desperately needed my caffeine, so I resorted to grabbing Levi's nipple and twisting. He yelped and stepped back, letting me go so he could rub the tender spot while Matteo roared with laughter, almost falling off the bench seat at the table.

"You play dirty, baby," Levi grumbled. I was barely listening, focused on pouring myself a mug of liquid heaven. "Lucky for you, I have no problem with getting dirty." I almost spit out my first sip of coffee.

I took another large swallow and with just that one shot of caffeine, I already felt more coherent. I rolled my eyes at Levi. "If come-ons like that are what stepping up your game means, then we have no problem." Levi grinned and took my cup, downing a healthy portion of *my* drink. I narrowed my eyes in warning. "You're playing with fire, coming between me and my coffee, especially the first one of the day." I glanced pointedly at where I'd pinched him. "Next time I may aim further south."

"I can take the heat, baby," he assured me with that fucking charming, panty-melting smile. "And, no, cheesy lines aren't a part of my plan. Just my inherent charm."

Damn him for being so adorable.

Matteo drew my attention when he stood, gathering up all of the papers from the table. "Teo, are you headed to tech?" I asked, swiftly walking toward him, or rather . . . away from Levi. I needed to get away from his overwhelming presence. I couldn't think straight when my sexually neglected body was constantly tingling with overactive hormones.

"Yeah, you want to ride with me?" Matteo asked absently as he picked up his jacket and a weathered guitar case that had been propped in a corner.

"Sure." I grabbed my things and scurried from the bus into the brisk spring air. It was nearing April, but New England weather has always been fickle and the wind still had a bit of a bite to it. I slipped on my leather jacket and followed Matteo to a rented sedan. The tour buses had to be parked just outside of Boston at the airport and since we got in at the ass crack of dawn that morning, instead of dropping us at our hotel, Noah had secured a couple of rental cars so we could be on our own schedule.

"You want to drop your shit at the hotel before we hit House of Blues?" he asked as he pulled out of the parking area.

I shrugged. "I'm good either way."

"You're so easy, B," he joked. "Though, that's not the way Levi tells it."

Laughter bubbled up and I smacked his arm teasingly. "Zip it and drive."

Chapter Sixteen

LEVI

The taste of Brooklynn's lip gloss lingered on my tongue and I stared at her ass as she walked out the door of the bus. Damn, that woman had me tied in fucking knots. My sad state of arousal made me sigh and I finished up the rest of the coffee while going over augmented scales in my head until there was finally a little breathing room in my jeans.

I was rinsing my mug when Noah popped in and looked around with surprise. "Since when are you the last one out?" It was a valid question. I was usually the first to get away from the tour buses when we arrived in a city where we would be staying in hotels. But, kissing the fuck out of Brooklynn while she was still doe-eyed and sleepy was too good an opportunity to pass up, so I'd stuck around.

Instead of explaining it to Noah, I shrugged and picked up my bag and guitar case from the sofa. He eyed me curiously but apparently decided to let it go and disappeared outside. He was already in the driver's seat of a rented SUV idling in front of the bus when I stepped out. I shut and locked the door behind me then circled around the vehicle and climbed into the passenger seat. We both sat silently on the drive to The House of Blues.

The venue was one of the smaller stops on the tour. The only real reason we were doing it was for fun. Those smaller, more intimate performances made touring a little more bearable when being on the road started to become long and tiring. More often than not, they were acoustic, without all the tech and pageantry. It reminded me of being in the studio or jamming in a local coffee house like we used to in college.

We ran a mic check and played around with a couple of songs before setting off to our nearby hotel. It was a modest sized place but the epitome of luxury and we always tried to stay there when we were in Boston, despite the grumbling from our security guys who would rather we stayed on the buses. They didn't have vacancies very often, but we'd gotten lucky this time, since we'd booked it the minute the tour manager, Caroline, mentioned a possible stop in Boston. At the front desk, I checked in and was given two keys. Normally, I just handed one back but for some reason, this time, I slipped them both into my pocket. Noah sent me a text to let me know everyone was gathering in the sushi bar downstairs, so I dropped my luggage in my room and made my way to the restaurant.

The first thing I saw and heard when I walked in was Brooklynn laughing, a sound that never failed to mesmerize me. She was so fucking gorgeous and I could feel the extra key burning a hole in my pocket. I sauntered over to the group and grabbed an empty chair from the table behind them. Brooklynn was sandwiched between Kristi and our publicist, Chloe, who was talking animatedly, her hands flying everywhere. Letting go of the chair, I leaned down and lifted Chloe's seat, with her still in it, and shifted her over far enough to make room for me. Then I maneuvered into the empty space and sat, ignoring Chloe's sputtering about what had just happened.

She sat forward so she could see around me and peered at Brooklynn dubiously. "You said you weren't seeing anyone," she accused.

Brooklynn shook her head at me before answering Chloe. "I'm not."

"Yes she is," I corrected nonchalantly, stealing a California roll from Sasha's plate across the table and receiving a smack on my hand for it. Glancing at Chloe, I pointed the seaweed covered rice at her with a look of warning. "Under no circumstances are you allowed to announce, leak, or even hint at this information." I didn't want even a whisper of a rumor of a relationship with Brooklynn going public until she was as invested in us as I was. Chloe pouted crossly and slumped back in her chair, folding her arms across her chest.

"I appreciate the fact that I'm not constantly bailing you guys out of trouble. But no news is not good news, Levi," she muttered. "Your love lives are pretty much all I have to work with and since none of you seem to have any inclination to have a relationship"—I opened my mouth to argue the point since I'd just claimed Brooklynn, but she glared at me and kept talking—"a *public* relationship. I can't even work that angle. Would it kill one of you to have a nasty break up?" Her short blonde hair was cut in a bob and fell in her face when she shook her head in frustration. Chloe was a tiny thing, barely five foot, with a lack of curves, and a sweet face. It was easy to mistake her for a teenager until you got close. She tucked her hair back behind her ears and the stubborn look on her face reminded me of a kid being told they couldn't play with their favorite toy. Her young appearance caused people to constantly underestimate her but the reality was, she was a fucking pit bull. She was right that we didn't go looking for trouble, but that didn't mean it didn't find us. When you're famous, scandals are around every corner and not having a publicist just because you think you are above that shit is a big motherfucking mistake.

"I'm sure Simon would be more than happy to provide you with a sex tape to leak." Simon grinned at my remark and gave me a double thumbs up.

"Sasha could probably find a Met fan to punch," I added. Sasha loved baseball almost as much as music and she was a born and bred Yankees fan. All I had to do was mention the Mets and she practically snarled.

Brooklynn was giggling beside me but Chloe was shooting daggers out of her piercing green eyes. She stood up and whacked me on the back of the head, prompting me to burst with laughter. "You're a pain in my ass, Levi Matthews," she snapped, but the corners of her mouth tipped up before she spun around and stomped out of the restaurant.

Brooklynn pinched my thigh, hard, and I hissed in pain as my head whipped in her direction. She was glaring at me and it was so damn cute, I couldn't help winking at her, earning me what I was sure would be another dark bruise on my thigh the next day. I was surprised at her strength, which immediately segued into thoughts of her strong hands gripping me tight as I fucked her delicious mouth. I told my cock to have patience and it pretty much gave me a double middle-fingered salute.

"Levi, don't tell people we are together," she whispered, her dark brown eyes narrowed in irritation. I shook off the fog of lust and focused on her demand.

"I didn't," I argued just as softly with a smirk. She scoffed and opened her mouth, but paused before shutting it, her brows furrowed in thought. The realization that I was telling the truth sunk in and she lost her bluster.

One corner of her mouth quirked up and she glanced at the ceiling as though praying for serenity. After a few seconds, she lowered her gaze to mine and the sparkle of amusement in them set my blood on fire. Every-fucking-thing about this woman set me ablaze.

"Don't tell them I'm seeing someone either, okay?" She formed it like a question, but her tone implied it to be a command.

It was cute how she thought she could order me around. "No." I popped the roll I'd been holding into my mouth and chewed on it happily. I hadn't realized how hungry I was. *For actual food.*

"No?" she repeated.

I swallowed and nodded firmly. "No."

She stared at me with her jaw hanging open and I gently grasped her chin and closed it. There was a fire igniting in her chocolate depths and I knew she was gearing up for a scathing response. I was saved by Sasha.

"Mimi is texting in all caps, Brooklynn," she sighed. "She's officially shouting at us to get our asses to hair and makeup."

I still had Brooklynn's face in my hands so I held her still and gave her a firm kiss. "See you later, baby," I murmured. With confusion clouding her face, she silently rose and joined Sasha, exiting the building but not without one last glance at me over her shoulder.

Polishing off Sasha's leftover meal, I talked music with the boys until it was time to leave. There was a large greenroom in the back and we congregated there to get ready for the show. My eyes immediately searched out Brooklynn and I saw her seated on a couch with two women. I knew right away that one of them was her sister, Baylee. They could've easily been mistaken for twins. The only real difference between them being that Baylee's hair was shoulder-length with long bangs, and there was just something about her face, an innocence that made it clear she was the younger sister.

The woman sitting with them looked to be a few years older than Brooklynn. She had beautiful, mocha colored skin, warm brown eyes, and wild black curls caught up in a ponytail behind her head. The three of them were talking enthusiastically but then Baylee's head turned my way and she froze. I gave her a welcoming smile as I made my way over to them. Three sets of brown eyes stared up at me and I couldn't help laughing at the picture they made. Brooklynn was practically glowing with happiness and warmth spread through my chest. I would've given anything to be the one who put that look of joy on her face.

Brooklynn looked at each of the other girls and laughed at their twin expressions of shock and awe. "Baylee, Cecily, I'm sure you know this is Levi Matthews," she introduced, then hurried on to add, "please keep the fangirling to a minimum."

I laughed and took Baylee's hand, pulling her to her feet and into a big hug. "Bullshit, I told her with a wink. "Fangirl away." She blushed to the roots of her hair. "It's great to meet you, Baylee. Brooklynn talks about you so much I feel like I know you already."

"Really?" Baylee breathed, her eyes widening with delight.

Noah's words about Baylee being the way too Brooklynn's heart swam around my head, but I didn't need them to push me to like Baylee. She was sweet and obviously worshipped her older sister. "Absolutely." I tucked her under my arm the way I did with my little sister, Lily, when I was home and turned to face the other woman. I reached out a hand and smiled. "Cecily. Too bad I didn't meet you first," I said with mock regret. "I would have run away with you in a heartbeat, but Baylee's got her hooks in me now." Cecily's hand was shaking when I took it in mine. Despite her dark skin, her blush stood out, and her brown eyes were a little glazed as she stared up at me. I gave her fingers a light squeeze and let go, though it took her a little longer to release my hand. She still hadn't said anything, but, not to be cocky, I was a fucking rock star after all, I was used to it.

Baylee giggled and Brooklynn beamed at me, turning the warmth into a slow burn. Mimi chose that moment to burst into the room and yell, "Showtime, people!"

Brooklynn stood and waved over one of the roadies who then approached us. She pulled Baylee from my side and hugged her, then Cecily, before guiding them to the girl in all black with long, dark braids of hair hanging over each shoulder. "Jeanie is going to take you to your seats and I'll see you after." Baylee clapped her hands and bounced on the balls of her feet. "Good luck!" she trilled before she skipping off.

I slipped my arm around Brooklynn's waist and brought her body flush to mine. "You know she just jinxed the whole show, right?" Wishing a performer good luck is the equivalent of putting a hex on their performance. Bad things always follow. Instead, we tell each other to "break a leg." It's a silly tradition, but one we all follow religiously nonetheless.

She laughed, filling me with warmth and making me crazy with how much I wanted her. "Baylee doesn't believe me and she informed me that she would never wish for me to break my leg."

I frowned in deep contemplation. "Hmmmm. We'll have to do something to counteract it." Threading my fingers through her hair I whispered, "A good luck kiss should do the trick," right before I slammed my mouth down on hers. We needed to get out to the stage in minutes, so I kept my impulses in check and didn't deepen it, but was still satisfied by the desire in her eyes, and the sight of her pink, swollen lips. "Break a leg, baby."

When we all returned to the greenroom after a fucking awesome show, the energy level was high and it was causing a familiar restlessness. The adrenaline rush from being on stage was overwhelming and it needed an outlet, to run its course before the performer could be calm again. However, with Baylee and Cecily there, I didn't know if Brooklynn would join us in our post-show activities. Normally, I was the one pushing everyone out the door and dragging them to the first of what was usually many, bars or parties. But, instead, I found reasons to linger until Brooklynn emerged from the bathroom in sweats and a t-shirt, her stage makeup washed off and her hair in a long ponytail that hung over her shoulder. I felt a spike in my pulse and I was taken off guard by the overriding desire to be with her, no matter what she was doing. If she went right to bed and I thought there was any way I could finagle an invitation, I'd have been the first one there. *There are all kinds of ways to burn through adrenaline...*

Chapter Seventeen

BROOKLYNN

I could feel Levi's gaze boring into me from across the room and that was the moment I decided I was too tired to fight it anymore. The way he'd treated my sister and Cecily smashed down my last remaining wall. Kristi drew my attention when she asked if I was going out with them to the Irish Pub they liked downtown. My eyes immediately sought out Levi and he raised an eyebrow, silently echoing Kristi's question. I nodded and he smiled wickedly like a satisfied cat that just ate a canary. I squeezed my thighs together, trying to relieve the ache he was causing.

"I'm going to get my sister and Cecily back to their hotel first, then I'll catch up with you guys," I told Kristi, but my eyes were still stuck to Levi's. My girls came prancing through the entrance to the room at that moment and it broke our connection. Baylee threw herself into my arms and squeezed me tight.

"You were awesome, Brooklee!" she shouted then danced around singing. Cecily joined us at a slower pace, not really watching where she was going because she was too busy mooning over Levi. He winked at her before turning to talk to Noah and she scurried over to us, her cheeks burning.

"I could just spread him on a cracker," she sighed. Baylee giggled and I laughed, threading an arm through one of each of theirs before moving toward the back door. We hailed a cab and once we arrived at their hotel, I walked them up so I could say goodnight and have a little pow-wow with Cecily before we went our separate ways.

I gave her some extra contact info, particularly for Sasha and Levi, since it was most likely they would know where I was if Noah or I couldn't be reached. There was a bit of separation anxiety and a little guilt plaguing me, hence the many, many ways of contacting me. We also went over the band's schedule and itinerary for the tour for the umpteenth time. "If anything changes I'll let you know and, you can always call Noah if you can't get a hold of me and it's an emergency. I've never seen him without his phone glued to his hand. But, now you have Levi and Sasha's cell numbers too."

Cecily stared at it, wide-eyed for a moment but then tucked all of the information into her planner and gave me a hug. "Thanks for bringing us tonight, I still can't believe we got to meet Stone Butterfly," she said dreamily.

"Yes! I love them!" Baylee exclaimed as she bounced over and gave me another big hug. "Goodnight, Brooklee! Safe travels!"

I gathered her close and kissed her forehead, already missing her so much it hurt. But, this whole situation was good for both of us. "Thanks, sweet girl. I'll miss you."

Tears filled her eyes and she clung to me for another moment. "I'll miss you too. But, no crying. We're too old for tears," she stated, jerking her head up and down for emphasis. Still, a few tears escaped. "Just . . . I'll see you soon." She gave me a watery smile and I hugged her tight one last time.

"Right," I agreed staunchly, drying the corner of my eye. "See you soon."

I found another cab and sent Kristi a text to get the name of the little Irish pub they were currently invading. When I arrived, the crowd was so thick, it was spilling out onto the sidewalk. I observed the masses for a moment, gearing myself up for the pushing and shoving I'd have to do to get through. Before I took one step, a tall figure with a familiar swagger came strolling around the corner of the building. Levi walked to where I was standing and stopped, took my hand and turned toward the pub entrance. "How did you know I was here?" I asked, bewildered.

"I was waiting out here for you. Wanted to make sure

you could find us." The words were said casually, as though it was no big deal, but to me, it was a giant gesture. Rock God, Levi Matthews stood out of the spotlight, literally in a dark corner, waiting for me to arrive. Shivers raced over my skin and my heart beat hard in my chest, while the butterflies in my stomach once again went mad. "And, to make sure nobody in the crowd tries to make a grab for what's mine," he added as he led me toward the sea of bodies. I rolled my eyes at his possessive, caveman attitude, but my heart sped up and I could feel it pulsing between my legs.

As we approached the door, the crowd parted like the freaking red sea, allowing Levi and I a clear path to our band mates who were holding court at the bar. Two of the guys on our security team, Luca and Cameron, were leaning grumpily against the walls closest to the bar, scanning the crowd. Stone Butterfly didn't always have security following them around, but Levi had mentioned that during concerts and at the after parties, they had been needed a time or two. They figured better safe than sorry.

Cooper was leaning on the bar a few stools down from Sasha, nursing a beer and glaring at her. She and Jonas were throwing back shots that were lined up in front of them, with the boisterous encouragement of everyone around them, particularly Simon, Matteo, Noah, and Kristi. We reached our group and Levi grasped my hips, lifting me onto a bar stool like I weighed nothing. I really had to wonder why I bothered to wear panties. *Down girl.* I chided my libido. *Climbing him like a tree in the middle of a public place would certainly give Chloe plenty to work with.*

He moved to stand protectively at my back, between me and the throngs of people. I could see him in the mirror above the bar and his aqua eyes were watching me with such intensity, I had to look away. In order to avoid swooning (there was just no other word for it), I spun the stool to my left and watched the entertainment. Sasha tossed back her last shot and banged the glass down on the shiny wooden surface. Jonas was only a half second behind her, but it was long enough to know he'd been defeated. "Victory is mine!" she shouted, her hands rising in the air, as though calling a touchdown. Levi laughed and stuck out his hand. Kristi, Matteo, Noah, and Simon all slapped cash down on his palm, grumbling and cursing. "Suckers," he gloated, pointing at each of them in turn. "Every one of ya." Then he leaned down and whispered in my ear, "I have a standing bet on Sasha and for some reason these fuckers are dying to see me lose."

Kristi glared at Jonas. "You said you'd been practicing!"

I snorted with laughter when he shrugged sheepishly and then kissed the frown off of her face. A few more guys from the crowd went toe to toe with Sasha until she started swaying and called a halt. "I need to dance some of this shit out of my fucking veins," she announced at the top of her lungs. "I'm headed to a club to shake my ass!" Faster than I could blink, Cooper had weaved his way over to her and was whispering something in her ear, prompting her to huff in irritation and plop down on a stool, sulking. He raised his hand and the bartender tossed him a bottle of water, which he opened and set in front of Sasha.

Levi's chuckle was soft in my ear and I glanced up to see him watching Sasha and Cooper as well. "Sasha is one of the most laid-back chicks I have ever known," he told me, his lips at my ear so I could hear him in the loud and boisterous bar. "I've never seen anyone rile her unless she felt like she or one of her family were being threatened. Until Cooper." He smiled down at me, his clear blue eyes filled with mirth. "He pushes all of her buttons."

"Is there something going on between them?"

Levi shrugged and took a swig from a beer that materialized on the bar beside me. After another swallow, he handed it to me and I tipped it back, the cool liquid feeling great in the heat of so many bodies packed into one space. I handed it back to him and our eyes met in the mirror again, his were dark with hunger. I swiped the bottle back and took another quick drink but the liquid didn't do much to alleviate the heat engulfing my body like it had just a few seconds before. He put his mouth to my ear again and whispered, "You want to get out of here?" His hot breath and the slide of his lips over the shell of my ear caused shivers to dance over me and the ache in my core to intensify. Shoring up my courage, I nodded firmly. Levi's smile lit up the whole freaking bar and all of my remaining worries ran for cover in the shadows.

Levi helped me hop off of the stool, then he leaned in close to yell something to Noah, receiving a chin lift of acknowledgement. Noah reached into his pocket and handed Levi a folder and then his kind blue eyes drifted to mine and he studied me for a moment, before cocking his head to the side. He wanted to know if I was good with the plan. It warmed me, the way he protected me like a big brother. I knew if I said no, he would have put a stop to Levi's plans without another thought. I smiled reassuringly, earning a quick nod before he turned back to his glass of dark amber liquid.

Making sure I had my purse and coat, I let Levi once again guide me through a throng of people who parted for the Rock God in their presence. He waved off Luca and kept going until we were outside and in the parking lot. He slipped a fob and key from his pocket and hit the button. The lights flashed on a dark SUV four stalls over and we strolled down to it. Levi walked me around to the passenger side and opened the door. He helped me up and into my seat, then pulled the seat belt over me and fastened it.

"Caveman, much?" I retorted.

He paused when his face was directly in front of mine and the proximity made my heart race, stalling my breath.

"Maybe I just wanted an excuse to kiss you," he murmured before softly touching his mouth to mine. "Or maybe"— one of his hands came up to cup my shoulder— "I might have been looking for an opportunity to cop a feel." He moved quickly and his fingers brushed, feather light, across the tops of my breasts. Before I could form a thought, my door shut and he was loping around the car.

Within a few minutes, he was settled inside and we were driving away from the pub. I'd regained the power of speech, but I didn't say anything, mostly because I'd been too turned on by his touch to protest it. He reached for my hand and laced our fingers together, kissing my knuckles once before resting them on his hard thigh. The drive was fairly short because, to my surprise, and a good dose of apprehension, he pulled the car up to the valet station at our hotel.

I wanted to take the next step with Levi, but I wasn't sure that my version and Levi's were the same. My body was aching for his and a little devil inside of me wanted nothing more than to drag him to his room and jump him. However, the logical part of me was still working for the moment, and it reminded me to take things slow. Make sure that things between Levi and I were more than our attraction. What if he got bored after the chase was done?

The little devil whispered that we'd spent six weeks getting to know each other and he'd proven himself. Logic rebutted that I was still facing the prospect of a bad break up and losing the best thing that had ever happened to me besides my sister. The impossible argument between my body and mind was interrupted when Levi opened my door and held out his hand. I took a deep breath, and—still unsure what I wanted and starting to get worked up over it—accepted his offer of help and exited the car.

He slipped an arm around my waist and we moved to the entrance of the hotel. "Baby, stop freaking out."

I glanced up quickly, startled that he seemed to have read my mind. His blue eyes were twinkling and he kissed my forehead before steering us toward the elevator. We stepped inside and I was grateful to see no mirrors. I couldn't look at Levi while I was in such a state of mess. He hit the number for our floor and my mind started swirling with how to get out of this and how to get him naked as fast as possible. I stifled a groan of frustration. I felt like Dr. Jekyll in the confrontation scene, a tug of war between two personalities.

The bell chimed and the doors slid open. He urged me with his arm to step out and we padded over the plush carpet. . .past my room. . .then past his. I wasn't sure whether to be relieved or disappointed. I landed on curious. Where were we going?

At the end of the hall was another door and he dug in his back pocket, producing another key card. He swiped it and opened the door, then swept an arm out, motioning for me to step inside. At first glance, it looked like the living area of a large suite. Except, on closer inspection, there were no doors leading to other rooms. I turned around, taking in the opulent cream and blue decor. It was gorgeous and had a calming effect.

"What is this?" I asked.

Levi grinned and removed his coat, tossing it on a table in a dining area. Then helped me remove mine and placed it in the same location. "It's like a suite, but without the bedrooms. An unattached gathering room. A lot of hotels have game rooms, or play rooms for little kids, a smoking lounge, all kinds of random rooms. This hotel has rooms set up for a group of guests to lounge, while keeping all of the rooms separate, so people aren't disturbed once they go to bed."

He gestured to the couch and I slipped off my Chucks before dragging my feet through the plush cream carpet as I walked over. I flopped down and leaned into a stack of pillows, sighing as I relaxed. Damn. I forgot how fucking exhausted I was. The comfy furniture and soothing atmosphere were quickly reminding me and making me drowsy.

"Hey," Levi grumbled as he sat. He set the folder on the opposite side of him before he snatched my hand and yanked me over to him. Lifting me up slightly, he plopped me down onto his lap. "You can sleep later. We aren't going to have sex"—he paused with a salacious grin—"unless you really, really want to…Otherwise I think maybe we should talk, yeah?"

I started to agree but had to stop when a big yawn overtook me. "Sorry," I said with a sheepish smile. He chuckled and looped an arm around my waist while the other played with my ponytail. His eyes stayed on mine, suddenly serious.

"I have something for you." He let go of my hair and picked up the folder, removing a sheaf of papers. He sighed dramatically. "To be fair, it's also from Noah. I can't believe I actually let that bastard guilt me into saying that when he wouldn't have known either way," he grumbled.

"Okay…" I trailed off, confused but smiling at how damn cute he was. I took the proffered papers. My mouth opened and closed like a fish as I scanned them, not sure what to say. "Sheryl is quitting permanently?" I clarified first.

He nodded. "We don't want your time with Stone Butterfly to be temporary, baby. The label has signed off on it and every member of the band is hoping you'll say yes. We want you to take her spot. Sort of."

"Sort of?"

"Read the contract, Brooklynn. You will be as much a part of the group as Sasha, Simon, Matteo, and me. This isn't for a backup singer, it's for another partner. Sasha suggested we also ask you to take over the piano on certain songs so she can add in additional instruments. In fact, we want to eventually hire *your* replacement. As a backup singer."

I sputtered a stream of unintelligible gibberish. "Um, I don't—"

"First," he cut me off. "Kristi was as much on board with this as anyone, she likes her smaller role in the group. It gives her the freedom to step back if she needs to. Did you know she and Jonas have been trying to have kids?"

I nodded, she'd shared their struggles trying to get pregnant with me.

"When it finally happens for them, she'll be in the same position as Sheryl. She isn't sure if she wants to continue traveling or dealing with the hard schedule the label puts on us when we are promoting a new album."

"This is, um, amazing, Levi. I'm not sure how to comprehend it right now"—I tried to move off of his lap but he caged me in with both arms around me—"but, if I'm going to accept, I think it's best we keep our relationship pro—"

"Bullshit, Brooklynn." Levi's hard tone ripped right through my words, his thunderous expression slicing through my heart. "I'm not going to let you use this to push me away again."

Pleading, I tried to make him understand my perspective. "I'm not pushing you away, Levi. It was one thing to give this a try when we had an expiration date because of the temporary contract. But, this means giving everything up for a permanent change to my way of life. One I'm excited to make. Except it means if things don't work with us, I have everything to lose. Everything."

He snatched the contract, flipping to a specific page and stabbing at a section. I read it and the heaviness on my shoulders from the weeks of tension and stress between us, from my worry and fear, all of the rocks on my chest, it all lifted away.

"The only way to fire you is the same way it is for any of us. The studio, band, and manager make the call together, with the reasons clearly cited, or your lawyer will kick all of our asses. And"—he lifted my chin so I could see the same lightness I felt reflected in his aquamarine pools—"I, specifically, have no vote. Unless it's to keep you around. Then I have all the votes." He finished with a lopsided smile.

I set the papers down beside us and cupped his face between my palms. "Levi?"

"What, baby."

"Will you have dinner with me tomorrow night?"

Chapter Eighteen

LEVI

I threw down a couple of poker chips and raised the bet. Simon, Noah, Matteo, and Cameron all eyed me with varying degrees of suspicion. They could look all they wanted, I had a stone-cold poker face. A good thing since I had a shit hand. My eyes wandered over to where Brooklynn and Sasha were sitting in the larger living area of the bus. Sasha was on the floor with her guitar, and Brooklynn was perched on the couch with pencil and paper. They were lost in the music, composing something new that they hadn't shared with the rest of us yet. Brooklynn hummed a few notes, then Sasha said something that made her laugh. I expected the thrill it caused to race through my body, but that didn't make it any less effective. She was beautiful all the time, but when she laughed, she was fucking magnificent.

It had been one of the hardest things I'd ever done in my life. Letting go of her last night, walking her back to her room, and leaving her with a chaste, goodnight kiss. After six weeks of wanting, with my feelings only growing stronger each day, I wasn't sure how long it would be before I snapped, threw her over my shoulder, and carted her off to the nearest empty room where I could seduce her.

After she asked me to dinner and I enthusiastically agreed, I kissed her and it quickly grew passionate. But, we were both aware of the boundaries for that night, at least on some level. She'd only just agreed to dinner, taking her to bed would have pushed her too far. Instead, we made out like teenagers for an hour, then said goodnight.

Checkout in the morning had been at eleven and by noon, we were on the road in the buses, headed to Pittsburgh. With traffic, we'd probably roll in around ten

PM. We were spending two nights in Pittsburg before a crazy stretch of concerts practically piled on top of each other, which meant a lot of time spent on the buses, and no hotels because we'd be driving through the night.

It would be late, but unless I wanted to take Brooklynn out after our concert the next day, this was our only opportunity to have some relaxed, un-rushed time together. We didn't need to be at The Vogue until four and could catch up on sleep in the morning.

Eventually, everyone grew hungry and Matteo, whose second passion in life was cooking, made dinner for everyone. We sat around the oval table on the U-shaped bench seat and talked about nothing in particular while moaning in delight over the delicious food. The buses came to a halt as we were finishing and the door swung open. Erin, one of our tour PAs, came in with a bag and manila folder. Incidentally, our other PA had the same name, except he was a guy and spelled it Aaron. So, we just called him 2.0.

"Erin!" we chorused. She was always a bundle of happiness and humor. She grinned and waved.

"Hey, Erin," Noah greeted. "Mail?"

"Yeah, and a report for you from Caroline," she answered cheerily, tossing the folder his way. "After you look it over, she wants you to have Cooper sign off on the changes." She smiled and dipped her hand into the bag, tossing out little bundles of mail to each of us one by one. When we were on tour, we forwarded all of our mail to the P.O. Box for the team that collected our fan mail and they would let us know about anything urgent, otherwise, they sent it ahead to all of the cities we stopped at. In order to make sure nothing got lost in the shuffle, we always started the forward several days before we left. So, when we got to Boston, Erin had picked up everything sent there early.

After passing it all out and making sure there was nothing we needed, she waved and hopped off the bus. Simon had a stack of at least ten letters and Sasha smirked at it. "More dirty letters from your harem of collagen and silicone?" she teased. "Material for the spank bank?"

I laughed when Simon turned a little green. I knew who they were from.

"Gross, Sasha," he spat. "These are from my family."

Sasha burst out laughing and patted him on the shoulder, somewhat apologetic. Though the sentiment was diluted by her continued snickering. "Sorry, dude. Didn't mean to put that imagery in your depraved mind."

"They're all from family?" Brooklynn asked in awe.

"Simon has seven brothers and two sisters," I told her, throwing my arm behind her, resting it on the edge of the seat.

She looked at Simon with wide eyes and a dropped jaw. "Nine siblings?" she choked out through her shock.

He shrugged. "Latin blood runs hot," he deadpanned. "Then again, I try not to think about my parents in relation to any baby-making activities." He grinned. "Latin storks, I guess."

Brooklynn giggled and, in what I liked to think of as an instinctive move, relaxed into my side, focusing on her own meager pile. Baylee was her only family and she hadn't been with us long enough to really start collecting fan mail. But there was an envelope from her sister and she brightened as though she'd received a hundred letters. She glanced up at me, her chocolate eyes sparkling. "Cecily must have had her write the letter and mail it even though I'd be seeing them in Boston. Just so I'd have something from them on the road."

I smiled softly and kissed her forehead, dropping my arm down onto her shoulders and pulling her a little closer. I ignored the raised eyebrows and sly looks from around the table and was grateful that Brooklynn was too engrossed in her letter to notice them. One handed, I sifted through the correspondence and snatched up one in particular when I caught sight of what appeared to be a postcard among the stack. Laughter bubbled up when I got a look at it.

"Another mash note from your chimp lover?" Matteo chortled. I raised an eyebrow at his old-fashioned term and he just shrugged with a smile. I laughed and gave him a chin lift. I had to give him that one, it was an antiquated term, but an accurate one.

I held it up to show him the front, which had a chimpanzee, dressed like a banana, swinging on a vine, blowing a kiss with big, red lips. Underneath it said, "Swinging by to say, I'm bananas over you!"

On the back was typed out:

Levi,

I hope I get to meet you in Boston, but I know you'll be busy.

Just know, I'll be watching and cheering for you!

Again, there was no call sign. "Damn, I wish I'd known they were going to be in Boston, I would've liked to meet this one. Eccentric fans are always fun." I laughed and slid it in under the pile.

Cameron was sitting on my other side and he grabbed my wrist before I could let go of the card. Taking it, he looking at the address and then inspected the stamp. "This wasn't sent to your P.O. Box, Levi," he stated gruffly. "It was sent directly to the hotel we stayed at in Boston."

I shrugged. "We've stayed there often enough, I guess. It wouldn't be a stretch for them to choose that one and hope they were right."

"Where is it postmarked from?" Noah asked.

"Some tiny town in Connecticut." Cameron tucked the card into his shirt pocket and stood.

"Hey, I wanted to add that to my bonobo collection," I grumbled good-naturedly. "They are an endangered species, you know."

Cameron frowned and turned, walking out the door without another word.

I looked at him curiously for a minute, then mentally

shrugged and let it go. It wasn't worth the brain cells, if Cameron wanted to obsess over it, at least it would give him something to do.

"Bonobo?" Brooklynn questioned with a laugh. "Did you seriously just pull the scientific name for a breed of chimpanzee out of your ass like that?"

I winked at her smugly and tapped a finger to my temple. "You'd be amazed at the things I have stored in this hat rack, baby."

Sasha snorted. "Sure. Chimps and sex moves he reads about in Maxim."

"If you want to think of me as an empty-headed rock star sex god, I have no problem with that. As long as you don't forget the second part." I wiggled my eyebrows comically.

There was a round of scoffs from the peanut gallery but I wasn't paying them any attention because Brooklynn's expression had snagged my eye. She was observing me with a single brow raised. "What?"

"Just wondering if it's true." Her head tilted as though she wanted to see me from a different angle.

"That I'm an intelligent human being?" I chuckled and grabbed my glass of water, still on the table from dinner and took a drink.

"No. If you are full of knowledge about fucking from reading Maxim and are now a veritable sex god," she whispered.

If you've ever seen a "spit-take" on TV or in a movie, I hate to break it to you, but it's rarely as over the top and hilarious as it seems, with a huge spray of liquid bursting from their mouth. It would make life a lot funnier, that's for sure. But, in reality, it's more likely the person will choke on what they are trying to swallow. Like I did at that moment.

I gasped in shock and inhaled most of the water in my mouth, throwing me into a choking and coughing fit. Although, Matteo, who was sitting directly across from me, did get water in the face. It just came from my glass when I jerked forward instead of being spit at. Brooklynn sat there and grinned, pounding me on the back, while Matteo wiped his face, and the rest of the table roared with laughter.

Once I could breathe and had some use of my voice, I bent my head to brush my lips over the shell of her ear while I purred. "You'll be finding out soon enough, baby."

I knocked on the door of Room 705 and then ran my clammy palms over my jeans. I felt like a fucking pre-pubescent teenager picking up his first date. Nervous as hell and sporting a constant erection. I was a rock star for fuck's sake. I didn't get nervous singing in front of millions of people but Brooklynn agrees to a date and suddenly, I've lost all my swagger.

The door swung open and for the second time since I met Brooklynn Hawk, I stopped breathing.

She was dressed in a snug, teal sweater that made her tits look even more mouthwatering and looked amazing against her tanned skin, a leather skirt that clung to her hips and dropped to just above her knees, and boots. Fuck-me boots. Black, leather and lace-up, with a tall, thin heel. Her hair hung down her back like an onyx waterfall and I could already feel the silky strands gliding through my fingers while our naked bodies slid together.

"You look fucking gorgeous, Brooklynn," I praised when I finally got some air back. Her cheeks tinged with pink and she gave me a brilliant smile.

"Thank you. I could say the same of you." Her eyes ran from the tip of my slightly messy hair, down over my black, cashmere sweater, on to my low-slung, dark, blue jeans, to my black, leather, Salvatore Ferragamo shoes. When her chocolate gaze slid back up, the hunger in them left a had all the blood in my body rushing straight to my groin.

One side of my mouth tipped up in a sardonic, lopsided

smile. "I'm gorgeous, huh? I think you just dented my manhood."

Brooklynn rolled her eyes as she stepped from the room and shut the door behind her. "You can take it, pretty boy."

I laughed and grabbed her hand, pulling her into me for a hello kiss. Her hands slid up to link around my neck and I gripped her butt cheeks, melding our bodies tightly together. After an indeterminable amount of time, I lifted my head a few centimeters from hers and whispered, "We have reservations. . .or, we could skip dinner, stay here, and devour each other."

"Um," she blinked a few times, seeming not quite focused on my words. "Dinner, please. At the restaurant," she clarified. I put on my best puppy dog look and she laughed, then moved one hand from the back of my neck, down to my ass and pinched it before slipping out of my embrace and walking backward toward the elevator. *Pace yourself, Matthews, it's gonna be a long night.*

We strolled hand in hand to a small bistro near the hotel. When I made the reservation, I specifically asked for a quiet, out of the way table with as much privacy as possible. I didn't want anything distracting or interrupting us except our food. They led us to a table for two, tucked in a corner, near a roaring fire. The lights were dimmed and candles flickered in the centerpieces around the room. I'd never been there, but it was everything people had said it was when I looked up romantic, local restaurants.

A young blonde woman hustled up to the table, her eyes as wide as saucers as she tried not to stare at me. "Um, w— what can I get for you this evening?" she squeaked as she whipped out a small pad of paper and a pen. She dropped her eyes to it so she wasn't as obvious, staring up through her lashes instead. I almost laughed, but I could tell she was trying to remain professional. Brooklynn's eyes twinkled with amusement, but she clearly didn't want to hurt the girl's feelings, so she kept her voice straight when she ordered roast chicken with sautéed vegetables and a glass of wine.

"Make it two." I smiled as I handed her our menus and she stumbled while backing up. Her face flushed bright red and she spun around, practically flying back to the kitchen.

Once she had disappeared, Brooklynn bubbled with laughter, and I joined her. "Poor girl," she sympathized. "It's easy to be dazzled by a Levi Matthews' smile." I grinned shamelessly at her, hoping for a similar reaction. She snickered, but that sweet shade of pink returned to her cheeks and she bit her bottom lip. She was adorable and. . . so fuckable, it was slowly killing me.

"Baby"—I stretched an arm across the table and laced the fingers of our hands together—"now that you've agreed to date me…" I trailed off when I saw the stunned look on her face.

"Date you?" she sputtered. "I agreed to a date, I never said we were a couple. I mean you're—and there's the band—and I don't know if I'm ready."

I frowned, frustrated that we seemed to be sliding backward. "Brooklynn," I said firmly, "I've let you steer this relationship every step of the way and I haven't minded. I've loved every moment I was able to be with you, getting to know you, and seeing how truly amazing you are. But, now I'm taking over. It's my turn to get in the driver's seat because I refuse to let you take us in reverse. Why are you fighting so hard to keep from moving forward?"

She dropped her gaze to her lap, her lip again being worried between two pearly white teeth. I used my free hand to tug it out and then caressed her cheek and chin, before putting pressure underneath to force her head up.

"Levi," she sighed. "I've only ever truly trusted one person in my life. Learning to let in another person or several, is a monumental task. But, as safe as I've been in my little trust bubble of two, I was also incredibly lonely. I know it seems like I'm fighting you, but I'm not. I'm simply fighting my own natural instinct to crawl back into the safety of my shell. Moving away from my hometown was the biggest leap I've ever taken and I was still reeling from the vertigo when you first started pursuing me and I couldn't handle the thought of it all falling apart if you and I went terribly awry. My world has righted itself since then and I really do want the next leap to be with you. I promise. But, it will take some getting used to. So, you'll have to be patient with me because for every ten steps we make in the right direction, I'm determined enough to only retreat a half step before closing the distance again."

Her face was so earnest, her eyes brimming with hope and resolve, it was the most beautiful she'd ever looked to me. Something in my heart shifted, like a boulder had rolled away and the space opened up and filled with strong emotions. Brooklynn wasn't ready to hear about them, which was okay with me for the moment, because I wasn't quite ready to name them. Still, I mentally acknowledged that they were there.

"I can do that, baby. I'll be whatever you need." I meant it. Every. Fucking. Word. My head cleared, as though sunshine poured into every nook and crevice and there was not a shadow of doubt in my mind. Brooklynn was it for me. The realization pumped energy through my veins. Unfortunately, it sent it hurtling straight to my dick. Fuck. I hoped she was ready to take that step. Every day I woke up wondering if my balls had permanently turned blue.

She beamed at me, only breaking my stare when our waitress returned with our meals. The girl stuttered through asking if we needed anything else, then scurried away. Brooklynn looked longingly at the basket of freshly baked bread as she dragged her salad closer to her.

I almost smiled at her forlorn expression, but instead, I hailed down the next server I saw and asked them to take it from the table, earning me a grateful smile. Brooklynn was, by no means, one of those girls who stayed thin by eating nothing. She loved food and I enjoyed watching her eat. The music industry isn't as judgmental as Hollywood and the acting world. Still, any job that puts you in the spotlight can be rough on your image. So, she was smart about what she put in her mouth and I knew she ran frequently and hit the gym a couple of times a week.

She'd found a balance between what made her happy and what others expected from her. That confidence was just another on a long list of things that made her so fucking sexy. I picked up my fork and stabbed a piece of lettuce, but paused with it halfway to my mouth. Brooklynn was removing the onions from the top of her salad and for some reason, I found it cute as hell. "Not a fan of onions?" She shook her head, peered into the bowl and then nodded with satisfaction and picked up her fork. I couldn't help laughing. "See, now this is something I would know about you already if you'd gone out with me sooner."

Brooklynn chuckled and took a bite, chewing and swallowing before asking, "What about you? What foods don't you like?"

"Well, I'm allergic to coconut, so I'm not really a fan."

Chapter Nineteen

LEVI

We talked and laughed all through dinner, but the sexual tension was growing steadily thicker and by the time we'd finished dessert, I wasn't sure how I was going to walk back to the hotel with a fucking baseball bat between my legs. The waitress brought our check and I smiled as I took it, making her blush.

Even though I was desperate to get out of there, I had one thing left to do. "Can you please bring your manager over?" I asked, trying to sound casual, so she'd know she wasn't in trouble. Apparently, I failed because her face bleached white and tears welled up in her eyes as she quickly spun away. "Fuck." I felt like a complete jackass.

"Levi," Brooklynn said my name reproachfully. "She did a great job tonight, not fawning over you, and waiting on us like we were any other customers."

"I know," I explained. "That's why I want to see her manager."

"Oh." Her frown immediately turned upside down into a brilliant smile.

A middle-aged man in a dark blue suit approached our table, his face concerned, with our waitress trailing behind him, clearly still fighting tears.

"I'm sorry, sir," the man said when he stopped at our table. "Was there something wrong with the service?"

I craned my head around him to see the little blonde and smiled, trying to ease her fears. Her nametag said Stephanie. "Stephanie, can you come over here, please? I didn't ask to see your manager to complain." She sagged with relief and warily shuffled closer. Looking up at the manager, I explained how she'd treated us throughout the night, not asking for an autograph or even acknowledging who I was.

"You should reward her, give her a raise or something," I suggested with a wink in her direction. If it's all right with you," I continued, "I'd like to get her address so that my assistant can send her a thank you." Stephanie's mouth popped open and the manager stood taller, his chest puffed up like he had been the one complimented.

"Absolutely, Mr. Matthews."

Brooklynn placed a gentle hand on Stephanie's arm to get her attention. "Thank you. You have no idea how much it meant to us, especially tonight."

The girl smiled and whispered, "You're welcome." She peeked at me again and I could see she wanted to say something but was too shy and stopped herself.

"Stephanie, can we take a picture together?" I asked, knowing she wouldn't. She slapped her hands over her mouth to muffle her yelp and nodded profusely. I laughed and stood, beckoning her over to stand next to me. Brooklynn asked for her phone and she eagerly handed it over. We smiled for the camera until it clicked. Then I held up my index finger to Brooklynn, asking her to take one more. She held up the phone and I crouched down next to Stephanie, who was so small, we were at eye level. "1…2…3." When Brooklynn reached three, I turned and kissed Stephanie's cheek.

"Thanks, Stephanie," I murmured. She sputtered, unable to form words, but her smile said it all. I thanked the manager again and took Brooklynn's hand, guiding her out of the restaurant. Once we were outside, I turned toward the hotel, but Brooklynn tugged on my hand. I stopped and in the next moment, she'd launched herself into my arms, her mouth pressed against mine.

"You're adorable," she mumbled against my lips. "And, that whole thing just made you even sexier. I'm starting to regret having put on underwear because they are probably ruined."

Well, shit. I came as close as I ever had to coming in my pants since I was a teenage virgin. I kissed her hard, my tongue sliding past her delicious lips, my hands squeezing her waist bringing her up on her toes. She plunged her hands into my hair and tugged on it as she moved restlessly against me.

"Baby, *fuck*," I panted. "You better back the hell up and stop touching me or I'm taking you to my room where there will be a whole lot more than touching."

She nipped my lip and I groaned, my cock twitching painfully. "As long as it includes spending the night in your arms, my vote is option two."

Choirs of angels started singing in my head. I tore my mouth from hers, firmly gripped her hand again, and practically dragged her down the street to the hotel. It was extremely late, so I didn't worry about anyone recognizing me as we rushed through the lobby and into an elevator being held open for us by an attendant. He began to step inside to operate it, but I waved my penthouse key, then put three hundred dollar bills in his hand and pushed him back out. He was laughing when the doors closed.

Our mouths found each other like magnets, unable to stay away. I couldn't find my finesse and roughly pushed Brooklynn's back up against the wall, shoving her skirt up and grabbing her thighs. She moaned and her hips bucked when I lifted her and her legs circled my waist. "I need you, Brooklynn," I rasped. "Need to be inside you. Tell me I can have that," I demanded. "Tell me I can fuck you."

"Yes," she breathed. Any remains of the dam that had been holding me back were washed away. If the elevator hadn't glided to a halt and dinged, I probably would have taken her right there, up against the wall. I didn't put her down when I stepped out, I kept my hands firmly under her backside, keeping her close as we stumbled into the hotel suite.

Normally, we didn't rent the big, expensive rooms. It seemed like a waste since all we did was crash there for a few hours. But this time, I told Noah to book me the penthouse. I wanted complete privacy when I brought

Brooklynn back to the hotel. Sure, it was a little cocky, but a guy could hope. I was a Boy Scout, so I believed in "always be prepared."

Brooklynn's hands traveled down my chest to tunnel back up under my shirt, leaving a trail of goosebumps in their wake. After descending again, she grabbed the hem and raised it until I was forced to stop kissing her so she could tug it over my head. Her legs were clamped tight around me, keeping her from falling in the few seconds it took to remove my sweater. Carefully, since my lips were, once again, ravishing hers, I made my way back to one of the bedrooms, kicking the partially open double doors out of my way.

I stumbled when my legs hit the bed and quickly turned so that we fell onto my back with her on top of me. More than ready to see all of her, I sat up and pressed kisses down along her jaw, then ran my tongue down the column of her neck, while my hands drew up her top. Leaning back, I whipped it over her head, then frowned because I could hardly see her. "Light," I grunted, stretching to my left, blindly searching for a lamp. Finally, I felt a plastic stick, more than likely a remote of some kind. Grasping it, I brought it close and hit the first button. The lamps on both sides of the bed flicked on, bathing the room in a soft glow.

I flung the remote somewhere and focused back on the woman in my arms. "You are so damn beautiful, Brooklynn." She was panting, the movement making her black lace covered breasts rise and fall. Her position, straddling my lap on her knees, put her tits at the perfect level and I licked my lips, eager for a taste. Moving in, I kissed the valley between the two mounds, both hands making quick work of the clasp on her back. I let it go and the lace fell away, baring the two most perfect tits I'd ever seen. They were full and lush, tipped with rosy red nipples, peaked by desire. I licked each tip and blew a little to make them harden even more. Then I drew her bra all the way off and dropped it to the floor before greedily latching on to one bud. Sucking, licking, biting, becoming more aggressive in reaction to her escalating cries of passion.

Her hands fisted in my hair, holding my head to her chest, while hers was thrown back, displaying the elegant line of her neck and her curtain of ebony hair hanging long and straight behind her. I released her nipple with a pop and a quick kiss, then switched to the other to give it equal attention. "Your sweet nipples taste like cherries, baby," I mumbled. "Did you know that I fucking love cherry?"

Brooklynn stilled and her hands pushed my head away. I flicked my gaze up with surprise to find her watching me warily. "Baby?" I asked as I sat up straight. "Brooklynn?"

Her eyes slid away and she cleared her throat, plopping her butt down on my knees and suddenly looking uncomfortable. What the fuck had just happened? Was it what I'd said? "Baby, if you don't like dirty talk, that's fine. You just have to tell me. I'll learn what you like a lot faster if you're honest about it."

"No," she muttered. "That was—um—I like it. It was a huge turn on."

I started to grin, but shook it off. We could get back to that later. I scratched my head, even more confused. "So, what happened?" She sighed and started to climb off of me but I wouldn't let her.

"It was your comment about cherries. I—well, you said I should be honest"—I nodded—"I hope you were serious when you said you like cherries." She gave a nervous little laugh, like she'd just made a joke.

"Brooklynn, I'm about two seconds from blowing my load and I'd like to be inside you when that happens, so spit it out, babe."

She glared at me and folded her arms under her tits, which elevated them and did nothing to help the current situation in my pants. "I'm a virgin," she announced, completely deadpan.

I reared back in shock. *What the actual fuck?* My mind started spinning. "A virgin," I echoed.

"Yes."

"As in, you've never had sex before."

"Correct."

"As in, I'd be your first."

"Yes," she snapped, clearly irritated. "Think about it, Levi. I've spent my life taking care of Baylee, protecting her, and working my ass off to get where I am. When exactly did you imagine I had time to get laid?"

I didn't know how to handle it. Her first. I couldn't take her virginity. I had to stop this, take her back to her room. And how the fuck was she a twenty-two-year-old virgin with the way she looked and her amazing personality and. . .*wait*.

I would be the first man to ever be inside her. To taste and pop her sweet cherry. A tide of possession swarmed to my surface and I swear to the king of rock, I got even harder. Hadn't I already admitted that she was it for me? Why the fuck would I turn her away and give some other motherfucker the chance to take what was mine?

Brooklynn was trying to scramble away again, but I was even more determined to keep her where she was. "You're mistaking my silence, baby," I guessed. She probably thought I'd landed on my first reaction. I was going to keep my mouth fucking shut about that part. "I was shocked, yeah," I conceded. "But, only because I don't understand how anyone as amazing and drop-dead gorgeous as you could still be untouched." She quit wriggling, but remained stiff.

"And, I don't really feel worthy—"

"Don't guys realize what douchebags that makes them sound like?" she spat. I honestly had no response to that. "It makes you sound like a pussy. And who the fuck put you in charge of who I decide to sleep with the first time? *Just* because it's the *first* time. Oh, but if it's time number two, it's full speed ahead." She was rambling and working herself up into a lather and it was damn arousing. "If I tell you I want your dick, who are you to question it?" she shouted the last part.

"No one, babe," I hastily replied. "It should be your call."

She harrumphed, losing a little of the wind from her sails. I bit off a smile and dipped my head, darting my tongue out to lick a circle around each nipple. Her little gasp shot a bolt of lust through me. Using one hand, I put light pressure on the back of her head, gently guiding her forward until my mouth neared her ear. "Do you want my cock, baby?"

She took my other hand from around her waist and slipped it between her legs, pushing it up until I was touching her panties. Her unbelievably soaked panties.

"What do you think?" she purred.

"Fuck yeah, you do," I groaned raggedly. I traced the edge of her underwear up to the top of her thigh, then back down, sliding one finger under the fabric. On the next sweep up, I dragged the digit in between her folds. A groan rumbled in my chest. *Son of a bitch...she's fucking bare.* She moaned and pushed her hips down against my hand. But I took it away and brought it to my lips to suck it clean. "Shit. Baby, you taste like cherries everywhere."

In one swift move, I flipped us over so she was on her back and I could straddle her waist. She stared at my chest hungrily, her eyes practically tracing the lines of my tattoo. It was an intricate, woven design of blues, reds, and yellows, that covered one pec and then trailed down my side and into my pants. What she couldn't see was that it then went down the crease of my upper thigh, ending about an inch from my cock. But, by the look she was giving the waist of my pants, I was confident that she wanted to find out where it led.

"It's beautiful, Levi."

I smiled warmly. "Thank you, baby. I'm glad you like it."

"I think I'd like to trace it with my tongue." Her voice was mostly thoughtful, but I caught the laugh she was trying to hold in.

"Maybe next time," I growled, tweaking her nipples, loving the way she gasped and arched her back. "This time,

I lick you." Her skirt was still bunched around her waist, so I straightened it just enough to access the zipper. I made quick work of it, then climbed from the bed to slide it off, catching her underwear along the way, down her leg and discarding them. I contemplated leaving the boots on, but left that for another day. They were the last thing to go, leaving her stunning body naked and laid out on the bed. Her tan skin stood out against the white comforter, her inky hair splayed all around her. I sucked in a breath, just staring at her and one thought came crashing down on me. *She was mine.*

Chapter Twenty

BROOKLYNN

Levi's aqua eyes were as dark as I'd ever seen them, roving over my body with a worshipful gaze. I'd never felt so beautiful as I did in that moment. After a few minutes of visual explorations, he bent and placed his hands on my neck, then dragged them down over my breasts to my stomach, and over to cup my hips, before moving them to my inner thighs. He gently pressed them apart, licking his lips when my pussy was fully exposed to him.

He climbed back onto the bed, lying on his stomach in the V my body created. The anticipation of what he was going to do had me strung tighter than a bow, leaving no room for being self-conscious. Slowly, touching all of my skin along the way, he moved his hands to my center and used his thumbs to part my lower lips.

"You're so wet, baby. Fuck, knowing I do that to you makes me go a little crazy," he murmured. "I love how pink you are here, it's so fucking pretty." In the next second, he was licking a path up the center of my sex with the flat of his tongue. I cried out at the intense sensations. I was already so primed and on edge that I started to spiral up, sparks shooting through my body. I tensed, attempting to squeeze my thighs together and hold off my orgasm. "Brooklynn, look at me." His voice was suddenly serious and commanding. I pried my eyelids open and tried to focus on him. "Don't hold back from me, do you understand?" I nodded. Or at least, I thought I did. "I want to hear every moan, every whimper, every scream, I want to know I've driven you so wild that you can't keep anything bottled up and unless I tell you otherwise, don't fight coming. If I want you to come, you will give it to me. And I want to hear you screaming in ecstasy while you do."

His words drove me farther up the cliff until I was balancing precariously on the edge. Still holding my pussy open, he licked again and again, then circled my clit before sucking it hard. I gave myself up to my instincts, screaming his name as I shattered. He continued to lick and suck, not allowing me to fall far before he drove me swiftly back up and over again. Finally, he sat up, wiping my juices off of his chin and licking it from his hand. "I'm never going to have enough of eating your pussy, baby. So be prepared for it to happen a lot." He grinned and came up on all fours to crawl over me and lay his lips over mine. I tasted myself on him when our tongues twisted around each other and we both moaned.

I was still shivering with aftershocks from my two orgasms, but his kiss fanned the fire in my core. With a last heated glance, he got to his feet by the bed then sat down to remove his shoes and socks. I gasped at the gorgeous tattoo that took up almost the entirety of his back. It was a phoenix, rising from the ashes, but in this case, the "ashes" were made of music notes. I sat up to inspect it a little closer and saw that if you were really looking for them, you'd see music notes built into the design of the phoenix itself as well. "Wow. Levi, your ink is amazing." He glanced at me over his shoulder with a happy smile before standing again.

That man had a spectacular ass, especially in a pair of well-worn jeans. *But fuck me running*, his naked butt was nothing short of perfection. Then he turned around and I got to see where the front of the tattoo ended. Right at his…*oh sweet mercy*. I swallowed hard as I got my first real look at his cock. I knew he was big, I'd felt it many times. *Understatement of the year.* It was huge. Levi was hung like a fucking horse. I was no small pony but, fuck, I still wasn't sure he'd fit.

"Lie back, baby," he interacted gently, dragging my attention from his shaft. Mostly. I met his gaze and he bit back a smile, gesturing to the bed. "Go on." His eyes narrowed in suspicion. "Stop freaking out, baby"—his voice turned soothing—"and trust me to take care of you."

I did as I was told and scooted up the bed before lying down. He grabbed a condom from the pocket of his pants and rolled it on. With that taken care of, he came down over me and covered me from head to toe, resting on his forearms on either side of my head and his body hovering just inches over mine. Heat radiated from his skin and his scent invaded my lungs, building my passion back up in an instant. He bent his head and kissed me until I forgot everything then he dropped down and our skin ignited wherever it touched. I felt like I'd been tossed into the sky during a firework show on the Fourth of July.

"Fuck, you feel good, Brooklynn," he sighed. I spread my legs farther apart to accommodate his size as his pelvis pressed against mine. "I've been dreaming of this since the moment I first saw you."

"Me too," I admitted with a whimper when he rocked his hips.

"Yeah?" he asked, sounding delighted.

"Don't let it go to your head, pretty boy," I managed to quip.

He thrust his groin forward. "Oh, it's gone to my head baby, just not the one on my shoulders."

I would have laughed if he hadn't dived down and sucked as much of one breast into his mouth as he could, his opposite hand going to the other, twisting and plucking my nipple. I was so caught up in what he was doing to me that I didn't notice he'd shifted, until I felt the broad head of his cock pushing in. I tensed as it stretched me, a little painful, but bearable. He switched breasts and continued to work his way in, centimeter by centimeter, stopping to let me adjust periodically. "You're so big, Levi," I whimpered.

"Trust me, baby," he groaned before taking my mouth in a deep, consuming kiss. One of his hands slid between us, down to where we were joined. He continued to ravish my mouth while he began to toy with my little bundle of nerves. He swirled around it, passed lightly over it, and essentially drove me out of my mind with need.

"Levi," I snapped.

"What," he grunted. "What do you want, baby?"

"I want you to stop teasing me. Make me come."

His fingers immediately honed in on my clit, his face returning to my breasts. He pressed hard on the little nub in my pussy and I cried out as the fire built to epic proportions. His hips had stilled, but I was barely paying them any attention anyway. He treated my clit to the same attention he'd given my nipples, pinching and plucking until I was writhing in ecstasy, then he pinched it incredibly hard, while biting down on my nipple and I screamed at the top of my lungs. I plunged head first into the strongest orgasm I'd ever had, multiplied by at least a hundred. My hands dug into his shoulders as I held on for dear life.

Levi shouted and pain suddenly sliced through the fog and I cried out at the feeling of my insides being ripped apart. At the same time, I was still in the throes of my orgasm, my body in a tug of war between pleasure and pain. As the waves receded, I felt my pulse pounding between my legs, still feeling a sharp ache with each throb, though it was getting duller with every minute that passed.

I realized Levi was practically frozen above me, sweat beading on his forehead, his face hardened with concentration. With both of us still, he slowly opened his eyes and studied me. "I hated hurting you, baby. I'm so sorry." Lifting my head, I brushed a wet kiss over his mouth.

"I'm okay."

"I knew if you were coming, it would help mask the pain, but, I'm so fucking big I still had to work my way in after I broke through." He dropped his forehead to my chest. "It took everything I had in me to stay still once I was all the way in"—he groaned like he was in agony—"the feel of your pussy clamping down while you came. Fuck, I wasn't sure I could keep from thrusting while you adjusted to my size."

I shifted experimentally and he sucked in a breath like I'd sucker punched him. "Tell me I can move, baby. Fuck, fuck, please," he begged.

The pain had been barely there when I moved before, when I did it again, pleasure radiated from where we were joined throughout my entire body. I'd never felt anything so blissful and so intimate. "Wow, that felt amazing," I breathed.

"Thank fuck!" he shouted as he picked up a slow, but steadily increasing rhythm, his head falling back and his eyes shut. "Fuck, baby, your pussy is so tight. Fuck! Yes! Fuck, fuck! Tilt your pussy, baby. Fuck yeah!"

His spew of dirty talk was the sexiest thing I'd ever heard and it sent shivers skittering down my spine and tightening my inner walls. "Levi! Yes! Yes! Oh, yes!" I screamed as I felt the buildup reaching its peak.

"Fuck, Brooklynn, you really do like it dirty, don't you," he growled. "I can feel your pussy tightening when I talk. Oh, yeah, baby, fuck! Just like that, yes! Fuck!" Levi started driving in fast and hard, the bed smacking into the wall with every thrust. I slapped my hands down on his granite ass and held tight, and when my nails dug into his flesh he bellowed, "Oh shit! Fuck!" Then he opened his eyes and looked down at me, his body still bucking into mine wildly. "Come, baby. Do it for me now. Feel my cock filling you full and let it drive you over the edge. I need to feel it again, I want your pussy to milk my cum and suck it dry." Like he knew it would, his filthy mouth tipped me over.

He got to his knees and wrapped my legs around his waist, then leaned over and grabbed onto the headboard, holding it for leverage as he slammed into me over and over. Until at last, he gripped my hips and yanked me forward as buried himself inside me as deep as possible. He roared so loud my ears started ringing and I felt hot spurts of cum filling the condom inside me. He continued to pulse and release more more seed until he finally collapsed on top of me. He was heavy, but it felt amazing, cocooned in his strength, both of us replete and exhausted.

After a few minutes, he rolled onto his back, taking me with him so I was sprawled over him, our bodies still tightly joined.

"Brooklynn, that was the single most incredible thing that has ever happened to me." His quiet, awe-filled statement made me practically glow with happiness.

"Me too," I murmured and kissed his chest.

"Oh, I know I rocked your world, baby," he said smugly.

"I'd smack you if I had the energy to lift my hand," I groaned.

He laughed and tapped my butt lightly. "We'll save that for another time."

We lay there until our heart rates evened out and our breathing regulated. Levi kissed my forehead and then gently moved me to his side as he pulled out. He dashed to the bathroom to dispose of the condom and clean up. When he returned, he had a warm, wet washcloth which he used to wipe away the blood and sooth the soreness. Then he climbed into bed and pulled me to him, wrapping himself around me, spoon fashion.

I was almost asleep when I heard him whisper, "Baby, you know this means we're dating, right?" Gasping, I sat up and stared at him with crazy eyes.

"What?!" I screeched. His stricken expression broke me and I fell into a giggling pile. For which I earned myself the sting of his hand slapping my ass. I couldn't fault him, I deserved it.

"Get over here, brat," he grumbled and pulled me back into position.

I pondered our situation for a moment, feeling mostly content, except for one thing. "Can we keep this between us for a little while?"

He leaned up on his elbow and frowned down at me. "What?"

"If we start telling people, the press will get wind of it

and then we'll be building a relationship between you, me, and the rest of the world. Let's see where this goes before we go public with it, okay?"

"I don't want to hide the fact that you're mine, Brooklynn," he objected angrily.

"I'm not asking you to pretend I'm not yours," I soothed. "We're just keeping it low key for a bit."

His anger ebbed, but he was still grumpy when he asked, "How long?"

"Not long, Levi. Just give me some time to adjust to taking another leap forward."

He sighed and lay back down, hugging me close. "Alright, we'll keep it private, *for now*." He reached over me to grab the remote and turn out the lights. Then kissed my temple before getting settled. "As long as you know, you're mine."

"Same goes, pretty boy."

He chuckled and held me close as we drifted to sleep.

Chapter Twenty-One

BROOKLYNN

The morning after we slept together, I woke up and the force of what we'd done hit me square in the face. I didn't regret it, not even the tiniest bit. But, my fears reared their ugly heads and I prepared myself for things to be awkward, and for the inevitable brush off that would follow it.

For the moment though, I was content to stay just as I was, with his body wrapped around mine. I scooted back a couple of inches, wanting to get even closer to his warmth, but froze when his hardened cock bumped against my ass. I was instantly wet and squeezed my thighs together. Shit. I groaned quietly when I felt how tender and achy I was between my legs. Levi shifted and I felt him brush my hair away from my neck before placing lingering kisses along my shoulder.

"You must be sore, baby." His voice was filled with sympathy, but I was pretty sure I hadn't heard any regret. "I'll start a bath and then order some breakfast. Eggs and bacon, okay?" he asked.

"Yes," I mumbled sleepily.

"Nothing too sugary or with dairy."

"How did you know that?" I twisted just enough to see his face.

He laughed and ran his fingers through my hair. "I pay attention, baby. I rarely see you eating those things, except when we have a day off and you're not singing."

His words filled me with a warm glow of pleasure, knowing he had noticed such tiny little details about me. "We have that in common," he continued. "They affect my voice too."

I smiled at him and his hand swept down my side, caressing my curves. He kissed my neck before gently disentangling himself and climbing off of the bed. I yawned and carefully turned over until I was sprawled on my stomach, wondering if we should just go back to bed. My eyes drifted to the clock on the bedside table and I sighed. *There went that idea.* It was almost two in the afternoon and we had to be at the venue by four.

The sound of running water drifted from the bathroom and after a few minutes, Levi came striding back into the room, still naked and. . .wow. Really aroused. I wondered what he tasted like, which sent a rush of liquid into my mouth and pussy. We probably had time for another round.

"Stop looking at me like that, baby," he growled as he changed directions to detour over to his suitcase. "You need to heal before we have sex again." Digging inside, he shoved things aside until he found what he was looking for, pulling black boxer-briefs from the bag. He quickly donned them, though he was careful as he tucked in his cock, which looked red and angry. Then he padded over to me, pulling the covers back and lifting me up. My arms went around his neck and I looked straight into his eyes, which were brimming with happiness. He kissed my nose and swiftly carried me to the bathroom where he lowered me into a luxurious tub filled with hot water and bubbles. My aches were immediately soothed and I sighed in pure bliss.

Levi made a pained sound and I glanced up to see his eyes glued to my breasts before trailing down to my center. He adjusted himself and started for the door.

"You're not getting in with me?" I asked, not bothering to hide my disappointment.

He looked back at me over his shoulder, his eyes dark and hungry. "You have no fucking idea how much I want to join you, baby. But, if I get in that bathtub with your wet, naked body, I won't be able to stop myself from fucking you and I don't want to hurt you."

I wanted to waylay his worries, but he was right. I was incredibly tender and I didn't think I could take his monster cock right then. He pivoted and came back to me, giving me a sweet kiss then beat a hasty retreat.

I used the time to call Baylee and check in with her. We talked about her trips into the city and the museums she'd been to. I told her about the cities I had been in and the audiences at the concerts, really anything at all. We just enjoyed sharing a little of our lives with each other while we were so far apart.

The concert had been incredible. When the audience is energetic and engaging, it makes all the difference in a performance and we'd blown the roof off that place. With the adrenaline high still pumping through my veins, I smiled wide as I entered the VIP gathering backstage. Levi and I were standing close, though I was careful not to touch him, talking to a group of teenagers who'd driven up from Kentucky, when I felt a tap on my shoulder.

I turned to find an attractive man smiling brightly at me. He was tall, with dark hair and eyes, tanned skin, and dark stubble on his carved jaw. His features reminded me of Matteo's, though not in a way that made me think they were related. Then he spoke and I knew why.

"Ciao. Mi Chiamo Bennedict. Ben."

His accent was thick, indicating that Italian was his first language. "Brooklynn," I replied. "Piacere di conoscerti?" I asked how he was while I stuck my hand out to shake his.

"Bene." He grasped my fingers and lifted them up, most likely to kiss the back, but he was stopped suddenly when a hand came down and clamped around his forearm.

"Hands off," Levi growled menacingly. Ben's eyebrows shot up and he quickly released my hand and stepped back.

"Scusa!" I gasped, then spun to face Levi. "Levi! What the hell?"

He was still glaring at Ben, who interrupted me just as I was about to tear into Levi. "Non c'è problema." He chuckled before switching to English. "I didn't mean to offend your boyfriend. I was speaking with Matteo and he couldn't say enough wonderful things about you, Brooklynn. When he told me you spoke Italian, I had to come over and say hello."

Levi had dropped his arm, but he settled himself firmly beside me, arms crossed, and burning holes in Ben with his scowl. I threw him a dirty look but he either didn't see it or had chosen to ignore it. *Fucking macho cavemen.*

"How do you know Matteo?" I asked curiously.

"Distant relatives of some sort," he laughed. "You know how Italians are. If you can find a connecting bloodline somewhere, no matter how remote, you're cousins."

We chatted for a few minutes, sometimes in Italian, but usually English because Levi became extra agitated if he couldn't understand what we were saying. Ben was apparently in town for business and Matteo's mother's sister's. . .blah, blah, blah, had put them in touch.

"It was lovely to speak with you. I rarely get to converse with anyone in my native tongue," he said eventually. "You are as charming and beautiful as Matteo described and I hope we'll meet again someday. Arrivederci." His eyes strayed to my hand but he wisely stayed back when Levi practically growled like a dog.

"Arrivederci," I murmured with a smile and a small wave. When he disappeared, I whirled on Levi. "What the hell was that?"

"I didn't like how he was looking at you," he stated without remorse.

"So you had to mark your territory?" I snapped "You might as well have come over and peed all around me."

Levi laughed and I was weak when it came to him, so I softened a bit. He took my hand and led me to an under-lit corner of the room. Drawing me into his arms, he tucked some of my hair behind one ear then kissed the sensitive spot just below it, eliciting a shiver from me. "Like I said, I'm not going to pretend you aren't mine. And, baby, I gotta say, when you speak Italian, it's hot as shit and it's taking everything in me not to fuck you right now."

I melted like an ice cream cone in the sun on a blistering July day. I was certainly dripping like one. My leather pants suddenly felt hot and very constricting, and I had the strongest urge to take them off. I was about to throw caution to the wind and attack him when he kissed the tip of my nose, took my hand, and led me back to the crowd. I was pretty speechless for the rest of the meet and greet. I spent most of the time undressing Levi with my eyes. It was so much more satisfying now that I could picture what he looked like underneath his jeans and snug, black T-shirt.

We spent another hour or so with the fans, then headed back to the buses. Indianapolis was our next stop and there was no break in between concerts so we were traveling overnight. Matteo went to bed immediately, Simon turned on a football game and vegged out with a beer, while Sasha, Levi, and I unwound around the kitchen table. After about thirty minutes, my eyes were drooping and I was ready to change out of my tight, leather pants, and the sparkly halter chafing my skin. I'd already ditched the six inch heels the moment we got on the bus.

"Okay, I'm officially dead on my feet," I announced. "I'm going to bed."

"Me too," Sasha agreed with a yawn and deep stretch. "I'll go with you." We scooted out and started for the stairs, Levi right behind us. At the top, I started to follow Sasha to our room but was yanked backward and spun around.

"Baby, where the fuck do you think you're going?" He was frowning at me, clearly irritated.

"To bed."

He pointed to the front of the bus where the other bedroom was situated. His bedroom. "Your bed is that way." His tone made it clear that he didn't expect an argument. He got one anyway.

"You agreed to keep this on the down-low for a while," I hissed, trying not to disturb Matteo.

"I did. But you sleep with me, this is not a negotiation." He kept his voice low as well.

"I can't sneak in at night and back out every morning so they don't know. That's ridiculous."

"It is. Which is why you won't be doing that. You're moving into my room."

I reared back in shock. "I can't do that! How is that keeping it under the radar? They'll all know we're sleeping together!

Levi sighed and put his hands on my shoulders, turning me so I faced away from him, then shuffling us until we were walking toward his room. "Baby, you're crazy if you think they don't already know. And, don't pretend what we were doing isn't more than casual fucking. It pisses me off."

We'd entered his room and he'd taken me all the way to the bed. He didn't bother with the light, just set about undressing me. I was too lost in my head to protest. On one hand, I was a little mortified at the idea of everyone knowing we were having sex. On the other, I was floating in the comfort of knowing Levi still wanted more with me.

I stood and stepped into him, suddenly realizing that we were both fabulously naked. My hands smoothed a path up his chest, over his shoulders, and locked behind his neck. Standing on tiptoe, I brushed my lips against his. He instantly took over, deepening the kiss, his tongue plunging into my mouth, his hands grabbing my ass and holding me tight against him. I moaned and he tore his mouth away, dropping his forehead to rest against mine. "We have to stop," he panted.

"No, we don't." I searched out his lips and sucked him into another soul-wrenching kiss. One of his hands blazed a trail down over my ass cheek, until he could touch my pussy. He rubbed a finger over my clit and I shuddered and moaned. Then he started to slowly push inside and this time, when I groaned, it was a sound of pain. He immediately removed his hand and I heard him suck it clean before sweeping me off of my feet and laying me on the bed.

"I was right," he grumbled, "You're too sore."

I wanted to argue, but damn it, he was right. I was still raw and when he'd entered me, the sting and burn had brought tears to my eyes.

Levi pulled the covers over me, then went around to the other side of the bed and joined me. He tucked me into his embrace and kissed my temple. "Sleep, baby."

I couldn't stop smiling. He was so sweet, unbelievably sexy, and I was starting to believe that he was truly mine.

"Levi, more monkey business," Sasha called as she stepped onto the bus. We'd performed in Indianapolis and had just finished our concert in Chicago before boarding the buses for the night drive to Atlanta. She must have checked in with Erin or 2.0 and took charge of the mail. We were all haphazardly sprawled around the living room, including Kristi, since Jonas had to head home for a couple of weeks. Levi sat in the corner of the couch with me tucked into his side.

Sasha tossed his stack in his lap and I snatched up the postcard to take a look at it. I rolled my eyes when I saw a chimpanzee sitting on a toilet, looking shocked like someone had just walked in on him. Ewwww. And, "him" wasn't exactly the right term. The sender had drawn on girly eyelashes and lipstick. There was no cute saying on the front this time but I flipped it over and saw the message in familiar typing.

Levi,
No matter what I'm doing, I'm always thinking about you.

"Good grief, I hope that's not true," I muttered, wrinkling my nose in disgust. Levi took the card and glanced at both sides, then laughed his ass off for a good five minutes while the card was passed around. There were varying reactions, generally the girls were grossed out and the guys thought it was hilarious. When it came back, I checked the mailing address and frowned when I realized it had been mailed directly to the P.O. box in Chicago that everything was forwarded to. It wasn't a public address like the one where fan mail and other band business was mailed to. Odd. The postmark was from a post office in the Bronx. I shook my head. There are weirdos everywhere, but New York City definitely had more than its share.

When I started yawning in earnest, Levi dragged me up to bed, all the while I blushed from head to toe and avoided all the watchful eyes. I wanted to be with him again, but I had to admit, I was really self-conscious about the possibility of our friends hearing us having sex. It didn't matter that night anyway, Levi could tell I was still a little sore and he refused to put me in any more pain. I was starting to feel sexually frustrated and restless, but, like the last couple of nights spent in his arms, I slept better than I ever had. I completely relaxed, feeling safe and (I hoped) loved.

Chapter Twenty-Two

BROOKLYNN

Levi was chuckling when I came down the stairs, still waking up and in serious need of coffee. The last week had been grueling. We'd played, Atlanta, Jacksonville, Miami, and Tampa. The concerts were back to back with the only break being an extra night in Tampa. Levi and I had made excellent use of that night though, checking into the hotel as soon as we arrived and with the exception of the concert, never leaving our room until it was time to board the bus. Thankfully, we were also getting an extra night in New Orleans, where we would be arriving in a couple of hours.

I poured a steaming cup of ambrosia and took a sip, sighing contentedly when strong arms closed around me. "Morning, baby," Levi crooned and nibbled on my ear. "Fuck, I love your body." One of his hands drifted up to cup my breast and I half melted, half freaked the fuck out.

"Levi!" I hissed trying to twist and go up on my tiptoes to peer over his shoulder and see if we were alone. His low chuckle in my ear had all the right places tingling.

"It's not like anyone would be surprised to see me groping my woman. I guarantee they all knew what was happening last night with all the noise you were making. Not that it bothers me, I fucking love it when you're loud."

I gasped, embarrassed but so fucking turned on. "That turns you on, doesn't it?" he purred, licking the shell of my ear. He moved both hands up under my shirt and tugged my bra down so he could palm both of my breasts and squeeze them. I moaned and tightened my inner muscles, trying to relieve the ache he was causing. "I bet I could make you so hot, you'd let me make you come right here in the kitchen where anyone could walk in on us."

Unexpectedly, the thought of someone catching us

made me burn even more and I bit my lip, trying to swallow my moan. He started plucking, pinching, and twisting my nipples and my hips involuntarily bucked in rhythm with him. He dropped a hand to the waistband of my yoga pants and slid down beneath it. One long finger dragged up the center of my pussy and I had to lift my arms and grab onto his neck when my legs turned to Jell-O. "You're so fucking wet, Brooklynn. All that honey for me. It's intoxicating."

He started to thrust his finger inside me, then two, sawing them until I turned my head into his neck to muffle my moans. His other hand left my breast and joined the first one in my pants. He used it to spread my pussy lips, while the other continued to plunge in and out, then he pressed the heel to my clit and I bit his neck to keep from screaming as I blew apart.

Without warning, he swept me up into his embrace and stalked to the music room, slamming and locking the door behind him. He carried me over to the piano and sat my butt right down onto the keys, tearing my shirt over my head. His mouth came down on mine and I gasped when I felt him rip the seam of my pants and then shred the panties that were ruined anyway. He yanked down the cups of my bra and bent his head to suck a nipple into his mouth. I moaned and the clinking sound of his belt being undone heightened my desperation to have him inside me.

His pants fell to his knees when he straightened and he gripped my hips, yanking me forward as he slammed inside me. I clapped my hand over my mouth to keep quiet but he snarled and ripped it away. "This room is sound proof, baby. I want to hear—fuck, I *need* to hear you." His eyes locked onto mine, neither of us able to look away as he slowly withdrew, then slammed back in, shoving my ass into the keys. My cry of pleasure drowned out their discordant notes. He drove in a couple more times then lifted me up a few inches and, staying inside me, he dropped down to the piano bench. He straddled it and I did the same to him. It kept my legs fully spread open so he could thrust up so, so deep.

"Ride me, Brooklynn," he demanded. With his hands on my hips, he helped guide me as I tried to figure out the best way to do what he wanted. Putting my hands on his shoulders for leverage, I began to rise and fall on his thick shaft. "Fuck, I could watch your tits bounce in front of my face all damn day." He pinched my nipples and then sucked and licked them, his hands returning to my hips. He bucked up every time I dropped back down and screams ripped from my throat.

"Levi! Yes! Yes! Harder! Oh, yes! Don't stop!"

"Keep it up, baby. Your screams are so fucking hot. Squeeze your pussy—oh, fuck! Yes! Oh, fuck, Brooklynn! Fuck, yeah, baby!"

"I'm going to come, Levi," I cried.

"Do it," he growled. "Your pussy is so fucking tight, but when you come on my cock, it's like a vise. I fucking love it. Give me that tight little pussy, Brooklynn." I fell apart with a shout and Levi followed a few thrusts later, roaring my name.

It took several minutes for us to come back to reality, our hearts still racing, taking in big gulps of air.

"Damn, baby. I could live inside your sweet pussy," he muttered with a satisfied sigh.

"I think we both need another shower," I observed, feeling sweaty and—uh oh—sticky between my thighs. "Shit, we didn't use a condom."

"You on the pill?" he asked.

I nodded and he shrugged.

"I'm clean. Haven't been with a woman in months and I got tested right after the last one."

"Okay." I realized in that moment that I completely trusted him.

"Sooooo," he dragged out the last syllable adorably. "Does this mean no more condoms?" His tone was hopeful and a little giddy. I laughed.

"Yeah, I'm cool with going bareback."

"Good, because you're going to be riding this stud a lot."

"Oh, sweet Mary," I snorted. "That was horrible! Beyond cheesy!"

"Ah," he said smugly. "Is it cheesy if it's true?"

I fell into a fit of laughter and he grinned, pulling me into him for a hug. My amusement reminded me of something from earlier. "Hey, what were you laughing at when I came downstairs?"

This made him snicker. "Another postcard."

"Was that, this is really funny, laughter or, I'm reverting to my twelve-year-old self, laughter?"

Levi threw his head back and busted up. "You're really fucking cute," he told me when he could talk again. "Come on, let's get cleaned up and you can decide for yourself."

The card wasn't gross, it was just as ridiculous as all of them. The chimp was lounging in a bubble bath, wearing one of those touristy top hats with the British flag on it and blowing another bubble through one of those tiny plastic rings. The caption said, "I know how to blow, Gov'nor."

"Okay, so it's somewhere in between," I said dryly. I flipped it over and read the message.

Levi,
I'd go anywhere for you. Even England.

"Even England?" I echoed. That seemed odd.

He shrugged. "Maybe they don't like the British," he quipped, taking a seat in one of the recliners.

I pretended to be incredulous. "But what about the sexy accents?" I was standing next to him and he slapped my ass before tugging me into his lap.

"Who's sexy?" he snarled. I grinned and didn't say anything. His next move was to dig his fingers into my ribs, making me giggle uncontrollably. "Who do you think is sexy, baby?"

"You!" I shouted through my laughter. "You! Please

stop! Please!"

He stopped tickling me and wrapped me up in his arms. "Damn fucking straight," he mumbled.

In New Orleans, we took an extra day and spent some time with the band, NOLA's Own. They were old friends of ours whom we rarely got to see. Then our tour stopped in Austin, then Salt Lake City, L.A., Sacramento, and San Francisco over the next eight days, so we had a little time to rest our voices and not get burned out too early. Then we moved on to several stops in the Pacific Northwest, up to Vancouver and then over to Montreal and Quebec. There was a postcard at almost every stop since Austin. The postmarks were from all over the North East and New England areas. Never from the same post office. They were starting to bother me a little, something about them just didn't seem quite right. Beyond the fact that they were getting more possessive and ardent.

One of them looked like a Valentine, the chimp in a pink dress with big red kissy lips and surrounded by red and pink hearts. The writing across the top said, "Wishing for you to Be Mine." The message saying,

Levi,
You have my heart forever. Please give me yours.

The next one was a chimp burning rubber in a shiny red Mustang. The caption said, "Playing it fast and loose."

Levi,
I know you've stopped seeing other women for me! Let's play together!

Then there was the chimp blowing out a birthday cake

with "Make a wish!" on a banner above its head.

Levi,
You're my every wish come true and I can't wait to make yours come true too.
Until then, I love you so much!

After that was a chimp fishing in a river, the flap of his waders having fallen down so you could see his hairy ass. He had a little text bubble that said, "You caught me."

Levi,
I caught you, you're mine. So, tell Brooklynn to stop trying to steal you. I don't like the way she sings that song with you. She's trying to make the world believe it's not about me.

Levi had brushed them off, but he'd looked a little grimmer than usual when he read the last one.

I mentioned my worries to Cameron and he said he was keeping a watchful eye on the situation. I had a feeling he was placating me and it pissed me off. I felt a little bad for reaming him out so I went back and apologized later, but he admitted that I'd been right. So, when I asked him about the fact that the postcards were being mailed directly to the package offices and contacts in each stop, he copped to being concerned about it too. But, so far, none of them had been threatening, they were only getting more ardent. They had no indication that the sender was even in the stalker category. Again, Cameron assured me that they were keeping vigilant about it and not to worry.

That night, Baylee seemed to sense something was off with me during our phone call and asked repeatedly if I was okay. I didn't want to tell her about the notes being sent, I was afraid that she would over react and it would scare her. So, I hadn't shared the situation with her and I wasn't about to. However, guilt at not telling her about Levi and me was poking at my conscience. When I really faced facts with myself, I owned up to the fear that things with Baylee would change. I didn't know how she would react and that bothered me. Would she like Levi as a permanent addition to the family (not that I was assuming we—not important at the moment), would she feel like I'd left her or was abandoning her? There were so many scenarios playing out in my head, so I just kept putting it off, which meant putting off going public with our relationship. Levi was getting frustrated by it too. I felt like I was stuck between a rock and a hard place.

"You'll always love me, no matter what. Right, sweet girl?" I asked her with a sigh.

"We're sisters, Brooklee. It's our job to love each other," she said solemnly. "But, it's okay to love other people too."

I'd been lying down, but when she said that, I popped up, completely alert. Was she referring to Levi and me? Had she picked up on something? I didn't want to ask in case she hadn't but I was eager to know if she was telling me that she was fine with a relationship between Levi and me.

Speaking of the devil, he walked into the room and smiled at me. "Who's that, baby?"

"Baylee."

He grinned and put his hand out for the phone. He liked to butt into my calls with Baylee and sweet talk her. It was absolutely adorable. However, he was usually chased away by Cecily's over the top fangirling. Which was pretty damn funny. I handed him my iPhone and he put it to his ear.

"Is this my Baylee Bear?"

I heard Baylee's giggle and my heart squeezed. Damn, I loved them so much. *Whoa! Whoa, whoa, whoa. Back it up there Brooklynn! You WHAT?!?* I loved them. Him. I loved Levi. I told the little voice freaking the fuck out in my head to shut up and sent it crying with its tail between its legs.

"She's *your* sister, Baylee Bear. Of course, I'll take care of Brooklynn," he assured her, giving me a dirty grin. I smothered a laugh in my hand. I listened to the rest of their call and then laughed hysterically when he started to get uncomfortable and disengage from the conversation. Cecily had clearly taken over the call. He finally managed to put me back on the phone, tossing it to me like it was coated in the plague.

I talked with Cecily for a few minutes about Baylee's progress with her activities and what their plans were. I was bringing them to the concert in Montreal, right before we left for Europe and I couldn't wait to see them.

Chapter Twenty-Three

LEVI

I stared deep into Brooklynn's eyes as we sang the final notes of "Sanity." A few concerts into the tour, we'd decided to close the show with it, instead of using it to end the first half. There was always an encore or two, but never enough time for the sexual high to completely dissipate. But, with Brooklynn being so careful about how we acted in public, I either had to drag her to my dressing room or the nearest closet for a quick fuck to take the edge off for both of us, or I walked around in pain and fucking grumpy all night, because she insisted if we left the others, we'd be "noticeably inconspicuous." We'd been together for nearly a month and I was tired of the cloak and dagger shit. I wanted to claim her, for everyone to know that she was mine, so every drooling fucker watching our show would know they'd never get a shot with her.

The lights went down and I grabbed Brooklynn around the back of her neck and sealed our mouths together. I knew the lights would go back up any moment and I was tempted to let them, she didn't seem to remember where we were as she threw herself into our embrace. But, at the last second, I pulled away, though I kept hold of her hand as the lights momentarily blinded us.

Reluctantly, I let her go and she returned to her stool, next to Kristi, behind us. Once we got to Europe, we were going to debut some of the new songs we'd been working on with Brooklynn. Which meant, we needed her replacement fast. I'd taken Noah aside a few days before to ask what the fuck was taking so long. He assured me he was working on it and we'd have someone in place by the time we flew to England. This singer wouldn't record with us, so we weren't concerned about her practice time. As long as she could pick up the harmonies and blend into the sound, I'd ceased to care. Before Brooklynn, I'd been picky as fuck about who performed with us. But she completed Stone Butterfly, when I hadn't even realized we weren't whole.

Kristi was a badass and we adored her, but the band wasn't her whole life like it was for the ret of us. She loved it, but it wasn't something she wanted long term. It had been the same with Sheryl. It had kept them from integrating into the very fabric of our foursome the way that Brooklynn had. Then again, I thought it was safe to say that no one else would have done what Brooklynn had because she was meant to be ours all along. We just had to find her. And yeah, that paralleled how I felt about her as my girlfriend too.

We had a two-day break after the concert, so I bought a couple of plane tickets and informed Noah that we would meet them at the next stop. Chloe was pissed as fuck because she'd planned a publicity event, but I didn't care. I waited until we were back on the bus and then told Brooklynn to pack a bag, we were going AWOL. She laughed and ran up to the bedroom, coming down less than ten minutes later with a small duffle, wearing shorts, a loose T-shirt that dipped low enough in the front to flirt with her bright red bra, and her hair pulled through the back of a Yankees cap. She was so fucking awesome, right?

Although, while I was drooling over her cleavage in that shirt, I wasn't very happy about the thought of anyone else getting a look at it. I almost told her to go change but she slipped her arms into a hoodie and zipped it up, so I kept my mouth shut and avoided a possible argument.

We took a cab to the airport and boarded for our first class, red-eye flight to Portland. I'd rented a little cabin on an island off the coast for us to hole up in until we met back up with the band for our Portland concert. The flight was quick and it wasn't long before I was unlocking the door to our lakeside retreat. We were fucking exhausted and fell into bed, too tired to do anything but sleep.

Late the next morning, I woke before Brooklynn and, like the whipped, love-sick pussy that I was, I spent a good thirty minutes just watching her sleep. She was so gorgeous. Her long, dark lashes rested on her high cheekbones, raised from the soft smile she was wearing in her sleep. My stomach rumbled and I kissed her temple before easing her out of my arms and climbing out of the bed. I grabbed a pair of jeans and threw them on, not bothering with anything else. I splashed water on my face and brushed my teeth before heading out to the kitchen. The caretaker of the island cabin had been kind enough to ask for a list of groceries and stalked the fridge for us.

I grabbed all the fixings for omelets, one of the few dishes Matteo had been able to teach me to make without destroying the food. Turning on the radio in the kitchen, I bopped my head in time with the music as I prepared breakfast.

"Hey." The soft greeting had me turning with a wide smile. Brooklynn stood at the kitchen door, adorably mussed and sleepy, wearing my discarded T-shirt from the night before. I sauntered over to her and wrapped my arms around her, lifting her off of her toes as I gave her one hell of a good morning kiss.

"Hey, baby," I said once I managed to release her delicious lips. "Hungry?" Just then, her stomach growled loudly, making us both laugh.

"I guess so. What can I do?"

"You can sit your ass on a stool at the counter and give me something pretty to look at."

Brooklynn smiled brightly and hopped up onto a stool, leaning on the granite island on her elbows. "Like this?" she asked cheekily as she batted her eyelashes.

"Not bad," I said thoughtfully as I observed her. "I think it might be better if you removed the shirt."

She laughed and shook her head. "I need food, man!"

I saluted her smartly. "Yes, ma'am."

Breakfast was ready in minutes and I joined her, sitting

on the stool next to her and we filled our bellies. "Mmmmm," Brooklynn moaned. "This is so good."

My food suddenly tasted like sawdust and I was hungry for something else entirely. Every slide of the fork between her plump, pink lips had images of them wrapped around my cock invading my mind. Damn, I was glad I'd left my pants unbuttoned as I shifted to make more room for my growing erection.

She glanced over and arched a single, black eyebrow. "You're not eating."

"Are you almost finished?" I croaked, my mouth completely devoid of moisture. I fucking hoped so.

Realization crept into her expression and my eyes narrowed when she smiled innocently. "Almost." Turning back to her food, she focused on cutting precisely and chewing each piece excruciatingly slow. After a few bites, I couldn't stand it anymore. I grabbed her around the waist and sat her on my lap, straddling me.

"Haven't we talked about what's going to happen if you keep teasing, baby?" I growled.

"Did we?" she asked coyly. "I'm not sure I remember."

Instead of responding verbally, I held her to me with my hands on her firm ass and rushed back to the bedroom. I dropped her unceremoniously on the bed and pointed at her. "Do. Not. Move." Going to my bag, I unzipped it and dug around to see if I had anything that would work for what I had in mind. There wasn't anything, then, I had an idea and moved to Brooklynn's bag. Quickly finding what I needed, I stuffed them in my pocket and returned to the bed where she was waiting, just as I'd left her.

I grunted my approval as I ran my hands up her smooth, endless legs. Her height was one of the things that made her so perfect for me. At six foot four, I was still a lot taller than her and she fit me just right. When I reached the hem of my shirt, I slid it up and over her head, my eyes devouring her incredible body. "Scoot all the way back, baby." She cocked her head curiously, but did as she was told, crawling backward to the head of the bed. "Lay down and grab onto the headboard." I watched her carefully as she complied, searching for any sign that this might be making her uncomfortable. Submission was a tricky area considering what she'd grown up with. I didn't want to ever give her even the illusion that what we did was being forced on her. But, her eyes burned with desire, so I proceeded with my plan. Taking her panties out of my pocket, I ripped them apart.

"Hey!" she complained. "Those were the only pair I brought, Levi."

"You won't need them." I bent a knee on the bed and hovered over her as I secured first one hand, then the other to the rod iron bars of the headboard. Before moving back, I looked her in the eyes and asked, "Okay?"

Her whole countenance seemed to soften and she smiled sweetly. "Yeah."

I nodded before stealing a chaste kiss. "You tell me if you get uncomfortable and I'll stop, no matter what."

Once she agreed, I stood and removed my jeans, mindful of my throbbing dick. Her eyes ran hungrily over me the way I'd done to her. When her perusal landed on my cock, she licked her lips and I groaned. I was fucking dying to feel that tongue on me. I'd planned to go right to eating her, but she'd blown that to hell with her little pink tongue. I got back on the bed, my knees on either side of her and stroked myself a couple of times. She wet her lips again. "Have you given a blow job before?" She shook her head. "Do you want my cock in your mouth, baby?" Her brown eyes flicked up to mine then back down to stare at my member.

"Yes," she whispered, almost shyly. I moved up until my legs were caging her in and put a hand down to run it through her hair before tucking it behind her ear. Then I traced her lips and groaned when she licked the pad of my finger. "Open," I commanded and she dutifully parted her lips. Hovering over her, I took hold of my cock and ran the tip across each lip, leaving it shiny with my pre-cum. Then

I slowly fed my shaft into the warm, wet cavern of her mouth. "Fuck," I gritted out, tensing from the pleasure and the pain of holding off my orgasm. "Lick the tip." She ran her tongue around it a couple of times, then flattened it against my slit, moaning from the taste when she removed it. "Fuck, that's good, baby. Now suck it, just the tip, oh fuck!" I breathed deep, trying to keep from thrusting into her mouth and coming down her throat. "Deeper now, baby," I instructed as I worked my way in the way I had with her virgin pussy. Feeding her a little more each time I pulled back. The girth of my cock filled her entire mouth and she sucked in air through her nose, her chest rising and falling rapidly. I finally bumped the back of her throat and her gag reflex started to kick in so I backed up to give her a break.

"Relax your jaw, baby. Good girl, I'm going all the way in again, ready?" She took a deep breath and nodded. This time, when my tip touched her throat, she was a little more prepared and she swallowed unexpectedly. "Oh fuck!" I shouted, almost blowing at that moment. At the last second, I reined it in. But, I couldn't stop my hips from moving, thrusting gently into her mouth. "Suck, baby," I begged. "Suck it hard, then swallow again. Fuck, yeah!" She dove into it with gusto and soon I was fucking her mouth, barely conscious of anything but the feel of her lips and tongue around my dick. "I knew your mouth would feel like heaven. It's almost as good at milking my cock as your tight pussy." I was reaching my limit, my spine tingling and my balls drawing up. I had just enough sense left to pause and drop my gaze to hers. "I'm gonna come. Do you want me to pull out?" She thought about it for what felt like a fucking eternity, then she shook her head and I was flooded with excitement, dying to come down her throat.

She sucked like a fucking champ and it wasn't long before I shouted with my release as hot cum poured out. She swallowed every fucking drop and when I pulled out, she licked it clean. "Fuck, Brooklynn," I panted. "I don't know if I could go through that again." Her face fell, misunderstanding me. "Baby, that was the best fucking head I've ever had. So fucking good you almost killed me."

"Really?" she grinned, turning cocky. "Are you going to let me go now?"

"Not a chance," I growled. "My turn. And don't think that got you out of your punishment for being a tease."

Her lips turned down in a ridiculously cute pout, but her chocolate orbs sparkled.

Settling myself between her legs, I used one hand to hold her pussy lips open while my mouth and fingers drove her to the brink, then let her orgasm ebb away before building her up again. It was hot as fuck, especially when she started writhing uncontrollably, begging me to let her come.

"Levi, please, I can't take anymore!" she yelled.

"Have you learned your lesson?" I asked around a mouth full of her pussy.

"Yes! Whatever I did, I'll stop, just let me come!" I chuckled at the idea that I'd driven her so crazy, she'd forgotten all about why I was doing this to her. The next time I took her to the peak, I moved up and swiftly drove my still hard cock inside her until I was buried balls deep. She screamed and I began to slam into her as deep as possible, hard and fast. She exploded with my name ripping from her lips. The second her walls clamped down in orgasm, I lost my shit and shouted my release, still pumping my hips while I emptied myself inside her. "Brooklynn, holy shit! Fuck, baby. You're so fucking tight! Fuck!"

We spent the majority of the day in bed, only coming up for air to get some sustenance. When the sun started to go down, we finally emerged from our little love cave. It was still a little chilly to us, not being used to the different climate of spring in the Northwest, so I built a fire and we cuddled up on the couch in front of it. The fireplace was the only obstruction in an otherwise completely clear wall of glass. It looked out over a lake and the setting sun reflected a beautiful kaleidoscope of colors on the water. I had one leg stretched out on the couch and the other on the floor, and Brooklynn was lying in between them, her back resting against my chest. I held her close with my arm banded around her, resting just below her tits, my other hand running my fingers through her long, straight black strands.

The quiet was peaceful and we didn't feel a need to fill the silence, comfortable to just be together. But, something had been on my mind and as much as I didn't want to break the serenity of the moment, I wanted it settled so the weight was lifted from my shoulders.

"Baby?"

"Hmmm?" She sounded content and drowsy, sexy as hell.

"Turn around and look at me, sweetheart, I need to talk to you." I didn't mean for my tone to sound so serious, but I was suddenly incredibly nervous. She sat up and rotated to face me, her expression worried.

"Is something wrong?"

I smiled tenderly and pushed her hair back behind her before caressing her cheek. "Not really, actually, there is one thing that is very, very right."

She smiled back at me tentatively. "What's right?"

Cupping her face, I got lost in the intoxicating allure of her deep chocolate eyes. "Us," I mumbled. "We're very right."

Her shoulders sagged and her smile brightened. "I think so too."

"Do you?" She nodded. "Do you also feel like you love me?" Brooklynn's eyes widened to saucers and she fidgeted nervously.

"Brooklynn?"

"Um." My heart started to sink only to take flight when she said, "Yes. I love you. So much."

"Thank fuck," I breathed, hugging her tightly. "I love

you too, baby. More than anything. I love you."

We kissed fervently, the confession freeing something inside of us, there was nothing left to hold back from each other. Still, there was one last thing that was keeping me from being utterly content. I separated our mouths and stared down at her. "I'm done hiding, Brooklynn," I told her firmly. "I love you and I'm fucking tired of pretending you aren't mine. I don't want to avoid touching you, I want to hold your hand, to kiss you whenever I want."

I prepared myself for her to argue but her eyes only brightened. "Okay. That's done. We're together and it's time the whole fucking world knew it. I'm sick of girls drooling over my man. I love you and I want to make it very clear that you're taken."

"Baby, that was the hottest fucking speech I've ever heard." I grinned before tackling her to her back on the couch and making love in the gleaming rays of twilight.

Chapter Twenty-Four

LEVI

I was on cloud fucking infinity now that I could be with Brooklynn in the open. I loved the fuck out of her and I was going to take every caveman opportunity to make it very clear that she was mine. At the end of the Portland concert, we sang our song and it was more amazing and emotion-filled than it had ever been. When the last note was done, I grabbed her and kissed her hard before the lights even had a chance to go down and I was still drinking from her mouth when they went back up. I didn't let her go until the audience was so loud it practically shook the stage.

They were clapping and screaming in approval (except the few fans who were crying hysterically like I had personally broken their hearts. But, I wasn't paying them any attention) and my face broke into a smile so fucking big I felt like it was splitting my face. I dragged her into the circle of my arms. "She's fucking awesome, right?" I shouted and they went wild. "I mean, how could I not fall in love with her?" I looked down at Brooklynn in my arms and despite her jaw being practically on the ground in shock, she was lit up like I'd never seen before.

"They're all waiting, baby," I teased. "They wanna know…" I trailed off as the audience started chanting, wanting her to tell me. She laughed and threw up her arms like she was giving in to a struggle.

"Yeah, I like the guy," she shrugged. The audience laughed.

"You don't deserve him, bitch!" someone shouted.

"Hey!" I bellowed. "Shut the fuck up for a second." The audience immediately obeyed. Brooklynn tried to tell me to ignore it, but I was fired up.

"We—" I started to gesture to behind me, but my arm

hit a solid body. I glanced to my sides and realized the rest of the band had flanked us, glaring at the audience. I started over. "We love what we do and you guys are a big part of that. We choose to live our lives in the spotlight so we can share what we love. Nothing is private anymore and we accept that. I'm not going to give you bullshit about respecting our privacy and letting us have a life. Because that's what it is, complete fucking bullshit." The audience started to clap and I held up my hand until they quickly silenced. "Our only choice is whether to accept that everything gets out there eventually, or to embrace it and instead, just fucking shout how much I love this woman. I chose to share it with you and by disrespecting her, you're just shitting all fucking over that." I let them have their reaction to my words for a few minutes before smiling again. "Now, where were we…oh yeah, Brooklynn was about to tell you how much she fucking worships me." I gave her a shit-eating grin and she laughed.

She looked out at the fans. "Yeah, I admit it, I fucking love him!" They laughed and clapped then chanted for us to kiss, so I dropped her into a dip and laid a big fat one on her. When I brought us upright again, she slapped my ass. "Doesn't hurt that he's fucking fine. Right, ladies?" I will deny that I blushed until my dying day.

We were both grinning from ear to ear as we stared at each other. Someone yelled for me to propose and Brooklynn laughed. I wasn't sure how I felt about that reaction.

"Let's not get ahead of ourselves people!" she griped good-naturedly. "I think we'll just enjoy making music and being in love for now." They applauded and she yelled, "Who's ready for more fucking music?"

We all moved back into position and played a couple of encores, quickly forgetting our anger and enjoying the rest of the show.

We performed a great show in Seattle and then officially ditched the buses to fly to Vancouver. We had two extra days there as well, but we hung out as a group. We all went out the day after the concert and did a little sight-seeing. We were a little silly, a little crazy, and more carefree that we'd been since going on the road. Noah always conferred with us about where we might like to visit for a little longer, getting to enjoy some of the places we visited rather than always being in and out. Then he made sure the tour manager worked in our requests as best they could. None of us had ever been to Vancouver, so we figured, why the fuck not?

It turned out to be a beautiful city and we had a lot of fun with the fans we ran into, even breaking out into an impromptu concert at a hole-in-the-wall bar we'd stumbled across. Doing stuff like this without getting mobbed was harder in the states, so we had four security guys with us just in case. It left us free to get drunk off our asses and we had a fucking blast. It was mostly Sasha's fault. Cooper had flown back to New York for a couple of weeks and she announced that since she had no babysitter, she was going to get pissed. Of course, that meant we all got sucked into shots. Even Noah let loose, well as much as Noah ever does.

Brooklynn and I stumbled into our room, high with energy and fucked the hell out of each other all fucking night long. It was amazing and I wanted to live in that blissful state. Unfortunately, the next morning, it was all shot to hell when the mail came.

I stared at a chimpanzee chain gang with the caption, "Working on a chimp chain. Join the gang!" That wasn't what had me ready to lose my shit. No, it was the note on the back.

Levi,

Tell her I said to leave you alone or I'll wrap a chain around her neck.

The card had come with three others, two of them

mailed on the same day, though the time stamps were different. All of them mailed after the concert where Brooklynn and I announced that we were together. The show had been up on YouTube within an hour of our last encore and in the next hour, it had garnered over two million hits. We expected the hate mail, but we didn't deal directly with it. We were prepared to stay off of Twitter and other social media sites for a while, until the hype died down and people stopped speculating, predicting, and slandering one or both of us.

The postcards had seemed harmless enough, but with the way they were escalating, the fact that this person was getting around the team of people we had shielding us from this kind of shit was starting to worry me. Noah had brought these to me and I forbid him from telling Brooklynn. None of this was her fault and I didn't want her stressing over it.

I picked up an envelope, surprised that one of the cards had been sent in it. I understood why when a printed picture from the internet fell out with it. It was a picture of me kissing Brooklynn on stage in Portland. The card had three chimps, a guy and two girls based on their clothing, cheesing it up in front of the Royal Palace Amsterdam with, "Sending our love from Amsterdam," across the top. One of the female chimps had been scribbled all over. On the back was typed:

Levi,
Three's a crowd. There is only room for you and me. Tell her YOU'RE MINE.

The third was a couple of chimps in hardhats doing construction. "Working like champs chimps!"

Levi,
I don't want to hurt her. But, I will.

The last one had chimps dressed in women's underwear.

On the top was, "Do you like my chimpanties?"

Levi,
Break up with that slut. She's not good enough for you.

The worst one was waiting for me in Quebec. The chimp on the front was a goth, dressed in all black with heavy dark makeup, a spiked collar and cuffs and it was saying, "I make this look good." The sender had drawn a knife in the chimp's hand.

Levi,
I'll be seeing you soon. Get rid of her or I will.

Chapter Twenty-Five

BROOKLYNN

I was so fucking excited I could barely contain myself. Levi laughed and pulled me into his arms so I would stop pacing. We were waiting at the airport for Baylee and Cecily to arrive and my arms itched to hug my sister. I'd missed her sweet embraces and our special sister time together. After this visit, I wouldn't see her for three months while we toured in Europe.

I felt him kiss my temple. "Look, baby," he said quietly, pointing at the exit from security. Baylee bounded out and looked around wildly until she spotted me, then she ran, full speed ahead. If Levi hadn't kept a firm hold on my hips, we would have tumbled to the ground when she crashed into me. I threw my arms around her, laughing and crying.

"I'm so happy to see you!" I hugged her tight. I'd missed her so much.

"Levi!!" Baylee shouted before leaping out of my arms and into his. He caught her and spun her around, making her squeal.

"Baylee Bear!" After a couple of spins, he set her down and kissed her cheek. "We're so glad you're here!" He slung his arm around my shoulder and continued to grin.

Baylee frowned and stepped back, looking between Levi and me. *Shit.* I'd hinted at my relationship with Levi but had been an absolute coward and hadn't actually told her we were together. When her eyes started to fill with tears, I knew right then that I should have. I was such an idiot.

"You're together?" she asked. She looked at Levi with accusing eyes and pouting lips. "You didn't tell me."

Levi had been talking to Baylee on almost all of my calls with her. They'd gotten really close, which I hoped meant she would be happy when she found out about us. I guess we'd both hurt her by not telling her.

"Hi, guys," Cecily's bright voice interrupted, breaking through the moment. I turned to say hello and rolled my eyes. Cecily was practically undressing Levi with her eyes. She was wearing more make-up and sexier clothes than usual and I had to hold in a laugh. It was kind of ridiculous that she thought she had a chance with him. That didn't have anything to do with her personally. It was just, beyond the fact that he was in love with me, he kept a certain distance with fans, trying to avoid messy entanglements and misunderstandings. And he had done the same with her, but I loved that he hadn't done that with Baylee. He treated her like she was his own sister and, even more, he didn't talk to her as though she were a child like a lot of people. Except for his nickname, but seriously, it was so damn sweet.

"Welcome to Montreal, ladies." Levi gave me a look and tilted his head to the left. I glanced over and saw the slowly growing crowd of fans as they recognized us.

"Time to go," I announced. Levi took both of their carryon bags and herded us out to the car. Baylee was quiet during the drive, but she didn't seem as distraught as before. When we arrived at the hotel, I helped the girls get settled in their room, then we made plans to have dinner. I was taking them out with the whole group for the first time. I was confident Baylee could handle the chaos at first, but after her reaction at the airport, I was a little concerned. I didn't want to make things worse by canceling either and decided to just keep the plans we'd made. I left them to unpack and went to Levi's and my room to do the same. We'd only taken the time to check in before heading out to pick up the girls.

He was just walking out of the bathroom in only a towel as I entered and I stopped short, staring at the delicious sight in front of me. "Wow, you really know how to make an entrance."

Grinning, he prowled over to me, tugging me up against his gorgeous, tatted, muscled chest. Unable to stop myself,

I leaned in and traced a line of his tattoo with my tongue. He suddenly bent and put his shoulder in my stomach, lifting me so I was dangling. . .with quite a nice view of his ass, I might add. I started laughing as he bound toward the bathroom and, because I could, I snatched the towel off to watch the tight muscles of his butt flex as he moved.

"You have a really fine ass, Levi," I complimented with a loud smack to said posterior.

We reached the bathroom and he set me down on the counter. Grinning smugly, he started to undress me. "You like my ass, huh?"

I shrugged with a grin. "It's okay."

He started tickling me until I admitted he had the best ass I'd ever seen, including Jamie Dornan's.

"Well, I kind of like your cute little ass too," he said with a mischievous twinkle in his aqua eyes as he grabbed my butt cheeks and squeezed. "I also like your kissable mouth." He nibbled at the corners before licking my bottom lip. "I love your tits." My shirt was off already, but he expertly popped the clasp on my bra and tugged down so he could wrap his lips around one of my nipples. An amazing multitasker, he loved on my breasts as he unbuttoned my jeans and slid them, and my thong, off. He'd shifted to the opposite nipple and he let it go with a pop, then dropped to his knees. "I love this adorable belly button," he said before licking all around it before sitting on his heels so his head was between my legs. "And I fucking love this juicy pussy."

"Levi!" I cried out when he buried his face between my thighs. He went to fucking town on my pussy, sucking, licking, biting until he'd wrung an earth-shattering orgasm out of me. Standing, he licked his lips and moaned at the taste. It was incredibly hot and I was already burning.

"I especially love the way I can make you fall apart," he mumbled against my lips. "I was gonna take a shower and I think you should join me now that I got you naked and dirty."

"No arguments from me." I put my arms and legs

around him, monkey style, and held on while he turned on the shower and kissed me while we waited for it to heat up. When we stepped under the spray, I felt it turn to steam the second it touched our overheated skin. Then we got all kinds of dirty before finally cleaning up and getting out.

We dressed and headed down to the bar where Sasha, Matteo, Cooper, and Noah were already waiting. Levi caught Noah's eye, lifted his brows and a cocked his head to the left. Noah nodded and headed toward us. Levi kissed my temple and murmured, "I need to talk to Noah for a minute, baby. I'll meet you at the bar." He gave me a tiny push in that direction and patted my ass to get me going. Over my shoulder, I raised a brow and gave him a smoldering look before putting a little more swing in my hips, knowing he was watching me walk away. I took a seat at the bar beside Sasha and glanced back to see Noah and Levi standing by the door having a very serious conversation, if the looks on their faces were any indication. I turned to face the bar and ordered an ice water. I didn't like to drink around Baylee, preferring to be completely clear-headed in case there was a problem. Sasha however, downed her glass of amber liquid and ordered another.

"You might want to slow it down, girl," I counseled. "The night is young."

She threw a dirty look over my shoulder before meeting my eyes and smiling like it hadn't happened. "You're probably right, B. I think I'll do that."

"I said the same damn thing ten minutes ago," Cooper grumbled, making me jump because I hadn't realized he'd come up behind me.

Sasha shrugged and blinked her green eyes, doing a pretty fabulous job of feigning surprise. "You did? I must have missed it." Cooper rolled his eyes. "Probably since most of what you say sounds like Charlie Brown's teacher," she added sassily.

"Wah wa-wah wah. Wah wah-wah. Wah." Sitting on my other side, Matteo mimicked the character she was referring to.

Sasha laughed and threw up her hands. "Exactly!" I couldn't help giggling and when Matteo deftly avoided Cooper's fist flying at his shoulder, I laughed harder.

"Watch it," Levi snapped as he and Noah walked up to us. "You accidentally hurt my woman, I hurt you on purpose."

Cooper nodded. "Fair enough."

I rotated the stool to the side and Levi's arm wrapped around my middle, his scent washing over me when he leaned over to give the bartender his order.

"B," Matteo called to me. "I forgot that your sister is your doppelgänger with short hair. That could seriously be you walking in the door."

I followed his gaze to see Baylee and Cecily just entering the low-lit room and scanning it for us. Raising my hand, I waved to get their attention and smiled when they saw me.

I laughed. "It's uncanny, right?"

"Or creepy."

I slugged his arm. "What?"

He grinned and looked between my sister and me again. "I just keep picturing you two as the twins from *The Shining*." I went for another punch and he reared back, chuckling. "But sexier," he amended. Levi landed a punch that time. "Ow!" he grunted glaring at Levi. "Sexy and creepy. It works."

"That makes no sense whatsoever, Teo," I snickered.

"Sure it does, it's like the crazy vs. hotness scale." I was about to ask what the hell he was talking about but then Baylee and Cecily reached us.

"Hey, sweet girl," I greeted Baylee softly. Levi let me go so I could put my arm around her in a sideways hug.

"Hi, Brooklee," she answered somewhat cheerfully. She seemed in better spirits than she had earlier though. Cecily gave a little wave at everyone, then blushed and giggled like a schoolgirl when she got to Levi. He smiled his, "fan smile," and turned to talk to Baylee. She blushed too, but it was way more adorable.

Simon, Kristi, and Jonas weren't far behind the girls, completing our group for the night. A lot of the crew and production staff were meeting us at the restaurant. We left the bar and, since we were far more recognizable as a group, took a back exit out of the hotel. A black stretch limo, the only way we could all go in one vehicle, was waiting to take us to the restaurant. Baylee lit up like a Christmas tree, shrieking with delight. "This is so cool!" She practically bounced inside and I couldn't help smiling hugely to see her so happy. Levi helped me in and then slid in next to me, with Cecily on his other side, and everyone else piled into the other seats.

None of us had ever been to Montreal, so we had the concierge direct us to a place to eat. He sent us to Dunn's Famous, a smoked meat restaurant. The location we were at was all dark wood and leather, giving it an almost historic feel. They set us up with a whole bunch of tables stuck together, which was pretty much all of them, spilling over into their booths, because by the time everyone arrived, there wasn't much room for anyone but our gang.

It was loud and boisterous, fun and so delicious. I kept a close eye on Baylee to make sure she didn't get overwhelmed, but she was eating up the attention being poured on her. She scooted a little closer to Levi, searching for the comfort of someone she felt comfortable with, making her feel safe despite being surrounded by strangers. I was on her other side and was a little disappointed that she'd turned to Levi over me, but it made perfect sense, so I had to get over myself. Between me and Levi, who was more likely to be able to protect her? He put his arm across the back of her chair and winked at me before giving her a quick hug. Then he stretched it out again, this time reaching my chair where he started to toy with the ends of my hair.

Cecily was next to me and kept straining her neck to see around me and stare at Levi. Her lack of attentiveness toward Baylee was starting to irk me, even though I knew that it was probably because I was there, so she didn't have to be as vigilant as usual. Still, her star struck fangirling was fraying my nerves a little.

"So, you guys are dating?" she whispered. I glanced at her and nodded with a smile. "Wow, you're so lucky," she sighed. "I bet he's totally packing, right? Like an animal in bed?"

I frowned and shook my head. Cecily was like family, but she was stepping over lines I wouldn't want even Baylee crossing. "Not appropriate, Cecily," I snapped quietly.

My tone seemed to shake her out of her head a little and despite her mocha skin, her cheeks turned bright red. "You're right I'm so sorry, Brooklynn." Her eyes strayed to Levi and then back to me. "Do you worry about all the women throwing themselves at him? I mean, I think I'd be a little frightened about how much they'd hate me for taking him away from them, you know?"

I was taken aback by her question and sputtered, not really knowing how to answer. Hadn't I thought about it? About the girls sleeping on his face, the women throwing themselves at him, even the guys who were in love with him. Levi had been very protective, but he couldn't keep every single negative post or comment from touching me. I'd seen some of the Twitter posts before he forced me to delete it from my phone for a while. I was the most hated woman in America at the moment. I hadn't let it get to me though. Levi had put permanent security on me since the Portland concert and they were following me fucking everywhere when he wasn't with me. And, I do mean *everywhere*. Cameron was usually my shadow, but I also had a woman, Lindsay, and she stayed on my heels all the way into the damn bathroom. But, I wasn't stupid. Until the hype died down, I figured, better safe than sorry.

"Um, no. I guess I haven't really thought about it," I mumbled.

"Wow. I totally would," she breathed. "I mean, the odds are that a crazy fan will get by the security one day, right?

I'd almost be afraid to date him."

"Well, I'm not. So, what adventures have you and Baylee been up to?" I asked, changing the subject. I talked to them at least every other night and knew all about what was going on with them, but I couldn't think of anything better to steer her in a different direction right that minute.

"Just the usual stuff. Not much new. She did well on the plane though, you'd have been proud of her…"

Success, I thought as she prattled on about Baylee and their trip. Sasha had started humming and Matteo started to tap out a rhythm with her. She switched to words, except she was making a hilarious parody of one of our songs. Simon started making guitar noises and we laughed at the dramatic faces he was making while he rocked out on his air guitar. Levi, Kristi, and I started to back her up like the Supremes backing up Diana Ross. Eventually, it morphed into another of our songs, with the correct lyrics that time. By that point, most of the restaurant was singing along with us. Baylee had tentatively joined in but with a little encouragement, I got her to join in with gusto. It warmed my heart to see her so happy, having so much fun. I still worried about being away from her, especially when we were headed to Europe where it would be a hell of a lot harder to drop everything and get back to her. But, this trip helped me feel more confident in her adjustment to a little extra chaos in her life.

Levi winked at me and mouthed, "I love you," over Baylee's head. I was so head over heels for that man, I mouthed it back, then blew him a kiss. Our merriment only died down when the manager of the restaurant apologized profusely at having to kick us out, but they'd already stayed open an hour past closing time and he had to get home. We thanked him for everything and gave him a signed Stone Butterfly photo to hang on his wall. He beamed and told us to come back anytime.

Baylee's eyes were drooping in the car and I pulled her close so she could rest her head on my shoulder. It wasn't long before she was sound asleep. I glanced up and saw Levi watching me with a soft expression before leaning over Baylee to give me a tender kiss. "You're amazing. You know that, right?" he whispered so he wouldn't disturb Baylee.

"Kinda," I quipped. He chuckled and kissed me again before sitting back. When we arrived at the hotel, Levi lifted Baylee into his arms and carried her to her room. As he laid her down on the bed, her eyes fluttered and a dreamy look crossed her face.

"Goodnight, Baylee Bear," he murmured. She giggled and mumbled a response before falling back asleep. Cecily had crossed to the other side of the room and was sitting in the chair at the desk, watching us.

"See you in the morning, Cecily," I told her quietly as Levi opened the door and ushered me out. "See ya," I heard her say as the door shut.

Levi leaned his back against the wall and tugged me into his arms, dropping his head to kiss me deeply. "The way you love, with everything you are. It's incredible," he murmured when his lips left mine. "Not to mention sexy as hell."

"Reeeeeally," I asked coyly with a comical wiggle of my eyebrows. He laughed and kissed my nose.

"Absofuckinglutely, baby. Every time you tell me you love me, I have to resist the urge to drag you to the nearest dark corner and fuck you."

Heat raced through me, a shiver skittering down my spine and bursting into flames when it reached my core. "We've got a room one floor up and I'm pretty sure there are some dark corners in there. How about you show me what you'd like to do whenever I tell you I love you." I tugged on the front waistband of his jeans and started walking backward toward the elevator. Levi's grin was so big, it looked like it might be in danger of breaking his face.

In the next second, I was dangling over his shoulder, fireman style, and giggling hysterically while he jogged to the elevator. The doors slid open and Levi came to an abrupt stop, quickly setting me down. I flipped around and saw

Noah stepping out with a grim look on his face. Luca, Cameron, and Lindsay were following behind in much the same state. "I need to speak with both of you," he said in a low, angry voice.

I shot Levi a questioning look but he didn't meet my eyes, keeping his attention on Noah. Levi grabbed my hand and held it tightly. Noah turned to Lindsay and gestured in the direction of my sister's room. She nodded in confirmation of whatever silent command she'd received and stalked down the hall with Cameron behind her. She planted herself in front of their door and Cameron knocked quietly.

"Maybe we should talk alone, Noah," Levi suggested with a meaningful glance I could only speculate about.

Noah shook his head. "This concerns both of you." His eyes strayed to me and they were filled with sympathy. *What the hell is going on?*

"Let's go to your suite," Noah urged and hit the up button, causing the doors to glide right open since the elevator hadn't left the floor yet. Glancing at Lindsay one more time, my sense of alarm began growing.

A million scenarios were assaulting me. Was Baylee in danger? Had some crazy fan threatened her? I was in a haze of worry and barely noticed when Levi put a hand on my lower back and guided me in. As we rode up to the next floor, I had the overwhelming sense that the shit was about to hit the fan.

Chapter Twenty-Six

LEVI

There was no doubt in my mind that Noah had news concerning the person sending the postcards. I was a little surprised at how quickly he'd come up with something since I'd only shown him that last postcard at the bar before dinner. It irritated the fuck out of me that he was going to bring Brooklynn into it. I'd kept the more recent ones away from her, only vaguely mentioning them as though they were harmless. Nobody but Noah and our security guys knew how threatening the last several had been. Technically, the threat was directed at her and I'd put extra security on her because of it. But, it was truly about me and she didn't need more stress than she was already under with all the recent changes in her life.

When we reached our room, we went to the sitting area and Noah dropped heavily into a chair, tiredness lining his face. I led Brooklynn to the couch across from him and sat, pulling her down with me and keeping her as close as possible.

"Okay, spit it out, Noah," I demanded.

He looked at Brooklynn sadly and shook his head. "Brooklynn, I'm so sorry you've been dragged into all of this. And, for what I'm about to tell you."

She sat up straight, tense and on edge. I lifted her ass off the cushion and plopped her sideways onto my lap, one arm banded around her waist and the other, rubbing slow circles on her back. She slumped against me a little, soaking in my strength rather than shouldering the burden alone. If it wasn't such a fucking shitty moment, I would have celebrated the way she'd come to trust me.

"When we left the restaurant tonight, Luca saw a stray bag that had obviously been forgotten by someone in our party. He grabbed it and brought it with him, planning to return it to its owner once we arrived back at the hotel." Brooklynn's brow furrowed and she glanced at me, but I shrugged, not knowing where Noah was headed. "Once he got back to their room, he opened it to find the owner's ID and"—Noah cringed and scrubbed his hands over his face—"he found postcards."

"Postcards?" Brooklynn echoed, confused. My spine snapped ramrod straight as what he'd said sunk in. Someone in our crew had been sending them? The idea had my fists and jaw clenching so hard they ached. But, at the same time, I recognized that the theory didn't make sense. They'd all been mailed from the East Coast.

"Postcards with chimpanzees on them. There were three, one of them written on and addressed to someone in Maine, named Gladys Turner."

"Turner?" Brooklynn parroted, seemingly unable to do anything else.

Turner? Then it hit me. "WHAT. THE. FUCK?" I shouted, immediately trying to move Brooklynn so I could stand.

"Levi, sit your ass the fuck down," Noah commanded. I was about to argue at an elevated level with a whole lot of fucks while I stormed out, but his minute nod in Brooklynn's direction cut through the red haze of my anger. I took several deep, calming breaths, before taking a seat again and cuddling Brooklynn close to me. I set her sideways again so I could see her face and run soothing fingers through her hair.

"Gladys…" Brooklynn mused as though chewing over the name. Slowly, I could see the light going on in her mind. "That's Cecily's mother's name."

She turned to me, her face apologetic. "Cecily's been sending them? Shit, Levi. I'm so sorry. I swear, I had no idea."

I grabbed her face and brought it inches from mine, staring into her gorgeous mocha eyes. "Do. Not.

Apologize," I gritted. "This is absolutely not your fault. I'm just so sorry about what this is going to do to Baylee."

"She can't keep working for you, Brooklynn. We'll be calling the police and filing a restraining order," Noah informed her.

"A re-restraining order?" she sputtered. "For some ridiculous postcards from a love-struck fan?" She shook her head in denial. "I get that you want me to fire her, and I respect that because she abused the knowledge she had of the band from me. But, you're acting like she was threatening Levi. I mean, she just complained about us as a couple—" Brooklynn cut off suddenly, her face becoming pensive. "Tonight though…"—she trailed off then her head spun to look at me, her accusing eyes piercing right through me—"You haven't shown me any lately. Were you hiding them from me? Are they that bad?" I wasn't sure what answer would get me in the least amount trouble so I looked to Noah for help.

"Brooklynn," he called. When she twisted back, he pulled those fucking cards from the inner pocket of his suit jacket. He held them out and she tentatively took them with shaking hands. The more she looked through them, the more horrified her expression became.

When she got to the one I'd received upon arriving in Montreal, she shot to her feet, dropping the cards. "Baylee! Fuck! She's fucking alone with *my sister*!" She started for the door in a panic but stopped when Noah spoke again.

"Cameron took Baylee to Sasha's room," Noah hurriedly explained. "Lindsay stayed behind and is keeping Cecily in her room until the police arrive."

Tears welled in Brooklynn's eyes, spilling over and making tracks down her cheeks. She dropped her head into her hands and said something, but her words were muffled and I didn't understand them. "Baby," I said in as appeasing a tone as I could muster. "Come here." Her hands fell to her sides and she looked at me, but didn't approach. To my surprise, the tears were drying and instead of sadness, her eyes were filled with fiery rage.

"I'm going to fucking kill that bitch," she spat. "Besides her behavior toward you, which is worth its own special brand of punishment. She's going to hell for what she's about to put Baylee through and I'm going to help her get there faster."

She was fucking magnificent when she was like that and my cock stirred. Of all the fucking times for me to be aroused. *Fuck*. I mentally sucker punched my hormones right in the solar plexus, cutting off their oxygen so they would go down without a fight.

"She's spent years taking care of Baylee," she shouted. "Who the hell knows what she's been teaching her and—fuck, has she been in danger this whole damn time? I can't believe I didn't see—DAMN IT!"

She was pacing and raging, jumping from one thought to the next, working herself up even more. She whipped around and pointed at Noah. "I want to see her."

"Brooklynn," I called her name softly. "I don't think that's a very good idea."

Furious brown eyes turned and practically burned me to ashes. "Excuse me?"

Yeah, I'd put my foot in my mouth with that one. I carefully worded my next comment to keep it from sounding accusatory. "I only meant that I think *we* should calm down before *we* confront her."

She seemed to accept my logic, though she continued pacing like a caged animal.

"Brooklynn, come here." I held out my hand.

She shook her head, the fury slowly converting into anxiety.

"Baby," I put more steel in my tone. "Come here. Don't make me ask again."

She tensed, but then her shoulders sagged, all of the fight leaking out, leaving only her clear devastation. She slowly trudged back over and sat on the other end of the couch. I rolled my eyes and clasped her hips, dragging her to my side.

"Stop it," I instructed as moisture gathered in her eyes again. "I can see you trying to blame yourself for this, thinking that it's your fault because you brought her into our lives." I took hold of her shoulders and shook her lightly. "That's bullshit. Complete fucking bullshit. You can't hold the weight of her actions on your shoulders just because I didn't personally know her before I met you."

I wrapped my arms around her and hugged her to me, placing a kiss on her crown. "Damn it, Brooklynn. I love the fuck out of you, woman. You mean more to me than anything and even if there was some blame to be laid at your feet—which there isn't. Just to be absolutely clear about that—I wouldn't care because I love you and nothing else matters as long as you love me back. You do, right?"

"So much, Levi," she mumbled into my T-shirt as her arms went around my middle, squeezing me tight. "I love you."

"Then, all this other shit is just stuff we have to deal with, but you and me? We're good. Better than good. We are fucking spectacular." She sighed somewhat contentedly and the sound was like a healing balm. It soothed the ragged edges left from my worry and anger.

There was a knock on the door and Noah went to open it. Sasha, Matteo, Simon, Kristi, and Jonas all filed into the room. Sasha rushed over to Brooklynn and yanked her up before throwing her arms around her. "Are you okay?" she asked, leaning back so she could see her face. "Baylee is sound asleep with your female security chick. Um, Lindsay. I figured she would be more at ease with her than Cameron if she woke up."

Brooklynn nodded her thanks. "I'm okay"—she looked around at everyone—"I'm so sorry guys."

"What the fuck ever, B" Matteo snapped. "None of this is your fault."

"See, baby." I couldn't help being a little smug. "Told you."

"That girl though," Sasha growled. "I am totally going to

kick her ass."

"Get in line," Simon said harshly.

Kristi hugged Brooklynn next, asking, "Is Baylee going to be, okay?"

"I think so"—Brooklynn shrugged—"It'll take a little time and she'll probably regress some and need more care for a while. But yeah, eventually. I'll take her home and help her get adjusted over the next few months, then we'll work on finding her a new companion."

I shot to my feet, suddenly furious. "What the fuck are you talking about, Brooklynn?" I exploded.

Brooklynn glared at me and I immediately softened my expression and tone. No fucking way was I leaving her for months. "We have to leave for Europe in a week, baby. If you need to, you can leave a week later and meet us right before our first concert." I felt a little guilty about demanding she be with me over Baylee, but fuck, neither of them would ever find the independence they were striving for if they let this throw them all the way back to the beginning.

"Brooklynn," Kristi said tentatively. "You're not just a backup singer anymore. We can't just replace you with a fill-in musician, honey." I nodded in agreement, happy that Kristi had brought that up so it wasn't all coming at her from me.

Brooklynn looked from one face to another, a little shell-shocked. I don't think she'd expected resistance. "Bu—but—"

"Baby, we need you too," I pleaded, making it clear I wasn't speaking only of the band. She softened and took a deep breath. "I promise, I'll do everything I can to help you get Baylee in great shape before we leave. And, you and I can fly back a little more often than we'd planned."

Another knock interrupted our discussion and Cameron stepped halfway inside. "The police are with Cecily now. They are asking for the two of you," he said as he pointed at Brooklynn and me, then stepped back out and let the door shut.

I laced my fingers with Brooklynn's and roamed my eyes over her face, really gauging how she was doing. "Are you up for this?" Not that she had much of a choice, but I asked anyway, worried about her.

She gave my hand a squeeze and a small tired smile graced her plump lips. "We can handle it."

We. Too fucking right.

Chapter Twenty-Seven

BROOKLYNN

Cecily was curled up in a chair, her eyes wild as they bounced around the room. She looked confused. Did she really think she wouldn't get caught?

I marched over to her, halting a few feet away when Levi's arm slipped around my stomach. The feel of his warm body behind me infused me with strength, knowing he had my back. Always.

"How could you, Cecily?" I exploded. "We fucking trusted you. I trusted you with my sister's *life*, Cecily. Do you know how hard that was for me?"

She cowered back, curling up into an even tighter ball. "I didn't—"

"You didn't think you get caught?" I accused acerbically.

"No, I meant I didn't do this," she pleaded, adopting a hurt bunny look. *What a load of bullshit.*

"You've spent enough time with Baylee to know what this will do to her. Did you even consider that? Her love is a gift and this will fucking crush her!"

"Brooklynn! I swear, I didn't do this!"

Disgusted with her, with the whole situation, I twisted around in Levi's arms and looked up at his beautiful face. "Get her the fuck out of my sight," I demanded. He nodded and directed his gaze to the set of police officers flanking her and lifted his chin. They immediately hoisted her to her feet and cuffed her, before shuffling her from the room.

"Ma'am," another officer spoke up. "We'll need to get a statement from you and Mr. Matthews, as well as speak with your sister."

"No," Levi barked. "Baylee isn't to be involved in this. Dealing with Cecily's abrupt departure is going to be hard enough."

"But—"

"Cooper!" he shouted, interrupting the cop. Cooper looked up from where he was talking quietly with Noah on the other side of the room. "Take care of this. Brooklynn and I will send in our statements, but I don't want anyone talking to Baylee."

He nodded and pulled his cell phone from his pocket, making a call. The conversation lasted about five minutes before he passed the phone to the officer. "Your Captain wants to speak with you."

The officer's conversation was even shorter and when he hung up, his face was beet red. "You're free to go."

I think my jaw dropped to the ground. How the hell had Cooper done that?

"Let's go," Noah said to us as he opened the door. "Cooper will handle everything from here and I've already alerted Chloe so she can control the story and try to keep it from leaking."

We exited the room and I couldn't help glancing back at Cooper, then to Noah as we headed down the hall. "How did he do that?" I asked, a little awed at Cooper's obvious power.

"He has connections everywhere and he wields more power than most people realize," Noah explained vaguely.

I threw a confused glance at Levi. "He's more than just a label rep," Levi answered my silent question. "You'll have to hear the rest from him."

The puzzle was a nice little distraction from the mess I was immersed in. But, it only lasted until we reached Baylee's room. *What the fuck am I going to tell her?*

Chapter Twenty-Eight

LEVI

"What do you think, Baylee Bear?" I turned to face her after Penny, the woman we were interviewing, left the room. It was our fourth interview that week. Brooklynn wanted to give Baylee time in between to really process the people she was meeting. We had told Baylee that it was really important for her to help us pick the right person and she'd glowed like I'd given her the keys to Disney World. It was helping us to gauge who she felt a connection with, someone she instinctively put a little trust in.

Dealing with Cecily had been hard on Brooklynn. Cecily swore up and down she hadn't sent the postcards. But, what else could she say? She was in a fuck-ton of trouble. We'd been fucking lucky that Chloe had been able to keep it away from the press, so it wasn't being spun and splashed everywhere. But telling Baylee had been even harder on Brooklynn. She hadn't known how to explain everything to Baylee when we were in Montreal. She'd settled on some half-truths, telling Baylee that Cecily had done some very wrong things and she needed to leave so she could be held accountable for her behavior. It was a simplistic description, but something that Baylee could 100% grasp. Baylee had cried and been sad until she'd finally gotten home. Brooklynn had been a little over protective in her worry and she hadn't left Baylee's side, day or night. I'd been understanding until we got back to New York and she kicked me out the first night.

After Baylee's hesitant reaction to us in the airport, Brooklynn didn't want to upset her any more than necessary. She'd vetoed most PDA too, forcing me to resort to stolen moments and schemes to get a few minutes alone to make-out with my girlfriend. I spent most of the last week with them during the day, then went home to my very fucking empty and cold bed.

Brooklynn came back into the room after showing Penny out and my tongue almost dropped out of my mouth like a cartoon. She looked so fucking sexy in tight yoga pants, a fitted T-shirt that teased me with a sliver of her flat stomach, her hair hanging long and wild down her back. Yeah, I was definitely on the verge of drooling, or grunting like a cave man and dragging her off to my lair. Fuck, blue balls was becoming a state of mind as much as a physical malady. Ever since the first time I'd fucked her, I'd been addicted and I was not handling the withdrawal well at all. I had to admit though, Baylee had bounced back faster than I'd expected and that helped curb my craving.

"She was super nice," Baylee said excitedly, pulling me away from my lust-filled thoughts. "She likes art, like me. And she likes animals! And she plays the piano like Brooklee and said she would teach me to sing!" Baylee clapped her hands and bounced in her seat. "Maybe she'll teach me to be so awesome I can play with you!"

I laughed and dragged her in for a hug. "I'm sure Brooklynn would be ecstatic. We all would be, Baylee Bear, but I don't think you'd like it."

"I know I would," she replied dreamily. Then she turned to Brooklynn and started extolling the virtues of Penny all over again. While she listened to Baylee, her eye caught mine and she smiled, a secret smile that she reserved just for me. The one that told me she loved me without words. The caveman went off to pout while the pussy inside me felt all warm and fuzzy. She was so fucking amazing and I was fucking head over heels for her.

Watching her with her sister that week had compounded on everything else I'd learned about her. Proving just what an incredible woman she was. The future began to flash in front of me at random times and it was filled with Brooklynn. Touring together, our wedding, making music together, our kids, growing old together. And, to my fucking shock, none of it sent me running for the hills. I wanted it. All of it.

"Do you want to spend a couple more days with her, sweet girl?" Brooklynn asked softly. To which Baylee fist pumped the air and shouted, "Yesssssssss!" Brooklynn laughed and hugged her, then stood and went to call Penny and invite her to the next step in the interview process.

"How about a game, Baylee Bear?" I smiled when she whirled around with a beaming expression.

"Mario Party?" She jumped up and down before running to the TV and getting the Wii set up. She was addicted to the game and I'd gotten pretty fucking good at it while playing with her. A lot. She was so cute when she worked at the games and scrunched her nose in concentration. It reminded me of Brooklynn.

We played for an hour before Brooklynn came to tell us that dinner was ready. She announced that she'd made tacos, causing Baylee and me to grin and high-five. After we ate, we ran through some of Baylee's lessons and activities that helped with her learning and coping skills. Then we cuddled up on the couch to watch a movie. Baylee fell asleep less than thirty minutes into it and usually, Brooklynn would wait until the movie was over to take her to bed, not wanting to disturb her in case she wasn't in a sound sleep. Baylee had a hard time when she was woken up like that, she would be very disoriented and it scared her. But, I'd gotten to know Baylee well, and I knew she wouldn't budge, so I ignored her whispered protests and lifted Baylee into my arms before taking her to her room.

"I love you, Levi," Baylee mumbled as I laid her down. I smiled and kissed her forehead.

"Love you too, Baylee Bear."

Brooklynn watched me with an unreadable expression when I returned and I smiled arrogantly as I sat down in my same spot. She snuggled up to me again and then leaned up to whisper in my ear, "You're pretty damn sexy, dude."

I reared back and quirked an eyebrow. "Dude?"

She grinned playfully and scooted closer. There hadn't been much space between us before, once she'd closed that distance, she was practically on top of me. Her tits pressed into my side, her warm breath bathed my ear, and her breathing picked up. My dick definitely noticed.

In two seconds flat, I'd twisted our bodies so that I was lying on top on her, my hands firmly holding her wrists up by her head. "What happens when you tease, baby?" I growled. Her eyes lit with fire and her pink tongue darted out to wet her lips. Her chest rose and fell with every pant, brushing mine with her hard nipples. I couldn't resist, I dropped my head and sucked one into my mouth through her thin T-shirt and bra. She moaned and her back arched. "Nine days, baby," I grumbled moving to the other breast. "I don't have much fucking control left."

I bit down and she whimpered, her hips bucking up against my hard as fuck cock. I tore myself away from her tits and rested my forehead on hers, my rapid breathing and racing heart matching hers. "I need you too." Her voice had an edge of desperation that I recognized, because I was right there with her.

"You were the one who set the rules, baby," I argued while grinding my erection into the apex of her thighs.

"Oooooh," she moaned. "It was stupid, don't listen to me, I clearly lost my fucking mind."

I chuckled and kissed her, my tongue licking the seam of her lips and sweeping inside when she opened right away. Our tongues rubbed together the way our groins moved against each other. Hot, hard, and slick. But, I wasn't a complete bastard. "I understand, baby. I do. But, fuck, I crave you like a fucking drug." I gave in to another deep, thrusting kiss and came up with a solution I was pretty sure we could both live with. And more importantly, my dick wouldn't shrivel up and die. "How quiet can you be?" I purred. A slow smile spread across her face. I reached past her to flick the light off, then dragged the blanket from the back of the couch to cover us. "Fast and hard, baby," I warned her. "It's been too fucking long. So, you better keep that pretty mouth shut."

"Now, Levi," she whimpered. "More fucking, less talking."

"How can a man turn down that request," I teased while practically ripping her clothes off. Once she was naked, I shucked my shirt, jeans, and boxers. "Ready?" I managed to ask around the ecstasy consuming me at the feel of our heated skin pressed together. I used one finger to enter her. "Fuck yes you are. Damn, you're fucking drenched. I think your little pussy wants my big cock as much as he wants her." She nodded and without preamble, I replace my finger with my dick, thrusting in balls deep and groaning at the feeling of her tight pussy gloving me so perfectly.

"Shhhh!" I almost laughed because it turned out to be me who needed to be reminded to stay quiet.

I sucked in a mouthful of her tit to keep from making more sound while my hips began to pump wildly. It was fucking heaven. In no time, I felt the telltale tingling in my balls as they drew up. Brooklynn was biting her lip to keep quiet, her legs squeezing the fuck out of me and her fingernails digging into my ass as she clung to me. She was close too, thank fuck. I kissed her and slid a hand between us to pinch her clit. I swallowed her screams as I buried myself as fucking deep as possible and came so hard, I was dizzy with it.

"Fuck, baby," I sighed as I placed little kisses all over her throat, shoulders, and chest. "I was about to lose my ever-loving mind. I needed you so damn bad."

"Me too," she agreed contentedly. "I gotta say, babe. You've got quite a bit of talent when it comes to wielding that monster between your legs. You could take that show on the road."

I laughed silently, my shoulders shaking, but couldn't keep it completely in when she muttered, "Never mind. That particular skill belongs to me. I don't know what I was thinking saying that."

"Your pussy inspires me, baby," I assured her, charmed and amused by how adorable she was. "I wouldn't be nearly as good with anyone else."

She snickered and pinched my ass. "Excellent answer."

"Brooklynn." My voice was hard as I stared at her with narrowed eyes. "We have to leave tomorrow if we are going to make it to London in time."

She bit her lip and shifted her weight to her heels, sticking her hands in her back pockets. She looked everywhere around the kitchen but at me. She'd been putting off this discussion for a few days. It was time to force the issue.

"I don't know, Levi," she hedged. "I'm not sure she's ready."

I sighed and walked over to her, lifting her up and setting her on the counter behind her. "Baby, you're not giving your sister enough credit. Penny moved in days ago and they've been like two peas in a pod. Baylee adores her. I think you hate the idea that she doesn't need you like she used to." Her mutinous expression confirmed my suspicion. "I get it, babe. I do. It was hard to admit that Lily wasn't a baby anymore and let her date that douchebag Flynn." My teeth ground together at the thought of my sister's new prick of a boyfriend. But, it wasn't the time to focus on that, one problem at a fucking time.

"She's doing great now, but what happens when I leave?" she argues.

"Then we'll come back." My response caused her eyebrows to shoot to her hairline. "I care about her too, Brooklynn."

She softened and cupped one of my cheeks in her warm palm. "I know. I'm sorry if I implied otherwise. You've been so amazing with her." She smiled sheepishly and admitted,

"I think you've been as much a part of how quickly she's gotten resettled as I have."

"Then why are you fighting me on going back on tour?" She shrugged and looked away. "Brooklynn, look at me," I demanded harshly. "If you want to be a coward, you'll do it looking me in the fucking eyes."

Her jaw hit the floor. "I'm not being a coward," she snapped.

"Really?" I asked with a sardonic raise of my brow. "You're not afraid that your sister won't need you anymore? You're not afraid that you'll be the cause for more crazy fans to threaten me? You're not afraid of the magnitude of what you feel for me? I see your little freak-out moments, baby. I see everything when it comes to you."

Her shoulders went back and she sat up straight. "It's not cowardly to have fears, Levi."

"No, it's human." She nodded and started to relax. "It's cowardly to give in to them and let them rob you of all the amazing things that could be in your future."

She tensed again, but I could see that I was getting through to her, one crack in her stubborn wall at a time.

"Remember what convinced you to try this whole thing in the first place? What would Baylee think if you explained that you were quitting because of her? She wants you to be happy doing what you love."

Direct hit.

"Besides, you'd be in serious breach of contract, Brooklynn. You'll burn a lot of bridges and set yourself back in your career."

Another hit.

Then I went in for the kill.

"I don't know how I'll survive those months away from you, baby. Isn't it enough that *I* need you?"

Bull's eye.

She melted into me, her arms going around my neck and her head tucking under my chin. "It is. I'm sorry, I don't know why I was letting everything get to me."

I kissed her forehead. "Completely understandable, baby. You've held up better than a lot of people. But, now is the time to be the tough as nails, confident, badass woman with a big ol' soft heart, that you really are."

She chuckled and hugged me a little tighter. "You're right. Baylee has always needed me, it's hard to accept that she's so independent now. On the outside, she's nineteen, but on the inside, she's still a child. But, even kids are more grown up than we give them credit for, right?"

"Absolutely, baby." I kissed her nose, then her mouth.

"Levi will yo—"

Brooklynn jumped and would have fallen right off of the counter if I hadn't been standing there, with my hands on her hips. Her face had drained of color as she looked over my shoulder. I was sporting a motherfucker of an erection, so I twisted at the waist to see Baylee and Penny at the entrance to the kitchen. Penny was grinning and gave Brooklynn a thumbs up. I laughed until I saw Baylee's face. Her expression had fallen like she'd just found out someone had stolen her best friend.

I felt guilt choking me and cleared my throat. (*Yeah, yeah, shame on me for that.*) I guessed I kind of had stolen her best friend.

"You're still together?" she asked, breaking my heart a little. "I thought you were just friends."

Brooklynn hopped off the counter and rushed over to pull Baylee into her arms. "You're still my favorite, sweet girl," she told her earnestly. Baylee's forlorn eyes stared at me from Brooklynn's embrace before she turned into the hug and closed her eyes. They squeezed each other tight, then Brooklynn whispered something and drew a small smile from Baylee.

"Baylee?" I called and she flicked her eyes back in my direction. "I don't like it when you're sad. You still love me, Baylee Bear?" I gave her my best puppy dog eyes and she brightened a little and walked over, throwing herself into my arms.

"Yeah, I still love you."

I kissed her head. "Thanks, sweetheart. I'm going to miss you."

She put her head back and smiled shyly at me. "Really?"

"I'll be devastated without my Baylee Bear." I figured there wasn't going to be a better or worse time to segue into our plans. "You know we have to leave tomorrow, right sweetheart?"

"I hoped you wouldn't go."

I hugged her again. "The rest of Stone Butterfly needs us too. But, they are just borrowing us from you."

She cocked her head to the side and studied me. "Are you just borrowing Brooklee?"

I laughed. "Yeah, I'm just borrowing her from you. But, I'm gonna have to do that a lot, okay?"

She shrugged. "I guess."

Brooklynn had her hands over her mouth trying to hide her giggles and her eyes were sparkling. I hadn't seen her look like that since the restaurant the night we found out about Cecily. I'd missed it more than I'd even realized.

"You're okay with me leaving again so soon, sweet girl?" she asked hopefully.

"Yeah." Baylee smiled and gave Brooklynn a quick hug before grabbing Penny's hand and dragging her off. Before she disappeared, I tipped my chin at Penny and mouthed "dresser," and she nodded in understanding. In anticipation of how difficult it was going to be for Brooklynn to leave Baylee, I'd asked Penny if she wouldn't mind bringing Baylee to Italy when we were there the next month. One of the reasons Brooklynn had liked Penny was because she also spoke Italian and had lived there for a few years and she had been excited about showing Baylee around Rome. I'd bought the tickets and paid a fucking fortune to get both of them expedited passports. I'd left all of the information on the dresser in her room.

When they were gone, I held out my hand and Brooklynn hurried over to me, letting me wrap her up in my arms.

"I missed you," I said, rubbing my nose against hers before kissing the tip, then pushing some of her hair behind her ear. "I love you and your unbelievably sexy body." My hands had slid down to her ass and I gripped her cheeks, lifting her to her toes so we were lined up just right. "When we get to London, I'll remind you all the things I love about you and your hot, delicious body."

Brooklynn shivered. "Deal."

Chapter Twenty-Nine

LEVI

"B!" Matteo shouted and ran to Brooklynn, scooping her up and swinging her around. I whacked him on the back of the head and pulled my woman out of his arms.

"Mine," I growled. Brooklynn pinched my arm but I just kept glaring at Matteo who put his hands up in surrender while laughing.

"Glad to have you back, B," Sasha said as she sauntered toward us. "Where'd you find the grunting caveman?"

I rolled my eyes and Brooklynn laughed. "He's a work in progress, he should turn into Levi Matthews any day now."

We'd flown into London last night and were meeting up with the rest of the band at a local studio. With everything we had going on, Brooklynn and I had been forced to leave finding her replacement in the hands of everyone else. Apparently, they'd been approached by the agent of a local musician, Emma something or other, and asked them to listen to her demo. Noah and Cooper had been impressed and arranged for the band to meet her in person. Sasha had called to tell me they'd found the one and of all people, Sasha was almost as picky as me. I trusted her judgment but she still wouldn't sign the girl without hearing her play with all of Stone Butterfly. Emma was going to fill in at the London and Manchester concerts anyway but we planned a jam session to get a feel for all of us as a group without the distraction of an audience.

Simon and Noah entered the room and immediately came over to welcome us back. I noticed that everyone seemed to have missed Brooklynn more than me. *You'd think I wasn't the fucking lead singer.* Then again, I couldn't really fault them because I understood what they felt. Brooklynn was. . .everything.

Cooper opened the door for a tiny, curvy, woman with big violet eyes and long, chunky blonde hair. She wore a tank top that showcased intricate tattoos covering both arms. Not quite sleeves, but the designed wrapped around them from shoulder to wrist. She smiled and walked to Brooklynn with her hand out.

"Brooklynn!" she exclaimed excitedly in a thick British accent. "I'm Emma! It's brilliant to meet you! I did studio work with Xavier Paxton last year. Right after he released Hallucinations. He couldn't stop singing your praises."

Brooklynn's cheeks bloomed and she laughed, shaking Emma's hand. "Xavier was a hoot. I don't know how he manages to be such a sweetheart and think he's God's gift to women at the same time."

"Right?" Emma exclaimed with a snicker.

I scoffed, my hand tightening on Brooklynn's waist and she threw me a curious look. I shrugged. "Xavier Paxton is a womanizing cradle robber." I kept my voice neutral. I didn't want to admit that the thought of Xavier hitting on my woman made me want to rip out his vocal chords. The guy had a reputation and I didn't believe for one minute that any of it had been exaggerated.

Brooklynn rolled her eyes. "He's harmless."

"I'm with Levi on this one," Matteo piped up. "I've met the guy too."

"Ditto," Simon tagged on.

"Jealous much?" Sasha tossed at them.

Emma laughed and tipped an imaginary hat at Brooklynn. "I have a knack for creating awkward situations. I don't always think before I speak. Bloody lucky I have a great accent, yeah? It makes my ineptness cuter and a little less dodgy."

Brooklynn was silently shaking with laughter.

"Anyway," Emma continued. "I'm chuffed to work with you."

She turned to me and cocked her head to the side, studying me with squinted eyes, as though she had no clue who I was. Then her eyes popped open with overly exaggerated shock. "Blast it! You're that singer. Levi Matthews, right?"

Just like that, any awkwardness or tension was diffused, as we all busted up with laughter. I shook her hand. "Great to meet you, Emma. I like you. I think you'll fit with us, but I reserve full judgment until I've heard you sing."

She grinned and bobbed her head. "Brilliant. Should we start then?"

Emma turned out to be a good fit for us. Her sound was unique but she knew how to blend. Her accent and random phrases made her even more fun. She and Brooklynn really hit it off, which sealed the deal for me. There wasn't much in life that I wouldn't trust going by Brooklynn's reaction.

At the concert the next night, we debuted "Like Her", the song Brooklynn had written with Sasha's and my help, and the audience went fucking ballistic over it. It was alternative rock but it was still a new sound for us considering we'd never had a powerhouse female voice like Brooklynn's. It was the best I'd ever heard Sasha sound. The song truly showcased her voice and Brooklynn's.

I was captivated by them, the way their voices blew through the mics. It was an upbeat, fun song, and they had the audience eating out of their hands. With Emma and Kristi backing them up, it was quirky in some places and had smooth, tight harmonies in others. I'd never heard anything like it and I was again, blown away by the depth of Brooklynn's talent. When I joined in as a complimenting harmony with lyrics that were in direct juxtaposition of theirs, it was like a tug of war between us and I fucking happily lost the war as they finished it out like the two baddass singers that they were.

"Did we hit the lottery with these two or what?" I yelled to the audience, then waited for them to settle before going on.

"You guys may have seen some of the YouTube videos out there, so let's just get this out of the way"—I held my hand out to Brooklynn and she walked over and took it, smiling brightly—"this wicked awesome chick with the smokin' body is the woman of my fucking dreams. I love the fuck out of her!" Brooklynn laughed before grabbing my face and kissing me hard. When She let me go, I'm sure I was sporting a goofy, lovesick smile.

"Okay, London! Enough of this mushy shit!" Brooklynn announced. "I think this is Levi's way of asking if you want to hear our new single!" Everyone was shouting, jumping, and screaming. The crackling energy in the concert hall was exhilarating.

"Brooklynn's right. I want to know who in here knows what it's like to be crazy in love!" The audience screamed and applauded. "I guess you want to hear us sing 'Sanity,' then?" I pivoted and pointed to Matteo who grinned and started to play. "Wait, wait, wait. Dude." He petered off with a disappointed look. "That's not how we start 'Sanity.'"

"Right. Cause that song makes me crazy! PUN INTENDED!"

"Teo, this is the only chance these two get to release their secret voyeuristic obsessions about doing naughty things in public," Simon hooted.

"Great, Simon," Brooklynn drawled sardonically. "Can't wait to see the stories all over the rags about that. I'm telling you right now, if someone speculates that you were involved in any of our escapades, I'm gonna tell them that your big guitar is compensating for something…tinier."

Laughter roared through the hall. "Hey fucktard," Simon hissed at Matteo. "Play 'Sanity' before Brooklynn lies to the whole world about the size of my massive dick."

"I'm going to need proof of this stonking todger," Emma announced.

Sasha almost fell over she was laughing so hard.

"Hey!" I hollered to the crowd. "I think you guys need to tell Matteo just how much you want to hear 'Sanity'!"

They almost brought the fucking roof down and this time, Matteo started the leading beat into "Sanity." And just like every time I performed the song with Brooklynn, I fell even more in love with her.

We walked off stage and Simon high-fived Brooklynn. "Fucking killed it out there, BK!" Then he twirled Sasha around before dipping her. "You too, Ginger." He flipped her back up. It was impressive considering Simon was maybe an inch or two taller than Sasha and she was wearing at least six-inch heels. After she was upright again, he smacked a kiss on her cheek. "Bout time you showed off those sexy pipes."

"You just won yourself a date for the evening, Simon," Sasha cooed. He perked up and opened his mouth, no doubt to say something crass but Sasha beat him to it. "A date where there will be, under no circumstances, sex for you at the end of it."

Simon's face and shoulders fell comically and he shook his head. "How sad for you. But, if you insist I'll give you a platonic pity date."

I watched all of that with a huge smile on my face, knowing how fucking lucky I was to be surrounded by these people. I wrapped an arm around Brooklynn and pulled her in close so I could kiss her forehead. "You know how I told the audience that I love the fuck out of you?" I asked cheekily.

"Let me guess, you want to go love the fuck out of my body?" She winked at me and grabbed my ass. "As long as I get a turn, I'm all in."

I threw my head back and laughed, the sound reverberating through the rafters. "Deal."

We still had the fan meet and greet, so we snuck off to an empty dressing room and she held to her promise and rode the fuck out of me. Afterward, we tried to straighten up as much as we could, then gave up and proudly wore the "thoroughly fucked" look with pride. When the interlude with the fans was finally over, we all piled into a couple of SUVs and they took us to our hotel. We were performing three shows in London before hitting Manchester for two nights on the way to a show in Dublin. It was a crazy schedule and it wouldn't get any better for some time. Which meant, the smart thing to do, was to get some rest. We decided to trash that option. We were in our early twenties for fuck's sake, we had a responsibility to be stupid sometimes. And yet, after hitting a couple parties and stumbling into the hotel at three in the morning, Chloe was still complaining about not having anything to work with.

"Chloe, I'm starting to wonder where all of this negativity is coming from," Sasha said, with only a slight slur. "Do we need to get you laid?"

"I volunteer as tribute," Simon called out, raising his hand in the air and leering at Chloe. She rolled her eyes and stomped off.

"Sasha, I think you may have hit the nail on the head, girl." Brooklynn and Sasha shared a look that, as a man, I would never be able to decipher.

"Speaking of getting nailed…" I said under my breath.

Brooklynn poked me in the side but she snickered and bit her lip to hide a smile. "Night, guys!" she trilled before making a beeline for the elevator.

The next two nights in London, the audiences were even better. By the time we got to Dublin, a lot of the negative hype about Brooklynn's and my relationship had died down and we started to relax. Also, "Like Her" had gained so much popularity over the internet, that they begged for it as an encore when it wasn't included in the line up.

When the lights went dark for the final time in Dublin, I dragged Brooklynn off stage and attacked her mouth. "I can't fucking get enough of you, Brooklynn Hawk."

"Someone find these two a closet before they start making babies right here on the floor!" Sasha's loud comment from right behind me caused us to jump, ending our mini make-out session. I shrugged unapologetically while Brooklynn smiled with a mixture of sappy and sheepishness. It was adorable.

Sasha's wise-crack had me thinking. Brooklynn and I were a long, long ways off from even thinking about kids. But, there wasn't a single doubt in my mind that she was it. The one. As we walked hand in hand to the green room, my eyes strayed to our laced fingers. I brought them up and kissed the back of her hand, then. . .I kissed the fourth knuckle. There was no hurry, but it was something to think about.

Erin was waiting for us and she discreetly waved a piece of paper and jerked her head toward the exit. I kissed Brooklynn quickly. "I need to grab something before we hit the rope line." She nodded and wandered over to talk with Kristi, Emma, and Matteo. I slipped out the door to the hallway that led to the back exit where we would eventually leave. Erin and 2.0 were waiting for me, looking decidedly freaked. "What's up, guys?"

Erin held out her hand and I reached out to take whatever—*no fucking way*. It was another fucking postcard.

Sone of a bitch!

"Brooklynn isn't to know about this, got it?" I stressed and waited until they nodded. I didn't want it weighing on her mind. They left and I was alone. Fury built inside me until I was consumed with it, feeling murderous. I banged my fist on the wall. "Fuck!"

Chapter Thirty

BROOKLYNN

It was finally starting to sink in that I was officially a part of Stone Butterfly, which was incredible enough, but to be sharing it with the most amazing man I'd ever met, it was a little surreal. Baylee seemed to be doing really well with Penny too, which set my mind at ease a little more every day. The first few days away from Baylee, I had second-guessed my decision a million times, but I spoke to her more often than I had before and that also helped.

We flew to Milan almost a month after rejoining the band and I was excited to visit Italy for the first time. I'd begun learning Italian in high school. Baylee heard it one day and she'd loved the sound and frequently asked me to talk to her in the language. I'd gone on to become fluent and even taught Baylee to speak it a little. In the process, I'd fallen in love with all things Italian and had vowed to get there some day. Now, not only was I going to check that off my bucket list, I was going to get to sing there. We wouldn't have much time in Milan, just the concert, then on to Rome where we would have a few extra days. Levi was so excited to take me around the city and his enthusiasm was adorable

The audience had been even more excited when they realized I spoke their language. We had a little fun with my band mates, teasing them in Italian, knowing they couldn't understand and treating it like a private joke between me and the fans. Emma spoke a little as well and she was cracking up and throwing in her own comments from time to time. "Ciao, Milan!" I yelled as we ended the concert and ran off of the stage. Levi grabbed my hand and without a word, dragged me away. He took me to a hallway behind the stage and tried every doorknob until he seemed to find what he was looking for. I found myself being shoved into a storage closet and then pushed up against the door once he'd closed and locked it.

"If I haven't told you before," he growled. "It's fucking hot when you speak Italian." His mouth crashed down onto mine and his hands went to my ass, pressing me into the large, extremely hard bulge in his jeans. "After singing our song together, and all that fucking sexy talking, I can't wait, baby." He lifted me and I put my legs around his waist and locked my ankles together. "I need to fuck you *now*."

His hips nailed me to the door while his hand yanked down the neckline of my strapless corset top. The boning held my breasts up like a shelf and Levi grunted his approval, palming them as he returned to kissing me fervently. My nipples were already pebbled but they tightened further as his thumbs brushed over them. I whimpered and slid my hands into his hair, clenching it in my fists as I arched into him.

"You have the most perfect tits, baby." His head descended and he bit down on a nipple, before soothing it with his tongue and sucking it into his mouth. At the same time, he trailed a hand down my body, tunneling it under my skirt. He ran a finger up the seam of my tights and underwear. "Fucking drenched." Somehow, he was able to pull the fabric away and twist it in his fist wrenching it until it ripped down the center. I heard the faint sound of his zipper and a second later, my head smacked into the door when I threw it back as he thrust his cock balls deep into my pussy.

"Levi!" I cried out as he began to slam into me, his mouth switching to my other nipple while his hand twisted and plucked at the abandoned one.

"I'm not going to last, Brooklynn," he said through clenched teeth after he let my nipple pop from his mouth. "Fuck!"

My hands fell to his shoulders and I held on, digging in for more leverage. "Yes! Harder Levi!"

He lost all rhythm and pumped in and out wildly,

bending his knees slightly to change the angle so he was hitting that sensitive spot inside me each time. He fucked me like a damn animal, even growling as dirty talk fell from his lips. I was yelling who the fuck knew what and bucking my hips to create even more friction. "That's it, baby. Fuck me back, yeah. Fuck! Squeeze that pussy! Fuck yes!"

"I'm so close, Levi! Yes! Don't stop!" He glided a hand down and on the next thrust, he pinched my clit hard while sucking as much of my breast into his mouth as he could fit and sucking, hollowing out his cheeks. I screamed and blew apart.

"Fuck, baby. I love hearing you scream my name when you come around my cock, it's—fuck! Fuck!" His voice was strained and he buried his face in my neck, sucking the skin as he drove in one more time before his head fell back and he bellowed my name.

We stayed like that, our harsh breaths the only sound around us. When the shudders began to subside, he kissed my lips, then trailed them down my jaw to my neck and nibbled on the skin there.

"I thought the first time I fucked you was the best I'd ever had, but damn, baby. It just gets better. I could live in your tight little pussy."

I grinned, basking in his words and the afterglow. "Fine by me." He laughed and nuzzled for another moment before giving me a quick kiss and setting me down.

"In that case." He straightened my clothes and tucked himself back in in record time, then grabbed my hand and starting dragging me again. *Such a* Neanderthal.

"Come on, let's get out of here. I'm ready to go back to the hotel and at least live in your pussy until we have to leave for Rome tomorrow."

Rome was even more beautiful than in any pictures, they hadn't quite captured the true magnificence. I stood on the balcony of our hotel room, unable to tear my eyes from the view. "It's absolutely gorgeous," I breathed.

Levi came up behind me and slid his hands around my to rest on my belly, hugging me to him. "Nothing's as gorgeous as you, baby." He pulled my hair away from my neck and nuzzled his nose in the sensitive area below my ear. "I'm going to take a shower, want to join me?" His voice was muffled against my skin since his mouth was busy kissing my bare shoulder causing little shivers to slither down my spine. I'd changed into a sundress when we arrived and we'd gone out to explore. We'd come back a few minutes before, leaving ourselves a few hours to relax and shower before the concert.

I turned in his arms and held his face between my hands while I kissed him. It was slow and easy, no less passionate than any other time, but more savoring, a silent exchange of love. "Damn, I love you," he mumbled against my lips before taking over the kiss, angling his head and deepening it.

When he finally let me up for air, I sucked in deep breaths. "I love you too, Levi," I replied when I could manage to talk again. Just then, there was a knock at our door. Levi frowned, releasing me as he stomped over to answer it. I could tell he wasn't in the mood to be nice to whoever it was because they'd interrupted our time together. So, I grabbed his arm and tugged until he stopped and looked at me. "Why don't you go get the shower started. I'll get the door and meet you in five minutes."

He threw another dark look at the door, then his blue eyes returned to my face, lit with a hungry fire. "Five minutes." He stalked to the bathroom and called out, "I'm fucking counting!" before disappearing.

I laughed, shaking my head at how ridiculous and adorable he could be, even when he was being so bossy. Opening the door, I smiled in greeting at Erin, who stood waiting on the other side. "Hey, Erin." I gestured for her to come in but she waved me off with a smile.

"I'm just dropping off the mail before 2.0 and I leave for a little overnight."

"I knew it!" I cheered, doing a little happy dance. "I appreciate you guys getting together, girl. Levi now owes me twenty bucks and a massage."

Erin laughed even as her face flushed red. "Happy to help." She winked and handed me the stack of mail before saying goodbye and practically skipping away. I shut the door and wandered to the desk, flipping through the stack. She'd brought Levi's and mine, the stack all mixed together. I tossed each piece on the table as I went through it then froze as I stared at the last one. It couldn't be. It was a postcard. With a chimpanzee standing in the rain dressed in a bright yellow raincoat, hat, and boots.

She wouldn't still be sending Levi postcards after we filed the restraining order, would she? I flipped it over and read the message.

Levi,

I don't want you borrowing her anymore. I don't like it. I'm learning to sing so I can come take her place and you won't need her anymore.

I read it twice more, something about the wording bothering me.

"Times up, baby!" Levi yelled. "Get your sweet ass in here!

"Um, give me just a few more minutes, babe!"

"Whoever is at the door better not be asking to borrow you because I'm not in the mood to fucking share," he added grumpily.

Borrow. A conversation popped into my head and I blanched. Levi asking to borrow me… It couldn't be. This had to be some kind of crazy coincidence. I lifted the card close and looked carefully at the postmark. Fucking shit on a fuckity fucking stick! It had been mailed from the town next to where my sister lived.

"Thirty seconds or I'm coming to get you and drag you in here whether you're naked or not. You know what? I take it back, stay dressed. I'm liking the idea of peeling your wet clothes off of you."

I jumped into action and ran over to my suitcase, shoving the card inside until I had more time to figure out how to deal with it. I knew I should tell him my suspicions but what if I was wrong? Quickly stripping, my bare feet padded over the carpet to the bathroom, silently promising to myself that if I couldn't confirm it one way or another in a couple of days, I'd tell him.

Levi knew me too well and for the rest of the night, he didn't buy my "I'm just tired" act when he asked me what was bothering me. At the concert, I left all of my anxieties backstage and lost myself in the performance. The high lingered when it was over, making it a little easier to mask the churning in my stomach and the ache in my heart.

I could tell Levi was worried about me and that night, we made love, soft and slow. I gave him everything, told him everything through my touch, my kisses. I poured out my heart to him as he moved inside me, whispering how much he loved me. Afterward, he pulled me close and I pretended to fall asleep immediately.

"Baby?" he asked doubtfully. I evened out my breathing and prayed he would let it go and sleep. "Don't think I don't know you're awake. But you obviously need a little time, so I'll drop it for now. Just make sure you're ready to talk tomorrow, I won't let you pull this shit. Shutting me out." He kissed my temple and laid down, spooning me and pulling me in close. "I love you too much to let anything come between us."

I blinked rapidly, trying to hold in my tears. I was fucking exhausted from keeping everything in and after silently crying for a few minutes, I fell into a fitful sleep.

The next morning, I woke to the sound of Levi's phone ringing. He gently untangled his limbs from mine and slid from the bed. "Yeah?" he answered in a whisper. "It can't wait?" he paused and then sighed. "Fine, I'll meet you in ten."

I heard rustling as he got dressed, then he was in front of me, bending down to tenderly kiss my lips. "Don't move. I'll be back in fifteen minutes and we'll talk, okay?" I didn't reply. He sighed and walked away. "I love you," he called softly before the door clicked shut.

I flipped over onto my back and stared at the ceiling. What was I going to do?

The only answer I could come up with was to find out if my suspicions were correct. We had a few days until our next gig. I needed to go home and see Baylee. Maybe I could fix the whole thing before he even knew about it all. There had to be some kind of explanation. Baylee wasn't the kind of person who could send these threatening letters. She had the biggest heart of anyone I knew. Unbidden, odd little memories snuck into my mind. Things I could have misinterpreted, her response to my relationship with Levi, especially when she caught us kissing... No. It had to be something else.

I jumped from the bed, grabbed my suitcase and set it on top, then started throwing my clothes inside.

Chapter Thirty-One

LEVI

"What the fuck is so important that you had to drag me out of bed at seven fucking thirty in the morning?" I groused when Noah opened the door to his suite. He said nothing, simply opened the door wider so I could come in. When he'd called, he'd been serious and adamant that he needed to see me right away. His lack of smartass comment was one more indication that something was very wrong. I became even more concerned once I got a good look at him. He appeared ruffled, suit jacket off, shirt sleeves rolled to the elbows, his hair a mess, obviously, the victim of his hands running through it.

Our security team was standing around the living area, faces grim. Cooper sat on one of the couches in much the same state. I ran my hands through my hair in frustration and stomped over to drop heavily into a chair. Noah walked to Cooper, took a file from him and tossed it to me. I caught it and leaned back in my seat, opening it. On top of a stack of papers was a postcard. I picked it up and lifted my head, looking at Noah and Cooper. "This is the one from Vienna, right?"

Cooper nodded. "We gathered all of the ones that were postmarked after we fired Cecily and filed the restraining order. We've had someone watching her as well, they aren't coming from her."

I'd figured that was the case. Focusing on the folder again, I went to the next document. It was a list of addresses, dates, and times. Again, I met Noah and Cooper's gazes, this time simply raising an eyebrow in silent question.

"Those are the dates, times, and post office locations for the last several notes," Noah explained. "There is one that has popped up more than once lately. Four times, in fact."

Studying the list, I noted the matching post offices and suddenly realized why they were significant and my attention flew back to Noah. "This is near where Baylee lives." His head bobbed in the affirmative. "Is this person stalking her to get to me?" Fear for her iced my veins. She had become special to me and not only because she was Brooklynn's sister. Damn, Brooklynn would fucking kill me if Baylee was in danger and I'd never forgive myself if she got hurt because of me.

"Look at the rest of the folder, Levi." Cooper rubbed two fingers from each hand on his temples.

I shuffled the top paper to the bottom, revealing a black and white, grainy photo. "What's this?" I picked it up, bringing it closer to my face and squinting to try and see the image clearer. A dark-haired woman was dropping something in a mailbox.

"Keep going," Cooper encouraged sounding as tired as I felt. The next photo wasn't much better as far at the grainy quality, but the woman had turned around and her unknowingly faced the camera head on. "Those photos are stills from the security footage of the post office."

I blinked a couple of times, then rubbed my eyes, unbelieving of what I was seeing. "That looks like Baylee."

"She's on the security tapes for this post office, always dropping something in the mailbox on days and times that match the postmarks for the postcards mailed from that location." Noah started to pace the small seating area, his hands buried in his pockets.

"Is this someone pretending to be Baylee?" I was wracking my brain to find any other explanation than the one clawing to the front of my mind. "It couldn't possibly be Baylee."

"I talked to the employees personally," Luca broke in, speaking for the first time. "They know Miss Hawk well and confirmed her identity."

Cameron spoke up. "The best we can figure, she's been sending them on day trips, but when you replaced Miss

Turner and ended her excursions, she began mailing them all from her nearest post office. It looks like she slipped her companion while they were at a bookstore."

"We've already taken steps to have her checked into a hospital," Noah added. "But, we decided to wait until Luca flew in this morning with concrete evidence. We thought it would be best if you were the one to break this to Brooklynn. Penny helped us get things in motion and she's still keeping an eye on her, she'll be a liaison for Brooklynn."

Fiery anger at Baylee shot through me but it was quickly extinguished by an icy feeling of dread. It spread everywhere and chilled my heart. What was this going to do to Brooklynn? She'd already blamed herself for this situation when we'd thought it was Cecily. I dropped the folder to the floor beside me and leaned forward, my elbows on my knees as I scrubbed my face with my hands. "Fuck. I don't know how I'm going to break this to Brooklynn."

"It's your call." Cooper mirrored my stance, his greenish blue eyes meeting mine, filled with sympathy. "If you want us with you, we've got your back. If you want to break the news alone, we'll wait here in case you need us to step in with the evidence. Chances are that she won't believe you at first."

I shook my head. "I need to do it alone. Can I take the folder?"

"Yes."

Noah stopped pacing near me, his face a mask of sadness mixed with frustration. "Make it clear that no one blames her. We'll do anything we can to help her with this situation. Just"—he broke off and swallowed hard—"let her know we're. . .here for her." He was letting his feelings for Brooklynn bleed through, but I didn't have an ounce of jealousy at that moment. I was too consumed with the task ahead. And, I knew exactly what he was feeling, except in my heart, it was exponentially magnified because my feelings for Brooklynn were more than a crush.

"I'll make sure." I gathered the papers that had spilled

out when I dropped the folder before standing. "If you don't hear from me in a half hour, you can stop waiting around. If something comes up later, I'll call you."

Cooper stood as well, walked over to me and laid a hand on my shoulder. "Another thing, her contract is not in jeopardy. Emphasize that." He removed his hand and stepped back, crossing his arms over his chest. I jerked my chin up in acknowledgment and strode to the door.

Sasha was standing in the hallway when I exited the room. "Do you want me to go with you?" she asked softly. I cocked my head to the side, giving her a questioning look. "Cooper was in the process of lecturing me about something or other I'd done wrong again—whatever. I wasn't listening anyway. When he got the call from Noah, I eavesdropped and put together a vague idea of what had happened by his half of the conversation."

I reached for her hand and gave it a squeeze. "Thanks. I've got it for now. She might need some reinforcement that we are all behind her eventually though. I'll call you guys when she's ready for it."

"Okay." She leaned against the wall, twisting the strands of her long red hair nervously.

I was never more grateful for the bond between me and my band mates. We loved and supported each other and Brooklynn was a thread in the woven fabric that made up this little family. Which meant, we did the same for her. "Thanks." She shrugged with a small smile, brushing off my thanks, making it clear she thought it was unnecessary.

With every step down the hall, my footsteps felt heavier. Something had been bothering Brooklynn since yesterday and I'd been prepared to drag it out of her today. Now, I had to drop this weight on top of whatever was already dragging her down. I hated going in blind, it left me no ability to prepare myself for her reaction.

Swiping my keycard, I walked into our suite. I made my way to the bedroom and did my best to keep quiet as I opened the door, assuming she was still sleeping. My brow lowered in a frown when I spotted the empty bed. A sound from the bathroom alerted me that she was still there. "Brooklynn? Baby?" I called softly. There was an extended silence and I wondered for a moment if I'd imagined the noise. I started for the bathroom but she suddenly appeared in the doorway. I smoothed my expression, not wanting to freak her out before I had a chance to ease into everything. Coming to a stop in front of her, I ran my eyes over her beautiful face before gathering her into my arms and kissing her sweetly. "Morning, baby." She leaned into the kiss, deepening it with a fervor that surprised me. There was almost an edge of desperation to it. I pulled back and set her a few inches away from me. "Let's talk, all right?"

Her brown eyes cleared of desire and became sad, but it was the wariness in them that surprised me. Taking her hand, I led her over to the sliding door to our balcony. There were two chairs situated in front of it and I guided her to one of them before dragging the other close and sitting across from her, our knees almost touching.

"Levi, you're making me nervous." Her fingers were tangled together and she was twisting them anxiously.

I didn't know how to fucking start. *Damn it all to hell.*

Handing her the folder, I decided to start with the postcards I hadn't been telling her about. "First, I want to remind you that I love you. You knocked me on my fucking ass and now, I'm head over fucking heels in love with you."

Her wary expression didn't change but she whispered, "I love you too."

"I didn't want you to worry, so I kept something from you. Maybe that was wrong, but my first instinct will always be to protect you." Her eyes narrowed, clearly conveying her irritation. *Shit.*

"Anyway, when we were in Dublin, I started getting postcards again." I paused, expecting an explosive reaction, but she didn't say anything. The only indication of her displeasure was in the darkening of her expression. "Like I said, I didn't want you to worry. But, we started looking into it again." I gestured to the folder and she opened it to find the latest postcard.

I went on to explain everything I'd been told, watching her carefully and waiting for the moment when she would either freak out or break down. The longer she went with little to no reaction, the more I felt that something was off. She was still holding back and it was making me suspicious.

When I finished explaining, I took her hand and gave it a gentle squeeze. "Baby, I know this must be incredibly hard to believe, but they wouldn't have come to me if they weren't one hundred percent sure. I'm so sorry, sweetheart."

Brooklynn shook her head, her face becoming blank. "I don't know what to say." She stood abruptly and turned away from me, stalking back inside and across the room. I followed slowly, cautiously, since I felt like I was stumbling around in the dark. The sense of wrongness about this was getting stronger, shrouding me in suspicion.

She whirled around suddenly, her body tense as a guitar string, her face a mask of resolve. "Look, we have a few days off. I'm going to go home and take care of this. I promise, I'll fix it."

I closed the distance between us and gently clasped her upper arms. "Baby, let's get something clear. None of this is your fault, no one blames you." Even as I said the words, my suspicions made them feel like sawdust in my mouth, but I ignored it. "Beyond that, it's not your responsibility to fix it either. Brooklynn, you can't solve this on your own. Baylee needs help and do you really think you'll have the strength to put her in an institution? I know you. You think you can care for her yourself, but sometimes, things are just out of our control. She needs professional help, baby."

Brooklynn shook her head emphatically and tore herself out of my hold. "You're wrong. I can do what needs to be done. I know what's best for my sister."

I sighed, hating the universe for making me the one to pull the wool from over her eyes. "That's just it, baby. Who

Baylee has become, she's not the sister you know. She's a stranger to you."

Brooklynn stepped back and almost tripped over something behind her. I made a grab for her, helping to steady her and that's when my eyes landed on what she'd stumbled over. "What the fuck are those, Brooklynn?" It was a rhetorical question, I knew exactly what they were. Two bright red suitcases sat on the floor, with her purse propped on top, clearly packed and ready to go. I wasn't sure I could trust my eyes because it seemed so unbelievable.

"I need to go. I was already planning it before you came back. There are some things I need to deal with."

Just like that, the suspicion blooming in my chest grew to epic proportions, mixed with a healthy dose of anger. "Brooklynn, what the fuck aren't you telling me? Why are you hiding something from me?" I steamed.

"It doesn't matter—"

"Bullshit," I spat. I marched around her and picked up a suitcase, tossing it on the bed and unzipping it. "You're not going anywhere until we figure this out. We are in a fucking relationship, Brooklynn. We need to be honest with each other."

"Like you were honest with me about the postcards?" Her voice was quiet, but it didn't need to be yelled, it pierced my heart in a direct hit.

I turned to her. "You're right, that was a dick move and I'm sorry. I promise to never lie or withhold anything from you again. Now, it's your turn to unload and we'll start over, with nothing between us."

Her eyes flitted to the suitcase on the bed and they widened. "No," she said frantically, moving toward it.

Frustrated, I spun back around and opened the case. I started throwing her clothes back onto the bed, determined to unpack and force her to stay. "Don't!" She lunged at the case just as I unzipped an upper pocket and stuck my hand inside. My fingers brushed something hard, thin and sharp, like heavy paper. Using two fingers, I pinched it and slid it out.

I barely registered Brooklynn dropping down onto the bed and putting her face in her hands. My focus was on the postcard in my hand, a card with chimpanzees and a postmark that matched those sent from Baylee's post office.

"What is this?" I continued to stare at the offending item, my voice picking up volume as I spoke again. "Brooklynn. Why do you have one of Baylee's postcards in your luggage?" Mistrust suddenly gave way to accusation and rage.

"Did you know? All this time?" I tried to find an explanation, but I was too far gone to be logical. "Fuck," I breathed. "You let an innocent woman take the fall for your sister." I finally looked at her and tossed the postcard into her lap. "How could you do that?"

She got to her feet, sticking her hands in her back pockets and pacing in quick, jerky movements. "You know me better than that, Levi," she argued, sounding almost as angry as I felt. I didn't know what the fuck she had to be angry about.

"Obviously, I don't know you at all. You certainly did a fantastic job of pretending to be the woman I fell for." I clapped mockingly. "You should go to Hollywood, Brooklynn. Really, your acting talents are wasted here. And making me chase you, wow. Fucking brilliant."

She came to a sudden stop and whirled to look me straight in the eye, her hands balled into fists and propped on her hips. "If that's what you really think, then fuck you, Levi," she snapped before pushing me aside to put everything back in her suitcase. "I'll just go and you can get over your imaginary Brooklynn that much faster."

I crossed my arms over my chest, my feet apart, a scowl etched on my face. "We've already got people taking care of, Baylee. You can't leave, Brooklynn."

She flung an incredulous look my way. "You don't want me here, why would I stay? And what do you mean they are 'taking care' of Baylee?"

"Noah informed Penny of the situation and she helped the people from the hospital take Baylee in. And, before you ask, we had already intended to send you home for the next few days to see her and come to terms with everything."

She finished packing and zipped up her suitcase, then lifted it off the bed. I put my hand out to keep her from passing. "You have a contract, Brooklynn. You'll be in serious debt if you breach it." Her face fell even further and I ignored the pain lancing my already shredded heart. "And, unlike you, I mean what I say, so I won't interfere if everyone else wants you to stay after the tour. But, our final concert in New York will be the last time we sing 'Sanity.'" I dropped my arms and pivoted, stalking to the door. "Stay here, I'll get another room."

"You're wrong." Her whisper reached me just as I was about to close the door. "If you'd only let me explain."

I slammed the door, shutting out the room and wishing I could shut away all of my memories of her, shut away my love for her, just as easily. Instead, they were so overwhelming that I stumbled into the wall, putting a hand against it to hold myself up.

Fuck this shit. You're Levi fucking Matthews. The world is full of Brooklynn's who will fall at the feet of a rock god.

I didn't really believe the voice in my head, but I kept telling myself the same thing hoping I'd believe it eventually. As I put distance between me and our—her room, a barrage of memories fell in front of me, one by one, like unique snowflakes, each with their own story to tell. Every one of them was a different moment with Brooklynn. They reminded me of why I fell in love with her and how genuine and honest she'd always been with me. By the time I reached the elevator, I'd begun to really doubt myself. When I got down to the lobby, I was convinced that I was the biggest fucking idiot in the world. Shit. I almost went right back up to apologize, but groveling alone wasn't going to make up for what I'd said to her, the things I'd believed, if only for a few minutes.

I'd been headed to the front desk, so I changed course and ended up at the bar. "Whiskey neat," I grunted to the waiter who seemed to materialize in front of me. "Make it three. And, throw a shot in there somewhere." The young guy eyed me with sympathy.

"Bad breakup?" he asked in stilted English as he poured.

"Not if I have anything to say about it," I growled. "First I have to figure out how to make up for a monumental fuck up."

"She is American?" he asked and I nodded. "You're in Rome, Signore. There are many inspirations for romance here. Best of luck, Signore." He nodded and moved on to help another customer. *Poor starry-eyed kid.* A romantic walk and a box of chocolates weren't going to cut it. I had a feeling I was going to need to bleed.

Chapter Thirty-Two

BROOKLYNN

I stared at the door where the man I loved more than anything had more or less just walked out of my life. The hurt wrapped itself around me so tight I was nearly choking on it. I sunk down on the bed, keeping my eyes trained on the entrance like he might walk back in and apologize any moment. Even if he did, would I really forgive him after the awful things he'd accused me of?

My next steps were fuzzy at best. I didn't really know what to do next. The instinct to go home was still there, but a strong part of me wanted to avoid the whole situation. I felt guilty for being such a coward and wishing I could avoid dealing with Baylee forever. Then there was the issue of my contract. By the time I got home, I'd have less than twenty-four hours before I had to be back for the concerts in Rome. We wouldn't have another extended break for four weeks, but then we had almost a week off. A much more reasonable amount of time to handle everything at home. I needed more information before I could make a decision.

Digging my cell phone out of my purse, I pulled up Penny's number and pressed call.

"Brooklynn?" her voice sounded strained and tear-filled.

"Hi, Penny. Are you okay?" I asked softly.

She sniffed. "Yes, I just, I'm so sorry Brooklynn. I don't know how she disappeared on me and…and I just don't understand how she could do such a thing. She talked about you all the time like you were her favorite person. The only other person she talked about like that was—well, you know. Anyway, I'm—I'm just so sorry." She was crying in earnest now and I wasn't sure what to say. It was hard to provide comfort when I couldn't find any.

"Penny, it's okay. Really. You didn't do anything wrong. I mean, if I could miss it, how would anyone else see it?"

"I guess." Her voice was small and sad.

I cleared my throat around the lump forming. "How is she?"

"She's all right, I guess. Mostly, she seems scared and lost." My heart squeezed, hating that my sweet little sister was—but then, did my sweet little sister only exist in my mind?

"Can you give me the information for her doctor? I'd like to check in with them."

"Oh sure." She rustled around for a moment, then rattled off all the information.

"Penny, I hate to ask, but I may be stuck here a little longer due to my contract. Would you stay on and keep an eye on her, stay in contact with the doctors and keep me updated?"

"Oh, of course, Brooklynn! I really think that deep down, she's the Baylee we know and love. I feel it, deep in my heart." I was glad she felt that way but I wasn't sure I had any hope that she was right. We said goodbye and hung up, then I dialed the number for Baylee's doctor at the hospital she was checked into.

"This is Dr. Arnold," a kind, female voice answered the phone.

I introduced myself and was grateful that the doctor seemed empathetic and showed a willingness to work with me. I asked for an update on Baylee and when she answered, I was relieved to feel as though she has really taken an interest in Baylee's case. New York mental hospitals didn't have the best reputations. If they'd taken her to Bellevue, I would have flown home just to drag her to a better place.

"Baylee was misdiagnosed for many years, Miss Hawk," she began to explain.

"Please," I said weakly. "Call me Brooklynn." I vaguely wondered how she'd come to that conclusion though. I knew that they'd taken Baylee to the hospital the day before, at least that was what I thought, the time difference was throwing me for a loop. "How can you know that so soon?"

"Good question. You'd be surprised what you can learn from someone's charts if you know what you are looking for. Baylee's been to a lot of doctors and other medical programs, and we all take notes. It looks like nobody ever stood back and looked at the big picture. A common mistake. But as I said, I had an inkling. Adding in your mother's depression, which is often hereditary, I was even more convinced what was happening, so I knew what to look for. Plus, after some time conversing with her over the last forty-eight hours, her answers and reactions were consistent with my diagnosis."

Guilt built the lump in my throat, why hadn't I found her better doctors? But she quickly went on as though she'd read my mind.

"Don't blame yourself, Brooklynn. Baylee's issue is not easy to diagnose. And, her situation is very unique. She has a borderline personality disorder. It's extremely severe, but not bad enough to be categorized as schizophrenia. She doesn't have multiple personalities, though it may seem that way because of the severity of what's actually happening. She's experiencing extreme mood swings. Patients with BPD are vulnerable to these mood swings not because there are necessarily differences with their brain chemistry, but instead because they possess rather fragile, developmentally-delayed and under-developed emotional coping skills. It can often appear as though the patient is a good or bad person with no in between, not seen as possessing those traits at the same time. Are you following me so far?"

I nodded, then realized she couldn't see me. "Yes, I think I'm understanding."

"Good," she said with a warmness to her voice that was incredibly comforting. "Young children tend to represent the world in this high contrast way, but to then grow out of this black and white thinking as they mature. With Baylee, it's unique because of the fact that she never mentally matured beyond the age of ten or twelve. She never reached that stage of growing out of it."

"So, this wasn't caused by her developmental delay?"

"No, it only exacerbated the situation. BPD represents a situation where that normal social and emotional maturation process becomes interrupted, due to trauma or difficult life circumstances that interact with temperamental—instinctual—emotional sensitivity."

"We—our parents"—I didn't know how to explain everything, nor did I really want to. I tried to be as succinct as possible—"Our childhood was incredibly rough. I—I assumed Baylee just didn't remember anything because she never mentioned it or asked about it. I hoped she'd blocked it all out."

"I'm not surprised. Again, Brooklynn, I really do stress that this isn't your fault, the signs are easy to miss. For anyone. Even the best doctors or therapists. But, I feel confident in saying that Baylee is carrying a lot of baggage from your childhood."

"So, can"—I mentally crossed my fingers and hoped— "you help her? Can she be rehabilitated?"

"Well, in some cases, therapy can be the only thing needed to keep it in check. But, as I said, Baylee's situation is quite dire. We are still in the process of doing tests and learning all of the facts. I do believe that we can get to a point where it's manageable. But, to what degree, I'm not sure yet. I can tell you that she would be better off living in an assisted living facility rather than on her own with a home companion."

My head was spinning with all of the information I'd been given in the last few minutes. But, I clung to one thing in particular, they would be able to help her. "So, my sweet sister isn't gone, right?"

"No," she assured me. "She just gets lost in the opposite side sometimes, when her mood swings the other way."

I sighed and some of the weight on my chest lifted.

"How long will she need to be in the hospital?"

"I imagine it will take several weeks to get her on a working regimen and she's safest here until it's under control."

I calculated the time in my head and came to the conclusion that the timing could work out fairly well. "If I need to come home right now, I will. But, I don't know what you recommend. I have a longer break coming up and I'm hoping it will be right around the time that you're ready to release her."

Dr. Arnold hesitated and when she spoke again, she was still sympathetic, but firm. "Honestly Brooklynn, it might be better to give her some time anyway. You are a part of her childhood; you're wrapped up in the trauma. With some intense treatment, she'll learn to cope better and then we can introduce you back into her life."

Tears were rolling down my cheeks by the time she finished. I sniffed and tried to keep from letting her know I was crying.

"I'm sorry, Brooklynn. But, for the most part, this is a good report." Swallowing my tears and doing my best to keep the tremor out of my voice, I thanked her and after a few more questions, I hung up. Giving in to the ocean of emotions I was drowning in, I curled up on the bed and eventually cried myself to sleep.

It was dark when a light knocking on my door woke me. Hope sparked that it might be Levi, but I quickly snuffed it out, not sure if I even wanted to see him. Sluggishly, I climbed off the bed and dragged myself to the door. I cracked it open and more tears sprung to my eyes (I was shocked I had any left) when I saw Sasha and Kristi on the other side. Words were stuck in my throat, I didn't think I could take their accusations and disgust on the same day as losing Levi. But, as I met their eyes, I saw only worry and sympathy.

"Can we come in?" Kristi asked quietly.

"I'm not giving you a choice." Sasha put her hand on the

door and shoved, making me stumble backward, the door opening wide. She stepped in and crushed me in a hug. My arms automatically went around her and I began to cry in earnest. She held me for a little while, then she led me over to the couches in the living area.

After we sat, Sasha next to me and Kristi sitting on the coffee table right in front of me, I looked between them confusedly. "You haven't talked to Levi?" I asked guardedly.

"I ran into him at the bar, well on his way to getting shit-faced," Sasha revealed. "He told me you needed us and you'd explain everything."

My confusion only intensified. Why wouldn't he explain what happened? For that matter, why would he send Sasha and Kristi to me at all? If he thought I was such an awful person, wouldn't he let me stew in my own misery?

"So," Kristi prompted, patting my knee. "Why don't you tell us what's going on?"

I didn't know what to say, but I opened my mouth and everything came pouring out in a rush, barely stopping to breathe. By the time I was done, Sasha and Kristi were both glaring at me, making me want to crawl under a rock. They obviously didn't believe my side of the story. "That fucking cocksucker said what?" Sasha snapped. At the same time, Kristi grumbled, "Motherfucking Levi."

"Wait, you're not mad at me?" I asked, more lost than ever.

Sasha rolled her eyes. "Open your eyes, B. He fucking steamrolled you and didn't give you a chance to explain." Her eyes narrowed on me. "And I don't know where the fuck your backbone went, but you've had your sulking time. It ends right now."

I opened my mouth to rebut her, then snapped it shut. She was right, I was being a complete pussy.

"You're made of stronger shit, B," Kristi added.

"Sometimes a girl just needs a good cry," I defended myself.

"Absolutely," Sasha agreed with a firm nod. "But you've had all day. Time to pull up the big girl panties and figure out what the fuck to do about this."

"There's nothing to do." I shrugged and flopped back against the cushions.

"Well, if anything, you at least need to show off the steel inside you and make sure he knows he can't take the music from you," Kristi said as she clapped her hands together and then pressed them on her knees and stood. "For now, Jonas said he'd be our chaperone so we can go out and get completely plastered."

Sasha shot to her feet, grabbing my arm along the way to pull me up as well. "Best fucking idea ever! We can get rowdy and stick it to Levi and Cooper at the same time. Two for one special!" She seemed overly excited at the thought.

"What is it with you two?" I was being nosy but figured, what the hell, if ever there was a time for me to get an answer, it would be now, while she was feeling bad for me.

Her eyes rolled so hard I thought they might get stuck in the back of her head. "Story for another day." *Damn it.* Kristi met my eyes and nodded, knowing exactly what I was thinking.

We moved on from all talk of anything of importance and focused on our night out. We agreed to meet in the lobby in half an hour, so I hurried to change and did my best to cover up the evidence that I'd spent the day crying.

That night, we did exactly what we set out to do and got completely falling down drunk before passing out in my room. The next day, we went sightseeing together and Matteo even joined us. He didn't bring up Levi or anything that had happened, he treated me as though everything was normal. It lightened my heart and I managed to have a good time.

The following morning was a little more difficult since we all went out in the morning, *all* of us. Then we had a publicity event and a shoot for the cover of the live album they would release before the tour next year. I studiously avoided looking at Levi, but I could've sworn I felt his eyes on me all day. Wishful thinking, I supposed.

Finally, it was the night of our first concert in Rome. The moment I walked on stage and the audience went wild, I was a little surprised. I always got a good reception, but I was becoming more and more well known, especially since I was officially a part of Stone Butterfly, rather than a backup singer. I took my place behind a shiny white grand piano that we'd requested for the concert.

A few weeks into the tour, I was working on a solo ballad in a small performance space in our hotel. Noah often tracked them down so we'd have somewhere to work while on tour without our buses. Matteo had walked in on me practicing and working the melody of a new song. He'd turned right around and went to find the rest of our band mates, herding them to the room I was in. He told me to sing what I had and I shrugged, then sat at the piano and began to play. When I finished, they'd all stared at me in stunned silence.

"It's not that bad, guys," I snorted. "I have to work to do still, but sheesh."

"When will it be ready?" Levi asked.

"I don't know, I'm just messing around," I answered, barely paying attention anymore, lost in changes I'd thought of while singing it for them.

"Rome." Levi's voice was firm and his tone had my head raising in surprise.

"Huh?"

"Can you get it performance ready by our first concert in Rome?"

"Um, sure, I suppose."

"Great, you'll close the first set."

My jaw virtually hit the piano keys when it dropped but before I could respond, they'd all filed out the door with huge grins on their faces. Levi had popped back in and run over to give me a hard kiss and then ordered, "Get to work."

The memory warmed me and the audience's excitement

heightened my ability to let our music take me sky high. To the music version of cloud nine. The only thing that tripped me up was not knowing how things would be between Levi and me on stage. We were professionals and knew how to keep the audience from sensing our tension and that's exactly what happened. Whenever I met his aqua blue eyes, you'd never know he wasn't still desperately in love with me, or that he harbored such ugly opinions of me.

The audience quieted after a long applause for our second to last song of the first set.

"We've got a treat for you guys tonight," Levi told them. "You all know that Brooklynn and I wrote 'Sanity' together, she also wrote 'Like Her' with Sasha. She's a brilliant musician and she's been working on a new song. Do you guys want to hear it?" They screamed and practically brought the roof down.

"This is 'The Road to Forever,'" I said. The piano was sitting on a low, mobile platform and when it went dark except for the spotlight on me, it started floating downstage to the center. As it moved, my fingers began to glide over the keys, playing a haunting, heartbreaking melody. Little by little, it strengthened until it was strong and full. Then, I began to sing. I'd written it in a lower key, showing off my husky alto that slid up through my mix into a clear belt. The song was a ballad, the melody fitting the words, captivating the audience in the richness of the tones and the lyrics. The song was about finding your way when you're lost, finding your way back to your perfect forever. It was meant to lift the listener up, to bolster their hope, to make them feel like all things are possible. As it crescendoed and my fingers alternated between chords and lyrical runs. My voice built until I was singing with every cell and molecule inside me. I closed my eyes and poured out my hope and love into every note and at the peak, I held out the brightest note, the vibrating strains of the piano going quiet and when I finally let the sound fade, there was complete and utter silence throughout the arena.

Then I slowly started the melody from the very beginning and transitioned to the stronger one within a few bars, I sang the chorus one more time before ending on a sweet and comforting note.

Once again, I was confronted with a reverent silence and about thirty seconds later, the arena fucking exploded.

Before the lights went down to signal the break in the concert, some kind of magnetic force pulled my eyes to Levi's. His sparkled and he nodded. If I hadn't known better, I would have thought he'd been bursting with pride. And he said I was a good actor. He could win his own academy award.

I was smashed in hugs from everybody as we exited the stage, everyone but Levi, who hung back. Still, his eyes never seemed to leave me. Part of me dreaded the final moments of the concert when we would sing "Sanity." But, there was simply no way to sing this song without being completely sucked into it. It fed off of emotion, no matter what kind. As the last notes were played on Sasha's cello, Levi brought me close like he usually did, and his head descended until it was only inches away. His eyes were intense and locked with mine. Then the lights went out and he held firmly for another couple of beats, before releasing me.

There was no way to avoid the high of performing, but, underneath was a soul deep hurt and it tainted the euphoria. Once we'd finished the encores, everyone headed straight to a meet and greet/jam session with some underprivileged kids who'd won the opportunity. I wanted to grab a bag of goodies I'd brought for them, so I told Noah I'd run to my dressing room and meet them there in a few minutes.

Chapter Thirty-Three

LEVI

The first time I heard "The Road to Forever," I knew it was a Grammy-winning song. I wanted to debut it on the tour to pick up steam, also because there was no better way to work out kinks, than to perform it live. It had been even more brilliant than I could have ever dreamed. From the audience's reaction, they were smart enough to think so too. Staying back and letting Brooklynn celebrate with everyone else had been torture. But, there was too much unresolved between us and I knew it would dampen her excitement to bring our tension into her moment.

I hadn't been able to take my eyes off of her all night. The only place where Brooklynn was more spectacular than when she was on stage was when she was falling apart in my arms. It was almost impossible not to kiss her at the end of "Sanity," but I knew it would only bring our attraction to the front of our focus when it needed to be minds and hearts first.

We had an event after the show, one we were all excited about. A local charity had held an auction for underprivileged kids, the younger ones drawing pictures as their way of bidding and the older kids had bid with "gift certificates" for community service. There was limited space for the get-together, but we'd made sure that every kid had a ticket to the concert. As we walked to the room to meet the kids, I glanced back and noticed Brooklynn wasn't with us.

"Noah."

"Yeah?" He didn't even lift his head from his phone as he answered so I punched his shoulder. "Fuck, Levi! What the hell was that for?"

I shrugged. "Felt like it. Where is Brooklynn?"

"What do you care?" he snapped.

"Just answer the question, fucker."

His eyes went back to his phone. "She brought a bunch of American junk food to hand out. She ran back to the dressing rooms for it."

Of course she did. Damn, I'd never get used to how big her heart was or how fucking adorable she was.

"I wouldn't count on her joining us too quickly, mates," Emma said with a smile. "She's got a cracking surprise waiting for her."

I gave her a curious raise of my brow. "A surprise?"

She nodded and grinned harder. "Yeah, her sister rang me and said she wanted to surprise Brooklynn. She told me you'd bought her a ticket and I guess Brooklynn had given her our numbers for emergencies and she couldn't get through to anyone else. I thought it was brilliant. She was right knackered when she arrived though so I took her to our dressing room so she could have a kip."

My feet were moving before I even thought about it, running as fast as they could.

Chapter Thirty-Four

BROOKLYNN

I dashed into the dressing room and over to my bag sitting on a counter with a mirror surrounded by lights. A loud bang caused me to jump a foot and when my head flew up I saw Baylee in the mirror, standing in front of the closed door to the room. I whirled around in shock but it was quickly replaced with anger. I walked over to her, my hands slamming down on my hips.

"Baylee, what are you doing here? How did you even get here?"

"Levi wants me here," she said sweetly. "He asked me to come and bought me a ticket."

I had no doubt that was true. Levi had known how worried I'd been about going so long without seeing Baylee. Bringing her to Italy made perfect sense for us. He must have forgotten to cancel the tickets when everything fell apart. That still didn't explain how she managed to get away from the hospital.

"You know I'm always happy to see you, sweet girl." I tried to keep my tone light and fixed a smile on my face. "Did someone bring you?"

She shook her head, her chin-length hair swinging with it. "I remembered how to use my bus pass to get to the airport. Cecily taught me when we went to Canada."

"Did the nurses tell you that you were allowed to do that, Baylee?"

Her sweet expression slipped and she glared at me. I'd never seen that look on her face before, especially not directed at me. "They don't like me. They won't let me do all the fun things that Penny and Cecily let me do. They said no, but I didn't want to disappoint Levi." She tapped her foot impatiently, her lips pursing and her brown eyes turning mutinous. "Penny said no too, so I locked her in my room and snuck out, like when Cecily and I used to play hide and seek."

Okay, definitely need to have a conversation with the hospital about their security. I was trying to figure out how to calm her down and then what to do, but she kept on ranting.

"I'm mad at you, Brooklee. Levi loves me but he likes to listen to you sing. I've been learning to sing, so he won't miss you if you're gone. I told you to go away from him, but you didn't listen. You're being bad and I think you need to be punished."

I didn't like where this was going.

"If you aren't punished, you'll never learn the lesson. You should have listened to me when I told you to go away. I don't like it when Levi borrows you, so now he doesn't have to anymore. He has me. And, you let them take Cecily from me. She got in trouble for something that was all your fault, Brooklee. You've been extremely naughty."

She met my eyes and her lips curled into an ugly smile. "You need a time out, then you're going home, young lady." Her hand came from around her back where I didn't realize it had been hiding. I gasped and took a step back as the lights around the mirror glinted off the knife in her hand. It was slightly smaller than a steak knife, but it looked plenty fucking sharp. "Go sit in time out and then if you're good, I'll send you home. But, if you keep misbehaving, I'm going to punish you like Daddy punished Mommy. She learned her lesson. She went away and didn't come back."

I wanted to scream. Fucking parents. They couldn't stop fucking with our lives even from the fucking grave. I was starting to panic. I didn't know this Baylee, which meant I had no idea how to handle her.

Bang! Bang! Bang!

"Baylee?"

At the sound of Levi's voice, Baylee turned her head toward the door and I took the opportunity to lunge for the knife. I wrapped my fingers around her wrist but she became enraged and started flailing. I lost my grip and the knife came down, slicing the skin on my arm, and causing me to stumble backward. I cried out in pain and as the banging on the door became more frantic, it was obviously that it was agitating Baylee. She screamed in frustration at the same time the door cracked and swung open. It pushed her forward and she went flying right at me.

A sudden pain in my chest stung like a bitch and I lost my balance, falling to the floor, with Baylee crumbling down on top of me. I tried to gasp but with every breath, the stinging pain in my chest got worse and my breathing became labored. I coughed and whimpered from the excruciating pain radiating to my shoulder and back. Baylee scrambled off me and into a sitting position. She maneuvered herself right behind me and dragged me up a little so my upper body was in her lap and she could curl her arm around my neck, cutting down what little air I'd been managing to draw in. Her free hand reached toward my body and my eyes followed it. They widened to saucers when I saw the knife sticking out of my chest, just below my right breast. From the position and the pain, it seemed likely that she'd punctured my lung when the knife stabbed me as she tumbled forward. She grabbed the handle and ripped it from my chest, causing me to scream in agony, my hands immediately covering the wound.

"She needs to be punished, Levi. Then we can go, okay? Just let me teach Brooklee her lesson."

My eyes had become clouded with tears and through the fog of pain, everything was blurry. I could just make out Levi getting closer. I tried to say something, but the words just wouldn't come.

"You can teach her a lesson without the knife, Baylee Bear," Levi soothed. His voice was deceptively calm but his eyes were wild as he glanced down at me. "Why don't you let me hold it for you?"

His hand slowly extended toward her, but she quickly moved her arm close to her chest. I couldn't see at that angle very well but it seemed like she was almost hugging it to her. Levi drew my attention when he scooted a little closer. "Baylee Bear," he said softly. "Why don't you let her go and we'll leave, okay? Don't you want to go with me?"

"Yes. But—" Baylee's muscles loosened just a tiny bit and her arm dropped a fraction. I was pretty sure it was enough. My hands moved as quickly as I dared until I was able to wrap my fingers around her bent elbow and yank it down. Levi sprang for the knife as she shrieked and ripped her arm from my hold. I didn't have the strength to keep a grip on it and the force of jerking her arm out of my hold sent Baylee rocking backward. I heard a scream and Levi's face contorted with horror. The arm around my neck went slack and I vaguely thought I heard the slump of a body. Someone else ran into the room as the edges of my vision started to turn gray.

Chaos had erupted around me but I could only focus on the pain. I felt myself being shifted and placed on something soft. Pressure was applied to my wound causing me to hiss from the pain. My hair brushed away from my face and Levi's voice was in my ear. "Baby, stay with me. Brooklynn, let me see those beautiful eyes." Were my eyes closed?

"Fuck! She's turning blue, Noah!" I did my best to drag them open. I wanted to reassure Levi that I was okay, but there were spots dancing in front of them, making me nauseous. I wanted to take a deep breath but it hurt like a bitch and caused me to cough, which was so, so much worse.

"Calm down, Levi. The last thing she needs is for you to lose it. The ambulance is on its way." There was a jumble of voices and all of it was giving me a fucking headache, but I couldn't make myself speak.

"I think Baylee will be fine, Levi. It's shallow." It sounded like Noah again. I pried my eyes open and tried to turn my head to confirm. It lolled to the side because I didn't have the strength to hold it up. It looked like he was leaning over something with someone standing behind him.

He moved and I could just make out Baylee lying on the floor, the knife buried in her shoulder. She wasn't moving. What had I done?

My eyes dropped. Damn, I was tired. My heart started to race, the nausea getting worse, and I felt clammy, cold and yet sweating, allthough I barely felt the pain anymore. "Brooklynn. Baby, open your eyes." I sluggishly lifted my lids but was disappointed when I couldn't see Levi. I wanted so badly to see his beautiful face. "Shit! Where's the fucking ambulance. Her eyes are dilated and—fuck! I think she's going into shock. Brooklynn!"

I was just too tired. I needed a nap, that's all.

Chapter Thirty-Five

BROOKLYNN

Everything hurt. It hurt a whole fuck of a lot. I moaned and tried to swallow but I felt like I had a mouth full of cotton balls.

"Brooklynn?" Callused fingertips brush hair from my forehead. I recognized the feel of those fingers, the calluses that came from playing the guitar. "Baby, please wake up."

"Levi?" I croaked. "Water." Lips brushed over my brow softly.

"Open your eyes, sweetheart and I'll get you some water."

I frowned. Seriously? Was it really worth it? I tried to swallow again. Okay, fine. I concentrated and managed to drag my lids up just a sliver. Then they slammed back down. Good enough, right? "Water," I requested again, my voice no more than a tiny whisper.

I felt the rasp of a straw on my dry lips and parted them to suck up a sip of cool water. I took another drink and sighed, damn that tasted good.

"Brooklynn, I need to see your beautiful eyes," he begged. I really hated to disappoint him, so I tried again and this time, I managed to get them open almost all the way, though they still felt droopy and sluggish. I slowly blinked and they started to feel a little lighter, so I did it again. After a few more, Levi started to come into focus. His aqua eyes stared down at me, the gems filled with worry. "There you are," he breathed. He dropped his head so his brow was pressed to mine, his minty breath blowing lightly across my mouth. "You scared the fuck out of me."

What? I tried to sift through my foggy brain and like a flood, the memories came crashing over me. "Baylee?" I asked, feeling the tears already building behind my eyes, my nose tingling.

"She's fine, baby. They flew her home yesterday. She's back at the hospital with a twenty-four-hour guard." Unwanted moisture leaked from my eyes and I was too weak to even lift my arm to brush them away. Levi did it for me, tenderly sweeping his thumbs across my cheekbones and catching each tear.

"Miss Hawk." A stranger's voice interrupted. "It's nice to see you awake." His accent was thick and the words sounded funny. He didn't use the right syllables, but somehow I could still understand him. I focused on the direction the voice was coming from and saw a tall, thin, dark-haired man with a mustache entering the room. He wore blue scrubs with a long white lab coat and a stethoscope hung around his neck. He was reading from a clipboard as he walked in but then he glanced at me and smiled. "How are you feeling? Are you in pain?" Those weird sounds again.

"Sì, un poco," I replied automatically. Oh, for the love of—I was such an idiot. He was speaking Italian. Evidently, we were still in Rome.

"English," Levi snapped.

"Scusa," the doctor said. "I apologize. Your friends mentioned that she spoke Italian, I wanted to gauge her response to it. She shows no sign of head injury, but we can never be too careful. Now, let's just check you over Miss Hawk."

A nurse had followed him in and she raised the bed so I was sitting and started taking my vitals while the doctor put on his stethoscope and placed it on my chest. "Breath, signora." I winced, remembering how much that had hurt the last time I did it. "It shouldn't be painful, just a little weak."

I slowly inhaled and found he was right. He moved the diaphragm around a few times, asking me to breathe each time. "Bene. You're sounding clear. We'll do another x-ray, but I don't think you are retaining any liquid in your lungs or developing any kind of infection. If it stays clear, we'll discharge you to go home tomorrow."

He wrote something on the clipboard and hung it at the bottom of my bed. "They'll be in to take you to Radiology shortly." Then he and the nurse were gone and I was left alone with Levi.

He'd stepped away while they worked, but when they were done, he came back and perched on the bed beside me. He was so handsome. I loved him so much. But the ugly memories of our fight were clawing to the surface with all the rest.

"I don't think I can take another scare like that, baby. Ever. It took at least ten years off my life." His mouth quirked in a cute, lopsided smile that I loved. It reminded me of when he used to smile at Baylee like that.

My throat seemed to close in an instant, choking me, but I didn't panic. I recognized it. The pain ripping me apart was in my heart and as the tears began to rain down, the choking feeling eased and was replaced by great big sobs. Levi scrambled onto the bed and carefully sat next to me, slipping his arms around me. He ran his fingers through my hair and kissed my head every so often. But mostly, he just let me cry.

I felt a great wave of guilt, self-loathing, and grief swallow me whole. I had hurt Baylee. If I had only figured things out sooner, it might not have happened. I'd been so fucking blind. And so fucking stupid to give my heart to anyone, even my sister. The almost unbearable heartbreak I was enduring was completely of my own making. I should have learned from my parents. It was clear from what fuck-ups they'd been, and how they'd messed with Baylee's mind, it was only a matter of time before I cracked too. The only way to protect myself and everyone else was to just stay away.

My fingers ached to feel the cool ivory keys of a piano under them. Music. It had always been my salvation. I needed to go back to the root of my soul and put my trust in the music that filled it. It was all I needed.

Don't look at me that way, I needed the lie. I needed it like I needed to breathe.

My sobs were quieting, losing strength, the tears drying up. Levi rocked me and hummed a sweet tune until I started to doze off. I hadn't quite fallen asleep when I was jostled fully awake as the orderlies came in to take me off to x-ray. It didn't take long and we went back to my room. Levi was waiting, pacing with his hands shoved in the front pockets of his raggedy jeans. He looked adorable in his Green Day shirt that said American Idiot and I almost laughed, knowing he was being ironic on purpose. I didn't laugh though, I was too physically and emotionally exhausted. They got me situated and hooked up to my IV, then Levi and I were alone again. He came back to sit beside me and brushed a few strands of my hair behind my ear.

"I'm not coming back," I told him softly. Preferring to be bluntly honest and get this over with. I pressed the button for the nurse, hoping she would arrive before things got too messy.

"To where, baby? Rome?"

"The band. I'm done."

He reared back, his face shocked. "What?"

"Us. Everything," I pushed on. "I'm done. It was all a mistake anyway, I don't know what the hell I was thinking."

I could see him gearing up to argue when the nurse arrived. She was a cheery looking woman with a swinging blonde ponytail, pink scrubs, and a smile bracketed with lines that showed she did it often. "Everything all right, signora?"

"I'm extremely tired," I told her in Italian. "I think visitors will just exhaust me." She nodded and glanced at Levi who was starting to look very frustrated at being left out of the conversation, before looking back at me. "Please," I begged. "Could you just tell him visiting hours are over or something?" I blinked back my tears, but she still saw them and her eyes filled with sympathy.

"Si, signora. We'll be giving you medicine soon anyway, it will pretty much knock you out. Should I tell him when he can come back?"

I shook my head. "I don't want any visitors, per favore."

She looked like she wanted to say something else, but she simply nodded and turned to Levi. "Signor, I'm afraid it is time for her medication and it will make her very sleepy. Visiting hours will be long over by the time she wakes. Let's let her rest, si?"

Levi turned to me, his eyes clouded with confusion and hurt lurking just behind it. I rolled to my other side, too cowardly to look him in the face while she kicked him out.

Chapter Thirty-Six

LEVI

The hospital had let me stay with her for the entire week she'd been there. Noah and Matteo had brought me clothes and Simon and Sasha had taken turns bringing food, all of them eager to visit Brooklynn. It wasn't the hospital kicking me out, it was Brooklynn.

I ran a hand over Brooklynn's head, down her hair, then stood and leaned over to place a kiss on her temple. "I'll go for now," I murmured. "But, you and I are far from over and we'll talk about the band tomorrow. I love you, sweetheart." I held my breath for a moment, hoping, but she didn't say it back and the air rushed out as my heart stuttered.

"Signore?" the nurse called softly. Her expression was filled with compassion, but she waved me toward the door. With one last touch to her head, I reluctantly left. When I reached the lobby, I stopped at the front desk to ask when visiting hours started. She gave me the time and I thanked her before exiting through the sliding glass doors. I sent a quick text to Erin and 2.0 asking one of them to send a car for me. I didn't feel like flagging a taxi and I had ridden there in the ambulance.

While I waited in the parking lot, I pulled out my cell and called Noah.

"How is she?"

"Talking about quitting."

"Fuck," he sighed.

"Yeah. Pretty much how I'm feeling, except with a lot more pain in the vicinity of my heart."

Noah was silent for a moment. "Wait, quitting the band or your relationship?"

I clenched my teeth, stifling the need to yell at no one in

particular. I felt like an animal that needed to howl in pain. "Both."

"Son of a bitch."

"We'll all go with you tomorrow and talk to her."

"No," I sighed. "I don't want to overwhelm her. Let me talk to her first."

"If you're sure." He sounded doubtful and it irritated the fuck out of me.

"I'm sure," I snapped as a black sedan pulled to a stop in front of me. "Car's here." I ended the call and opened the door, climbing in and practically collapsing on the seat. I was fucking drained, but I wasn't looking at much rest. I'd discovered an inability to sleep well without Brooklynn in bed with me since the night of our fight. I just hoped she would be in a better mood tomorrow after she got some sleep.

But, the next morning when I arrived at eight AM on the dot, I tried to sign in to visit her and was told that she wasn't taking any visitors. I must have stared at the woman dumbly for several minutes because eventually she waved her hand in my face. "Signore? Pronto?"

I shook my head and stepped back, still a little stunned that Brooklynn had basically banned me from her. If I was being honest with myself, I had expected what Brooklynn liked to call a "movie moment." She would wake up and tell me she loved me and all would be forgiven and we'd ride off into our happily ever after. Instead, she effectively shut all of us out of her life. Whoever said that tragedy brings people closer together was a fucking idiot. Complete bullshit.

I stewed at the hotel the rest of the day trying unsuccessfully to come up with some kind of game plan. Depression was starting to settle over me as I wondered if I'd truly fucked this up for good. Simon called to see if I needed to get good and drunk. I considered it, but it would only delay the inevitable. The heartbreak would have to be dealt with eventually, might as well get a jump start on it. My door suddenly opened and Sasha came marching into my room, looking at me with disgust.

"Really? Sitting around in the dark feeling sorry for yourself?" She planted her hands on her hips and glared at me. "A couple of stupid idiots, the two of you. You know that? Do I have to do *everything* for you people?" She huffed and stomped over to flip the lights on, making me wince. "Serves you right," she muttered under her breath as she moved to a chair and flopped down into it. "You just going to be a pussy and let her walk away?"

"What exactly do you want me to do, Sasha? She won't even let me near her."

"Yeah, you're a colossal fuck up, Matthews. Still, you've got some good qualities, or I wouldn't love you like a brother." Her voice softened and she reached out to grab my hand, giving it a squeeze. "Come on, dude. You really going to just let the best thing that ever happened to you, to us, run away?"

Something in her voice perked my ears and I cocked my head as I studied her. "You sound like you've come up with a plan."

"Well. Ideas more like." She let go of my hand and leaned back in chair with a smug smile making it look remarkably like she was a queen sitting on her throne. "First of all, I don't want you to let her get away, but you do need to give her some space." She leaned forward conspiratorially. "Then…"

I listened and wasn't sure about some of her ideas, but I sure as fuck didn't have any better ones.

"What makes you the expert on this?" I asked, only half kidding. "You can't even deal with your own fucked up relationship."

She glared at me. "You want my help or not?"

I sighed. "Yeah."

It about killed me, but I took Sasha's advice and gave Brooklynn some space. We sent out a press release that she was leaving the tour temporarily for medical reasons. Speculation ran rampant, the assumptions that she was pregnant hurt my heart more than I expected them to. It wasn't that I was ready to start a family, but my greatest fear was that I would never have the opportunity to have one with Brooklynn.

I mostly adhered to Sasha's suggestions. But, I did send her flowers to have waiting for her when she got home. In the note, I told her that our story was an unfinished song and someday, we'd have no choice but to give in to the music and follow the melody where ever it led.

We continued with our tour and every time a show ended, with the noticeable absence of our duet, I fought the desire to drop everything and go get my girl. I didn't completely leave her life though. I meddled when necessary and planned for the right day. The one when I would claim her for good.

In the meantime, I lay awake at night without her and missed her like crazy every fucking day.

Chapter Thirty-Seven

BROOKLYNN

The day I arrived home, a bouquet of purple roses showed up at my door. Levi's note was beautiful and I burst into tears. I'd gone to bed and cried myself to sleep.

I'd always heard that heartbreak was deadly. There were endless songs dedicated to warning you to avoid it, some lamenting it, some making you feel it with them, and every other facet of it. If you asked me, I'd say they were right *and* wrong. I didn't feel the pain they always described, but I suspected that was because they were right when they said it was deadly. Every day, I woke up and went through the motions of life, but I don't think anyone could classify what I was doing as living. The day of the flowers was the last time I remembered feeling anything.

Though, the lack of feeling may also have had something to do with me becoming more familiar with my pain pills than I should have over the next few weeks. But, despite everything that had happened, there were things I couldn't continue to neglect. Mostly, I had to face the demons of my past. Baylee had only me, I couldn't just walk away. You didn't walk away from family when they were in need. That definitely wasn't something my parents ever grasped and even if I did have some of their darkness inside me, I would never let it consume me the way they had.

Eventually, I dragged my ass out of bed, tossed the pills down the drain, and started making phone calls. The first thing I did was get on the phone to a realtor in my home town. I didn't know why it took me so long, but I was determined to shed my parents' baggage. The first step was selling the property where the house we grew up in still stood. We hadn't lived there since we went to foster care, but it had been paid off by my dad's life insurance and without a will, it had gone to the next of kin when they died. Me. It was kept in a trust until I was eighteen and for some unrecognized reason, I hadn't sold it. I still paid the property taxes every year, but that was it. I never saw it again. I could only imagine the shape it was in. I contracted to have the place demolished and put the land on the market. Their first opening wasn't for six weeks, but a demolition date was set and it was one thing to check off my list.

I was going through the motions, feeling almost nothing. The only thing there was a spark of fear that kept me from facing Baylee until I couldn't put it off any longer. Dr. Arnold had told me it was best to stay away for a while anyway. That's the excuse I used most days. Then she left me a message to tell me that I needed to make a decision about Baylee's long term care. I'd been waiting for the hospital bill to show up, and I was sweating about what it was going to cost for the kind of facility she needed to be in. But, I hadn't gotten any mail or phone calls from the billing department. One more thing I could procrastinate.

Standing at the doors to the hospital, I stared at them for a good ten minutes. Still nothing. I couldn't muster up dread, guilt, certainly not happiness. I gave up and walked inside, asking where to find Dr. Arnold and following the directions to her office. Her door was open and I took a moment to study her as she stood by a filing cabinet, reading from a folder. For some reason, I'd pictured a tall, statuesque woman, blonde and beautiful. In reality, she was pretty average. Medium height, light brown hair caught up in a twist at the back of her head, average weight. Then I knocked and she looked up and I was struck by her eyes. They were hazel, nothing truly spectacular in color, but they were brilliant, or rather she was brilliant and it was clearly reflected in her eyes. They were also filled with kindness and for the first time in weeks, I felt a little warmth seep through my bones.

"You must be Brooklynn," she said with a smile. "Baylee looks so much like you."

I nodded and shuffled in to take a seat in front of her desk. "I hear that a lot," I mumbled. She sat behind her desk and picked up a different folder, and handed it to me with the one she'd been reading when I knocked.

"The blue folder is information about Baylee's condition and her progress reports. The second one is brochures for some facilities I recommend for Baylee. I'd like to go over everything with you if you have some time."

For the next hour, we talked about Baylee's future, her progress and the plans for what was next. When we got to the brochures and their pricing estimates, I wondered how the hell I was going to pay for it. Especially when I wasn't sure what the fall out over my contract with Stone Butterfly was going to be. I'd figure it out. Whatever Baylee needed. Family, I reminded myself.

"I'm not sure what I can afford right now," I admitted dispassionately. "I haven't even seen the hospital bill yet."

Dr. Arnold tilted her head and looked confused. "What do you mean? It was my understanding that the hospital bill had been taken care of."

I shook my head and sighed. "Nope." I didn't even have the frame of mind to freak out about it.

She picked up her phone and made a call, when she hung up, she tapped on her computer and then the printer spit something out. Snatching it, she handed it to me across the desk. "Here's a copy of your bill."

I frowned as I took it. The first thing I saw was the billed amount. Even a dead person's heart would start pounding at the sight of that number. Holy fucking shit. I'd still be paying that off for multiple lifetimes. Then my eyes dropped to the bottom where it gave the amount due.

$0.00. Paid in full.

"What the fuck?" I shouted then immediately slapped a hand over my mouth. "Dr. Arnold, holy crap, I'm so sorry."

She waved off my concern and laughed. "It's a warranted reaction."

"Do you know who paid it?" I asked. I had an idea, but

I wanted her to confirm it.

She shrugged. "I asked and all they would all me was that it was an anonymous donor."

Sure, it was. Part of me wanted to tell them to send it back and set up a payment plan with me. The other part, the one in control, wasn't that stupid (thank goodness) and it kept my mouth shut. The reality was, as much as I didn't want to owe him, I couldn't handle this on my own. The kind of facilities the state would assist with were scary on way too many levels. And, the truth was, as hurt as I'd been by Levi's accusations, I knew he would never do this with any expectations of payback. He'd never accept it either.

"Okay, thanks," I mumbled and shoved all of the papers and folders into a tote bag I'd brought. It also had a couple of things for Baylee. I cleared my throat and shifted uncomfortably. "Um, I brought some things for Baylee. Should I—can I take them to her?"

Dr. Arnold tapped her lips with one index finger as she considered my question. "I know you are each others only family. It's always one of my goals to try and keep those ties strong. She's doing very well and I'm hoping she'll be happy to see you. But, I'm more concerned about you than her if she isn't."

"I'll be fine," I told her, knowing I wouldn't feel it either way. She nodded and led me down a sterile white hallway, hanging right at the corner and then stopping at a thick, white door, with an oblong window in the top half. She swiped a key card on the pad next to it and I heard the gears shift and click. Opening the door, she motioned for me to wait while she went in first.

"Good morning, Baylee."

"Hi, Dr. Arnold."

Baylee's sweet voice sliced through the numb. I grabbed my chest and bent over, the feeling shocking me, reminding me why I preferred not to feel at all.

"Your sister is here, would you like to see her?"

"No, thank you. Mommy doesn't visit when Brooklynn

is here."

I squeezed my eyes shut, trying to ignore the burning behind my lids.

"She brought you a present, are you sure you don't want to see her for just a minute?"

"I guess," she grumbled.

Dr. Arnold opened the door wide and I plastered on a fake smile as I stepped inside. Baylee was sitting in a rocking chair by a window that over looked a garden, reading a book. She was dressed casually in jeans and a pink T-shirt, her growing hair tied back in a tiny ponytail. She looked like a typical nineteen-year-old girl, but fresh and innocent, like the Baylee I remembered. The room was surprisingly homey, with pretty art on the walls, colorful bedding, and normal furniture. You wouldn't know it was a hospital or basically a prison cell. Nor would you notice the specific absence of any items she could hurt herself or someone else with.

Her face turned my way and her brown eyes perused me from head to toe. "Hey, sweet girl," I said softly. I reached into my bag and pulled out a book of Madlibs. "I thought we could do a couple of these when I visit."

She held out her hand and I walked forward, setting them in her hand. A small smile cracked her straight face when she looked at the booklet. "Thank you." Then she set them on the table next to her and opened up her book, effectively dismissing me.

"You're welcome," I whispered. "I'll come back soon, okay?"

"Okay," she responded carelessly.

I debated giving her a hug, but. . .I could pretend all I wanted, the truth was, I was scared to get too close to her.

I backed up a few steps, then pivoted and crossed the short distance to the door. Dr. Arnold smiled and followed me out, making sure the door latched correctly before facing me. "Believe it or not, this is progress for her. When she first came back from Italy, she was angry almost constantly.

She's been slowly reversing the ratio and the fact that she took your present is a good sign."

Nodding, I rubbed my chest, trying to stop the ache in my heart. "Thanks. I'll try to come back in a few days. When do you expect her to be ready to transfer to a full-time care facility?"

"Next week," she answered as she walked beside me down the hall. We talked a for a few more minutes until we reached her office. "It was nice to meet you, Brooklynn. I'm happy to know Baylee has you."

"I'll call you to schedule her transfer." I shook her hand and scurried from the hospital. Once outside, I bent over, clutching my chest and trying to suck in deep breaths. After the clamp on my chest had eased, I stood and looked at the city hustling all around me, New Yorkers doing what they do best. Moving from one place to the next as quickly as possible, completely focused on their destination, or lost in their music, on their phones, or simply wandering. It was familiar and steady, soothing the tear in my shell. I hopped on the subway and went home.

After a lot of research, I chose the facility I thought was best for Baylee. And, it was in Brooklynn, not so far from me. It was extremely expensive but I was determined to make it work. I had put feelers out for studio jobs, but so far no one seemed to need me. I was damn fucking good at what I did, so it made absolutely no sense. I put the worry aside for that moment while I dealt with getting Baylee settled.

Penny and I met at the hospital the day they moved Baylee. I stayed in the background, unwilling to upset her during the transition. She shouted happily when she saw Penny and went running to her for a hug. Another slice of pain ripped through my chest.

Over the next few weeks, I started to visit Baylee for a few minutes a couple of times a week. At one point, I even made her laugh. My visits with her were the only time I couldn't keep every emotion shoved behind a wall. As much as I wanted to keep my heart protected from loving anyone, I'd never stopped loving her. No matter what, she was my sister and I would always love her. It also gave her the power to deeply wound me and some days, her indifference hurt. A lot.

When I approached the facility about financial options, they informed me that Baylee's care had been paid in full for the next five years and that they had instructions on who to contact when the time was up. *Fucking Levi*. I was grateful, don't get me wrong. But the feelings that came with it, they were incredibly unwelcome.

Demo day for the house arrived before I knew it. It was a good thing the realtor had sold the land because I'd only managed to book a handful of studio gigs, even commercial and voice over opportunities seemed to dry up. I needed the money from the sale and it wouldn't go through until the house had been leveled and cleared away.

I dashed into Baylee's home, shaking off the rain and checked in before heading back to the activities room. She wasn't there, so I stopped to talk to her nurse for a few minutes and found out Baylee was in her room. When I reached the small but pleasant space, I peeked in to make sure she wasn't taking a nap. She was standing at one of her two windows, watching the rain so I knocked softly.

"Hey, sweet girl," I called softly, so I wouldn't startle her.

She whipped around and screamed, "GET OUT! GET OUT! I HATE YOU! YOU TOOK EVERYBODY FROM ME! I WANT MOMMY! GET OUT!"

I stumbled backward from the force of her anger and slammed the door shut before taking off at a run. My protective walls came crumbling down. Outside, I stood in the rain and sobbed as pain radiated through my body. I missed my sweet sister, I missed Levi, I missed everyone so fucking much.

Unexpectedly, I realized there was something I needed to do. I pulled out my phone and found an hourly rental car in a garage nearby and booked it. Ten minutes later I'd picked it up and was on the road. Two hours after that, I pulled up to a place I'd hoped never to see again. The rain hadn't come this far north yet, so the demo crew was there working. I sat and watched as they worked. When the roof caved in and the structure fell in on itself, I was done. I started the car and headed to the other place I'd never expected to visit again.

The black gates were open, but with the weather coming, the cemetery grounds were pretty deserted. I remembered exactly how to get to their plots and as I pulled to a stop and parked, I second-guessed what the fuck I was doing there. Determined, I opened the door and alighted from the car. I walked around the the front and onto the grass, trudging forward until I found the graves I was looking for.

Marie Hawk

An angel in heaven

.

I almost snorted. *If you say so.*

David Hawk

Beloved husband and father.

That time, I actually snorted out loud. *Beloved is a bit of a stretch.*

"Do you assholes know what you did to her?" I snapped. "What you did to me?" I yelled this time.

Remember how we talked about movie moments? They aren't always sappy and lovey-dovey. Sometimes, they are full of hurt and rage. Well, I had one right then. At the very moment every emotion I'd been hiding from came crashing down on me, thunder boomed so loud it shook the ground. Then the sky opened up and rain drenched me from head to toe in seconds. The rain stung my skin as it pelted me, hard and cold, but I barely felt it beyond the agony that had been unleashed inside me.

"Dying young was too good for you," I spit. "You should've had to live the rest of your motherfucking lives in the same way you lived the beginning of it. Minus the poor defenseless children unfortunate enough to have your fucking genes. The ones whose lives you continued to shit on from the fucking grave!" I was screaming now. And, I didn't give one fuck about it.

"I hurt her, do you understand? Because of you, I hurt her. Now she mixes me up with you fuckers in her head! Can't you leave me the fuck alone?"

Chapter Thirty-Eight

LEVI

I pulled the car over a few feet from the dark sedan hidden by a crop of trees. Grabbing my umbrella, I braved the torrential rains and quickly jogged to the darkened windows. Using the umbrella to shield myself and the person inside the window, I knocked and it slid down.

"What the fuck is she doing out there?" I yelled to be heard over the rain. "You're supposed to protect her. If she gets pneumonia and dies, you won't have done your jobs very well, fellas."

Luca glanced in Brooklynn's direction and then back. "This just didn't seem like the right time to step in."

I peered over the car and saw her staring at a grave or graves. She was making jerky movements and as everything tuned out but the rain, I could faintly hear her voice. Shit, she had to be fucking screaming for me to hear her from that far away in the roaring rain. "Is she where I think she is?"

Luca nodded.

"Fuck," I sighed.

I'd waited long enough, I was done with this shit, being away from her was slowly killing me. I'd stayed away for the rest of our tour in Europe and we'd finally gotten stateside a couple of days ago. Sasha had some crazy ideas throughout this whole ordeal and I'd shot down most of them, but when she blew into my hotel room the other day, she brought gold.

I ran back to my car and quickly grabbed the papers I'd brought, sticking them in the inside pocket of my coat. Then I made my way toward my woman. As I got closer, it confirmed I'd been right. She was screaming at their graves. I couldn't say I blamed her after the kind of life they'd given their daughters.

She appeared to have screamed herself out because by the time I was only a few steps away, she was silently staring at them, her shoulders slumped. I still heard her tears though, her small sniffles and the occasional sob. Every natural instinct I had begged to go and comfort her. But, she wasn't ready for that. She was still grieving everything that had happened and coming to grips with her upbringing, finally letting go of it.

I was positive that she needed to rediscover the Brooklynn I fell in love with, not that I didn't love this one too. I loved every fucking part of her, but she'd lost the confident, sassy woman somewhere in the clusterfuck that was our lives. So, I was doing the only thing I could think of to help her find herself again.

"Brooklynn." I had to call her name loudly so she would hear me. She gasped and whirled around, slipping in the mud and landing on her ass on the wet ground.

"Fuck, baby. I'm so sorry, I didn't mean to startle you," I said as I tossed my umbrella down and reached out a hand to help her up. "Are you all right?" We were both soaked through, so I didn't bother picking up my umbrella again.

"Couldn't get any worse," she shrugged. "So, yeah, I guess I'm okay."

Luca and Cameron had been thorough in their reports over the last two months and the lifelessness in Brooklynn's eyes in every picture they sent broke my fucking heart all over again. I was filled with relief when I wasn't met with that same empty look. I hated to see her in pain, but it was better than knowing she wasn't feeling anything at all. I needed her to open herself up again, to lay her heart vulnerable like I was willing to do. To give it to one other person wholly and completely to care for.

"Um, thank you for everything you—"

"Stop," I cut her off. "I don't want your gratitude."

"Okay." She turned to glance at the graves once more then plodded away toward the little road where our cars were parked.

I quickly caught up and grabbed her arm, spinning her around to face me. "That's not why I'm here."

"Then why are you here, Levi?" she asked coldly, her head down, refusing to meet my eyes.

Taking her chin between my thumb and forefinger, I forced it up so she was looking at me. "Your time is up."

She shook her head like she hadn't heard me right. "Pardon?"

"You heard me. Your time is up. I told you I'd back off a little while. And I did. We gave you two months, Brooklynn. It's longer than your contract stipulates."

"My contract…" She was clearly confused.

"Cooper told me to inform you that you're expected to return to the tour for the final concerts. Starting with D.C. Next weekend."

She straightened her spine and glared at me. "I told you. I'm done."

"Did you ever read the full contract, Brooklynn?" I asked, knowing very well she hadn't read ALL the fine print. Noah and I might have been a little underhanded with it. And if she had read it, she would have confronted me about it a long time ago.

"What are you talking about?" she asked warily.

I pulled the papers from my jacket and quickly stuffed them in hers so they wouldn't get too wet. "Go home and read it thoroughly, Brooklynn. Seems like you aren't fully aware of all the details. And we'll see you on Friday. Or you'll be in breach of contract and I don't think you want to be in that hornet's nest with the label."

Then I held her chin a little tighter and covered her mouth with mine. I kissed her with all the love I'd been storing up for the last two months. When I finally let her go, she stood in a stupor and stared at me.

"We'll never be done," I whispered before giving her one more hard kiss and walking away.

Chapter Thirty-Nine

BROOKLYNN

"Brooklynn, what were you thinking signing this without having a lawyer look over it?" Ollie, my lawyer, rubbed a hand over his shiny bald spot and then adjusted his glasses, peering at the paper again.

I shrugged and slumped back in my chair. It had been two days since I saw Levi and I was a fucking mess. Why did he have to show up at the very moment when I was the most vulnerable? Now I couldn't stuff my love for him back in the box I'd been keeping it in. I made an appointment with my lawyer and brought him my contract with Stone Butterfly and the label.

"I was excited and I stupidly trusted Noah and Cooper."

"I'm sorry to tell you this, but you're shit out of luck if you want out. It's ironclad. You're locked in for five years and—"

"FIVE YEARS?" I screeched and shot to my feet.

He leaned away from the force of my scream and winced. Then patted his ear and blinked. "Watch the lungs, Brooklynn. You're going to pop an eardrum one of these days."

"Sorry, Ollie. But get back to the five years."

He pointed to a line on the paper. "Your contract is for the length of five years and has an option for three more. It includes two albums, another tour, the composition of at least one new song a year and—" he paused and looked closer. "Um, that's unconventional."

I sighed dejectedly, flopping back down in my chair. "What is?"

"It also stipulates that you share at least eighteen hundred meals with the band's front man, Levi Matthews. Breakfast, lunch, and dinner are acceptable, no snacks or dessert runs included."

A bark of laughter escaped before I could swallow it. "What other bullshit did that fucker slip into the contract?"

"You, um"—a chuckle slipped out but he quelled it when he saw my dark scowl—"Sections C 7.4 stipulates that you agree to forgive Levi of at least, I'm quoting, 'one fuck up a month.' As well as an addendum that informs you he has agreed to the same stipulation and he initialed it here."

Ollie pointed out a few other ridiculous things that Levi had clearly wrangled into my contract and I couldn't help laughing.

"He said something about giving me two months longer to stay away than my contract stated. What was that about?"

"Oh, there is a provision for you to take a temporary leave if an emergency arises involving your sister, Baylee. It gives you six weeks at the most and if more is needed, you can work it out with the label on a case-by-case basis. Oh, and you have a non-compete."

"What the fuck?" I shouted then immediately apologized when Ollie winced. "Sorry." Now I knew why the fuck I hadn't been able to get another gig.

He'd really covered all of his bases, hadn't he? I was going to kick Cooper's ass for getting the label's lawyers to agree to this ridiculous document. I sighed. Apparently, I was still a member of Stone Butterfly whether I wanted to be or not.

I couldn't deny that a part of me was doing a tiny little happy dance. I'd missed music and performing, but mostly, I missed the family I'd become a part of when I joined Stone Butterfly. And, I felt ready to let go, to find freedom from the chain around my neck that was my past. I'd finally let it all out during my visit to the cemetery. I wasn't going to let those people have an effect on my life anymore.

"BK! For fuck's sake, girl. You look terrible." Simon had come running when he saw me but as he came to a stop in front of me, a frown marred his handsome face. I'd just arrived at the arena for my first concert since Rome. I was nervous, a new feeling for me. I'd never been nervous performing, just the occasional jitters after it was over. Simon's familiar greeting went a long way in soothing my nerves.

"Thanks, Simon," I responded dryly. "Just what every woman wants to hear."

"No worries. We'll pack some meat back on these bones." He picked me up into a bear hug, then set me down and grinned. "I'm seriously glad you're back, B. Levi's been a real motherfuckering bastard while you've been gone."

"Hey, Brooklynn," Matteo beamed at me as he walked up and swept me up into a hug, spinning me around before putting my feet back on the ground.

I put an arm around each man's waist and squeezed them to me. "I missed you guys too."

"Brooklynn!" Kristi practically skipped over and threw her arms around me. Sasha sauntered up behind her, grinning broadly. "Welcome back, babe."

Emma was hanging back, biting a nail and looking on with anxiousness. "Hey, Emma," I greeted her with a warm smile. "It's great to see you."

She smiled back tentatively and walked forward. "Welcome back. Um, I'm —I'm so sorry you…"

I shook my head and patted her shoulder. "Emma, I hope you haven't been letting this eat at you. How could you have possibly known? You aren't in any way responsible for what happened."

"I'm still sorry."

"Okay. Unnecessary apology accepted."

"Brilliant." She hugged me and stepped back.

I heard a door shut and my eyes lifted, expecting to see Levi, but it was Cooper and he was watching me almost as warily as Emma had been. Ah, Levi must have warned him about spilling the beans on the contract. Noah walked in next and came to a stop, immediately adopting a sad puppy look. Ugh, I fell for that every time and he knew it, the bastard.

"You two," I said firmly doing the "FBI" double-finger point. They looked to each other and I could see their silent exchange, both wondering if they could escape. "You'll have to face me eventually boys, might as well get it over with."

They both shrugged in grudging agreement and approached me. When they got close enough, I stepped over and whacked each of them once on the backs of their heads. "Next time you try and pull shit like that with me, I aim lower and use the heel of my stiletto boot. Am I making myself heard?"

Noah grinned. "So noted." Then he hugged me. "Welcome back. We missed you."

Then it was Cooper's turn. "I'm just the label's mouthpiece," he tried to argue with a laugh.

"Then I'd invest in a really sturdy cup," Sasha quipped. "Probably a good idea, you know, just in general."

The rest of the crew filtered in a few at a time and soon, it felt like I'd never been gone. With one notable exception. Levi was nowhere to be found. I tried not to let it hurt and failed miserably.

Chapter Forty

LEVI

I let her have her reunion with everyone uninterrupted, wanting her to be comfortable and at ease. Staying away sucked, but I was playing the long game and I hoped I'd be rounding the eighteenth hole sooner than later. *That came out dirtier than intended. Sort of.*

As the time for curtain approached, I was standing in the wings letting a tech attach my wireless mic when Brooklynn walked in. Suddenly, I could breathe with more freedom and my heart beat harder. Other parts of me hardened in happiness too, but I ignored them. It was definitely not the time.

Her hair was pulled up into a high ponytail, hanging long and straight down her back. It highlighted the structure of her face, showing off some of her most beautiful features, clearly declaring her Native American heritage. Long feathered earrings dangled to her shoulders, which were bared by a red, strapless top. Her ass looked amazing in her leather pants and her black, stiletto boots brought back fantastic memories of fucking her with nothing but those on. Fuck, I needed to get some control over myself or I'd be going on stage with a fucking chub.

I grabbed a cold bottle of water and chugged it down, feeling only marginally better when it was gone. Wandering around backstage, I focused on getting pumped and did a few vocal exercises to make sure I remained loose. Then, it was time to go on. At the last second, Sasha grabbed my arm and pulled me aside. "You're not planning on singing her a song, right? Because that's just too fucking cheesy man, and so not the way to Brooklynn's heart."

I rolled my eyes. "First of all, I think I know Brooklynn better than anyone else and second, I'm not a complete fucking idiot, Sasha."

She grunted. I wasn't sure if that was an agreement or not. "Good, now get your ass out there."

"How are you guys doing tonight?" I shouted as I walked on stage with Sasha. She smacked my ass and jogged over to her instruments. "Are you ready for us?" They clapped, screamed, whistled, and made all kinds of noises of approval.

"Tonight is a celebration. We picked up a lost band member on our way here, how about you guys show her how glad you are that she's back!" The audience's response to Brooklynn as she walked on stage was phenomenal. The roar of approval nearly took the roof off the joint. "Let's do this!"

We launched into a fan favorite and the show was off, barreling down a familiar path. It felt like coming home, having all of us on stage together, again.

I couldn't keep my eyes from constantly straying to Brooklynn. She was so fucking gorgeous. Seeing her come back to life on stage made every moment of hell worth it. I made sure to have Noah ask her if she was comfortable performing "The Road to Forever," before suggesting it during the concert. The audience went fucking ballistic. This would only be the second time she'd performed it live, but the first one was all over the internet and the reception from the fans had been overwhelmingly positive.

Just before the end of the first set, they lit her piano and she played "The Road to Forever." Listening to her, watching her in her element as she sang her own words, I fell back into the same cycle, falling even more in love with her. As we exited the stage, I smiled at her and put my hand over my heart, letting her know I'd been touched by the performance. She lit up and smiled brightly, then shrugged like it was no big deal. I laughed and almost stepped toward her, but she was swallowed up in the praises of our band mates.

Mimi called out five minutes and we all downed more

water, wiped off with towels, and got ready to go back out there. The lights dimmed and we took our places.

"You didn't think we were done, did you?" Simon asked, scratching his head. They laughed and he shrugged with a wink. "Great, because it feels like the right time to sing 'It's Not Over'!"

"It's Not Over?" Matteo repeated, confused. "That's not one of our songs."

"So?"

"Sooooo," Matteo dragged out the vowel condescendingly. "We can't sing other people's stuff, dude."

"Fuck that! We're Stone Butterfly—" He had to stop for the thunder of the audience. —"We can sing whatever the fuck we want. But, I guess these people did come to hear our stuff."

Sasha started plucking a melody on her violin. "Sounds like we're playing 'Unmasked', boys," she drawled. Brooklynn picked up her part on the piano. "See?" Sasha continued. "The piano agrees."

"Bossy," I murmured in a stage whisper to the audience. "'Unmasked' it is!" I lifted my guitar from its stand and put the strap over my head. Then my chords joined in with the sound before I started singing.

The show neared its end, and right at the point where Brooklynn and I would normally perform "Sanity," I set down my guitar and walked to the edge of the stage. I waited until everyone quieted down.

"So, I've got a problem. I fucked up. Like big time, colossal fuck up. I said some hurtful things that I truly regret to the woman I love. I would get down on my knees and tell her how sorry I am. I would tell her that I was a complete asshole and beg her to take pity on me for being an idiot. Now, I'm sure a lot of you are thinking, 'I hope he's not about to sing her a song.' I'll put your minds at ease, I'm not. However, I'm not above using every tool in my arsenal to get her to forgive me. And, singing together is how I got her to fall in love with me in the first place. So, I need your help." I waited for the applause to die down again before going on. "It just so happens that I fell in love with Brooklynn Hawk while we wrote a song together. I think you guys have probably heard of it?" I grinned and gestured for them to get louder. "Let her know you want us to sing it!"

The audience began to chant for "Sanity" and I turned around, praying I wasn't about to see the face of an enraged Brooklynn. To my relief, her eyes were shining and a beautiful smile graced her lips. I ran over and grabbed her hand, bringing her downstage, like I had at that first concert. "The first time we performed this song, I told the audience that they had no idea how fucking lucky they were. But, the truth is, it's me who didn't know how fucking lucky I was. And, chances are high, that I'll fuck up again in the future, a lot. But, if she'll give me another chance, I promise not to ever again forget how fucking lucky I am to have her love. Now, I've put her on the spot, so understand, you guys are going to get to see how this plays out. Especially because we'd go to jail if you were allowed to watch how I'm hoping this resolves."

I grinned and shrugged sheepishly when Brooklynn whacked me on the arm. Relieved to see her laughing when she did it. "Do you want to hear 'Sanity'?" I finally shouted.

The music started to float to our ears from upstage and when the time was right, we sang, staring into each other's eyes.

When I make you crazy
When your love has an edge
When we lose our minds
Together, we lose our sanity
Ooooh, oooh, oooh,
Can we find it?
Is our love enough?
Can our love be the key?
To finding our Sanity.

Oooh, oh, oooooh

The last notes reverberated through the rafters and I gave in to the rising desire in my head and heart. Pulling Brooklynn to me, I kissed her. I poured every ounce of my love, every facet of my soul, into that kiss. I gave her everything.

The lights went out and when they slowly turned back on, I released her lips. I barely noticed the roar of the crowd as I kept her close, looking deep into her eyes. The chocolate orbs were swimming with tears, but I had no fucking idea if they were the good kind or the bad. *In my opinion, all tears are fucking terrifying and my woman should never cry.*

Matteo vamped with the audience until we snapped out of our little bubble. Brooklynn stepped back, then turned and jogged to the piano. I refocused on the moment and threw myself into our encores. When the lights went down for the final time, I was buzzing with even more energy than usual at the end of a concert. I swiftly exited into the wings and ripped my mic off and tossing it to a tech, ignoring his deadly glare for mistreating his precious equipment.

I looked frantically for Brooklynn and then made a beeline for her. Grabbing her around the waist, I swung her around to face me. She stared, caught off guard and I used the moment to get out what I needed to say before she could get her bearings.

"I don't expect all to be forgiven at once. I know I need to earn your trust back, but I'd like to do it with you, rather than for you. Do you understand?" She nodded mutely. "I'd also like to remind you about Section C 7.4 in your contract." A smile played around the corners of her mouth, but she firmed her lips and simply nodded again.

"With those things in mind, I'm hoping you'll meet me back at the hotel. I'm in Room 1222. Before you say anything, I'm not expecting anything to happen. I just want a quiet place to talk so I can apologize and we can try to figure out how to move forward, become stronger together. Don't answer now. Just think about it. I hope you'll give me another chance."

I planted a chaste kiss on her lips then let her go and rushed to my dressing room. I needed to get my ass back to the hotel so I had as much time as possible to get everything set up.

Chapter Forty-One

BROOKLYNN

There wasn't really a question about whether or not I would meet Levi in his room. For my own pride's sake, I pretended to think it over for approximately sixty seconds. Then I hurried back to the dressing rooms and changed into my street clothes. It occurred to me to stay in the sexy outfit from the show, but for this, I wanted to just be me. So, jeans, peasant blouse, and sandals were my attire as I flagged down Noah and told him I was grabbing a cab back to the hotel.

I showered as fast as I could before running out the door. I felt bad for ditching the fans waiting out back by taking a side entrance, but this was too important and they wouldn't have had my attention anyway. A cab was coming down the street with its light on so I raised my hand and flagged it down. Sliding onto the bench seat in the back, I gave him the name of the hotel and fidgeted through the short ride. I paid and dashed from the car, only slowing down when I hit the lobby so I wouldn't draw attention. Fans were mingling around, trying to catch a glimpse of a band member, but I'd tucked my ponytail into the back of my shirt, put on a pair of sunglasses, and kept my head down as I strolled to the elevator. When I stepped inside, I blew out a breath, removed the glasses, and punched the button for the twelfth floor. Just as the doors were closing, one of the girls in a small group of teenagers looked over her shoulder and met my eyes. She yelled to her friends that she had spotted me and they ran full speed in my direction, but they were too late and I was alone as the elevator ascended.

Once I was on the right floor, I checked the signs for the numbers and turned left to find Levi's room. With every step closer, I took deep, calming breaths. I didn't think I'd ever been that nervous and when I spotted the gold lettering that announced I was at room 1222. My heart began to beat so hard, I felt like it was going to burst through my chest. With a raised hand, I knocked and waited. He didn't make me wait long, swinging open the door after only a few seconds.

"Hi," he rasped with a soft smile. His eyes roamed over me from head to toe, drinking in the sight of me just as I was doing to him.

Finally, I asked, "Are you going to let me in or are we talking in the hallway?"

He chuckled a little sheepishly and stood back, holding the door open for me to enter. My body brushed against his as I passed him and we both sucked in air at the electric jolt from our bodies touching. After shutting the door, he followed me into an open space, set up more like an apartment than a hotel room. A small table sat to the side of a kitchen, right in front of a wall of windows that looked out over the city, showing off the magnificence of D.C.'s monuments. But, I didn't do more than glance at the view, my eyes were glued to the candles, the beautifully set table, a vase of lavender roses, and a medium sized package wrapped in silver paper with a white ribbon.

"How did you know I would come?" I asked curiously.

"I didn't," he said from directly behind me, his warm breath blowing across my exposed neck. "I hoped. And I wanted to be ready in case the universe decided to grant me an undeserved wish."

Levi was so damn good with words, he was always making me melt, my heart and my panties. *Such a cheater.* I felt a gentle touch on my arm as he grasped my bicep and turned me to face him. "Brooklynn, you can't possibly know how much I regret what I said and how I treated you. By the time I reached the lobby, I'd already realized how unbelievably stupid I'd been. But I knew it would take more than a simple apology after the way I hurt you. I foolishly hoped that when you were injured and in the hospital, all would be forgiven and we could just move on. Yet another example of how foolish I was being. Letting you go was agonizing and all I could do was pray that I'd done the right thing." Everything he was saying strummed my heart strings in a beautiful melody.

He leaned in and brushed a sweet kiss over my lips. "I'm not asking for you to forgive me overnight, but would you give us another chance?" His fingers slid down to tangle with mine and he led me over to the table. I tugged on his hand to bring him to a stop in front of it.

"Levi, I'm not going to pretend what happened didn't break my heart. But, nobody is perfect and by refusing to forgive, all I'd be doing is hanging on to something toxic that would eat away at me until I'd be nothing but an empty shell. I'm ready to grab onto life and let it take me on a thrilling ride. There is nobody I'd rather have strapped in with me. The reality is, I forgave you a long time ago. And, you deserve an apology too. I shouldn't have tried to keep the truth from you, I should have told you the minute I figured it out. I was doing what I'd always done, trying to handle everything alone. I hadn't completely put my trust in you."

I cupped his cheek with one hand and he closed his eyes, turning his face to lean into my touch. "How about we wipe the slate clean and give each other our whole selves?" I whispered. "I'm ready to trust you and remember that we're both flawed. Which means that even when your words or actions hurt, I need to give you the benefit of the doubt and assume you've simply lost your fucking mind."

Levi tossed his head back and laughed, the sound joyful as it washed over me. I loved his laugh. "What do you think?" I pressed.

He smiled wide, his aquamarine gems sparkling with happiness and love. "I'm in, baby. I'm all in." I threw my arms around his neck and went up on my tiptoes. He met me halfway, dropping his head forward to capture my lips in a deep kiss. "Fuck, I missed this. I missed us." He slipped his tongue into my mouth and it danced with mine, while his hands palmed my ass and tugged me into his body. My hands delved into his hair and I clung to the soft strands. Before things could get out of hand, much to my disappointment, he tore his mouth away. He stared into my eyes with an intensity that I felt in my soul and in my core. "I love you, Brooklynn."

I beamed at him, so happy to be back in his arms, to hear him declare his love. "I love you too, Levi. I was miserable without you." He kissed me again, but ended it much too soon. His hands traveled up to rest at my waist and he slowly rotated my body until I was facing the table.

"Open it," he urged, referring to the prettily wrapped present. I stepped closer and took ahold of it. The bottom and top of the box were separately wrapped, so all I had to do was untie the ribbon and lift the lid. Inside was a sheaf of papers that, upon closer inspection, turned out to be sheet music. It was titled, "Forever Found." Reading the notes, I realized it started out with the basic melody of my song, "The Road to Forever," but quickly transitioned into something new. It was a duet and every now and again, the female part slipped back into the melody of my song. The words were about what happens when you reach the end of the road. When you finally find your forever. It was essentially, the happy ending to my song.

I glanced up at him and he smiled nervously. "I said I wouldn't sing a song for you on stage, I never said I wouldn't write one for you." He turned me so he could cup my face in his hands and lean his forehead against mine for a reverent moment. Then he brought his head up and pushed a piece of hair that had escaped from my ponytail behind my ear. "You're my forever, baby."

"Sounds good to me." I grinned and he swept me up into another perfect melding of our mouths. I was on fire and feeling desperate to have him wrapped around me. To feel our naked skin pressed together. "Levi."

He was panting when he stopped kissing me to ask,

"What, baby?"

"Fuck dinner." He stared blankly at me for half a beat then bent at the knees and lifted me by the backs of my thighs so my legs circled his waist. I leaned over and blew out the candles then sealed my lips back over his. He stumbled a little as he tried to navigate to the bedroom, but we managed to make it there without injury.

Lying down on the bed, his hungry eyes seemed to be glued to my face, as though he couldn't bear to tear them away for fear I would disappear. My hands found the hem of his shirt and I tunneled them underneath, going up until he was forced to lift his arms so I could pull it off. I was struck by the familiar sight of his beautiful tattoo. I'd forgotten just how stunning it was, the colors bright and brilliant as they swirled and weaved over his muscular, ripped chest and abs.

"I want to make love to you, baby," he grated. "But, if you don't stop looking at me like you want to eat me for dinner, I won't be able to control myself." He laughed when he could tell I was obviously weighing both options. "We'll compromise, okay? Let me make love to you, then I promise to the fuck the hell out of you."

"Deal."

His smile turned soft and sweet, so full of love it made my breath catch. He moved down and removed my sandals before placing tiny little kisses all over my feet. Then he methodically worked his way up my body, removing an article of clothing and then kissing and licking all of the uncovered skin. When I was naked, he scooted back on the bed and simply looked me over. "You're so fucking gorgeous."

"If I remember correctly, you're not so bad yourself. Of course, you'd need to shed the rest of your clothes for me to truly make a determination." He chuckled as he climbed off the bed, kicked off his shoes and removed his pants and boxer briefs. "Looks like I was correct," I said cheekily.

He moved until he was hovering over me, his hands

bracketing my head and his knees at my sides. The mood shifted into something heady and thick with passion. I'd been heated, but I began to rage with fire, it's flames licking my skin and causing a restless need inside me.

Finally, he lowered himself until he was pressed against me from chest to toes. "You feel incredible, baby," he moaned before he kissed me. His lips found their way down to nip and suck on my nipples, before continuing their journey until he reached the apex of my thighs. He spread my legs wide and licked his lips as he looked at me. "I love how fucking wet you get for me." He ran a finger up my center and I whimpered. "So pink and swollen," he breathed as his finger brushed over my engorged clit. Without warning, his mouth was suddenly on my pussy, his tongue driving me wild, until his fingers entered me and with a few quick thrusts, sent me hurtling into a cataclysmic orgasm.

He crawled up my body and watched me with awe as I came. "This is the only time you are more beautiful than when you are lost in your music." The shudders began to ebb but he didn't give me long before his cock was playing with my entrance. I was a little concerned about how long it had been since I'd had him inside me, worried about the pain from his large shaft stretching me to accommodate him after two months. "Trust me," he whispered.

Inch by inch, working in and out, being unbelievably gentle, he slowly pushed inside without causing me pain. I felt stretched and full, but not uncomfortable. At last, he was fully seated from root to tip and he stopped, letting me adjust to his girth. He loved on my breasts again, building the good kind of tension, the kind that relaxed my walls just enough so he could move. "Fuck, I can barely move your pussy is gripping me so tight," he grunted. "Oh fuck, that feels good."

"More," I moaned and wrapped my legs around him. He sped up a little, but kept to a steady, maddening pace, building up to my orgasm gradually. As impatient as I was, I could feel the difference from our hard and fast fucking.

The fire was being stoked with precision meant to build it to unimaginable heights. "I can't take this, Levi!" I cried, thrashing and trying to urge him to adopt more vigor.

"No, baby," he growled. "Let me make love to you, sweetheart."

It was sweet and I loved every second even as it drove me fucking crazy. But, I was ready to move it along before he killed me. I plunged my hands into his hair, kissed him with fervor, and squeezed my inner walls. "Fuck!" he shouted. One more clench around his dick and he lost control speeding up and hammering into me. The force of his thrusts knocked the bed into the wall and each time he bottomed out, I screamed with ecstasy.

"Yes! Levi, oh don't stop! Yes!"

His mouth attacked my breasts, biting and sucking on my nipples and all around, leaving his mark. Then he threw his head back and shouted, "Fuck, baby! Fuck, yeah. Give it to me, Brooklynn, that's right. Tilt that pussy, baby—oh fuck yes! Fuck!" He changed the angle of his thrusts as I lifted my hips so he was driving inside even deeper, hitting both of my most sensitive spots. It wasn't long before I was screaming his name as I came in an orgasm that left the last one in the fucking dust. He buried himself as deep as he could, bellowing my name as he exploded, his hot seed filling me and sending me into a third orgasm.

A long while later, we lay wrapped around each other, breathing hard and trying to recover. "You cheated," he growled.

I snickered, then looked up into his aqua pools and smiled lovingly. "We'll try it your way again some other time, we've got forever."

Epilogue

LEVI

I was sweating, so fucking nervous I could barely stand still. We were half way through our final concert of the *For Your Sanity* tour at Madison Square Gardens in New York City. I'd been planning this for months, long before I knew if I would ever have the opportunity. Still, I worried that I was rushing it. We'd only been back together for a week. But, fuck, I needed to make her mine.

We were called to the stage for our second set and I shoved away the nerves, becoming the rock star I was every time I walked on stage. Then we were at the pivotal moment. Fuck, I hoped I wasn't making a mistake. I turned to Brooklynn and held out my hand, like I always did when it was time to sing "Sanity." She popped up from the piano and made her way to me with a bright smile. Taking my hand, she walked downstage with me. Normally I would be revving up the audience and she threw me a questioning look when I remained silent. Then I took a deep breath and jumped off a cliff, hoping she would be there to catch me.

Facing the audience, I raised Brooklynn's hand to my mouth and kissed the back. The audience clapped and got excited, thinking they knew what was next. "You know, I first met Brooklynn shortly before we started touring. I fell in love with her when we wrote a song together, a song that lays our love at the audience's feet. I declared that love for her on stage. I royally fucked up and gave her a public apology on another stage. Since you've been with us from the beginning, I decided to let you be a part of the next verse in our song."

I turned to Brooklynn and grasped both of her hands tightly. She was smiling but her eyes betrayed her confusion. "I may have been a little underhanded in the contract we gave you to sign when we asked you to become a permanent member of Stone Butterfly. So, this time, I'm just going to lay my cards on the table. I want another contract. Except this one is just for you and me. I want a piece of paper than we both sign to seal the deal so we belong to each other forever."

Her eyes widened as understanding dawned on her face. I dug what I needed from my pocket and dropped to one knee.

"Brooklynn Hawk, I love you more than I ever imagined was possible. And, I'm going to continue to love you every day for the rest of our forever. What do you say? Will you accept the terms of the new contract and marry me?"

The audience fucking roared their approval. Tears overflowed from Brooklynn's eyes, making tracks down her cheeks and I started to panic. Until her smile lit up the whole fucking arena and she leaned down to cup my cheeks. "Where do I sign?"

The End

Books By Elle Christensen

The Fae Guard Series
Protecting Shaylee (Book One) – Available Now!
Loving Ean (Book Two) – Available Now!
Chasing Hayleigh (Book Three) – Available Now!
A Very Faerie Christmas: A Fae Guard Novella (Book Four) – Available Now!
Saving Kendrix (Book Five) – Available Now!
Forever Fate: A Fae Guard Novella (Book Six) – Available Now!

The Fae Legacy
Finding Ayva: A Delta Force: Operation Alpha Kindle Worlds Novella (Book one) – Available Now!

Stone Butterfly Rockstars
Another Postcard – Available Now!
Daylight — Coming Soon!

Miami Flings
A collection of standalone novellas
Spring Fling – Available Now!
All I Want: A Sex, Vow & Babies Kindle Worlds Novella - Available Now!

Standalones
Love in Fantasy – Available Now!
Ranchers Only: A Lone Star Burn Kindle Worlds Novella – Available Now!
Say Yes – Available Now!

Books Co-authored with K. Webster
Erased (Standalone) – Available Now!
Give Me Yesterday (Standalone) – Available Now!

Check out Elle Christensen and Rochelle Paige's co-written books under the pen name Fiona Davenport!

http://www.fionadavenport.com

About Elle Christensen

I'm a lover of all things books and have always had a passion for writing. Since I am a sappy romantic, I fell easily into writing romance. I love a good HEA! Music is my second language, I'm a huge baseball fan, and an obsessive reader.

My husband is my biggest supporter and he's incredibly patient and understanding about the people is my head who are fighting with him for my attention.

I hope you enjoy reading my books as much as I enjoyed writing them!

www.ellechristensenauthor.com
elle@ellechristensenauthor.com

@authorellec
Facebook | Instagram | Twitter | Pinterest

Made in the USA
Columbia, SC
30 September 2017